A NOTE FROM THE AUTHOR

Like the others in this series, this book is a pastiche of real events strung together via fiction. In fact, it's the most unbelievable elements of all that have the most basis in truth. While the protagonists are my own creations, the lore of Billy the Kid, the Skinwalker, the Santa Fe Ring and the rest are all real. Though I didn't nail the dates or names down to a tee, a man named Brushy Bill Roberts really did pop up in New Mexico seeking a pardon from the governor in late November of 1950. That same year, Billy the Kid's tombstone was stolen from Fort Sumner and not recovered until 26 years later in Granbury, Texas, very near to where Roberts lived and died. As far as the historical record goes, that's just coincidence, but it had the makings of a great story. Furthermore, though there were no skinwalkers loose in Fort Sumner in 1950, the legend of the Navajo witch is still very real to many New Mexico and Arizona residents who are reluctant to even utter the word. And, as strange as it sounds, New Mexico witches really are said to ride fireballs. As for the fantastic places explored in this novel, notably the haunted Dorsey Mansion and Fort Stanton Cave's snowy river, they, too, are real. Though some historical figures are mentioned and a version of Billy the Kid appears in this book, otherwise, all the other characters are purely fictitious and none are based on any person, living or dead.

OTHER BOOKS BY THIS AUTHOR
Tall Tales and Half Truths of Billy the Kid
Tall Tales and Half Truths of Pat Garrett
Hidden History of Southeast New Mexico
The Man Who Invented Billy the Kid:
The Authentic Life of Ash Upson
Cowboys & Monsters: Vampires, Mummies,
and Werewolves of the Wild West

OTHER BOOKS IN THE 21 GUNS SERIES
The Noted Desperado Pancho Dumez

21 GUNS

VOL. 1 BOOK 2

JOHN LEMAY

WITH ILLUSTRATIONS BY
LOGAN PACK

BICEP BOOKS ·
ROSWELL, NEW MEXICO

An *Original* Publication of BICEP BOOKS.

Copyright © 2022 John LeMay.
Cover art and interior illustrations © Logan Pack
Published by Bicep Books, Roswell, New Mexico.

Printed in the United States of America

ISBN: 978-1-953221-32-2

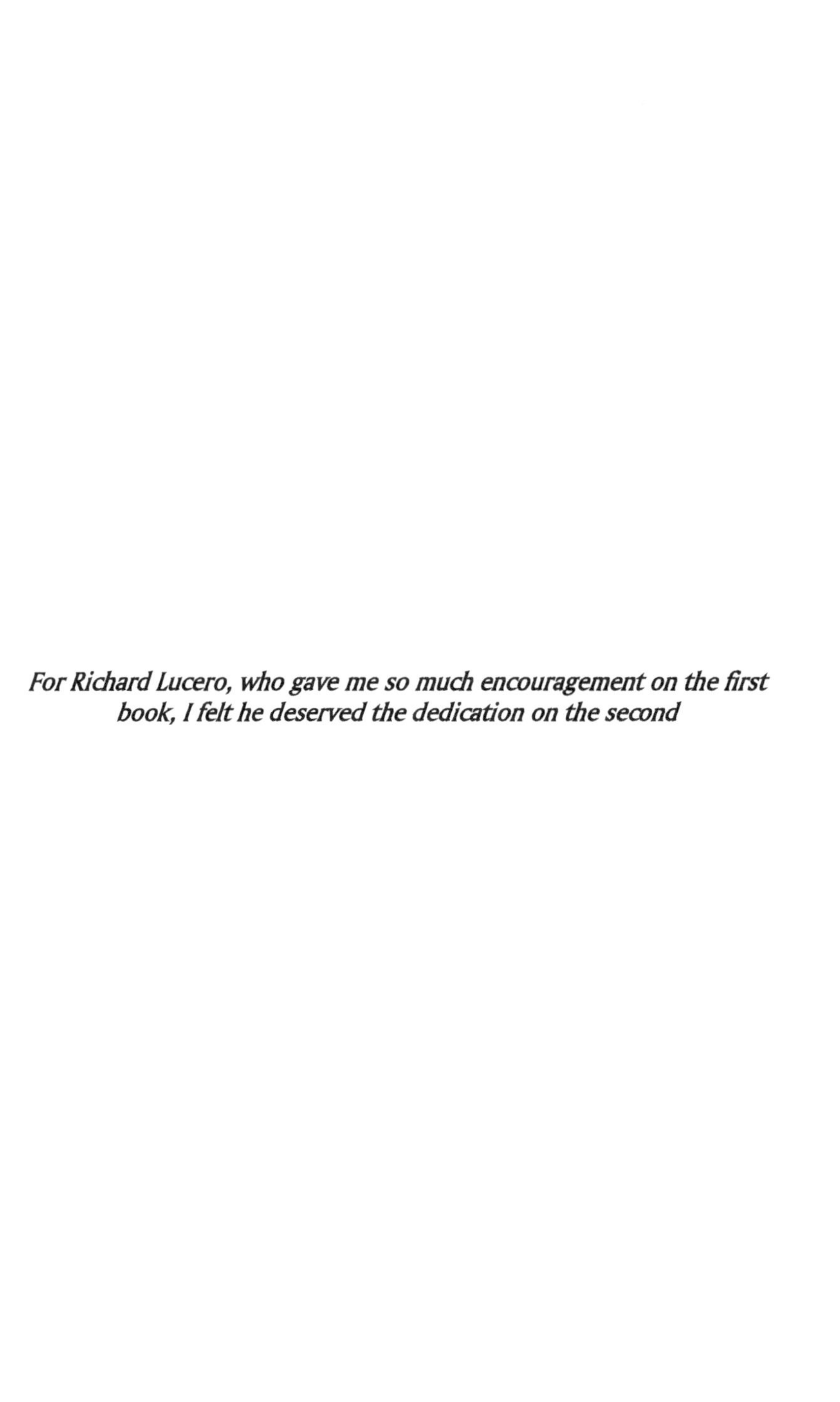

For Richard Lucero, who gave me so much encouragement on the first book, I felt he deserved the dedication on the second

KID AIN'T DEAD SAYS FORT SUMNER OLD TIMER

11-1-1950

NEW MEXICO –In addition to being the Land of Mañana, New Mexico is also a land of tall tales. Take the fabled Lost Adams canyon of gold, wherein a whole party of prospectors was massacred by the Apache to keep its location a secret. Today, only the Indians know where it is, and they aren't telling. Tales of gold seem popular with all races, while others are more distinctive to the background of the teller. Indians, it would seem, have a legend to go along with every big rock jutting from the desert floor. Their favorite will usually go that it's the remains of some monster or giant slain by the Hero Twins of their tribal mythologies. Meanwhile, the Spanish still tell superstitious tales of witches who ride fireballs, while the Anglos seem to prefer to sit upon the ground and tell sad stories of the death of outlaws, to paraphrase Shakespeare.

One town in particular offers a distinct mix of all three of the state's cultures, that being Fort Sumner. In the old days, the Navajo and Apache were sequestered there at Bosque Redondo until they were moved elsewhere. Soon after, the Lucien Maxwell family bought up the old fort properties and the place achieved another token of fame when the so-called "Boy Bandit King" himself, Billy, the Kid, was killed there around 70 years ago on the windswept plains. He died at the hand of Sheriff Pat Garrett in the home of Pete Maxwell on the night of July 14, 1881. There Garrett gunned the Kid down about midnight and was promptly buried the next morning.

Not so, says Fort Sumner old-timer Kit Carson. No, not that Kit Carson. This man claims to be the more famous Carson's nephew and moved to Fort Sumner several years back. According to Uncle Kit, as he's affectionately known, history has it wrong. According to him, Garrett let the Kid go and helped fake his death. Why?

"Garrett and the Kid were pals," says Carson from his small, Fort Sumner abode outside of town. "Garrett helped Billy get away. That's why no one ever saw the body. In fact, I hears they put a few bags of sand in the casket to give it some weight and buried it right quick!"

Carson's claim is vehemently disputed by old-timer Salvador Miranda, who lived in Fort Sumner when the Kid was shot. Not only that, Miranda made the Kid's tombstone, which has become a tourist attraction in Fort Sumner since tales of the Kid gained a resurgence of popularity in the 1920s, largely thanks to books like Walter Noble Burns' *The Saga of Billy the Kid.*

But just what proof does Carson have that the Kid isn't resting in the Old Fort Sumner Cemetery? Carson claims to have ridden with Billy the Kid, not during the Lincoln County War of the late 1870s, but down Mexico way during the Revolution. According to Carson, he and the Kid were both some of Pancho Villa's top fighters.

This strange claim seems to gel with reports that Billy the Kid has recently been unearthed in Granbury, TX, by a lawyer named Charles Burleson. Burleson was settling a court case when he came across 90-year-old William "Tumbleweed" Williams, who claims he fled to Mexico after his alleged assassination in Fort Sumner all those years ago. Could he be the same surviving Kid that Carson knew? Or are Tumbleweed Williams and Uncle Kit both just another in a long line of Old West impostors such as J. Frank Dalton, who claims he is Jesse James? They aren't the first, and they likely aren't to be the last, either. In any case, like wise old sages from the fairy tales of yore, we can only hope that the old timers will keep spinning their tall tales until they can spin them no more.

II
ONCE
UPON A TIME
FORT
SUMNER

PROLOGUE
THE LONG WALK

WINTER 1864

Everywhere the boy looked, he saw nothing but blue-tinted snow. Inches of it had settled onto the flat plains ahead and more fell unceasingly from the evening sky. Ten minutes ago, he could still see his people and the soldiers prodding them along. He had kept sight of them until the mile long procession had turned into a tiny black speck, and then, finally, nothing. He and his mother had lost them, or rather, the group had chosen to leave them behind to die. Now they were alone in this strange, flat land where the ground currently mirrored the sky and seemed to blend together. Perhaps that was what he hated most about this foreign new land, it was flat and boring.

Over a month ago, he and his people were forced to leave behind the fierce, red rocks of their country in Arizona for New Mexico's Fort Wingate. As it turned out, that was only the start of their hellish journey from one fort to the next. From Fort Wingate they were forced to march across the jagged black rocks of the lava fields that the Spaniards called the malpais. To them, it was simply lava rock, but to the boy and his people, the landscape had been created not by an erupting volcano, but by the blood of the giant Yé'iitsoh, slain by the Hero Twins on the sacred mountain. Though it hadn't been pleasant to cross, it was still fascinating for the boy to traverse a land of legend. After that, the journey became more monotonous. Supposedly they were being led to a place of trees outside of another fort, Fort Sumner, that they called Bosque Redondo, or Round Woods in the tongue of the Spanish. The boy had hoped it would not be as boring as the other places, but now it no longer seemed to matter.

Though they were only one day away, the soldiers had still left them behind. Actually, that the soldiers didn't care wasn't a surprise to him. Even at five years of age, he knew they didn't consider Navajo to be real people like them. That his own clan had decided to leave him and his mother behind stung much worse. Without his father, there was no one to help his sickly mother through the snow. Soon—within an hour perhaps—he and his mother would freeze to death.

He struggled to help her up from the snow, but she was too feeble and his young, starved body was weak as well. She muttered several times for him to leave her, but she was all he had ever known. He would rather die with her than face the world alone.

He looked ahead again in a vain hope that help would come. In the distance, blurred by the snow, he could make out a figure coming toward them. Any other time seeing a stranger in the middle of the plains would be cause for alarm, but not when one was close to death. In that case, the dread of death outweighed the fear of the oncoming stranger. The hope he felt dissipated once he saw it was not a man, but a wolf slinking toward them in the snow. He could see its blue eyes even through the icy flurry.

His heartbeat quickened as the form of the wolf loomed larger and larger. Relief washed over him when he realized that it wasn't a wolf, only a man wearing an animal pelt with his head hung low. The man stopped and peeled back the wolf's head to reveal a fellow Navajo. It wasn't a man from the Long Walk, though. His people never wore the pelt of a predatory animal. Only a witch would do such a thing. But even now the witch was a welcome sight.

"Do you know what I am?" he asked the boy in their native tongue.

The boy nodded wordlessly.

"And you are not afraid?"

He shook his head defiantly. He was about to die. What thing worse than death could the witch inflict upon him?

The witch sniffed the cold air. "You speak the truth. I am impressed."

The witch walked past him to his mother and knelt by her side. The boy watched as the witch whispered something in her ear, her eyes still glued to him all the while. She nodded and the witch looked back to him.

"Your mother has given me her permission to help the both of you. Will you let me?"

The boy nodded.

"You already know I am a witch, but do you know what else I am?"

The boy nodded. "You're a skinwalker."

"Weren't you taught not to say that word out loud?" the witch asked.

The boy's people feared that in uttering the word, they would draw the attention of a skinwalker and rarely said it. "Yes, but you are already here, so it doesn't matter," the boy answered.

He smiled again. "Very clever." He crept over next to him and drew a bone dagger from his wolfskin cloak. "This is going to hurt, but it's the only way."

The boy's heartbeat quickened when he thought the skinwalker would stick him with the dagger. Instead, he used it to slice his own palm. He looked from his bleeding hand to the boy. "You know what comes next?"

The boy nodded and took out his own knife, preparing to cut into his palm.

The man waved his finger at him. "No, it has to be this one. It is special."

The boy winced as the bone dagger cut into his flesh. As soon as he had withdrawn the dagger, the witch clasped his bloody palm into his. He looked into his eyes. "You are like me now."

The boy nodded even though he didn't feel any different.

"What is your name, boy?"

He told him and the witch looked pleased.

"Wolf. How very appropriate." But then the witch shook his head and added, "You must trust no one with your real name ever again. Only other witches. Do you understand?"

He didn't, but he nodded just the same. The witch studied him as if he knew the boy didn't fully comprehend what he'd asked. "Come on, let's go."

The boy pointed back to his mother, who lay motionless in the snow.

The witch shook his head. "She's dead."

"But you can do magic," the boy pleaded with teary eyes.

"I can't raise the dead. Now come along."

When the boy lunged to embrace his dead mother one more time, the witch snatched him up into his strong arms. The boy pounded on the witch's back with his fists and screamed as he watched the only true home of his nomadic existence slowly fade into the snow. Eventually, shock and rage subsided into exhaustion and the boy's face settled into the wolf's pelt. Even though it shouldn't have, the coarse fur began to feel strangely comforting as the boy drifted off into unconsciousness.

I.

THE BODY

Everywhere Hondo Dumez looked he saw dirt. There was dirt on the desert floor stretching endlessly towards the horizon on either side of him. There was dirt behind him, stirred up into an angry cloud from the dusty road he was currently flying across. Even the sky was dirty today; its usually clear blue obscured behind hazy red dust carried on an ugly wind.

New Mexico was a land of wind and great gusts it seemed. It blew winter and summer both. The only difference was that in the summer, the wind was hot, and in the winter, it was cold. Today was a blustery fall day, though, which was unusual. Fall typically wasn't too bad for wind in these parts. Hondo wasn't superstitious, but a part of him couldn't help but feel like the weather was a bad omen, because today, Hondo was on his way to the scene of a murder.

Hondo worked as a Deputy Sheriff for De Baca County, the second-least populated county in the whole state, to which the vast stretches of nothingness on either side of him were a testament. His hometown, Fort Sumner, was the county seat, but since it was the only real town in the county, there was no other option. Being a small-town deputy sheriff, murders weren't something Hondo dealt with much. Car accidents out on Route 84, rabid dogs, rowdy drunks, minor squabbles over property lines and irrigation ditches—those were his daily bread and butter.

But not today. This morning a local had phoned the station with so much terror in her voice the dispatcher could barely make out the call. She had recognized the caller's name, as Fort Sumner was still small enough that most everyone either knew each other or at least knew of each other. It was Shirley Nelson, a basic do-gooder who was also a little nosy and prone to gossip. Shirley was known for delivering meals to some of the shut-ins in the area, which served a two-fold purpose.

One was feeding the less fortunate, and the other was spreading old rumors and obtaining new ones. But what she was spewing on the other end of the phone that morning wasn't gossip—the terror in her voice made that clear.

Between the panicked gasps, the dispatcher was only able to make out two things, luckily those being the "what" and the "where". The what was "murder", and the where was "Uncle Kit's place". So far, that was all Hondo knew, but he had to wonder if old Uncle Kit had just dropped dead and Shirley's overactive imagination had done the rest.

Hondo squinted through the hazy dirt, expecting to see the metal glint of Uncle Kit's trailer reflected in the sunlight at any moment. Uncle Kit was the perennial hermit common to the Southwest, and every town had one. They all looked basically the same; long hair and unkempt beards wearing ratty clothes like they had just stepped out of the Old West itself. And they all had crazy names, too, like Sombrero Jack or Pecos Bill and so on.

Fort Sumner's Uncle Kit was no exception. He looked like you'd expect with an unkempt beard and long hair which he sometimes did up in braids like an Indian, even though he wasn't Native American. Kit was a drifter who had chosen to settle in Fort Sumner because it had enough solitude to suit his needs when he wanted to be alone and enough people to get attention when he wanted to be seen.

He was probably best observed during the Fourth of July parade. He'd wear his best buckskins and wave around a big flag as he rode by on horseback. It was a pretty good show for a man of his age; if he was actually as old as he said he was, that is. Uncle Kit claimed to be nearly a hundred but looked more like he was seventy. Everyone called him Uncle Kit because he claimed to be Kit Carson's nephew. Hell, if he could've gotten away with it, he probably would have claimed to be *the Kit Carson* but was smart enough to do the math on that one.

Among his various claims to fame, in addition to being Kit Carson's nephew, was that he had been in Buffalo Bill Cody's old Wild West Circus, that he had fought in the Mexican Revolution beside Pancho Villa, that he met Jesse James once, and so on. And, like every other old-timer along the Pecos, he had either ridden with, shot at, or been shot himself by Billy the Kid. Whether or not he shot with the Kid or at him depended on the listener. If they were of the opinion that the Kid was a ne'er-do-well thief, Uncle Kit had shot at him. If the listener was of the persuasion that Billy was a modern-day Robin Hood, then Uncle Kit shot alongside the Kid.

William H. Bonney, alias Billy the Kid, was easily New Mexico's best-known outlaw, having fought in the Lincoln County War. The bloody range war had erupted over land, cattle, and—what else?—politics. The Kid had fought on the side of the poor folk while the other side was backed by the Santa Fe Ring, a group of corrupt, upper-crust politicians. The war ended in defeat for the Kid and his compadres, who turned to cattle rustling after it was all said and done. This led to the Kid becoming a wanted man. He had been captured at Stinking Springs, jailed in Santa Fe for a while, then was sentenced to be hanged in Lincoln. The Kid miraculously slipped out of his shackles and made a death-defying escape from the courthouse though, cementing himself as a legend before fleeing to Fort Sumner, his favorite spot in all of New Mexico.

In addition to hanging around Old Fort Sumner in life, the Kid had made Fort Sumner his permanent residence upon his death. The scourge of cattle barons across the land, they had elected Pat Garrett as sheriff to go and hunt him down. And that he did on a moonlit night in July of 1881, ending the Kid's alleged reign of terror among the cattle barons. The Kid had been buried in the Old Cemetery near Bosque Redondo. The Kid's grave was the main reason that anyone that didn't live in Fort Sumner or didn't plan to live there stopped on their way through.

The Old Fort Sumner Museum outside of the cemetery had made a killing in the last few years as books and movies on the famed outlaw became more prevalent. The museum was so successful that there was even talk of another family building a "Billy the Kid Museum" across town soon. The real kicker was that the new museum planned to build a replica of the Kid's grave. If that didn't beat all, Hondo thought.

The Kid's grave was the town's bread and butter, and that's one area where Uncle Kit had recently made waves. As of late, Uncle Kit had started making noise that Billy wasn't really buried in the cemetery. That's because, according to Uncle Kit, Garrett faked the Kid's death and Billy was alive and well and living in Texas. Hondo shook his head just at the thought of it. It was nearly as nutty as building a replica of the Kid's grave when the real thing was only a few miles away.

Though nobody necessarily believed Uncle Kit's recent claims about the Kid, it did make some folks angry. Afterall, if it turned out the Kid wasn't buried where they said he was, that would be bad for Fort Sumner. For a split second, Hondo halfway wondered if someone could have offed Uncle Kit just for that. But no, people around Fort Sumner didn't have that nature.

A glint of hot, shiny metal in the distance coupled with a violent bump from a pothole jarred Hondo from his thoughts. He cussed at the bump and then squinted through the dirt to confirm that what he was seeing was Uncle Kit's trailer. The reddish dirt of the valley that had gusted into the air gave the scene a hellish tint, but he could discern the outline of a long, dilapidated airstream. He had seen it before on a welfare check a while back, and from the look of things, it hadn't improved.

The trailer had settled onto the desert floor long ago when the tires went flat. Years of dust storms had piled up red sand along the bottom so that you couldn't even see the tires anymore. It had also sandblasted the once shiny metal into a dull grey that somehow still managed to reflect the sunlight. When he had settled here, Uncle Kit had never gone to the effort to put the trailer up on blocks, which is what one did when they intended to park for long periods of time. Uncle Kit hadn't bothered for one of three reasons, Hondo assumed. One was that he was lazy, or another could have been that he was unable to do so, but Hondo figured it was because he had known when he settled here that this would be his last stop along life's trail.

As he pulled closer and angled around the trailer to park, he spotted the sheriff's patrol car and cussed again. The old man had beaten him, naturally, and would be sure to rub it in that he had. The sheriff, in this case, was also his father, Harold Dumez. One would think that working with one's father would make matters easier, but not for Hondo. Even though he felt he had job security with the old man in charge, he was also under his constant scrutiny.

Hondo parked his patrol car next to his father's. He glanced over and could see the old man inside reading over a clipboard. He looked up at him and lowered his sunglasses, his beady brown eyes boring into Hondo's even through two windowpanes and a dirt storm.

Hondo stepped out of his car while his old man did the same. "Nice of you to roll out of bed and join me this morning," his father grumbled as though he was late. Technically, he had been on time for work, which was 7:30, but it took nearly thirty minutes to drive out to Uncle Kit's place due to the rough terrain. Plus, the old man liked to wake up at 4:00 AM every day, so to him, anyone who got up past six was a beatnik.

His father slammed the door of his cruiser shut and cinched up his pants, which were already too high for Hondo's liking. The old man had a proud, hawkish nose and a paunch belly. Unlike the paunch, which Hondo noticed grew in increments every few years, the hair atop his head seemed to get a little thinner each year. Even though he was pushing sixty, he looked older. To Hondo it seemed his dad had been born an old man.

Hondo slammed his door shut. "What have you been here for, Dad, all of five minutes?"

"I told you when we're on duty to call me Sheriff," the old man huffed as he staggered against a particularly strong gust.

"There's no one out here right now, old man," Hondo shouted over the wind.

"Bah," he grumbled with a wave of his hand. "Let's get this over with. Besides, got better things to do than stand out in the damn wind all morning."

Despite his apparent haste to get inside, the old man stopped in front of the trailer with a hint of trepidation. When Old Lady Nelson had left, she had been in too much of a hurry to shut the front door securely. Now it was flapping open, the screeching grate of the hinges complimenting the hellish howl of the wind.

Father and son stared at the flopping door as though a ghost were inside until Hondo broke the silence. "You really think somebody killed him or that Old Lady Nelson's been watching too many murder mysteries?"

Hondo's father harumphed. "It was probably Old Lady Nelson's cooking that got him." But for all his bravado, like his son, the old man hadn't dealt with many murders himself. In fact, if his memory was right, the last one had occurred when the post office got robbed forty years ago. When the door flew open and slammed against the trailer once more, the old man pinned it down and marched inside.

Immediately upon following his father through the doorway, Hondo's hand flew up to his nose. The smell was ghastly and familiar, because even if he hadn't investigated a murder, he had retrieved decomposing bodies before. However, most of them had been outside. In the small, enclosed space, the perpetual warmth of New Mexico's Indian Summers had made it even worse.

"Well, he's dead alright," the old man remarked with his usual lack of tact. "The only question is, where is he?"

With one hand still over his mouth and nose, Hondo used the other to point ahead to a little sleeping area at the back of the trailer. An old buckskin hung from a rod obscuring the bed that lay behind it. Uncle Kit had to be there.

The old man withdrew a handkerchief from his pocket to place over his nose and approached the old buckskin curtain. He pulled it back and immediately began cussing up a blue streak, revealing the grisliest sight Hondo had ever laid eyes on. For a split second, the body didn't register as Uncle Kit. It wore his clothes and had his face and beard, but he was bald. No, Hondo suddenly realized he wasn't bald. He'd been scalped. That wasn't all. A large red splotch on the sheets drew his attention to the fact that Uncle Kit's right hand had been cut clean off.

Hondo looked away and was suddenly thankful for his empty stomach. If it was full, he might have thrown up. And even if it was only his father there, he still didn't want to be *that guy* at the crime scene. If you couldn't handle dead bodies, you were in the wrong line of work. However, with a sight like this, he wasn't sure that anyone would judge him. Hondo returned his gaze to the deceased.

Even if there wasn't any blood at the scene, it would still be apparent to anyone who saw it that Uncle Kit had not died peacefully. His mouth and eyes both gaped open in terror. The hand might have been cut off when he was still alive. Hondo felt sick and angry. The old man may have earned his meal ticket on lies, but he had never set out to hurt anyone. And he didn't deserve to die like this.

No, no one from town could have done this. If anyone around here wanted to kill Kit, they'd probably have just shot him. Had to be a sick drifter of some sort. A serial killer they called them, he thought.

"What do you think, Dad?" he asked, and this time the old man didn't correct the way he addressed him.

"God knows, son." The old man shook his head in disgust. Even with all his years in law enforcement, it was clear he'd never seen anything like this.

For a moment they stared at the corpse in stunned silence, the only sound being the hellish cacophony of wind outside the trailer.

The old man lowered his handkerchief from his face. "Come on. Let's go outside and look around while this place airs out." Hondo's father walked past him and then added, "We can haul him out and look around in here later. We'll need to see if anything's been taken."

That last remark raised Hondo's hackles, but he'd given up on saying, "I know, Dad," a long time ago. He'd been doing this job with the old man for the past two years now, and his dad still felt the need to state the obvious to Hondo. In this case, the obvious being that they'd look around the trailer to see what the killer had taken. Hondo suddenly stopped in his tracks as he glanced around the trailer, which looked awfully neat if any type of robbery had occurred. What if the killer hadn't taken anything? If that were the case—

"Hey, pin the door open, would ya?" His old man hastily cut into his thoughts.

"Yeah, sorry," Hondo answered, still running through motives in his head as he latched the door open so that hopefully some of the smell would dissipate. He noticed suddenly that the wind wasn't fighting him on the door.

Hondo stepped outside and was relieved not to have his eyes assaulted by a flurry of dirt. Strangely enough, the wind was gone. It was as if it had done its due diligence in setting the stage for the murder, and now that that part of the play was over, like an actor, it had exited stage left.

Hondo stood next to his father and looked down at the sandy earth. "Damn wind's probably already blown away any footprints."

"Well, look around just the same. You never know what you'll find."

The old man walked towards the west to circle the back of the trailer while Hondo faced east. Outside of the trailer were a few junk items that wouldn't fit inside, mostly Indian paraphernalia like a reproduction totem pole, things of that nature. There was also a rudimentary corral which Hondo noticed that Uncle Kit's horse, Geronimo, was absent from. Someone, probably the killer, had either taken it with them or let it go. Kit had never learned to drive a car and preferred the old ways, which in this case meant a horse.

Hondo knelt to examine the sandy red earth for hoofprints just in case the killer had ridden the horse, but as he feared, the loose earth had blown away in the dust storm. Not only had the wind helped set the stage for the murder today, it had also been an accomplice.

Hondo stood and began to walk around to the backside of the trailer when his boot caught something in the dirt and he nearly tripped. He looked down to find a wooden stake pounded deep into the earth. Hondo kicked around the stake, only it had been driven so far into the dirt it looked more like a mini-tree stump cut off close to the ground.

"Uncle Kit didn't have a dog he kept tied up, did he?" Hondo asked, wondering if that was the former purpose of the stake.

His father walked from behind the trailer and looked at him like he was an idiot. "What?"

"The stake." Hondo pointed at the ground.

"I don't know, but there's three more of 'em all around the property and that makes four," the old man responded.

Hondo contemplated the purpose of the stakes. The intuitive side of his gut told him that they might be important, while his practical side told him he was overthinking things. For all Hondo knew, every strange detail mattered in a murder case. Or, at least, he thought they should.

The old man leaned up against the trailer to scrape some horse dung from his boot. Hondo settled back against the trailer next to him. He pulled a toothpick from his shirt pocket and was soon twiddling it in his mouth. He'd found that when he was deep in thought it was best he found something to chew on; a stick of gum, a blade of grass, whatever he could find, because if he didn't, he'd just end up biting his lower lip. "You find anything out back?"

His father ceased scraping the dung from his boot to shoot him an irritated look.

"Other than horse shit, I mean," Hondo added.

"Nope." The old man shook his head and went back to scraping. "Just like you said. Any tracks to be found were blown away in the wind."

"I just don't get who'd want to kill Uncle Kit. What's the angle?" Hondo wondered aloud.

The old man ceased clutching his boot and stood up straight again. "Well, he did choose to name himself after public enemy number one as far as Indians are concerned. And they hated it out there at the Bosque."

It was true. Kit Carson, the *real* Kit Carson, had led the main campaign that subjugated the Navajo and the Apache into surrendering. This, in turn, resulted in the legendary Long Walk to Bosque Redondo just outside of town from 1864 to 1868. Many had died on the journey. Hondo remembered one story in particular that always stuck with him about a young Navajo mother and her little boy being left behind on the trail to freeze to death. Things weren't any better when the Indians arrived at the Bosque, and within a few years all were allowed to return to their homelands.

"You suggesting an Apache did this?" Hondo asked since the Navajo weren't known for scalping, then added, "No Apache has lived in these parts for nearly a hundred years."

"Musta been passing through is all I can figure. Besides, who else scalps anybody anymore?"

"Nobody." Hondo shook his head. "Not even Apache. More likely I'd think it was some sicko who's watched too many Westerns."

"Could be. But just the same, I might go down to the Mescalero Reservation this weekend and ask around."

"That's out of our jurisdiction, isn't it?"

"To arrest somebody, yeah, but to get some consultation, no. Besides, you got any better ideas?"

It wasn't a challenge this time, just an honest question. In fact, that he'd even ask nearly gave Hondo the warm and fuzzies.

"No, I reckon not." Hondo looked up at the sky, finally able to see its normal clear blue, the dark wind now gone as if it had never been there at all. "Well, you want me to head back into town and radio for the coroner as soon as I'm in range?"

The old man stared off into the distance and then spit. Spitting seemed to be a prerequisite for him when it came to answering a question. "I reckon. I'll look around the trailer for a bit, see if anything's been taken."

Hondo nodded and walked towards his patrol car.

The old man suddenly stopped him with a question. "Hey, what else you got going on in town other than fetching the coroner for me?"

Hondo turned around and could tell from a rare look of orneriness on the old man's face that he knew exactly why he was anxious to get back into town.

Hondo grinned. "Nothing. Gotta see a man about a horse is all." It was an old joke between him and the old man that was code for "None of your business."

"Or to go ogle that new waitress at Patsey's?" The old man gave him a half-amused, half-irritated smirk. "I have been a cop for over half my life, son. Besides, your mother is getting antsy about grandchildren."

"She's already got one!" Hondo threw up his hands. His younger brother Jerry and his wife had just had a baby boy first thing that year.

"Yeah, but you're the oldest. She's getting worried."

"Well, tell her it'll be nine months at least."

"Better be more than that!" The old man hollered at him with a pointed finger as he crawled into his car.

"I haven't even asked her out yet. If she's even the one," Hondo said as he shut the door and started the engine.

The old man waved his hands in disgust. "Bah, the one! You kids today believe what you see in those awful moving pictures. Your mother and I were practically forced into our marriage and look how we turned out."

"Exactly!" Hondo shouted and then tore out of Uncle Kit's place, stirring up another angry dust cloud on his way back to Fort Sumner.

II.
THE GIRL

It was a quarter past nine, and Debbie Madrid was still waiting for the jingle of the diner's front door to herald the entrance of a certain handsome stranger. Not that he was really a stranger anymore. She had learned his name, Hondo, and his occupation, a sheriff's deputy. She was new in town and still getting a sense of the place. But for the past two weeks, watching him walk into the diner to get his coffee had been the highlight of her morning. For the first four days, she didn't attempt any real conversation with him. Patsey, the owner, did most of the talking. Like everyone in small towns, they had known each other for life, or since "you were knee-high to a grasshopper" in Patsey's terminology.

When Patsey wasn't around, Hondo wasn't unapproachable, but something in his demeanor always seemed to give the impression of someone who was deep in thought. Someone who didn't need to be distracted by inconsequential chatter about the weather, or whatever she could think of to talk to him about, and she was dying to talk to him. Only about what? She wasn't sure how to approach him outside of taking his order, which was always the same, black coffee, no sugar. But finally, on the fifth day, he started to make small talk with her. It was the usual, "I don't think I've ever seen you around town before?" followed by, "Not until the last few days, I mean."

Debbie had responded, "I just moved here a week ago." She made sure to stress "I just moved here" as opposed to we. As in she was single. "Still trying to get the lay of the land and all that," she added, a perhaps not-so-subtle hint that she would love for someone like him to show her around. Their little conversation had continued, and he had been nice but hadn't taken the hint. Maybe she was overthinking it, but she had taken it as a rejection and had decided from then on to be friendly but guarded where Hondo was concerned. Maybe he didn't like forward girls? Maybe he preferred girls who played hard to get?

She was hoping that maybe he was mixed like her. Her father had been Hispanic, and her mother was white, which was still taboo. That made things harder for her when it came to finding a man of her own. She wasn't dark enough for the Mexican boys that dreaded bringing a white girl home to their mama, and she wasn't light enough for the white boys who seemed to fear their mamas nearly as much as the Mexicans did.

But, if he was mixed like her, he'd be perfect. Not that that was the only reason she had her eye on him. She would have been over the moon for Hondo either way. He was what she would call lightly-olive skinned with dark brown, almost black hair, and the oddest but most attractive eyes she'd ever seen on a man, light green with a golden rim right around the pupil that she'd never seen on any other human being. His broad shoulders oddly made him look shorter than he really was, which still wasn't quite six feet, but she didn't mind. She was only 5'6", so he was still plenty tall for her. Debbie glanced up from the counter to the windows. A few cars passed by on the street, but no one walked past the diner at the moment.

"Don't worry, I'm sure he'll be in eventually," Patsey said.

"Who?" Debbie said, hoping she came across as innocent as she scrubbed the countertop.

Patsey gave her a look that said otherwise. "Really, Debbie?" Patsey picked up a few saltshakers from the counter. "If you want him to make a move, you'll have to give him a few more signals."

Debbie shrugged and swept some crumbs off the counter. "I don't know. I don't think he's interested in me. Or maybe I'm just not pretty enough for him."

Patsey let out a smoker's cackle as she proceeded to refill the shakers. "Honey, there's nothing more irritating than a pretty girl who pretends like she doesn't know she's pretty."

Patsey had gotten her there. "Okay, so I'm not the most hideous girl in town, but I still don't think he's interested in me."

"Or maybe you've just been trying so hard to hide how bad you have it for him that he thinks you're not interested." Patsey paused to let it sink in. "Hondo's polite. If that boy doesn't think you're interested, he's not going to ask." Patsey set the saltshakers back on the counter and walked down to the other end.

Debbie had never thought about it that way. Before she could contemplate the matter further, the door jingled, and this time she just knew it would be him. It was. The only thing that surprised her was that he was out of uniform today, wearing a black shirt with a dark brown jacket over it. As he walked towards the counter, she decided to take Patsey's advice and show some interest.

"You're late today, Hondo." Debbie made sure to say his name right away. She had read in a magazine that when people liked you, they used your name more often in conversation.

He offered a weary grin as he slid down onto the stool. "Had a tough case this morning."

"Like what?"

He plucked a toothpick from the counter and started twiddling it around in his mouth. "Can't tell you, too gruesome."

Debbie shrugged. "Well, I know it's a little late for coffee, Hondo, but I take it you still want your usual?" She hadn't waited for a response and was already pouring black coffee into the cup before him.

When she finished, he pushed it back towards her with an uncharacteristically cocky look in his eyes. "Nah, today I think I need some sugar."

Debbie turned away as she felt her face blush. She looked over at Patsey down at the other end, who gave her a sly, mischievous grin. Debbie pretended to be looking for the sugar even though it was under the counter behind her as she waited on her blush to fade.

"I think it's under here." Hondo leaned over the countertop to grab it. He smiled mischievously when her eyes met his, as if he knew why she'd turned away.

He slid back behind the counter and poured the sugar in his coffee. "So, what's new?"

"You're ornery today."

He sat the sugar down. "And I asked you a question."

"And I answered it. That is new. You're not usually this… interesting." Debbie had debated whether or not to say the last part, but if he was teasing her, then maybe she should tease him back.

Hondo practically spit out his coffee laughing. He and Patsey exchanged a look as though they had an inside joke going that Debbie wasn't a part of.

He wiped the coffee from his lip on his sleeve. "Not usually this interesting, huh? Wow, I didn't realize that talking to me every day was that rough."

Had he been drinking? He seemed like a completely different person today. She'd say he was putting on an act, except acts didn't usually work, hence why they were called an act. But, even though this wasn't the Hondo that she'd gotten to know over the past two weeks, it somehow didn't seem fake, either.

"It's just... I've never seen you like this," Debbie said with a shrug.

Hondo didn't miss a beat. "Well, how'd you like to see me like this again tonight at seven?"

The question shocked her. "See me again?" She picked up a clean glass and started shining it just to be doing something with her hands. "You won't see me here if that's what you mean. I'm not working tonight."

"I know you're not. That's why I asked. I was thinking we'd go somewhere..."

Hondo paused as her eyes met his.

"A little nicer?" Debbie finished his sentence and immediately regretted it since Patsey was within earshot.

Out of instinct, Debbie looked over at her with a deer-in-the-headlights expression. "Sorry, I didn't mean—"

Patsey cocked an eyebrow and then grinned. "It's alright. I ain't gonna fire ya. I know what ya meant," she said before sauntering off.

"I was actually gonna say somewhere a little crummier," Hondo broke the awkward silence. "Ever hear of Sunnyside Up?"

Debbie had. It was a little bar on the outskirts of town. She couldn't believe Hondo would invite her there, though. "Funny, I wouldn't have figured that for your kind of place."

"I go there all the time. To drag the drunks out, I mean. I just thought I might rather experience it as a customer for once. Try something new."

He finished his coffee. "Besides, tomorrow's Thanksgiving and bars are great the night before Thanksgiving. People drift back into town for the holiday. Old friends, long-lost relatives. You never know who you're gonna see walking in." He paused for a second. "Or see stumbling out." He grinned and twiddled the toothpick around some more. "So whattaya say?"

It wasn't what she had imagined when she pictured him asking her out on a date. She wasn't even sure she wanted to go to a bar. But since Hondo had asked her… "Sure."

"Slip me your address and I'll pick you up."

Debbie took the pen from behind her ear and wrote it on a blank ticket, then slid it across the counter.

He put it in his jacket pocket, stood up, and plucked a donut out of the glass cake stand on the counter. "Catch ya later, sweet stuff." He winked at her and then turned towards the front door as Debbie watched in disbelief. Suddenly she realized she had never given him his actual ticket.

"Hey, you didn't pay," Debbie called out as he neared the door.

"Put it on my tab!" he garbled through a mouthful of donut and walked outside.

"You don't have one!" she yelled as the door jingled shut.

Patsey walked back behind the counter and grinned at Debbie's confusion. "What was all that about?"

"Oh, let's just say you saw another side of Hondo Dumez today, darlin,'" Patsey answered cryptically.

What did that mean? Did he have a split personality or something? The matter continued to confuse her for the next few minutes until Hondo walked in again, this time in his uniform.

"You're back already?" Debbie said. "And you changed, too."

"I changed?" Hondo crinkled his shirt collar between his fingers.

Patsey broke the awkward silence. "Your brother was here."

"Brother?" Debbie muttered.

"Pancho was in here? How long ago?" From the way Hondo was clutching the door handle, it was clear he was about to fly back outside.

"About ten minutes or so," Patsey said. "And guess what else? You owe me fifty cents."

"Geez. I'll pay you back in a little bit. I mean, get him to pay you," he said before bolting out the door.

Patsey turned to Debbie. "Don't feel bad, honey. Even their mama can't tell 'em apart sometimes."

Feeling slightly embarrassed, Debbie picked up Hondo's—or Pancho's—empty coffee cup. Hondo suddenly burst back into the diner and ran up to the counter. He wasn't coming for Patsey, though. He was coming straight for her.

"I'm sorry," he said, literally sliding up to the countertop.

"You want your coffee to go?" she asked, assuming that was what he wanted.

"No, I actually came in here to ask you a question, and if I didn't have such a crazy day, I'd just come back when I had more time, but... I was wondering... if you'd like to go to dinner with me tonight?"

Debbie nearly dropped the mug.

"I mean, unless you're already seeing someone," Hondo said, mistaking her look of shock for one of awkward disinterest. "It's just you said you were new in town and..."

"Oh no, it's not that. I want to. It's just..." Debbie paused, wondering if she should tell him who had just asked her out, but a sudden impulse told her not to. "...someone else already asked me tonight and I had said yes. I mean, I'd rather go with you, I just already committed and..."

"I understand. Friday night, maybe? So long as you don't end up marrying him or something before that," he said with a smirk.

"It's okay. He doesn't seem like the marrying type," Debbie blurted out, then suddenly regretted it, realizing how it sounded. Nice girls usually didn't date guys who "weren't the marrying type" since men like that usually only had one thing on their mind.

"Oh," Hondo nodded awkwardly as if he were mapping out the scenario in his head.

"I mean, it's not like that. It was sort of a misunderstanding. It's a really long story." Debbie sighed and glanced to Patsey for help, but she only offered the look of a spectator who was enjoying the figurative car wreck unfolding before her eyes.

"Okay," Hondo began, a hint of awkwardness still apparent in his voice as he backed away from the counter. "Well, Friday night, if I don't see you before then. Anyways, I better go try to find my brother. See y'all later."

Patsey walked by once he was out the door and gave Debbie a gentle snap with her dishtowel. "How you like that, honey? Now you got two to choose from."

***

Hondo strutted swiftly along the sidewalk of Sumner Avenue. Like a random tumbleweed blown in on the wind, Pancho would choose today of all days to tumble back into his life. Ordinarily, Hondo would have been nothing but happy to hear that his brother was back. Today wasn't ideal for Pancho's arrival for a few reasons. One was the murder, of course, which was distracting in its own right. Two was that Pancho had thrown off his concentration on the very day that he had finally decided to make his move on Debbie. And three, which was the reason he had rushed out of the diner, was that the fifty cents at Patsey's was small potatoes compared to what Pancho owed other folks around town. Hondo had been told by more than a few of the ne'er-do-wells in the vicinity that they'd clobber Pancho when and if he rolled back into Sumner.

Pancho's knack for getting in trouble was just one of many reasons that Hondo frequently wanted to clobber Pancho himself. But then again, as different as he was from him, Pancho had been his other half growing up. They had done everything together, from school to the war, which the U.S. was entering just as they graduated.

Hondo had a few guesses as to where Pancho might have headed after leaving the diner, but he scanned the concrete sidewalk for clues just the same. Considering a cup of coffee only cost a quarter and he'd racked up a fifty-cent bill, he probably snatched a donut on the way out. And like a rat, he'd left a small trail of crumbs along the way.

Hondo soon realized he didn't need to follow the crumbs; he could follow the noise. A commotion was coming from the pool hall, and something told him it wasn't the billiard balls thwacking into each other. The McPherson clan hung out there and were among those who had threatened to clobber Pancho upon his return to Sumner, which wasn't good considering that the McPhersons were the biggest men in the valley. Hondo crossed the street for the pool hall, the noise growing louder with each step. Hondo only became nervous when the noise suddenly ceased.

Hondo swung the door open anxiously, and every head in the room—about half a dozen or so—shot in his direction. Slim McPherson had Pancho pinned by the neck against the wall with a pool cue, while one of Slim's cousins had a hold of Pancho's right hand, probably to break his thumb. That's how pool hustlers were dealt with.

"Hondo," Pancho hissed through his blocked airway, "if this is about the fifty cents at Patsey's—"

"Pancho, shut up." Hondo turned his vexed gaze from his brother to the man holding him against the wall. "And you, just what in the hell you think you're doing?" Hondo asked, even though he could imagine. Being a pool shark, Pancho had no doubt swindled one of them the last time he was in town.

"It's not what it looks like, Deputy," Slim intoned in his distinctive, nasally voice. Though easily the biggest man in the valley, Slim was also notorious for having the most nasally voice in the valley as well, probably due to his nose having been broken many times over the course of his life.

"I know exactly what it looks like. You're about to break the thumb of a pool hustler," Hondo said.

"Maybe I am, but this is between me and him, Hondo, and I got every right," Slim said.

"Got every right? Didn't you know better than to play him for money?" Hondo responded since Slim had lived in Sumner his whole life.

"Well o' course I did, but my little nephew Bean Pole didn't." Slim cocked his head in the direction of his "little nephew," who was close to seven feet tall and sat in the corner glaring at Pancho with his arms crossed.

"Now hold on, Slim. That may be, but it ain't fair the way you got him outnumbered."

"Ain't fair the way that Pancho swindled Bean Pole outta $100 either."

"Maybe not." Hondo held up a finger. "But he still beat 'em one on one, mano a mano."

A contemplative expression crossed Slim's face. "Well, I suppose that's a reasonable point." Slim abruptly released Pancho from the wall and he tumbled to the floor, gasping for air.

"Thanks," Pancho rasped in the direction of his brother as the color returned to his face.

Hondo walked to his twin and helped him off the floor, then to Slim, said, "Now, contrary to what you might be thinking, I don't have a problem with you breaking his thumbs."

"You don't?" Pancho interjected, a look of horror and betrayal on his face.

"It's that if you do it, it needs to be in a good ol' fashioned one-on-one fight first," Hondo continued.

"That still don't get Bean Pole back his $100," Moose McPherson, the shortest and squattiest of the bunch, said.

"Moose, you're right," Hondo replied. "And, as deputy of Fort Sumner, I propose a solution to our little problem here."

"Yeah, what's that?" Moose asked, clearly the brains of what little brains the McPherson operation had amongst them.

Hondo turned to his brother and smiled. "I propose a little bet. Slim knocks Pancho the hell out and you get your $100 back. But Pancho knocks Slim out first, you owe us $200. Double or nothing as they say."

"What the hell are you doing?" Pancho whispered to him. "I can't beat Slim."

"I know." Hondo gave him an ornery smirk and slipped out from under Pancho's arm, letting him stand on his own again.

Moose answered for his kin. "Alright, Deputy, we'll take your offer seeing as how there's no way in hell your brother can take Slim." All the McPhersons nodded in agreement.

Slim pounded his pool cue into the floor. "Damn right! Now somebody count to three so I can knock this s.o.b. the hell out!"

"Wait just a minute," Hondo said sternly, holding up a hand. "If this is gonna be for money, then it has to be a fair fight."

"Well o' course it's gonna be, Hondo." Slim butted the pool cue into the ground again like a judge over a contemptuous court.

Hondo shook his head as he walked towards Slim. "I don't know about you McPherson boys." Hondo turned his gaze to Slim's cousins as he continued his walk towards Slim. "Remember that time at the 4th of July picnic that Slim did this to me?"

Hondo suddenly kneed Slim in the groin and he doubled over. "Now, Hondo, we was just kids then! I wouldn't do that now!" Slim squeaked out.

"Well, maybe not, but you mean to tell me you didn't plan on doing this with the pool cue?" Hondo grabbed it and smashed it over Slim's shoulder.

"Hell no, I wasn't gonna do that!" Slim said, sinking a little lower to the ground.

"What about this?" Hondo twisted his nose between his fingers and Slim let out a particularly girlish scream as he sank to his knees.

"No, I ain't gonna do that!" he wailed like an angry child being accused of a crime he didn't commit.

Hondo let go of his nose and gave Pancho a knowing look. "Well, if you're gonna fight fair, then I say one, two, three—go!"

Pancho didn't miss a beat and clobbered Slim across the face while he was still down on his knees. Slim let out another girlish yelp and collapsed like a rock tower onto the floor.

***

After collecting their winnings from the dimwitted McPhersons, who were what the city people might call inbred, Hondo and Pancho strutted out of the pool hall. Slim glared at them from the open doorway like an angry cat that had just been given an unwanted bath.

"I'm gonna go lock him up now, Slim. Don't you worry!" Hondo called in jest as he counted their winnings.

Pancho didn't feel too bad for what had just transpired considering that when they were kids the Mcphersons' favorite game was to hold them face down in the irrigation ditches until they nearly passed out.

"There's gotta be something in the water at their ranch, I swear." Pancho shook his hand, which was already sore from impacting Slim's fat head.

"Well, you know how Ma used to warn us not to play with those McPherson boys," Hondo said.

"Yeah, well, we showed them, didn't we?" Pancho said and then launched into an impromptu imitation of Slim: "'Hey, you brokended my dose!'"—those being Slim's first words upon returning to consciousness.

"Hey, where's my cut?" Pancho held out his hand expectantly.

"Your cut? I did 90 percent of the work."

"Well, what about my ten percent then, smartass?"

"Twenty bucks, let's see… let's call that interest on the fifty cents you racked up on my tab at Patsey's." Hondo stuffed the money into his wallet. Pancho didn't suppose he could argue with that. Hondo had been the one to come save his bacon, after all.

"Why if it ain't the Dumez boys back together," Pancho heard a familiar, aged voice say. He looked up to see one of the old-timers, Boots McGee, walking in their direction. The old man had lost all his teeth since he'd seen him last.

"And in trouble already." Boots shook his head, taking notice of Pancho's limp. "You the one who beat him up, Deputy?"

Hondo shook his head. "No, someone else beat me to it."

"Yeah, what about you, Boots?" Pancho joined the exchange. "You lose that last tooth in a fight, or you just bite into some hard candy recently?"

A sour look crossed Boots' face. With a "Bah!" and a dismissive wave of his hand, he was off along the sidewalk again.

"Yeah, yeah, nice to see you too, Boots," Pancho hollered, trying a little harder to hide the limp.

"So, what brought you into town today anyways, the wind?" Hondo asked.

Pancho shrugged. "Turkey tomorrow, I reckon."

"Shoot, knowing you, I was worried you might be gone by tonight. That mean you'll come by for dinner later at Ma's?"

"Actually, I'm meeting a friend tonight at Sunnyside." The thought of what Hondo didn't know yet made him grin. "You should come along. Besides, night before Thanksgiving, gonna be all sorts of people rolling back into town. Maybe even one of your old high school girlfriends or something."

Hondo laughed and grabbed him by the neck, wringing it only slightly. "Yeah, you son of a bitch. Most of them are my ex-girlfriends thanks to you," he said since their identical appearance had caused more than a few mishaps and misunderstandings with the opposite sex.

Pancho shoed his hand off his neck. "Yeah and you should be thanking me. Probably would've settled down with one of the Lobley girls and be out picking cotton right now if it weren't for me."

"Yeah, yeah," was Hondo's only response.

When their rapport didn't continue after a moment, Pancho asked, "Something on your mind? You got awfully quiet."

Hondo paused pensively before responding. "Dad and I found a body this morning… Uncle Kit."

Pancho was surprised in the sense that everyone is when someone they've known their whole life dies, but at the same time not surprised considering Kit's age. "Uncle Kit, huh? What was he, a hundred?"

"Who knows? But it wasn't natural causes that got him."

"It wasn't?"

"Nope." Hondo made a slitting motion across his throat.

"Who the hell would want to kill Uncle Kit?"

"That's what I said."

"How—"

"I'll tell you later. I don't feel like talking about it now."

Even though Pancho could tell his brother was shook by the murder, somehow he could sense that wasn't what caused the awkward silence earlier. Pancho put two and two together when they walked past the diner and felt his brother's demeanor change.

"Uncle Kit isn't the only thing that's bothering you, is it?"

Hondo didn't respond.

"Come on. You can keep secrets from Mom and Dad, but not from me. What's eating you?"

Hondo glanced briefly in the direction of the diner. "I asked out the girl that works in the diner—you saw her, I'm sure—but she already had a date."

"Psh, don't sweat it." Pancho stopped him. "You know why?"

Hondo turned to face him. "Why?"

Pancho gave him a knowing look and slapped his shoulder. "Because whoever he is, I bet he ain't half the man that Hondo Dumez is."

III.
THE HUSTLER

Pancho twiddled his toothpick as he searched for his turn. It was 6:58, so he was on the verge of being late on his way to the girl's. He was also caught up in a drive down memory lane as he cruised up Sumner Avenue, recollections of his youth washing over him like warm, relaxing water. He had spent the first part of his life in Hatch, but his family had moved back here when he turned thirteen. That was the year that he discovered two things: girls and fighting. While girls provided him with an intellectual challenge, fighting provided the physical one. Fighting didn't stem from any repressed anger or resentment towards anyone in particular—he just enjoyed the challenge and intensity of a fight. That's why he so often provoked Hondo.

During high school in particular Pancho had gone to extra pains to torture him. He'd check and see what Hondo was wearing for the day, then pick out an identical set of clothes and hide them in his backpack. They'd go to school together dressed differently, but at some point in the day, Pancho would change, impersonate his brother, and then do something horribly embarrassing in his disguise, which would then be blamed on Hondo. Then the fight would be on. Sometimes their younger brother, Jerry, would join in, too, even though he had nothing to do with their drama. He just wanted to be included.

Pancho scanned Sumner Avenue for new businesses, of which he still didn't see any. The only new trend he noticed was that some of the businesses sported a few of those "Better Dead Than Red" posters warning against communism—as if Fort Sumner would ever play home to Soviet spies. Even the local theater was playing only one movie, and it was *I Married a Communist,* which Pancho noted was already a year old.

Things might have gone different for Fort Sumner if not for the Great Depression. Back in the twenties, the Transcontinental Air Transport began building an airfield there until the stock market crashed. After that, it was abandoned and now only functioned as a small municipal airport. Time hadn't been terribly kind to their town, at least not in terms of population which barely hovered around 2,000 people. But, then again, maybe time was being kind by not increasing its numbers. Big cities bred violence as far as Pancho was concerned. Of course some people would consider the episode in the pool hall to be violence, but it wasn't the same as violence in the big cities somehow.

The animosity between the Dumez brothers and the McPhersons was mutually beneficial in his opinion. Like the good book said, as iron sharpens iron a friend sharpens a friend. That was Pancho's somewhat distorted view of it, at least. In his mind, he had taught Bean Pole a valuable life lesson about hustlers, and Bean Pole's uncles, in turn, had taught Pancho not to get too complacent and cocky.

Pancho viewed his date as "Hondo" with Debbie in a similar light. First thing he had done when he came into town that morning was to go and see Ma. Hondo and the old man were already out, and as Ma gave him the scoop on what was new, she had told him how Hondo was dragging his feet in asking out the new girl. Pancho had decided it would be fun and beneficial to just do it for him. After it was all over, it would just be a funny story. Or another fight, maybe, but that would just be a funny story one day, too.

Pancho had nothing but good intentions when he had gone into the diner. Maybe those good intentions were mixed with just a slight bit of orneriness, but they were still good just the same. However, when he had seen her, he could tell why Hondo liked her. She had dark skin, hair, and eyes that reminded him of a doe somehow. She was a true Fort Sumner fox if ever there was one.

It wasn't just the looks, though, but the purity and innocence she seemed to exude. Hondo was probably better suited for her in that regard, but then again, they did say that sometimes complete opposites made the best matches. Not that Hondo was an angel, it was just that in comparison to him, he seemed that way. If Pancho wasn't around, Hondo would probably have a reputation himself.

The figurative devil on his shoulder was currently whispering in his ear that maybe the girl would like him better, and if that was the case, so be it. It was her choice, after all. He tried to block the temptation from his mind. He was doing this for Hondo, both as a prank and a kind gesture and it was too late to turn back now. Besides, he had invited his brother to join them, and after he got there, he'd let him take over.

At 7:02, Pancho pulled up to a small pink house on Lantry. It suited her, he thought. He didn't have to get out of the car. When he saw the inside light switch off and the porch light switch on, he knew that meant she was coming out.

He was still debating whether or not to keep up the charade that he was Hondo as she walked towards the car. He leaned over to open the door for her, and when she slid inside, he had his answer.

"Hello, Hondo, or should I say Pancho?" She slipped into the passenger seat with a challenging gaze. "I am speaking to Pancho now, aren't I? Unless you two have switched places yet again and you're actually Hondo now?"

Pancho smirked. "Why? Do I seem boring already?"

She held up a finger as she shut the door. "I never said Hondo was boring." She sounded defensive. Clearly, she really liked his brother.

"That is what you said. You said my brother was boring," Pancho said with a shrug.

She settled into the seat and fastened the safety belt. "I didn't say that. I said you were just more… talkative."

"No, you said I was more interesting." He started the car and pulled out of her driveway.

"Well, he's more polite, that's for sure. Besides, I only agreed to go out with you because I thought you were—"

Pancho gave her an "Oh really?" look and Debbie suddenly stopped herself, her eyes turning apologetic. "I'm sorry. I didn't mean it like that."

He grinned. "It's okay. This isn't really a date."

"It's not?" There was a hint of alarm in her eyes, as if he might be about to drive her out to the middle of nowhere and then leave her for dead.

"I mean, not between us. I invited Hondo," Pancho clarified.

"Oh." Her eyes seemed to brighten, which suddenly bugged him. "Does he know?" she asked hesitantly.

"No. It'll be a surprise." After a beat, he added, "I have one question for you, though. If you'd met me first and I asked you out, would you have said yes?"

Pancho watched her bite her lip from the corner of his eye before she finally responded. "Maybe." After a beat, she added, "I have a question for you."

"Yeah?"

"You ever stop stirring the pot?"

"Never." He looked away and bit down hard on his toothpick. The devil on his shoulder was currently winning.

***

Hondo inspected his face in the steamy bathroom mirror. It was clean now. Earlier, the weather of the day had darkened it with smudges of dirt which had stuck to his skin thanks to the perspiration. But then again, his face was a little darker than a typical white man's anyways. That was just one reason that Pancho had gotten it into his head once that they were adopted. Their skin was olive-toned compared to their mother, father, and siblings, who were all lighter.

Hondo remembered the argument they had about that back when they were just starting high school.

"Look at them, Hondo, they're all white as sheets compared to us," Pancho had said.

"We're white, too."

"Yeah, but we're a much darker white, stupid."

"We're probably just throwbacks. We probably have some Indian blood somewhere and it just happened to manifest in us. That's all."

"Twins don't run in this family, either," Pancho continued his argument.

"Well, there's a first time for everything," Hondo had answered.

"But what about our eyes?" Pancho wasn't about to let it drop. "Nobody in our family has got eyes like us."

It was true. Pancho and Hondo both had a condition known as central heterochromia, where there were two distinct colors within the iris of their eyes, in this case, a gold-brown ring just outside the pupil, while the outer rim was light green. In fact, the only difference people could tell between the two of them, and that was only if they got up close and squinted, was that Pancho had a big dark spot in the golden ring around his left eye that Hondo didn't. But so far, their mother was the only one to notice that. He didn't think his old man had ever even noticed.

Their little argument had come to a head when Pancho wondered if, rather than being adopted, Ma had an affair. Hondo had chased him down and gotten him into a headlock until Pancho promised to drop it, though he suspected it still lingered somewhere in the back of his mind. It lingered in Hondo's too, sometimes.

Hondo finished drying himself off and exited the bathroom. It was 7:05, so he was already late to see Pancho and whoever his "friend" was, not that it mattered. It was probably a date, and Pancho only said it was a friend so Hondo wouldn't feel like a third wheel. But like Pancho said, it was the night before Thanksgiving. Even if it was a date, he wouldn't feel too out of place since Thanksgiving was typically a time for family reunions.

Hondo got dressed, snatched his cowboy hat, and marched across the yard towards his parent's house. He lived in a guesthouse on his folks' property, so he had privacy when he wanted it but could also go and raid Ma's kitchen when it suited him. Besides, it wasn't an empty nest just yet.

In addition to their younger brother, Jerry, they also had a baby sister named Patricia. She was born late and was only ten. Seemed like the old man almost had a heart attack when he found out Ma was pregnant with her. Poor Dad, Hondo thought. In three years she'd be thirteen, and his father would be 63. It'd be too much stress for an old man. Maybe he'd have to step in and do the boyfriend handling for him. But, of course, that said, Patricia was also the old man's favorite. Jerry was definitely the second favorite, so the way Hondo reckoned it, his father went from newest to oldest when it came to playing favorites.

"What are you all gussied up for tonight?" the old man asked as soon as he walked in. He was perched in his recliner like a big fat bald eagle in the living room while Ma did the dishes in the kitchen.

"I'm gonna go meet Pancho at Sunnyside Up." Hondo dug into the refrigerator.

"Boy can't even stop in and see his own family. Would rather go to the bar first thing," the old man grumbled, and even though Hondo had his back to him, he could tell he was shaking his head.

"He did come by, Harold. You were already at work. And he'll be home later tonight," Ma hollered.

"Sure, at 3:00 in the morning!" the old man retorted.

"See, old man, all you gotta do is wake up one hour earlier and you can see him first thing tomorrow." Hondo had cobbled together a crude baloney sandwich and was trying to choke it down as quick as he could and get going.

"He's probably out with a girl." Patricia was sitting at the kitchen table, combing the hair of her dolly. She looked up at him. "When are you gonna get a girl, Hondo?"

"You're my girl, don't you know that?" Hondo garbled through his sandwich.

"It's just you can't wait forever to settle down and have kids," Patricia said with a shrug, and Hondo knew that she was parroting something she'd heard Ma say. He shot Ma a look and she gave him a guilty smile from the sink.

"Oh, so you and Ma want grandkids? Well, you'll just have to make do with Jerry's little…"

His mother shot him a look.

"…bundle of joy. Christopher? Colton?" The kid was brand new and he still had trouble with the name.

"Cade," Patricia corrected him with a look.

"Well, I did finally ask Debbie out today."

"And?" his mother asked.

"And she said yes. We're going out Friday." Hondo deliberately didn't mention that she had a date tonight. In his mother and father's generation, if a girl had a date with two different men in the span of a week she might as well be what Ma called "one of those girls".

Hondo wanted to get going, but at the same time, he knew what a night out with Pancho would likely entail and decided it might be best to eat a few extra slices of bread to soak up the alcohol. As he chewed on the bread, he peered over the old man's shoulder as he read the paper. "So what's new in the world, Pop?"

"Oh, just some crazy loon that thinks he's Billy the Kid."

"What?"

"Hails from Granbury, Texas, of all places. Texas!" The old man shook his head in disgust and continued. "Claims Garrett let him get away and the whole thing was faked. Says his name's Tumbleweed Williams. Can you believe a name like that? What a squirrel. And he's getting a meeting with the governor next weekend to boot! If it were me, I'd send him straight to the nut house."

"What's he meeting the governor for?"

"Says he wants a pardon for the crimes he committed as Billy the Kid. Maybe I should go up there and threaten to arrest him, see if he still wants to say he's Billy the Kid after that." The old man straightened the paper angrily, then added, "I ever tell you my grandmother used to cook meals for the Kid at her place on the Hondo River?"

"Only a thousand times, Pop." Hondo's mind suddenly drifted to Uncle Kit's recent claims about the Kid being alive. "You think this Tumbleweed Williams guy might've known Uncle Kit?"

"Probably. Birds of a feather and all that." After a moment, he added, "And speaking of Uncle Kit, don't go telling everybody about him, at least not how he died, I mean. We're lucky Old Lady Nelson's been too ill to spread the word yet."

"Ain't that the truth?" He looked at his watch. "Anyway, I better get going. Pancho's probably wondering where I am." Hondo finished the last of his bread and slipped on his jacket. He walked over to the fridge and gulped down some milk from the bottle while Ma had her back turned and managed to get it back in by the time she turned around.

Ma got on her toes to kiss him on the cheek and then grabbed him by the shirt collar. "Just don't go beating him up when you see him, ya hear?"

"Why would I do that?" he said as she let go.

Ma shrugged, turned around, and began drying the dishes as though she had something to hide. "I just know how you boys are. Slightest little thing gets your blood to boiling and it's off to the races."

"Alright, see y'all later." Hondo headed for the door.

"You're taking your truck, aren't you? I don't want you booze cruising in the cruiser," the old man said.

"Yes, Dad," Hondo sighed, irritated.

"And don't forget, you're the sheriff's son!" the old man hollered at him—that was code for don't get too drunk. Hondo didn't respond and let the door slam behind him.

As he drove to Sunnyside Up, Hondo wasn't sure if his happiness for Pancho being in town outweighed his disappointment that Debbie hadn't been able to go out with him, but it was a nice consolation prize. For a split second he wondered if he might run into Debbie and her date there. No, she didn't seem like the type that would go on a date to a bar. At least he hoped not.

Debbie was important to him because she was one of the only single girls in town that looked to be his age. The rest were either too young or so old that they were taken or widowed. Not that that was the only reason he was interested in her. He felt like even if there were hundreds of girls to choose from in town, she'd still be his favorite. He had wanted to ask her out from the moment he'd seen her, but she hadn't seemed interested. He had told his mother, and she had said that maybe she was just shy or playing hard to get. Besides, he was the man, he'd be the one to ask one way or the other. But he'd waited too long, and now he was paying the price.

By 7:30 he was at Sunnyside Up. It was so named for an old settlement called Sunnyside that had long since gone belly up, so to speak, hence the bar's name. It was crowded just like Pancho said it would be. As he walked inside, even amidst the noise of friendly chatter and country music, Pancho had sensed his presence and locked eyes with him immediately. Hondo's suspicions had been right, he was here with a girl. Pancho waved and Hondo made his way over, bumping into several high school friends on the way there, which, as Pancho predicted, had come back into town for the holiday. It must've taken him five minutes to make it to Pancho's table.

His twin stood. "Hondo, where ya been? I've been dying for you to meet my friend, Debbie."

That was a funny coincidence, he thought, until he looked down at the pretty girl at the table and realized that it was Debbie.

"Hi, Hondo." Debbie offered him a guilty, sheepish wave, then added, "I was going to tell you this morning but—"

He switched his gaze from Debbie to Pancho. "This… This is your date?" His blood pressure went up and his left hand tightened into a fist.

Pancho held up his hands as Hondo inched closer. "She didn't know. I was pretending to be you, so technically, this is your date. Surprise."

Hondo cut his advance short and shot Debbie a confused, semi-suspicious look.

"Like I said this morning, it was sort of a misunderstanding," Debbie said with a look that pleaded her innocence.

Hondo offered her an awkward smile and then turned to his brother. "Can I have words with you for a moment?"

"We'll be right back," Pancho said to Debbie.

Hondo grabbed Pancho by his jacket collar and marched him over to the bar. "Pancho, what the hell are you doing?"

"Hey, Ma told me you were having trouble working up the courage to ask her out, so I thought I'd just do it for you. See, and here you both are."

"And you brought her to a place like this?" Hondo said, his voice filled with disgust.

"What? It's funny. Besides, it'll be a great story to tell the kids one day."

Hondo looked Pancho in the eye. He couldn't tell if he was playing games with him or being sincere. "Hey, I like her, man," Hondo said. Even though it was only five simple words, Hondo knew Pancho would understand that as a nice, coded way of saying, "I saw her first, she's mine, and you better stay away."

"Then go get her. She's right there." Pancho grinned and cocked his head at the pretty girl staring at them from the table where they left her.

IV.
THE OLD TIMER

*A*fter a few minutes, Hondo's blood had cooled. It was by now apparent that his twin had been telling the truth about setting up their date. In an odd way, Pancho had served as a good icebreaker. First dates could be awkward, and Pancho's meddling had actually served to make it less awkward in a way, as they were both victims of his prank. They had bonded more in those first few minutes discussing the strange circumstances of the evening than they had in the entirety of the first two weeks at the diner.

Pancho came back to the table with three drinks just as "If You've Got the Money, I've Got the Time" started to play.

"Well looky here, they're playing your song and everything. Speaking of which," Hondo said turning to Debbie, "he tell you I saved him from having his thumbs broken this morning?"

"No, he failed to mention that." Debbie took a sip of her drink.

"And Hondo tell you I made him $200 when I knocked out Slim McPherson with only one punch?"

"I made us $200 after I got Slim down on his knees for you," Hondo corrected. "But don't take that to mean being a delinquent pays off."

"I don't know about that," Pancho said and pointed at the jukebox. "Lefty Frizzel wrote that song while he was jailed down in Roswell. Now he's a millionaire." After a second, he added, "Hey, I guess this gives the term double date a new meaning?"

"This is not a date." Hondo leveled a finger at Pancho.

"It's not?" Debbie looked disappointed.

"I mean, yes, you and I are on a date," he said to Debbie, and then to Pancho, "And you're just—"

"The third wheel? I get it. I'll leave." Pancho stood.

"No." Debbie grabbed his hand. "You stay. From what I understand neither of you ever see each other. Besides," she looked at Hondo, "I learn more about you from him than I do you."

"Is that so?" Hondo could see he needed to be more aggressive. He stood up and held out his hand. "In that case, come dance with me, and you can ask anything you want."

Debbie looked a little surprised, and so did Pancho.

She took his hand and they walked to the small dance area. "Goodnight Irene" by Moon Mullican was playing now.

"So, have you lived here your whole life?" she asked her first question.

"Just half of it. We were born and raised in Hatch 'til we were thirteen, then we moved here. You?"

She smiled. "Cimmaron, of all places."

"Oh yeah? You still got family there?"

When she looked away, Hondo could see he had touched on a sore spot. After a moment, she answered. "No, not anymore. Our dad ran out on us," she said with a tinge of shame that he could tell still stung. "And mother passed away earlier this year."

"I'm sorry to hear that," Hondo said.

"Anyways, I just wanted to go somewhere new. Start over." The tone in her voice made it apparent she wanted to change the subject. "And now I'm here in this strangely named bar that I initially mistook to be some kind of breakfast joint."

Hondo spun her, then explained, "Well, long, long time ago, there used to be two towns side by side, sorta like twins, actually." He nodded at his brother. "They were called Sunnyside and Fort Sumner."

"What happened? Did one eat the other?" Debbie joked.

"Not exactly. A windstorm blew Sunnyside off the face of the earth forty-five years ago." Hondo looked over at his brother and hollered, "Kinda like me and Pancho here. Area ain't big enough for the both of us, is it, little brother?"

"Little brother? You both look the same size to me," Debbie said.

"He was born one minute before me," Pancho hollered from the table. "And he won't ever let me forget it, either."

"Darn straight, that's why I'm always on time and he's always late," Hondo answered.

"Says the guy who got here late," Debbie told him.

"That's before I knew this was a date, though. If I knew that, I woulda been on time," Hondo replied.

"Well, you're kind of right. He was late," she said in a whisper.

Hondo looked into her eyes. "Well, one thing I can promise is I'd never leave a girl like you hanging."

From the reaction she gave him, something told Hondo he could have kissed her then if he wanted, but somehow it didn't seem appropriate—both the location and all the people watching. But he could tell Debbie was thinking about it, too, on some level hoping he would. He gave her a knowing smile. "Come on. I think Pancho's getting lonely over there."

***

Time flew by, and before Hondo knew it, hours had passed. And, as much as he hated to admit it, he hadn't had this much fun in years. Maybe it was because by now he was slightly drunk, but he felt like Debbie was already his steady girlfriend. Drinking did that, made time pass different and made people you barely knew seem like family you'd known your whole life.

"Hey, so you said you were new in town, right?" Pancho asked Debbie, but Hondo could tell the question was really a set-up for something else.

"Yes, I've only been here two weeks."

"You got family here?"

"No." She shared a look with Hondo.

"What are you doing for Thanksgiving then?"

Debbie seemed to become embarrassed and crinkled her napkin. "Um, Patsey invited me to her house."

Hondo knew she was lying. Patsey had already driven to her sister's house in Eunice by now.

Pancho grinned. "You're a terrible liar."

Debbie let go of the napkin. "How did you know?"

"Because Patsey never sticks around here for Thanksgiving," Hondo answered.

"But you're welcome to come to our place for Thanksgiving," Pancho said, then shot Hondo a look that made it clear he was trying to help him, not make a move on her.

"Oh no, really I couldn't intrude," Debbie said, looking at Hondo even though it was Pancho who had invited her. Pancho gave Hondo a look as he sipped his drink, letting him know the response would need to come from him.

"Well, that's the thing," Hondo began. "Knowing you're home alone on a holiday is gonna make me feel bad and I doubt you'd want to ruin my Thanksgiving, right?"

"Well, I suppose if you put it that way, then... yes." Debbie smiled.

"Then it's settled," Pancho said. "You're spending Thanksgiving with us."

Hondo looked at his watch. It would be coming up on 10 o'clock soon. "And on that note, we had better get you home."

"Ah, come on. It's still early," Pancho whined.

"I won't turn into a pumpkin, Hondo," Debbie said.

"Come on. Just one more shot," Pancho pleaded. "Then we'll go home."

Four shots, three beers, and nearly two hours later, they were still there. Hondo was telling the story about the night that Pancho wanted to take two different girls to the movies and had impersonated him to do so.

"Lost my girlfriend over that one when she found out I was 'cheating' on her," Hondo concluded the tale.

"Oh, you act like you had it so bad?" Pancho slurred. Then, turning to Debbie, said, "You know what he did to me when we were kids?"

She grinned. "What?"

"He told all the kids at school that for the first four years of my life that Ma used to put me in dresses and call me Panchita."

Debbie grinned and swatted Hondo on the shoulder. "You did not?"

Hondo shrugged bashfully.

"He did, and so then to get even I told all the kids that Hondo was actually projecting his gender dysphoria onto me, and what really happened was that when he was born, his little wee-wee was so small that the doctor mistook him for a girl," Pancho said squeezing two fingers together.

"Hah!" Hondo drunkenly tipped up his hat with his beer bottle and leaned forward. "If it's true for me, then it'd be true for you, so joke's on you, too." Then Hondo turned worriedly to Debbie, shook his head, and whispered very seriously, "It's not true, by the way."

A few minutes later, when the conversation finally suffered a drunken lull, Hondo leaned back in his chair and surveyed the bar. They were the only revelers left. From behind the counter, the bartender, Charlie, glanced longingly at the clock, waiting for the long hand and the short hand to strike 12 so that he could kick them out. Charlie let out a sigh as the front door creaked open with the wind.

Hondo turned to see Old Man Miranda teeter in along with his grandson, Hugo, who was about Hondo's age. Salvador Miranda had lived around Sumner longer than anyone else currently still alive. And whereas most old-timers just claimed to know Billy the Kid, Salvador had made his tombstone not long after Garrett gunned him down. In fact, that new Billy the Kid Museum had even hired Miranda to make a duplicate tombstone for display, which was impressive considering that the old man was currently pushing 100. His secret to vitality, he claimed, was one shot of tequila a day.

"We didn't miss last call, did we, Charlie?" Hugo asked as his grandfather shuffled up to the bar.

"You did," Charlie lied and shrugged. "But, for the oldest man in the valley, I'll make an exception."

Charlie had already poured Salvador his usual as he reached the bar. The old man caught Debbie's eye. "Who's that?"

"That is the oldest hombre in Sumner, Salvador Miranda. Knew Billy the Kid and everything," Hondo answered.

"It's true, even made the Kid's tombstone," Pancho whispered, then shouted to the old man, "Hey, Mr. Miranda, how's it going?"

Salvador put his empty shot glass down and turned from the bar, pretending to do a double take at the twins. "If I deed not know you boys since you were *pequeño*, I would theenk the dreenk already get to me."

They all laughed. It wouldn't be that funny of a comment from anyone else, but it was somehow coming from a nearly hundred-year-old man. Salvador tottered over to their table, and Hugo stepped in to steady him. Hondo and Pancho both stood at once to shake his hand and Hugo's, then introduced Debbie.

After the introductions were made, Salvador sat next to Hondo, while Hugo pulled up a stool from the bar and perched atop it as if to stand sentry over the ancient patriarch.

Looking at Debbie, Salvador remarked, "Thees ees good. We need more pretty girls in thees town." Then motioning between Hondo and Pancho, asked, "Which one do you belong to?"

"Well, neither yet, but I think I'm leaning towards this one." Debbie settled back against Hondo's arm and patted his chest. Her touch made his alcohol-laced blood go especially hot and he was glad that he was sitting down at the moment.

"I'm gonna get us all one last drink," Pancho said abruptly and headed for the bar.

"I hear Uncle Keet is dead. Very sad how it happen," Salvador said, shaking his head.

Hondo nodded in somber affirmation until he reflected on that last part. "You mean you heard how he died?"

Salvador nodded. "Yes."

Debbie looked at Hondo. "What happened to him?"

"Scalped like in the old days," Hondo answered solemnly. "And they chopped off his hand for some reason, too."

Debbie slumped back in her chair with a bewildered look on her face, probably wondering what kind of a town she'd just moved to.

"You've lived here longer than anybody," Hondo said to Salvador. "What do you think? Could it really have been an Indian?"

Salvador looked pensive and began to shake his head. "Yes and no. I think it sounds like a *brujo*."

"A what?" Hondo asked, unable to place the word.

Salvador tried a word he thought Hondo might know. "A weetch."

"A witch? Like in *Wizard of Oz*?" Hondo was picturing Margaret Hamilton in green greasepaint.

Salvador looked mildly frustrated at his gringo interpretation of the word and shook his head again. "No. In our culture a weetch can be a man, too. I think he might have been a…"

Old Salvador's words trailed off as Hugo placed a hand on his shoulder and shook his head.

"A what?" Hondo looked at Hugo.

"We don't like to say it out loud," Hugo answered.

"Say what?"

Salvador motioned for Hondo to come closer, then whispered, "A skeenwalker."

"A skin-what?" Hondo blurted out drunkenly.

Hugo shot him an angry look. "As I said, we don't like to say it. It can draw… unwanted attention."

Pancho stumbled back up to the table with a tray of shots. "One more shot in memory of Uncle Kit. It's what the ol' boozehound would have wanted," Pancho said since Uncle Kit, too, had been a regular at the bar. Pancho plunked the shots down noisily, diffusing the lingering tension from the unutterable word.

"Okay, but this really is the last one," Hondo said, holding up a finger. It was a statement, not a question.

"Hugo, Mr. Miranda, I got you one too," Pancho said and handed them over. Pancho raised his glass. "Well, here's to Uncle Kit."

They all took their respective medicines, Hondo and Debbie being the only two to wince from the effect.

"Okay, folks, show's over," Charlie called from behind the bar.

Even though he knew it was long past due that they leave, Hondo was still disappointed that the night was coming to an end. They all stood and started to shuffle out together. Hondo turned his attention to the old man again. "Mr. Miranda, one more thing. Before he died, Uncle Kit claimed that the Kid was still alive. What do you say to that?"

The question seemed to agitate him for some reason, and he shook his head profusely. "Eh, Uncle Keet, he full of lies! Beelee thee Keed, I see hees body! He's dead! He dead!"

"Come on, Granddad. Let's get you home," Hugo said and began herding the old man through the door. "Thanks for the drinks," he added, and they stepped outside. It was clear Hugo wanted to be shed of them.

"What was that about?" Pancho asked.

"I don't know," Hondo said, still pondering the old man's strong reaction to the question.

Charlie, the bartender, cleared his throat, a signal for them to quit loitering in the doorway and get out.

"Okay, I heard you. You're a real buzz kill, you know that, Charlie?" Pancho said as they walked out.

Outside, Hondo took in a breath of cool breezy air, his lungs finally free of the bar's smoky ambiance. He heard a jingle as Pancho drew his car keys from his pocket. "Alright, howsabout both you kids ride home with me since I'm the most experienced of the bunch?"

Hondo swiped at the keys. "You're not driving."

Pancho held the keys away from Hondo's meaty hands. "You saying you are?"

"I'm saying none of us are. We're all too drunk." Hondo swiped at the keys once more.

Pancho threw up his hands and backed away. "It's Fort Sumner, Hondo. What is it, six miles to the house on empty streets?"

Hondo drunkenly pointed his finger in his brother's face. "Yeah, but Dad'll beat your ass if he finds out you drove home drunk. Or me."

Pancho shoed the finger away. "The old man's gotten so fat he can't see his own pecker anymore let alone whoop both our asses."

"What about Ma?" Hondo countered.

Pancho's expression changed from cocky to sullen. "Okay, you have a point." He put the keys back into his pocket. "How the hell are we gonna get home then?"

"Maybe we could take that," Debbie said.

The sound of hoof beats suddenly joined the rustling breeze. Hondo turned in disbelief to see poor Uncle Kit's horse, Geronimo, come trotting into the parking lot. Uncle Kit had come here often enough that the horse probably came out of habit.

"She's got a point. It's not drunk driving if you're on a horse," Pancho said.

***

After a few minutes, Pancho had managed to get himself and his passengers onto the horse. Being under six feet and lean, him and Hondo weren't too much of a strain on the animal, and Debbie couldn't have weighed more than 120 pounds. Still, he felt sorry for Geronimo.

"Oh, I hope no one sees me like this," Debbie blurted out from in between them as the horse trotted down the street.

Pancho grinned at her torment. "Why? You worried what'll happen when somebody sees the new girl in town sandwiched between two men on a horse at one in the morning?"

"Pancho…" Hondo said with a warning tone.

"Well, don't worry, darlin'," Pancho continued. "In this sleepy town, I can guarantee you that not only is everyone asleep, but if they ain't and they see us, they'll just think they're hallucinating."

"Just one more drink," Hondo grumbled. "How do I always fall for that with you?"

"Hey, it's not my fault you two teetotalers can't hold your liquor. If the bothofyas exercised your liver a little more often, you'd be sober right now. Like me," Pancho said and then steadied himself when he nearly slipped off the horse. Luckily, Hondo didn't notice.

"I'm a man of the law. Drinking isn't becoming of me," Hondo started grumbling again.

Pancho stopped the horse when a familiar billboard caught his eye.

"Why are we stopping?" Debbie sounded tired, the happy buzz of alcohol having deteriorated into crankiness.

Pancho nodded towards the billboard, reading SEE BILLY THE KID'S GRAVE. "It's the middle of the night, perfect time to go dig it up and see for ourselves if Uncle Kit was telling the truth."

"No." Hondo reached around him and took the reins, smushing Debbie between them as he prodded Kit's horse onwards.

"What's the big deal about Billy the Kid anyways?" Debbie asked.

"The big deal?" Hondo guffawed. "You've just insulted Pancho's number-one idol. After me, of course."

"The big deal," Pancho began, "is that to this day, people don't know for sure that he's buried out there."

"Why wouldn't he be?" Debbie asked. "Didn't the sheriff shoot him?"

"Not necessarily," Pancho answered.

"Here we go," Hondo muttered.

"I don't understand, though. Why wouldn't the sheriff shoot him?" Debbie asked.

"Well, before I go into that, let's take me and Hondo as examples. You've got Hondo, a sheriff, and me—"

"A delinquent," Hondo blurted out.

"Thank you," Pancho replied, then continued. "If Hondo was ordered to hunt down and kill his own brother, do you reckon he'd do it?"

Hondo started to say something, but Pancho cut him off. "Shut up, Hondo."

"Well, I don't suppose so," Debbie answered hesitantly.

"That's the thing. One of the Kid's best friends was the same sheriff, Pat Garrett, that supposedly shot him. Only plenty of people whisper that Garrett helped the Kid fake his death and run off to Mexico. I bet you $100 if we dug up that grave tonight, Billy wouldn't even be in there."

"You calling Old Man Miranda a liar?" Hondo asked.

"No. I think he's in on it and is just trying to keep the Kid's secret. That's why he got so defensive earlier. How's that for an answer, Mr. Detective?"

"I think... I think... I'm going to be sick," Hondo croaked out. Pancho suddenly felt Debbie clutch his shoulder for stability. He glanced behind him to watch her pat Hondo on the back as he began to throw up. Pancho laughed at his brother's misery and said to Debbie, "Think you can hold my little sister's hair for him while he throws up, sweetheart?"

Hondo answered by threatening to kill him in between heaves while Debbie comforted him, or tried to. He might've been too drunk to notice. By the time they reached Debbie's house, Hondo was passed out cold. It'd be up to Pancho to get her inside.

"Will he be okay?" Debbie asked as he helped her off the horse.

"Him? Oh, he'll be fine," Pancho said as Hondo slumped face-first into the horse's massive neck, drool running down his chin.

Once she started walking up the sidewalk, Debbie stumbled and Pancho had to steady her. "Where are we?" she mumbled.

"Oh boy, we better get you inside before you fall down," he said as they walked to the door. Since she'd only lived here for two weeks, he figured this house was still so new to her that her drunken mind expected to see her old house in Cimmaron. As he steadied her with one arm, he fished through her purse for her keys with the other.

They stumbled through the house together until he found his way to her bedroom. He laid her down on the bed gently, and as he was pulling away, her arms suddenly shot around his neck. She kissed him. It was a brief but hard smack, followed by, "Hondo, I think one day I'm gonna marry you."

Pancho started to say that he wasn't Hondo, but when she fell back onto the bed and passed out, he realized she probably wouldn't remember doing it anyways. Hopefully, neither of them would ever find out, and it was an honest mistake… for a drunk person, at least.

When Pancho got back outside, he wished he had a camera. Hondo had shifted his position and was now laid out sideways like a corpse on the back of the horse which was grazing itself on some of the neighbor's shrubbery.

"Fort Sumner's finest indeed," Pancho muttered with a grin. "It's good to be home."

V.
THE TREE

THURSDAY, NOVEMBER 23, 1950

Pancho's head was pounding, and at this point in his life he didn't know if it was from the liquor last night or the fight at the pool hall yesterday morning. He was on his parent's couch and a blanket had somehow found its way onto him in the night. Either Ma had put it on him or his drunken mind had acquired it while he was on autopilot.

Suddenly he got the feeling that he was being watched. He peaked over the couch. The old man was leering at him from the kitchen in his flannel boxers and white undershirt, steam rising from the coffee cup in his hand. What stood out more than anything to Pancho, though, was the old man's gut, which had grown another inch since he'd last seen him.

"Geez, Pop, I thought you were supposed to be putting away bad guys, not donuts."

He ignored his son's rude remark. "What in the hell is Uncle Kit's horse doing in the front yard?"

Pancho stood and stretched. "Me and Hondo did some detective work, thought it'd make you happy."

The old man gave him a look that had "horse shit" written all over it.

"Okay, so he was our designated driver when he wandered up to the bar." He patted the old man on the shoulder as he stumbled into the kitchen towards the coffee pot. "Speaking of which, think you could give us both a lift to get our cars from Sunnyside Up here in a bit?"

A wave of the hand and "Bah!" was the response as the old man trudged into the living room. "Where's your brother?" he asked as he plopped into his recliner.

Even though that was the question spoken, Pancho knew he was actually asking, "How drunk did he get and how late is he going to sleep in?"

"He's right where I left him," Pancho responded casually as he poured himself some coffee.

"What's that supposed to mean, that you dumped him in the gutter somewhere?"

"Just that gutter you call a guest house in the backyard." Pancho poured another cup for Hondo. "I'll go see how he's doing."

Pancho exited the sliding porch door and strolled through the backyard, taking note that it still wasn't too chilly for a fall morning. However, sometimes it got the warmest before a cold front, and something told him the cold would be coming soon enough.

He entered the guest house and found Hondo sprawled out on the bathroom floor where he'd left him. Figured he might as well leave him near the toilet in case his stomach wasn't totally empty yet.

Pancho nudged him with his foot. "Hey, rise and shine, sleeping beauty."

"Ugh," was the only response Hondo could muster as he stirred himself into consciousness. Pancho kneeled down and offered him the coffee.

Hondo looked at him suspiciously before accepting it. "No sugar in it?"

Pancho shook his head. "Black. Just like you like your men."

Hondo sneered at his brother for provoking him when he was in no condition to clobber him. "How bad was it?"

Pancho stood. "You mean you don't remember?"

"No." Hondo shook his head and took a sip.

"Good, then hopefully, neither will she."

Alarm crossed his face. "It was that bad?"

A couple false scenarios crossed Pancho's fiendish brain to embarrass his brother, but he didn't rattle them off like he would've in the old days. He was getting soft. "Nah, not really. You threw up on the way home is all."

Hondo finally got up off the floor. "And Debbie?"

Pancho cocked his head in the direction of the house. "She slept on the couch with me. Ma's making her breakfast right now."

Hondo's bleary eyes finally flashed with life. Pancho jumped backwards out of instinct and pointed at him. "I knew that one would finally get you! We dropped her off at her place, remember?"

"Vaguely." Hondo rubbed his eyes. "Did we ride a horse?"

"Yeah. I got him tethered up in the front yard. You shoulda seen Dad's face when he asked me about it." Pancho headed for the door. "And hey," Pancho turned suddenly serious, "you need to reign him in on those donuts."

"Heh, you're the one that likes sweets. You'll probably look just like him when you get that old."

"Don't count on it," Pancho said and exited the guest house. Pancho had known in his gut that the old man wasn't their real dad for a long time. He loved him, sure, but he was positive that couldn't be their biological father. He had shared this theory with Hondo once, but he'd gotten pretty upset, so he didn't bring it up again. For Pancho, it was pretty simple considering Jerry looked quite a bit like the old man, whereas he couldn't find a single physical trait that they shared. Patricia only resembled their mother, though, thank goodness.

He decided to go check on the horse and rustle him up some food. He deserved something for getting them home safely, after all. His folks lived in a decent house on the outskirts of town in the farming area, even though they didn't farm. Their nearest neighbors were about a mile down the road, so they had plenty of privacy apart from the occasional passing car. They lived along Main Canal Drive, which, as the name suggested, ran parallel to the main irrigation canal.

"Pancho!" the familiar voice of a little girl cut into his thoughts. It was Patricia running at him through the dry grass, kicking up fallen leaves as she did. She was the same spunky, dark-haired little girl he'd last seen six months ago, only a little taller now.

He caught her and spun her in the air. "What's up, Patty Cakes?" Pancho sat her down and cocked his head in the direction of the guest house. "Am I still your favorite brother over ape-face in there?"

"I don't have a favorite," she giggled.

"It's okay. I know you don't want to hurt Hondo's feelings. Besides, I got you a pony, didn't I?" He pointed to Uncle Kit's horse tethered in the front yard.

"That's not a pony. That's a full-grown horse. And Daddy said we couldn't keep it because it was evidence," she said as they approached the horse.

"Well, you never know. Maybe when he's done being 'evidence' we can keep him?" Pancho patted the horse's neck and it neighed gently.

"What's his name?" Patty asked, running her hand across its smooth hide.

"Geronimo, like the Indian Chief."

Pancho watched Patty inspect the horse and wondered what it would be like to have kids of his own. Suddenly, and perhaps not randomly, his thoughts of children switched to that of Debbie kissing him the night before.

"Where you been anyways?" Patty asked, snapping him out of the memory of last night. "Ma says she's surprised you're not in jail."

"Jail? Is that where you think I should be?"

"No, we just know how you are. So, where ya been?"

"All over the place. I been making most of my money at the pool halls and the poker tables."

"You think you'll ever come back here and settle down?"

"Maybe. But enough about me," he said, mostly because he wanted to change the subject. "How many boyfriends you have already?"

"None," she laughed again. "But I kinda like Jimmy down the road. I don't think he likes me, though."

Pancho momentarily racked his brain for who Jimmy was until he realized it was the Patterson boy, which he approved of. "Don't worry. He's not old enough to like you back yet. Just give him another couple years, then you'll be the one trying to keep him away. Just don't ever hang around any of those McPherson boys."

"Yeah, they remind me of you," she said.

"Hey!" Pancho gave her a look and she flashed a wicked smile, knowing full well how to push his buttons.

She shrugged innocently. "What? They're always in trouble."

"I am not always in trouble. Just most of the time, there's a difference," he corrected her.

"Speaking of that, you still got your switchblade?" she asked, and he assumed it was going to lead into another critique of his character.

"Yeah. What of it?"

"Can you still do that trick with it?"

Patricia was referring to Pancho's precision aim with a knife. He had been known to pin a falling leaf to a tree before it could hit the ground. Whereas most men around Sumner liked to do target practice with a gun, when Pancho was younger, he'd taken to throwing his switchblade around when he was bored. The remedy to boredom had eventually resulted in skill, and now he was able to hit just about anything with a knife. He didn't feel up to doing it just then, though. "I just woke up."

She looked up at him with her hands on her hips. "You mean you're too hungover?"

"Hey, where did you learn what a hangover was?"

"I'm looking at you, aren't I? Besides, the Pancho I used to know could pin a leaf to a tree before it even hit the ground hungover or sober."

"You think I can't do it?"

She shook her head. "I bet not."

Pancho was proud of her. She had already learned how to manipulate a man's ego. "Well, bet again, sister."

They walked towards a White Ash tree that stood alone in the big field that separated them from their neighbors. It had been planted on the property long ago. Pancho didn't know how old it was, but it was clearly ancient. Its trunk of pale bark was thick, and its roots crawled into the ground in such a way that reminded him of a giant octopus. It was always particularly striking in the fall like this, with its leaves having already shifted from a shimmering gold to a purplish maroon. It wasn't native to the area, and his mother claimed one of the Indian chiefs had planted it back in the days of the Bosque. Pancho loved that tree. It had been his escape as a boy as he climbed into its branches. It had been the hiding place for the little trinkets he imagined to be treasure, too, whether he stuck them in the nook or buried them in the earth between its roots.

Pancho held up his knife. "Okay, the next leaf that falls, I pin to the tree, in which case you have to shovel up that horse poop."

"Hey, that's no fair. You brought him home."

"You said you bet. That's the bet."

"Yeah, what if you miss?"

"I ain't gonna miss." Pancho threw the knife as a leaf drifted to the ground, pinning it to the trunk of the White Ash.

"Aw, man!" Patricia said, disappointed rather than delighted under the new circumstances.

Pancho was about to tell her that was why one should never set a bet before determining the parameters when a gunshot rang out and another falling leaf burst into dust. They both jumped and turned in alarm to see Hondo holding the smoking gun.

"Now that, that was impressive." He blew on the barrel like he was in an old Western, then holstered it.

"Great, now Ma's gonna come out," Pancho said.

"Exactly. And I made sure not to hit the tree." Hondo smiled deviously. "Unlike your knife."

Ma came screeching out of the house, wringing her dishtowel as predicted. "Hey, don't be filling my tree full of holes!"

"I didn't, Ma, honest," Hondo said. "But Pancho…" Hondo nodded at the knife stuck in the tree.

"That tree's older than me and you both," she said as she hustled past them.

"Sorry, Ma, I won't do it again," Pancho said as he plucked the knife from the trunk.

Ma ran her hands up and down the bark. "Anyways, I got a little breakfast cooked up. Not a big one, mind you. We'll save our appetite for dinner tonight mostly," Ma said, turning back to face them.

"Hey, speaking of that, we kinda invited a guest last night," Pancho said, figuring he should warn her.

"Oh really…" Pancho could tell by Ma's tone she knew who it was, but she still asked, "Who is it?"

"It's that girl I was telling you about, the one from the diner," Hondo answered.

"Which one of yas invited her?" Ma asked with a hint of concern.

"Both of us," Pancho said before his brother could answer.

Ma grabbed both of them by the ears and pulled them down to her level. "You just hear this. If there's any fighting to be done, you'll do it after dinner. I won't have you tipping over the table with the turkey on it like back in '36. Ya hear?"

"Ow, we're not little kids anymore," Hondo whined while Patricia giggled.

"Heh. That's exactly what worries me," she said.

"Now, no rough housing over that girl, promise?" she asked again, giving their earlobes an extra squeeze.

"Hey, she's Hondo's girl," Pancho said. "I got no interest in her. I was just the matchmaker."

Ma's gaze drifted back and forth between the two of them, her eyes acting like a human lie detector which Pancho hoped he passed. Her stare didn't render a clear verdict, but after a second, she finally let them both go. "Well, alright then."

Then, as her way of apologizing, pinched both their cheeks and added, "I love the both of yas, but sometimes you're enough to drive a woman to drink."

"Whataya mean?" Pancho asked.

"I mean you always off doing Lord knows what Lord knows where," she said, looking at Pancho and then to Hondo, "and then you following in your father's footsteps in that awful job. You know how happy it'd make me for the both of you to settle down with a couple o' nice girls and nice, regular jobs?"

"We'll see what we can do, Ma," Hondo said.

"Eh, I'll believe it when I see it," she said and grinned, sauntering back to the house with Patricia trailing behind her. She shooed her in, and then turned back around and hollered, "And one more thing. I heard about yesterday morning. If I told ya once I told ya a thousand times, don't be hanging around those McPherson boys!" Ma harumphed and then went inside.

"Tattletale," Pancho said to his brother.

"Hey, it's a good story."

"Yeah, but I bet you didn't tell her how you swindled those poor hillbillies out of $200?"

"Hell, no, I didn't. Hey," Hondo said, stopping Pancho as he walked towards the house. "You telling the whole truth when you said you're not interested in Debbie?"

Pancho caught himself pausing and then said, "Yeah, she's all yours, man." After a second, he added, "Besides, it's clear she likes you better anyways." It was only after he said it that he realized that comment gave him away.

VI.
THE KISS

Debbie looked to the sky. The moon was shining through what looked to be storm clouds as unfitting as that might be for Thanksgiving. However, in New Mexico the weather was always moody, and it looked as though the stubborn heat and the oncoming cold were nearing their final clash for dominance. She hoped the looming thunderstorm wasn't a bad omen as she stooped over to get the cake out of her car. She felt like she needed to bring something over. It wouldn't be proper not to, so she had whipped one up that afternoon. It hadn't been easy for several reasons. One was the hangover, of course. The other was that her kitchen was a mess. She hadn't been satisfied with it when she moved in and was in the process of retiling it herself. But, by some miracle, she had cobbled a cake together amidst all the mess.

Still, she approached the Dumez home with some trepidation. It was the kiss that was bothering her. She felt like the date went well up to then. What had she said to Hondo after she kissed him? She couldn't remember—just the kiss itself, then mercifully passing out. Not that Hondo would mind a kiss, he was a man, after all, but she didn't want him to think that she wasn't proper. Or that she was too desperate.

Maybe Hondo wouldn't remember? Or maybe he would remember but not say anything? Had he told his mother about it? For some reason that horrific thought popped into her head the moment the door opened to reveal a short woman in an apron.

"Well, hello," she said friendlily enough. "You must be Debbie. Come in, come in."

Her fears were abated by the warm welcome as she stepped through the door. "Thank you again for having me. I can't tell you how nice of you all it is."

"Oh, it's nothing," the woman said and waved her through the hallway towards the living room.

"Oh, and I made this, too. I hope you don't mind?" Debbie offered her the cake.

"Mind? Lands no, girl." She took the cake as they continued towards the living room. "Hondo and Pancho are in the guest house getting dressed, but come and meet the rest of the family," she said and then hollered, "Harold, come meet Hondo's new girlfriend!"

Within moments, Debbie was immersed in a whirlwind of introductions and names that she tried desperately to remember. The father's name started with an H. For Heaven's sake, the mother had just called it. Howard? Harold? But she should probably call him Mr. Dumez or Sheriff, anyway. Then there was the little sister, Patricia, the younger brother, Jerry, his wife Marlene, and their baby. She didn't get the mother's name, she had introduced everyone but herself, but she figured she'd just call her Mrs. Dumez as well. Lastly, there was a grandmother or great-grandmother that they called Mamaw, but she didn't know what to call her herself not being family.

She examined them all as they made small talk. The mother was a short little woman, and even though Hondo and his brother weren't what anyone would consider terribly tall, they still seemed too big to have come from her. The father didn't resemble them either. It was also clear that both of the parents were white, so there went her theory about Hondo being mixed. But, then again, it didn't look like it mattered considering that the mother liked her. If it stayed that way, then the biggest hurdle had been cleared. The father was much nicer to her than she expected from the way that the brothers had joked about him last night. But, then again, she noticed the men that were the gruffest with other men could be the gentlest, warmest men she knew whereas women were concerned.

She felt like she could at least see some resemblance between the twins and the little sister, but not Jerry. He was the same height as them but didn't have their skin or hair color. He was lightly freckled with a head of wispy, coppery red hair that looked like it would curl if it got long enough. Jerry's way of speaking was also distinctive from his brothers, more country-like, almost like a Texan. His wife, Marlene, had big black Texas hair and was prettier than her large, horn-rimmed glasses made her appear.

Finally, Hondo and Pancho came loping in through the sliding screen door. Since they were both dressed up for dinner, for a split second of panic she couldn't tell which one was which. She waved at them both, hoping one of them would do something that gave their identity away. She quickly realized that the more bashful-looking one was Hondo since Pancho was never bashful.

"Hi," Hondo said with a sheepish look.

"Hi, Hondo. Happy Thanksgiving."

"You too." He leaned in to give her a hug. "Thanks for coming."

"My lands," Pancho said, plopping a hand on both their shoulders. "You saw his ugly drunk side last night and now here you are meeting the parents. Y'all getting married in the morning?" He slapped his brother on the back, soaking up the awkwardness with glee. She couldn't deny that a little part of her did like Pancho. Maybe more than a little, but she still liked Hondo more. But the question he had asked her last night lingered. What if she had seen him first?

"Isn't he wonderful?" Hondo said with a sarcastic grin as he grabbed his brother by the neck.

"Hey, like Ma said, no fighting 'til after dinner," Pancho said, slipping from his grasp.

"What's that supposed to mean?" Debbie asked.

"It means he's worried that—"

Before Pancho could finish his sentence, Hondo had slapped his left hand over his mouth and his right arm under his neck, dragging him backwards.

Hondo grinned at Debbie. "We'll be right back."

About then their mother stepped in. "Okay, time for dinner. Boys, let each other go or I'll make you eat outside with the horse."

That was all it took for Hondo to release his brother and they both headed for the table, "Yes, Ma," being their unified response.

Hondo pulled out the chair for Debbie to sit, and she noticed him give Pancho a look as he sat next to her. The dinner was about what she had expected, a blessing followed by some catching up and lots of family stories. It was the usual "Remember that time…" and then everyone would laugh.

"And then Dad finally yells, 'No, Boots, hell no!'" Mrs. Dumez slapped her hand on the table and everyone roared. Debbie hadn't entirely understood the story but laughed along with everyone else anyway.

Jerry finally decided to tell one of his stories. "Hey, remember that time I sewed that rattlesnake's mouth shut and then set it loose in the house for y'all to find?" He looked around the table eagerly expecting raucous laughter, but they all shot him dirty looks instead.

"Well, I guess some can tell 'em and some can't." Jerry shrugged and went back to eating.

After an awkward silence, the grandmother, who was hard of hearing and probably hadn't heard a word of what had been spoken the entire night, finally started getting in on the conversation.

"So, when are you two getting married?" the woman called Mamaw asked her through a garbled voice.

Debbie froze, not knowing what to say.

"Oh, Mama, they just started going out," Mrs. Dumez said and then whispered, "You're embarrassing them."

"Well, they're out together after dark, aren't they? It's only a natural assumption," Mamaw said loudly to her daughter, and then turning back to Debbie and Hondo, "Back in my time, a man and a woman weren't allowed to go out together after dark until they were engaged, at least."

"Her boyfriends probably wished it was after dark so they didn't have to look at her," Mr. Dumez muttered from under his napkin.

"What was that?" Mamaw said, pointing her butter knife in Harold's direction.

"Nothing," Mr. Dumez grumbled and cleared his throat. "Must be hearing things again."

"How long have you and Hondo been courting?" Mamaw asked.

Debbie gave Hondo an awkward smile. "Well, just since last night, I suppose?"

Mamaw's eyes got wide as saucers. "You went out at night on your first courting unsupervised?"

Pancho raised his hand. "I supervised, actually."

"You got them drunk and then took them home on a smelly two-bit palomino is what you did," Mr. Dumez corrected, and Debbie blushed.

"Harold!" Mrs. Dumez hissed.

"He what?" Mamaw asked.

"He said Pancho was a good chaperone, Mother, that's all." Mrs. Dumez patted her hand.

"I chaperoned Harold and Edith here in the back of our buckboard with a shotgun. And only before nightfall," Mamaw added with a raised finger. "You remember that, don't you, Harold?"

Mr. Dumez didn't respond, but the look on his face was response enough.

"This young man's lucky I didn't kill him." She lowered her voice as though what she was about to say was scandalous. "I caught those two holding hands once before marriage." Mamaw turned her gaze from Debbie to Harold and raised her voice again. "Slapped your hand with a willow switch, didn't I, Harold?"

Pancho and Hondo were shaking and turning red-faced without making a sound. Debbie covered her mouth with a napkin.

"Of course, I'm one to talk. Homer, that was my husband's name, he held my hand once while we were courting, and if my daddy had known, he'd a killed him. Bam!" She slammed her hands down on the table, rattling the plates. "Woulda shot him dead right there on the front lawn. And if he had, none of you'd be here right now." She pointed a finger around the table.

"Mama, maybe you ought to go and lay down for a while?" Mrs. Dumez stood to help her mother up.

"Well, alright then. It was nice to meet you, young lady," she said, rising slowly. "You watch 'em, make sure they're not touching hands under the table," she said to Pancho, who was about to fall out of his chair.

"I hope I don't live to see Edith turn into her mother," Mr. Dumez muttered and shook his head as his wife helped her mother stagger down the hallway.

Jerry suddenly got a bead on Debbie. "You're not one of them vegetable-inarians are you?"

"A what?" Debbie asked, perplexed.

"I just noticed you didn't hardly touch the meat on your plate and was worried you were one of them that didn't hardly never eat meat?"

"Oh, no, I eat meat. I just wasn't super hungry tonight," she said instead of saying she was hungover.

"Thank goodness. One of the guys on the base is one of those vegetable only people." Jerry glanced around the table, then added, "Worst gas I ever smelt."

"Jerry," his mother hissed as she came for his plate.

"What? It smelt like burnt lettuce. It was awful!"

"So what's new at Holloman, Jerry? Other than the farts, I mean," Pancho said, still stifling a laugh.

"You are never gonna believe it." He pointed his fork in the direction of Debbie and his brothers. "They're thinking about sending monkeys into space."

"As if they didn't waste enough of our tax dollars already," Mr. Dumez harumphed.

"Well…" Marlene interjected, "they figures they better make sure it's safe for monkeys to go there before us humans. Might even get a monkey onto the moon, who knows?"

"But don't worry, Daddy," Jerry explained, "I'm gonna make damn sure they're monkeys born right here in America. Ain't gonna have no commie foreigners getting launched into space on my watch."

"On your watch? Don't you just mop the floors right now?" Pancho said, stifling another laugh.

"Very funny, Pancho. No, I'm a staff sergeant now for your information."

"And he's working his way up." Marlene patted his arm. "Might even be those monkeys' boss one day."

"Well, that's one job you're suited for," Pancho said, then reached behind Debbie to slap Hondo on the back, who was laughing, too.

"Ma!" Jerry yelled. "They're doing it again!"

"Who's ready for cake?" The mother bolted out of the kitchen, diffusing the situation with an offer of food like she had before. "Debbie made us all a cake. Jerry, would you be a doll and grab it off the table behind you, please?"

Jerry did as told but seemed perplexed by the weight. "Is this a pound cake?"

"No, just a regular white. Why?" Debbie asked.

"Just… heavy," he answered as he set it down.

Debbie had noticed it was a bit heavy herself but wasn't sure why. Now she was starting to get nervous.

"You divvy it up and I'll get dessert plates," the mother said to Jerry.

"This is some crispy icing you got here," Jerry said with some strain in his voice. The knife finally cut into the cake and slammed into the bottom of the pan loudly, making Debbie jump.

"Wait a minute." Jerry sniffed the cake as a mortifying realization was settling in with Debbie. Jerry wet his finger and ran it across the icing, then stuck it in his mouth. "Is this…" He smacked his lips in contemplation. "Is that tile grout?"

"Oh no." Debbie's hand shot to her mouth. She had been so hungover when she made the icing that she must've mistook some of the grout for sugar. "I've been regrouting the tile in my kitchen, and I had some tile grout laying around and I guess… I was in kind of a hurry and I got it mixed up with the sugar for the icing."

Before she knew it, they were all laughing again. But she didn't feel like they were laughing at her, but more so with her.

"It's very good when you can break through the surface," Jerry said a little later, eating another mouthful of the cake sans the grout icing. So far, he was the only one eating it, but eventually his mother took it away from him.

With dessert officially over, the father made a beeline for a recliner in the living room. "Edith, call the undertaker, that meal did me in," he hollered as he plopped down.

Debbie offered to help with the dishes, but the mother wouldn't have it. She didn't make Marlene help either, though she figured it was because that baby she had was a real handful and seemed to scream its lungs out anytime it wasn't being held. While Pancho talked to Marlene and Jerry was in the bathroom, she finally found herself alone with Hondo.

"I'm so embarrassed about that cake I could die," she said.

"Are you kidding? That thing was the hit of the evening. They're gonna talk about that cake for years to come."

"Oh, gosh, I hope not."

"And if you think you're embarrassed, how do you think I feel about my grandmother?" Hondo said and she laughed.

"It's only our second date and we've already had two people asking us when we're getting married," she said.

"I know, and we still haven't gotten to have a regular date yet, what with all my relatives always hanging around. You handled my family like a pro, by the way."

"Oh, it's nothing. I mean, at least you still have a family."

Mamaw came staggering in on a cane about then, already done with her lay down period. "Honey, I'm sorry if I embarrassed you earlier. You know I can't hear well," she said as though that was to blame. "But I want you to know I think you're a fine young woman. I'll even let you wear my wedding dress one day if you want."

"Oh, thank you, that's very sweet."

"It's white, of course," the old woman added and hobbled over to the table to harass her daughter.

When she was gone, a red-faced Hondo apologized again. Debbie felt now was a good a time as any to address the elephant in the room from last night.

"Um, Hondo?" she began nervously. "Actually, I'm the one who should be sorry, about last night, I mean."

"No, I'm the one who should apologize for not cutting us all off after the third shot."

"No, I didn't mean that. I mean, I hope you don't think I'm that kind of girl?"

"What are you talking about?"

Debbie lowered her voice even lower. "The kiss. You were so sweet when you carried me to bed—"

"Wait, I didn't carry you to bed…" Hondo's eyes slowly drifted to Pancho and Debbie realized she'd just made a horrendous mistake.

As if by the telepathy some people claimed that twins possessed, she watched as Pancho's eyes met his brother's from across the room. It was clear from the look on his face that not only did he remember the kiss, but that Hondo was now aware of it as well. They looked like two dogs in the wild, one getting ready to pounce and the other getting ready to run for its life.

"You!" Hondo said with an accusing finger pointed at his brother.

"Hondo, I didn't know…" Debbie began, but it was too late. Hondo bolted for his brother.

Debbie watched in horror and embarrassment as the twins circled around the dinner table like two wolves as Mrs. Dumez and Patricia were trying to clear it off.

"What in tarnation?" Mrs. Dumez grabbed Patricia protectively. "What's going on now?"

"He ruined my date!" Hondo hissed from the other side of the table. "Just like I knew he would."

"Are you kidding? The both of ya's probably would have barely said hello and goodbye if it weren't for me!" Pancho snapped. "Besides, she must really like you to try and kiss you after all that barfing you did."

"You threw up in front of her?" Mrs. Dumez asked.

"You kissed on the first date?" Patricia said.

"No, she kissed me," Pancho clarified and Mamaw started to faint.

When Hondo saw that he wasn't likely to corner his brother, he picked up the cake and launched it at his head. Pancho ducked as it imbedded itself in the wall and then made a mad dash for the kitchen. Debbie thought she heard Mrs. Dumez tell one of them to put down a carving knife.

The father looked up from his paper and shouted, "Y'all take it outside onto the lattice. I've been meaning to tear it down anyways."

Mrs. Dumez slid the porch door open just in time for both of them to go sailing outside. She slammed it back shut and muttered, "At least they waited until after dinner," before marching back into the kitchen.

Debbie watched in disbelief as the twins crashed through the lattice work on the porch and went rolling through the wreckage. Marlene sidled up next to her.

"Shouldn't we do something?" Debbie clutched Marlene's arm, terrified that one would kill the other and it would all be her fault.

"Oh no, they do that all the time," she said casually as she bounced the baby, who seemed to be watching the fight intently.

Jerry came out of the bathroom, his eyes lively. "Did I hear there's a fight already!" His face appeared joyous rather than worried as he darted towards the sliding porch door.

"Now, Jerry, my mama bought you that shirt and you know it's gonna get torn up!" Marlene yelled at him as he ran outside, while Debbie marveled that it was only the shirt she was worried about.

For a moment, Debbie thought he was going to break the fight up. Instead, he joined it.

"Y'all couldn't o' waited for me?" Jerry shouted and jumped into the two-man dogpile.

"This isn't your fight, Jerry!" Pancho hissed best he could from the headlock Hondo had him in.

In no time, Hondo had maneuvered Jerry into a headlock as well. "Patty, you might as well get in here, too, so I got all three of my little sisters in a headlock," Hondo shouted to Patricia, who had sidled up next to Debbie to watch.

The phone rang, cutting into the moment.

"Quiet!" their father snapped from the phone, and all three finally stopped. Hondo let them go, and they all listened intently. Clearly, whatever the father was listening to on the other end wasn't good.

Mr. Dumez looked solemn as he hung up. "That was Hugo's wife. She says Old Man Miranda is dead. Can see him out floating in the Pecos by the old petrified forest."

"We just saw him last night," Hondo said, shocked.

"Well, you're about to see him again, so grab your coat," Mr. Dumez ordered.

"I'm coming, too," Pancho said.

"Well, if he's going, I'm going," Jerry added.

Debbie followed Hondo to the front door, where he was getting his coat from the rack.

"I'm so sorry about before, Hondo. I just—"

He gave her a knowing smirk. "It's okay. They don't call us identical twins for nothing."

She touched his arm. "Be careful."

"Don't worry, I will," he said. "Hey, and soon we'll have a proper date. Just the two of us." Suddenly, he looked around the room slyly and muttered, "But before that…"

He leaned in and kissed her.

VII.
THE KILLING MOON

ondo's mind raced with possibilities as they sped up Route 84 past Lake Sumner. Two deaths in two days, and like Uncle Kit, Salvador Miranda was an old-timer with a connection to the Kid. Was it just coincidence? Regardless, those were the only similarities that Hondo could draw between the two victims.

That said, Uncle Kit had claimed that the Kid wasn't dead, while Salvador adamantly asserted just the opposite. Another thought suddenly crossed Hondo's mind: the witch. Salvador had said a word that his sober brain couldn't retrieve from his drunken memories. It had started with an 'S' and Hugo had become angry when his grandfather uttered it, as if it would bring bad luck. And now the old man was dead. Surely that was just old-time superstition, a coincidence?

The Mirandas' ranch was located along a particularly interesting stretch of the Pecos River, where the half-submerged remains of a petrified forest lingered. It wasn't anywhere near as grand as the famous Petrified Forest of Arizona and covered much less ground. It was just a small marsh littered with the tipped-over remains of giant cedars lying there in the water. There was a movement to turn it into a state park in 1911 as Hondo understood it, but it never gained any traction. Now the forest was mostly forgotten.

"No need to hurry, boy. He's already dead," his father reminded him from the passenger seat as they flew over a bump.

"Sorry," Hondo muttered. They were off the main road, or the beaten path as it was, and were currently flying down the rocky dirt trail leading to the Miranda's property.

"You think the killer'll still be hanging around somewhere, Daddy?" Jerry asked, his voice tinged with excitement.

"What makes you think there's a killer?" the old man replied.

"Well, what with that body yesterday and all—"

"Probably just coincidence," the old man cut him off. "We'll learn soon enough."

Hondo cast a sideways glance at the old man and could tell from the way he bit his lip that he wasn't so sure of that. Hondo's father was thinking all the same things that he was, he just wasn't saying them.

As Hondo pulled up to the spooky stretch of river, his headlights illuminated Hugo sitting along the shore of the marsh clutching a shotgun. Hondo wondered why he hadn't gone to fish out his grandfather himself until he saw his pantleg. It was torn and bloody.

Swiftly they exited the car.

"Hugo, you okay?" Hondo hollered as they approached him.

He nodded his head. "I'll be alright. I sent my wife to call you and then for a doctor."

"What happened?" the old man asked as they helped Hugo up.

"Something spooked our cows. We all came out here to look for one of the ones that ran away. Grandfather and I were out here while my wife waited in the truck when something… something ran by and tore at my leg. Before I knew what happened, I got knocked out. When I came to, my wife was screaming, and Grandad was… was…" Hugo pointed out to the marsh where the old man's limp body floated face down in the pitch-black water.

Suddenly, Hugo's eyes, full of sorrow, transitioned to anger directed at Hondo. He grabbed him by the jacket and shouted, "It's your fault. You made him say it! You made him say the word!"

"Hey, he didn't know," Pancho said gently, pulling Hugo off of his brother.

"What did this?" the old man asked.

"They know," Hugo shrugged Pancho off with fire in his eyes.

"Know what?" Jerry asked, confused.

Hugo spat at the ground. "Just go out and get my grandfather already."

The old man nodded at Hondo to do as he said. Hondo surveyed the area, wondering if who—or what—had wounded Hugo and killed the old man was still out there. It was odd. It sounded like Hugo had been attacked by a predator, but an animal wouldn't drag Old Man Miranda out into the water and leave him there. Did the old man run into the water because he thought it wouldn't attack him there? Who was he kidding? Old Salvador couldn't run at his age, even if he was healthy for being damn near 100. Salvador wouldn't have swam out there, the killer had to have dragged him into the marsh. It felt like a trap.

Hondo shone his floodlight across the water just as the distant sound of thunder broke the eerie silence. The surface of the water was pitch black aside from the moon's gigantic reflection. He could see a few leafless, dead trees jutting out of the inky blackness, like something out of a fairy tale… or a nightmare. He waded out into the cold depths, which luckily only came up to his waist. He wasn't afraid of water. There wasn't anything in the Pecos River to be afraid of except for snakes; they were probably holed up somewhere by now.

But still, the inexplicable fear of not being able to see below one's waist in the blackness was unnerving. Even if it wasn't getting cold, his hair would still be standing on end. Pancho was by his side, for moral support more than anything. Dragging the old man out of the water wouldn't be hard. Poor old man couldn't have weighed any more than Debbie. It was odd that she suddenly crossed his mind in his moment of fear, and he realized that more than anything, he feared not seeing her again. Infatuation was already turning into love and taking root. That'd be his luck. To finally get the girl and then die.

As Hondo neared the old man, he wondered if there was a chance he'd find him mutilated like Uncle Kit, if it was the same killer, that is. As he came closer, he could see the old man still had his scalp, though he was bald to begin with. Maybe Indian serial killers didn't scalp you if you were bald?

Hondo flipped him over with apprehension, greeted with the grim mask of death that he expected. He glanced at the arms and could see that the right hand was gone, just like Uncle Kit. It had been the same killer. Hondo looked back to the shore, dreading Hugo seeing his grandfather like this. Hondo and his twin trudged through the black, muddy waters. Streaks of lightning began to dance across the inky surface in jagged arcs and Hondo was doubly glad to be nearing the shore again.

Hugo's horrified reaction was about what Hondo expected as he clutched the old man's wet body. "Why? Why would someone do this?" he asked, taking notice of the hand, or lack thereof.

"I don't know, son," Hondo's father said, doing his best to be a comfort.

Hugo laid the old man's body out on the sandy shore of the Pecos. He was the last of the true old-timers. In a way, between him and Uncle Kit, it was like the Old West was really dead now. The thunder began to increase in volume.

The old man put a hand on Hugo's shoulder. "Come on, let's get you back to the ranch."

A dark cloud drifted over the moon and the atmosphere suddenly changed, like there was electricity in the air, but not from the storm. It felt like time was passing differently now, too. Hondo looked at Pancho. He could sense it as well, but somehow Hondo knew that the others didn't.

There was a funny whooshing sound and their father clutched his neck. "What the hell?"

When he took his hand away, there was a smattering of blood.

"Daddy, you been shot?" Jerry asked, even though there had been no noise.

"If it'd been a bullet, it would've made more of a mess. And noise." Hondo clutched his father's shoulders, examining his neck. It wasn't a bullet wound, that was sure. It was too small. What was it, a dart?

Their father wavered. "I'm fine. It just stings. What was—"

"Look!" Hugo shouted over a clap of thunder.

Before Hondo could fully comprehend what was happening, Hugo had aimed his shotgun into the trees above them. There, illuminated in a flash of lightning, was a figure akin to something he'd seen in an old tintype of a medicine man wearing an animal skin atop his shoulders. It uttered a weird cry similar to a fox. In a flash, Hugo fired, and the being was gone as though it had never been there to begin with.

"What the hell?" Pancho muttered.

"Where'd it go?" Jerry shouted.

"There!" Pancho pointed at two taillights buzzing away in the distance even though Hondo could hear neither the sound of a motor nor tires peeling out of the dirt. Right about then, two headlights suddenly appeared behind them. It was Hugo's wife in their truck with another man that Hondo recognized as a local doctor. His father and

Hugo would be left in better hands than his own, freeing him up to chase down the bastard that had killed Old Man Miranda.

"Jerry, stay with Dad and make sure the doc looks at him," Hondo said as he steadied his father into Jerry's grasp. Hondo grabbed Pancho's arm and they bolted for the cruiser to catch up with the strangely dressed perp.

"Up ahead!" Pancho exclaimed as they both slammed into their respective seats. He pointed at the taillights as they sailed down the dirt road, heading north. Hondo gunned it, gaining on them until he was matching their speed. For now Hondo would have to be content with not losing them. It wasn't like on the highway where you could go as fast as you wanted on flat pavement. This was a county dirt road, bound to be filled with potholes and rocks. Fortunately, the perp's car wasn't stirring up a ton of dust, though. If it had, they might lose sight of their taillights for sure.

Hondo rubbed his eyes. The taillights seemed uneven, but perhaps it was the excitement of the moment coupled with the bumpy terrain. Or maybe, Hondo suddenly thought, they weren't the taillights of a car. Maybe there were two perps, and they were riding a pair of motorcycles? Somehow, the strangely dressed man he had seen didn't seem like the type to ride a motorcycle, or drive a car for that matter.

"What do you make of that thing?" Hondo asked his brother.

Pancho shook his head in a daze. "It looked like a man's body with a wolf's head. You got any silver bullets?"

"It was a coyote pelt, I think. Uncle Kit was scalped like an Indian would do in the old days. I think whoever this is fancies himself as some kind of perverse medicine man or something."

It still didn't make sense, though. Something animal-like had either slashed or bitten into Hugo's leg. Had the perp been carrying a weapon around to do so with? Did he have an attack dog with him? So much of this wasn't adding up.

"Skinwalker," Pancho blurted out. He turned to look at Hondo. "That's what Salvador called it last night."

"What the hell is it?"

Pancho shrugged. "Beats me."

After a few moments of silence had passed, and it was clear that they weren't losing sight of their pursuit, Pancho added, "Hey, I'm sorry I didn't tell you about the kiss. She was so mixed up, she thought I was you. I didn't think she'd remember it, and I thought we'd all be happier and better off if I didn't bring it up. Honest."

Hondo bit his lip. "I'm sorry I jumped to conclusions. I just really like her."

"Well, I don't know if I should repeat this or not, but the last thing she said before she passed out was, 'Hondo Dumez, I think I'm gonna marry you one day.'" Pancho grinned, even if he was a little jealous.

For a moment they nearly forgot they were on the trail of a serial killer, but then they both noticed the lights veering off in the direction of a small village. "Looks like they're headed for Puerto de Luna," Pancho said.

Puerto de Luna had been a hangout of Pat Garrett and Billy the Kid at one time and translated as Gateway to the Moon, which Hondo couldn't deny was strangely fitting on this night. The perp's car was headed towards the skeletons of some old, rock-walled ruins. Only a few of them were semi-complete, those being a small church and part of the jail. All the other buildings no longer had their roofs, and the ruins jutted out of the ground unevenly. Some comprised of a simple doorway or a few empty windowpanes flanked by rock walls, which turned a ghostly blue whenever they were illuminated by the lightning. It made Puerto de Luna appear as if it were a ghost village phasing in and out of a different dimension. A blinding flash of lightning whited out the sky, and when it was over, the taillights were gone. The car had to have shut them off, which is what it should have done to begin with.

Hondo cursed. "We lost them."

"No we didn't." Pancho pointed ahead, and Hondo saw the shadow of what appeared to be a coyote slink across one of the old stone walls.

Hondo stopped the car and looked at his brother. "You don't have a gun."

"Neither does it, apparently. Besides, I have this." Pancho flipped out his switchblade.

They both got out of the car. Hondo drew his pistol and scanned the abandoned village, which was becoming obscured by a dirty spray of wind littered with fallen leaves and tumbleweeds. Whenever a flash of lightning illuminated the place, Hondo would scan it as quick as he could for movement. Seeing nothing, for a moment, Hondo worried the man had gotten away, but then he heard that foxlike tittering again, as if it was mocking them. In the distance, another flash illuminated the being as it stood in one of the vacant windows of the old jail. Once again, it revealed a silhouette that looked just like a man aside from the head, which had a snout and two pointy, canine ears. And then, in the blink of an eye, it vanished.

Every fiber of Hondo's being seemed to tingle; every hair stood on end. But it wasn't the same feeling as abject terror like most would experience. It was tangent to excitement, a strange, righteous anger directed at the abomination he'd just seen, like the fire of God was welling up inside of him. He had no desire to run away from it, but rather to run towards it. He looked at Pancho and could tell he was feeling the same thing. He nodded silently at his brother, knowing that he understood they were going to split up to cover more ground and search the ruins. They both turned their gaze to the ghostly village before them and advanced, Hondo veering to the west and Pancho to the east.

Hondo cursed the thunder. Even though it masked the sound of his own footsteps, it also covered that of the enemy's, though something told him that the man might be silent even without the thunder. Then he saw it; a form crouched in the darkness. He was planning to fire and was seasoned enough to close his eyes just as he pulled the trigger. His eyelids were shielded from the bright flare of gunfire that would have resulted in a brief bought of flash blindness at night. He heard an animal screech and opened his eyes to see a black cat darting away and scaling up a rock wall.

Suddenly, a searing hot pain tore into the flesh of his back. Before he was fully aware of being attacked, he was knocked into the dirt. He could hear that tittering laugh again and a smattering of footfalls in the dirt. The man was toying with him. If he'd wanted to, he could have stabbed Hondo in a vital spot and finished him, but instead, he felt like he'd been slashed by claws. As Hondo started to right himself it felt as though an animal ran across his back, trampling him back into the dirt. He flipped onto his back, feeling the open slashes in his skin burn as they made contact with the dirty ground. He looked frantically to his left and right, but it was gone. Hondo spun around like a madman when he heard it coming again and leveled his gun right at Pancho, who instinctively threw his hands up. "I heard the gunshot. You okay?"

Hondo nodded, his eyes wild as he lowered the gun. Pancho helped him up.

"It get you?" he asked, noticing the claw marks that had shredded his shirt.

"I'm okay. They're just scratches, I think."

The strange titter broke the night air again, and both spun around to see the coyote-like being leering over them from atop the old chapel, clutching the steeple as it was illuminated in another burst of lightning. The brothers didn't hesitate to act. Pancho threw his knife and Hondo shot his gun. The figure toppled and fell to the earth, and it somehow didn't seem to be a coincidence that the storm began to dissipate. The dark clouds obscuring the moon parted to reveal the form of a dead man wearing a coyote pelt sprawled before them.

Pancho's knife protruded from his abdomen, raising up and down with the man's last breaths, while Hondo's gunshot had gotten him in the upper chest. When the strange man breathed his last, Pancho nudged the coyote scalp with his foot, tipping it off the man's head to confirm that it was just that, a simple animal skin. Odder yet, this was an old man, not as old as Salvador, but clearly in his 70s or more.

"How the hell did an old man move that fast?" Pancho asked.

"I don't know. But let's see if we can find his car," Hondo said, even though he couldn't imagine that man owning or driving one. What he really wanted to confirm was whether it had been a car or two motorcycles. If there was a cycle, it would imply that there was another perp on the loose. However, try as he may, neither he nor Pancho could find any trace of a car or a bike. The driver of the car had to have dumped the old man out for some reason and then sped off, seeming to confirm Hondo's fear that an accomplice was still out there somewhere.

"I'm gonna go radio this in," Hondo said as he walked in the direction of the cruiser. However, when he got there, dispatch was already trying to contact him. Probably the old man, worried out of his mind.

"Deputy Dumez, this is dispatch. Do you copy?" the fuzzy voice said over the radio.

Hondo picked up the transceiver. "Dispatch, this is Deputy Dumez. We've got a 10-55 out at Puerto de Luna. I repeat, a 10-55 at Puerto de Luna. Over."

"Copy that, Dumez. We need you to come on back. Over."

"Dispatch, you don't want me to wait for a coroner? Albuquerque isn't that far away."

After a moment, a different voice broke over the comms. "Hondo!" It sounded like Jerry.

Hondo's grip on the transceiver tightened. "Jerry, is that you?"

"Hondo, get back here as quick as you can."

"Why? What happened?"

"Our father, he's dead!"

VIII.
THE REPORTER

Hondo watched in disbelief as the casket was lowered into the snowy ground. It was a miserable day for a funeral—icy cold— which hadn't done the gravediggers any favors when they carved out the plot from the hard, frozen earth. Nearly the whole town was there to pay their respects it seemed like. Pancho and Jerry stood on either side of their mother, while Patricia was on the other side of Hondo, clutching his hand tight. Debbie was there for him just like he was there for Patricia, her hands wrapped around his arm.

He had taken the old man for granted. He wasn't exactly a bundle of fun to be around, but Hondo would miss him terribly just the same. It wasn't just that. This made him the man of the family now. The patriarch he thought they called it.

He looked down at Patricia. A few days ago he had thought to himself that he'd have to help the old man out when she started dating. Now looking after her would be his job. Before this, he had thought about getting a place of his own. Now he'd want to stay close to watch out for his mother and sister, especially with Jerry having a family of his own and Pancho being, well, Pancho. He had also worried that this newfound responsibility might hinder his relationship with Debbie. Poor girl, all she wanted was a boyfriend and now she had to run the gamut of a grieving family.

However, if anything, the tragedy had only strengthened their relationship. She had cleaned and dressed his wounds the night he came home since his mother was too upset. She had cooked meals for them and been to their house nearly every night. To say that all of it had accelerated their relationship would be an understatement. They still hadn't managed to go on a regular date, though.

More than anything, Hondo still thought about the strange circumstances under which his father had died. Other than a scratch on the neck, he had seemed fine. Irritated and confused when Hondo last saw him, yes, but not near death. Jerry later told Hondo that their father had become hot and feverish, muttering incoherently until he suddenly passed out. And then he never woke up again. Whatever had embedded itself in his neck had been laced with poison—poison that acted quickly enough to kill him within hours.

They hadn't found out what it was until Hondo met with the coroner in Albuquerque a few days later. The same coroner examined all three bodies, those being his father's, Uncle Kit's, and Salvador Miranda's. Hondo had gone to see Uncle Kit's body first since it was already done. As far as they could tell, Uncle Kit had died from a strain to the heart, likely from terror.

"Anything else I should know about?" Hondo had asked the coroner.

"Yes, this," he said, holding up a small piece of bone.

"That a chip off of his humerus or something?" Hondo asked.

The coroner gave him an odd look. "This isn't his bone."

"Then who's is it?"

"I don't know, but I found it embedded in his neck."

The minute the coroner said it, Hondo's mind went to his father and Miranda. "You find one of those in Miranda, too?"

"He'll be up after your father. I'll let you know."

Several hours later, it was confirmed that his father and Miranda had one of the strange bone darts in their necks. Since Hondo's father hadn't been mutilated like the other two, it quickly became evident that whatever poison tipped the bone had killed all three men.

But still, the case wasn't closed. The body of the killer from Puerto de Luna couldn't be identified apart from being Apache. Not that anyone would come forward to claim the body of a witch. It was taboo. If he had any relatives or accomplices, they would stay hidden. Nor did the man's fingerprints match any records. Plus there was the matter of the missing car, which proved that an accomplice was still loose. This was confirmed a few days later when a drifter named Cactus Jack was found mutilated near Fort Stanton. Like Miranda and Carson, he was another old-timer.

The age was still the only common denominator that Hondo could see between the victims. As for his father, he had simply been in the wrong place at the wrong time, though Hondo wondered why the perp had chosen to shoot him out of everyone there. Hondo also wondered if he was obsessing over the investigation to bury his grief.

Pancho seemed to be taking it rougher than him. Maybe it was because Pancho didn't see the old man as much and regretted it, whereas Hondo had spent nearly every day of his life with him apart from the war. Jerry was even worse, though Hondo suspected it was because Jerry was barely out of his teens and just entering his early twenties. And as for poor little Patty, he wasn't sure if the reality of the situation had set in yet.

After the pastor finished the last prayer and the casket had been lowered into the ground, Hondo and Pancho stood over the open plot while Jerry took the girls to the car.

"What do we do next?" Pancho asked.

"What do you mean? We got the guy that did it." Hondo shrugged. That wasn't the truth, but he didn't want Pancho mucking up his investigation. He wasn't a cop, plus he was a hothead. He didn't have the temperament or finesse for this line of work.

"I'm not stupid, Hondo. There was another person in that car that got away. Whoever it was could be dangerous." He eyed him determinedly. "Look, I know how you are. You don't want me getting in the way. I get it. But I have to do something."

Hondo nodded. He had never been able to fool his brother and even if he didn't want to admit it, he understood his need to be in on the case. "I'm going to the reservation in Mescalero to ask some questions tomorrow morning. It's what Dad had suggested after we found Uncle Kit. Can you stay here and look after the girls?"

"Jerry can do that, can't he?"

"Jerry has to get back to Alamogordo tomorrow, so Ma and Patty'll be all alone. And Debbie," he added after a second. "Besides, even if he wasn't going, you'd still be the one I consider more capable of looking out for them." It was partly the truth and partly a way to placate his brother.

Pancho nodded reluctantly. "You'll tell me what you find?"

"Of course," Hondo said, even though that all depended on whether or not he felt Pancho could handle what he found.

"See you at the wake?" Hondo asked.

Pancho nodded. "Of course."

***

Pancho stared miserably into his beer glass, now half empty. He should have been at the wake, but he just couldn't stand to deal with all the long-lost relatives and town folk there. Each of them assuring him of how sorry they were while also managing to be nosy and pry some information out of him about his life, where he'd been, all the stuff that was none of their business. Besides, Ma had Jerry and Hondo.

Pancho had never gone out drinking when he was sad. He had always been happy and didn't realize that depressed drinking only made things worse, not better. He never resented Harold Dumez for anything. He spent most of his teenaged years thinking that his father was someone bold and exciting who looked just like him instead of the cranky old man who had raised him. Now he felt ashamed for all the years he spent believing that he wasn't really his father.

Pancho's mood was made worse by a stranger in the corner. He could feel the man's eyes boring into him even though every time he cast a sly glance in his direction, he was already looking away. He was older than him, probably in his late fifties. He had a haunted, paranoid look in his eyes. Pancho couldn't tell if it came from a lifetime of seeing too much or just a disturbed mind in general. He didn't look homeless, though. He had on not what he'd call a nice suit, but a decent one. A seersucker suit he thought it was called. If he had to peg him for anything, he'd pick either a mortician or a reporter. "Take a picture, old man, it'll last longer," Pancho said when he looked again.

The man stood and began walking towards his table. "I'm sorry, it's just that I couldn't help but notice that you look a great deal like your father."

That was bull. Pancho didn't know what the guy's angle was, but he was obviously grasping at straws to try and talk to him. Pancho slammed his glass down. "Mister, ain't nobody ever told me that I look like my old man."

The man paused awkwardly before responding, as though what he was about to say would warrant some consequence. He sat down and leaned in close. "I meant your real father."

The words nearly stopped his heart from beating. Pancho grabbed him by his shirt collar. "My old man's dead, and you got the nerve to imply I'm some sort of bastard. That my mother—"

"She's not your mother, either," the man said, and then glanced in the direction of the bartender. He was eyeing them, so Pancho let him go. "Look, I know that my timing couldn't be worse, and I'm sorry for your loss, but—"

"Who are you?" Pancho asked, irritated, intending to get a feel for the man before asking him the questions that really mattered.

"I'm sorry, how rude of me. My name is Jamison Tilley, and I'm a reporter for the *Albuquerque Alibi.*"

"Well, if you want a quote about my old man's death, you can forget it."

He shook his head. "No such thing. I always let grieving families be. I'm not a bloodsucker."

"What are you still doing hanging around town then? Ain't been any more murders around here."

"You're right. In fact, I should have moved on to Fort Stanton a few days ago."

"Was there a murder there?"

Tilley nodded. "An old drifter named Cactus Jack was found just like the other two."

"Son of a bitch," Pancho muttered under his breath. Hondo didn't tell him that, and he had to have known. He was already keeping secrets from him.

"I'm sorry?" Tilley asked, confused by the outburst.

"You didn't answer my question. What are you still doing here?"

"Truthfully… I had gotten a quote from your brother about the murders when I first came to town. But after seeing him, I noticed a certain resemblance to someone that I used to know. Only, I didn't exactly know how to breach the subject with him."

"And what was it exactly that you recognized in dear old brother?" Pancho took another drink and eyed the man suspiciously.

"It's your eyes. You've never seen anyone else in your family with eyes like you, have you, Pancho?"

Pancho couldn't deny it, and he had pointed that out to Hondo himself.

Tilley continued, "What if I told you that I met someone down in Mexico with eyes just like yours? Your father, to be exact."

The words made his hairs stand on end.

"My father, huh?" Pancho tried to sound skeptical, even though deep down his instincts were screaming that the man spoke the truth. "You knew him well?"

"I met him when we fought in the Revolution. Well, he fought in the Revolution. I was just a war correspondent. Dorado Dorantes was your father's name. He even knew Pancho Villa."

"Bullshit," Pancho said, leveling a finger at him. "You feed me any more fairytales, old man, and—"

"If you don't believe me, I know someone who you might."

"Who?"

"I only knew your parents fleetingly, but there's someone else who knew them much better." Tilley paused before continuing, "That man from Granbury that's made the news recently... The one that's meeting with the governor this weekend, Tumbleweed Williams."

Pancho stood up. For a second the man had him, but this was too much. "Pancho Villa and now Billy the Kid, huh? Listen, old man, you've got until the count of three until I bust your head in, got it?"

Tilley stood and started to draw something from his wallet. "Clearly I picked the wrong time to approach you. But take this, it's the number of the motel I'm staying at." Tilley slid the card across the table. "You may change your mind when you're sober." Tilley backed away and grabbed his coat from the table he previously occupied, then headed for the door.

Pancho picked up the card. It was Tilley's business card, and he had scrawled the motel number on the back beforehand, so clearly he had planned on approaching him from the moment he set foot in the bar. He pocketed it and looked at his watch. It was seven o'clock and well after dark. The mourners and the busybodies should have cleared out by now. Pancho walked towards the bathroom in the back to take a leak before he drove home but saw a line beginning to form. He swore and walked out the back.

As Pancho wet a weed outside by the dumpster, he examined the card one last time. Just as he was about to let it drop to the ground to be carried away in the breeze, a familiar voice broke into his thoughts.

"I was hoping I might find you here." It was Hugo.

Hugo had been angry the last time he had seen him, and they were alone out behind the bar. Was he here for a fight?

"I'm not quite sure how to take that, Hugo," Pancho said as he zipped up. He turned around to face him.

Seeming to read his mind, Hugo said, "Don't worry. I'm not here to fight, just to talk. Is your brother around?"

"He's at the wake with everyone else."

"Why aren't you?" Hugo asked.

"Didn't want to deal with the doo-gooders and busy bodies."

Hugo nodded and offered him a cigarette. "I understand. Smoke?" Pancho didn't smoke on a regular basis but did so when the occasion suited it.

"I came to apologize for my anger the night grandfather died." Hugo extended his lighter.

"It's fine, Hugo. I understand." Pancho inhaled on the butt to get it lit.

"No, you don't." He shook his head and then lit a cigarette of his own. After taking his first drag, he continued. "Your customs are not ours. Besides, now I realize this thing was here before Grandfather uttered the word."

"You really believe that's why it happened?"

"Maybe. I don't know." He shook his head. "The Navajo that used to live here with the Apache, they were the ones who first taught us about these creatures. But only in whispers, only in the day, they would never utter that word at night."

"I'll admit I thought you guys were just superstitious at first. But what we saw…" Pancho let his words trail off and then took another long drag.

They both stood there, just leaning against the wall of the bar, each thinking back to that night. Hugo took one last drag and then tossed the cigarette onto the ground, grinding it into the dirt with his boot. "We're selling the ranch and moving somewhere else."

"I'm sorry to hear that." The Mirandas had been in the valley longer than anyone he knew.

"Before we go, I wanted you and your brother to know something."

Pancho nodded and Hugo continued. "The night before he died, here in the bar, you saw Grandfather become upset when Hondo asked him about burying the Kid. On the way home, Grandfather told me something he'd never told anyone before."

"What?"

"He said he lied. He said Billy the Kid's alive."

IX.
THE TOMBSTONE

Pancho's mind was racing, the wheels in his head quite possibly outpacing the ones on his car. Even though he had been reluctant to believe Tilley's claims, his talk with Hugo Miranda shortly after had changed that. Pancho had half-joked to Hondo the other night that he thought Salvador helped fake the Kid's death, and Hugo had just confirmed it. But that wasn't all…

They had walked over to Hugo's car in the parking lot. He had wanted to show him something, though Pancho would have never guessed what.

"The tombstone…the real one," Hugo clarified since Salvador had made a duplicate for the new Billy the Kid Museum. "Grandfather got worried about it when Uncle Kit was murdered for some reason. He told me we needed to protect it, like he thought someone might steal it or something."

Pancho had nodded. "Why are you telling me this?"

Hugo's answer had been to pop his trunk.

"Is that the replica?" Pancho asked upon glimpsing what looked to be Billy the Kid's tombstone.

Hugo had shaken his head.

"That's the real one?" Pancho asked, shocked.

"I switched it with the duplicate at the cemetery. No one will know the difference."

"Who else knows?"

"Only you. My wife and I are leaving Sumner tonight for good, but this belongs here. I hoped since your brother is the new sheriff, he could keep it safe until things blow over."

"Safe from what?"

Hugo had shrugged. "I don't know. All I know is that I've fulfilled my promise to Grandfather. Now, will you help us?"

Pancho had agreed, and the tombstone now rested safely in his own trunk. Maybe Old Man Miranda's worrying about the grave marker was just the eccentricities of a senile old man, but Pancho would honor his last wish and hide it away until things calmed down. But first, he was going to have a talk with Hondo.

When Pancho pulled up to the house, Hondo was sitting on the front porch swing like a father waiting for his wayward teenager to come home. It reminded him of the old man. Patricia was splayed across his lap, asleep. Pancho could tell he was in a bad mood as he stepped out of the car.

"The hell have you been?" Hondo whispered and got up gently, seeing to it that he didn't wake Patricia.

"Hondo, you're not gonna believe this—"

"You missed the wake," Hondo said as he walked to meet him in the driveway.

"I'm sorry. I just didn't feel like being around a bunch of looky-loos, okay?"

"Ma—"

"Ma had you and Jerry."

"That still doesn't make it right."

"I saw Hugo tonight." Pancho cut to the chase.

Hondo's expression tensed. "And?"

"Remember the night before Thanksgiving in the bar? When Salvador got upset?"

Hondo nodded. "Yeah…"

"Well, Hugo says they had a little talk on the way home about that. Hugo says the old man didn't just help cover up the Kid's death back in 1881, he claims the Kid is still alive."

Pancho could tell from the look on his brother's face that he was trying to connect this new information to the murders. Hondo bit his lip, and Pancho said aloud what he knew he was thinking. "What did Uncle Kit say, Hondo? The same thing, that the Kid isn't dead. And guess who's coming to Santa Fe tomorrow."

"Now look," Hondo held up a finger, "I believe that Uncle Kit thought the Kid was still alive, and apparently Salvador did, too, but that doesn't prove that's the reason why they were murdered. Or that this Tumbleweed Williams guy is the Kid."

"Just the same, don't you think you ought to be there when he comes to Santa Fe?"

"I can't do that."

"Yes, you can. You're the sheriff now."

"Listen, that the murderer is after people because of the Kid is just a theory. I have to go based on what I know, which is that somehow this ties into the Apache. I've got to go to Mescalero."

"Then let me go see Williams. I could pretend that I'm you."

"No," Hondo cut him off decisively.

"Look, that's not the only reason I think one of us should meet Williams," Pancho said. "I met this reporter tonight. Wild-eyed guy. Says he talked to you a while ago."

"Was his name Tilley?"

"Yeah, the same one that got a quote from you," Pancho said, and Hondo looked like he wanted to say something. Before his brother could interrupt him again, Pancho continued, "Listen, you're not gonna like this, but he says he knows who our real parents are."

Patricia stirred and Hondo shot him a dirty look. He grabbed him by the scruff of his jacket and led him further away from the porch. "Not this bull again, especially not now," he hissed.

Pancho shrugged him off. "Don't be pissed at me. I'm just repeating what I was told. He said our real father fought in the Revolution in Mexico and this Williams guy can tell us about him."

"Hold on a second." Hondo held up a finger and gave him an angry smirk. He marched over to his patrol car and rifled through a mess of papers in his passenger seat. Hondo walked back to him and handed him a flyer. "Take a look at this. Came in a few days ago, before I knew."

"Knew what?" Pancho looked down at the paper. It was more of a missing person's type flyer than a criminal wanted poster. It had the reporter's face and his name on it. Pancho read it aloud. "Jamison Tilley—escaped from New Mexico Insane Asylum at Las Vegas on 11-17-50. Suffers from schizophrenia and other mental delusions."

Pancho felt like an idiot. Maybe the man had been full of it after all.

"You have any idea where he is now? I need to send one of the deputies out to get him if you do," Hondo said.

Pancho sunk his hand into his pocket, fiddling with the card. "No. I ran into him at the bar and that was it."

"Well, if you see him again, call one of the deputies to go round him up. Guy is a nutjob." Hondo rubbed his temples. "Like I said, I'm heading to Mescalero first thing in the morning, so I need to get to bed." He slapped Pancho on the shoulder. "If I can break away from Mescalero in time, I'll do my best to get up to Santa Fe to check this Williams guy out, okay?"

"Okay," Pancho responded, even though he knew his brother was just trying to placate him. Hondo turned and began to walk back up the porch. "Hey, there's just one more thing…"

Pancho was about to tell him about the tombstone, but Hondo turned and held up his hand to stop him. "Panch,' it's been a really long day. Unless somebody's life is on the line, can it wait?"

Pancho was already irritated, but that last comment made his blood boil. Okay, you smug bastard, he thought to himself, I'm fine with knowing something that you don't. Besides, Hondo had deliberately not told him about the murder at Fort Stanton, so…

Pancho nodded. "Yeah, sure. It can wait." He did his best to hide the resentment in his voice, but Hondo still picked up on it and shot him a look before scooping Patricia up off the porch swing.

"Goodnight, brother," Hondo said irritably as he jimmied the screen door open with his foot.

"Goodnight… dick," Pancho said under his breath when he disappeared inside. He took Tilley's card out of his pocket. After he hid the tombstone away somewhere safe, he had a phone call to make.

***

Pancho dialed the number for Tilley's motel tepidly. If he was wrong, if he was about to willingly have a meeting with an escapee from an insane asylum, then Hondo would lose all respect for him when he found out. Even though logic screamed out at Pancho from the flyer, his gut told him there was something to Tilley's claims worth looking into before he wrote them off.

"Hello?" said the voice he recognized as Tilley's, a hint of paranoia in it.

"I've sobered up. How'd you like to head back to Sunnyside Up? Nine o'clock."

"I'll be there."

When Pancho got to the bar, he found Tilley already seated at the same table as before.

"I have to admit. I was surprised to get your call this soon," Tilley said, standing to meet him.

"Yeah, well, things have changed." Pancho sat down at the table.

Tilley sat. "What's that mean?"

Pancho looked around the bar. It was crowded now, being later in the evening. It was harder to hear, too, but that was a good thing. He didn't want anyone overhearing their conversation.

"First, I want you to explain this." Pancho nudged the folded-up flyer to him.

Tilley unfolded it and immediately shot him an expression of disgust. "This isn't what it looks like."

"Looks like a wanted ad for the nut house to me."

Tilley shook his head and pushed it back across the table. "They're out to discredit me."

"Who are they exactly?"

He leaned over the table. "The Santa Fe Ring."

Pancho had heard of the Ring. It was a group of corrupt politicians that ruled the whole territory during the Old West. They were one of the main factions in the Lincoln County War, backing the side that fought against Billy the Kid and the Regulators. So far as Pancho knew, the Ring had died a slow death, figuratively speaking, when New Mexico achieved statehood in 1912.

"You've heard of them?" Tilley asked.

"Yeah. They can't still operate, though," he said dismissively.

"Oh, I know they do. Being a reporter, you stumble onto things sometimes."

"Oh, yeah? Well, being a reporter, why is it that you don't expose them?"

"Are you kidding? I'm not suicidal," he hissed. "Besides, no paper would run that story."

Inwardly, Pancho rolled his eyes. Clearly, this kook was cut from the same cloth as people who believed in flying saucers. But he still needed to hear what Tilley had to say about his parents. "Let's get to it. My alleged parents from Mexico, are they still alive?"

"I honestly can't say. They were when I left Mexico, but that was thirty years ago. That's why I suggested you go see Williams in Santa Fe before it's too late."

Pancho took that last statement to mean something other than before the old man left town. It sounded more urgent. "What's that supposed to mean?"

"Here's the thing, Uncle Kit, Old Man Miranda, Cactus Jack, they're not the only ones connected to the Kid to turn up dead in the last few years."

"What are you talking about?"

"In 1937, two old-timers died within a few months of each other. Know what they had in common? They both at one time claimed to be a surviving Billy the Kid. One was called Walkalong Smith, the other was…" Tilley snapped his fingers, trying to recall the name. "John Miller, from Ramah, I believe. He's buried at the Old Pioneer's Home in Prescot. And I bet you that if you got your hands on their autopsy reports, you'd find the same anomalies in them that were found in Carson, Miranda, and your father."

"I don't have the authorization to—"

"Yes. But you look just like someone who does." He gave him a knowing look.

"Alright. But first, tell me what the big deal is about Billy the Kid living past 21 anyways? It's interesting, sure, but not something worth killing over."

"It's not about the Kid. It's about what he found before he quote-unquote died in 1881. In fact, that's the real reason he had to go into hiding."

Tilley paused awkwardly as the waitress came by to bring them their drinks. Once she was gone, he resumed. "What the history books won't tell you is that back in 1881, the Kid made the acquaintance of a certain man called Adams."

"Adams who?"

"Exactly. Just Adams." Tilley gave him a look as though he should know what that meant.

"The Adams?" Pancho answered incredulously. He had heard the story of the Lost Adams Diggings as a boy. It told of a canyon of gold guarded by the Apache. It was discovered in the 1860s by a man simply known as Adams. Or, at least, Adams was the only one to survive. There had been a whole party of prospectors that he was a part of, but all of them but Adams were slaughtered by the Apache, hence it being called the Lost Adams Diggings.

Tilley nodded. "That's right. The story goes that shortly after his escape from jail, the Kid met Old Man Adams by chance and saved his life from a group of ruffians. In return, Adams told Billy the location of the lost canyon. What if I told you that not only did Billy the Kid find the Lost Adams Canyon, but he even made a map to it?"

"If that's true, and he's still alive, then why the hell hasn't he shared the wealth already?"

"There was an accident that sealed up the canyon shortly after the Kid and his compadres found it. Some act as though God Himself did it so that it would never be found again. That's why you have to have a map to find the area. It's unrecognizable now. Not even the Apache can find their way back.

"Not just that. It's also the Santa Fe Ring. The Kid's been in hiding for over seventy years now because of them. That's why Pat Garrett helped him fake his death in 1881, and now he's resurfaced after all this time... to smoke them out before he dies. See how many of them are still out there before he can reveal the location."

Pancho tried to tie that to the recent killings. "Do you think the Santa Fe Ring ties into the murders somehow? Like maybe they're staging these killings to just make them look like the work of an Indian?"

Tilley shook his head. "I don't think so. That canyon was a taboo spot for the Apache. I think it's a real Apache that's behind the murders, either because they're trying to help keep the canyon hidden or rediscover it themselves.

"Anyhow, if you want to ask Williams about your parents, your real parents, you need to get to him before either the Ring or the murderer does because they're both after him."

Tilley took a well-deserved drink to calm his nerves. The calm didn't last long. Suddenly his eyes darted to the doorway and he put his beer down. "Oh no."

"What?" Pancho looked behind him.

"Those men, see them?"

Pancho nodded. Seven men in suits too nice for this crowd had just walked inside. As if they couldn't be any more obvious, a few still wore dark sunglasses even though the sun had set hours ago.

"They're from the Santa Fe Ring… someone must have talked," Tilley hissed in a panic.

They certainly looked like government men, or G-men as some called them. But were they really from the Ring? Again, logic and his gut-instinct played a tortured game of tug of war in his mind. Logic told Pancho that the men could be from the asylum, but his gut told him that they were exactly who Tilley said they were. Afterall, the other night he and his brother had chased down a man who thought he was a skinwalker. Why couldn't the Ring still be in operation as well?

The men took notice of Tilley but didn't approach the table. Three parked themselves near the front door, while three more situated themselves by a rear exit near the bathrooms. The last one moseyed on over to the bar and leaned against the counter, staring at them.

Tilley grabbed Pancho's arm. "A fight. You need to start a fight that gets the whole bar into an uproar. Then we can get out."

Pancho bit down hard on his toothpick. This was the moment of truth. Did he really want to risk his neck for an old man who might be a mental patient? Pancho studied the men again. Since they hadn't come to collect Tilley right away, Pancho was guessing that they intended to follow him out and then grab him when he left. If these men were from the asylum, they'd probably go up to Tilley first thing and not be so secretive about it.

Pancho turned back to Tilley. "Alright, but what's the plan after we split?"

"You get to Santa Fe to meet Williams and I go on the lam until things cool off. Just get me out of this bar." Tilley tightened the grasp he had on his arm. His wild eyes did make him look a little crazy.

"Alright." Pancho wrenched his arm away and scanned the room, calmly twiddling his toothpick. A "Better Red Than Dead" poster on the wall along with a glimpse of the McPherson clan yukking it up in the corner was all he needed to formulate a plan. Between the current Red Scare paranoia and the McPherson's hot tempers, he'd have the bar in an uproar in no time.

"Watch me work, old man." Pancho stood and swaggered towards the lone G-man at the bar. Pancho pounded his fist onto the counter. "Attention, everybody, attention!"

The revelers quieted down and stared at him with a mix of curiosity and resentment for bringing their revelry to a halt. "As most of you know, I buried my father today, so I just wanted to take a moment to raise a glass in memory of my old man, the sheriff of Fort Sumner, and one of the best who ever lived!"

The bar cheered in agreement and raised their glasses. Pancho glanced over at Tilley, who looked mortified. This wasn't how one typically started a fight. Pancho winked at him and turned back to the crowd. "And, while I got y'all's attention, I might as well tell y'all a really funny joke I heard today."

Pancho turned his gaze to Slim McPherson and his giant kin over in the corner. "Y'all hear the one about why the McPhersons had to start wearing dresses around the ranch?" Pancho didn't wait for a response and fired off the punchline. "Because the goats can hear a zipper drop from a mile away by now."

The drunk men guffawed and laughed while some of the women gasped in shock. Everyone else braced themselves for the storm.

"Hey!" Slim pointed at Pancho. "You take that back! We wouldn't never lease goats on our ranch!"

It was true. Goats were the bane of ranchland because they ate the roots along with the grass, ruining the land. Pancho was more taken aback that Slim was more concerned with what type of livestock it was as opposed to what he had accused him of doing with it.

"That's not what he's getting at," Moose hissed at Slim, then whispered the real meaning in his ear. Slim's eyes lit up like a fire.

"You're a dead man, Dumez! Dead!" Slim screamed and picked up his beer bottle. Pancho stepped in front of the G-man at the bar as Slim took aim, then swiftly stepped aside when Slim launched it. The bottle hit the G-man in the head just like he planned. A hushed silence fell on the room as the man went limp.

Pancho clutched the now unconscious G-man in his arms, watching as his brethren reached into their suit coat pockets, presumably going for their guns. He needed to act fast. Feigning a great deal of urgency,

Pancho shouted, "Slim, do you have any idea who you just knocked out?"

Pancho didn't wait for an answer. "The suit. The dark glasses at night. Isn't it obvious? He's a soviet spy. They're all commies!" Pancho pointed to the other G-men and the crowd gasped in unison.

"Commies right here in Fort Sumner! I don't think so!" one old man shouted.

That was the spark to ignite the powder keg. The good ol' boys were rearing for a fight on Saturday night anyways, and now Pancho had just made it their patriotic duty. Within seconds, the G-men were beset upon and a barroom brawl was in full swing.

Pancho dropped the unconscious G-man to the ground and surveyed the chaotic room for Tilley. The biggest G-man was successfully fighting his way toward the old reporter in the chaos. Pancho had to get to him first. There was a problem, though. Slim was swimming through the sea of people like a shark straight for Pancho. Slim didn't care about the commies. He still wanted him.

"Pancho, now you get over here and take your medicine like a man!" Slim yelled as he drew near. Pancho watched helplessly as Tilley tried to get to the front door and away from the G-man, which wasn't easy in the frenzied crowd. Before Pancho knew it, Slim was upon him.

"Slim, I didn't mean it! I just needed a little distraction." Pancho ducked Slim's swing, a whoosh of air rushing over his head. "I'll explain one day. It'll be a real funny story, I promise!"

Pancho ducked and weaved his way to the south wall near the front door as he watched Tilley make it out, but the G-man was still hot on his trail. Suddenly, Slim grabbed Pancho by the shirt collar and slammed him against the wall. His head battered into a picture frame, the broken glass cutting his scalp.

"Hey, I didn't really think you guys would ever touch a goat, okay?" Pancho said, wincing through the pain as the meaty fist pinned him to the wall. Pancho realized there was no way to talk himself out of Slim's grasp. It'd be quicker to get knocked out of it. Pancho held up a finger. "Now, a sheep, on the other hand…"

Slim smashed Pancho so hard it sent him flying right into the doorway just as the G-Man came upon it. He tripped over Pancho as he tumbled through the exit. When the man stood to resume his pursuit,

Pancho grabbed his legs as Tilley disappeared into the parking lot. The man turned and quickly gained the advantage over Pancho due to his size and the fact that he was still lightheaded from getting slammed by Slim. The man pinned him to the ground, his hands on his throat.

"Your friend, what did he tell you?" the man hissed.

"Hey, he's mine, ya damn commie scum!" Slim yelled from behind. In an instant, Slim knocked the man out cold with a blow to the head.

Pancho jumped to his feet. "Slim, if you wasn't so ugly, I could kiss you!" He slapped him on the shoulder and then darted away into the night.

"Hey, you get back here and finish this fight like a man!" Slim yelled.

Pancho watched a car peel out onto the road and could only hope it was Tilley. Pancho ran for his own vehicle, and he knew exactly where he would go next. There was only one person who could help him now.

***

A ringing doorbell at this hour was never a good thing. Debbie had stayed up later than she planned after having left the wake and was exhausted. She peeked through the curtains and was relieved to see it was Hondo rather than some stranger.

As she opened the door, she was shocked to find his clothes torn and his hair a mess. "Hondo, what happened?"

"Sorry, not Hondo," the twin she now knew to be Pancho said with a hint of guilt.

"Oh." Debbie caught a whiff of alcohol in the air. "Have you been… Are you drunk?"

"I was about two hours ago." Then, getting her drift, added. "That is not why I'm here. Listen, I'm sorry to do this, but I need a favor…"

A few minutes later, Debbie's mind was reeling from everything Pancho had just told her. Right now he was sitting on a swivel stool in her kitchen as she sewed up a scrape on the back of his scalp as he recounted his wild night.

She didn't feel uncomfortable with Pancho. She had seen him every day for the past week along with Hondo. She was practically one of the family now. No, she definitely wasn't uncomfortable so much as she felt strange about being alone with him, like it was tangent to cheating somehow even though it wasn't. She wondered if she'd feel this way if it was Jerry here instead and suddenly realized she felt awkward because a part of her was attracted to Pancho.

"Do you think I'm crazy?" he turned and looked up at her with pleading eyes, and for the first time, he reminded her of a boy.

"About Billy the Kid, maybe. But not the bit about your parents. Your real parents, I mean."

She turned his head back around so that she could continue sewing the flap of skin down that had torn loose when Slim McPherson knocked him against the wall. "The minute I saw Hondo, my first impression of him was that he was mixed like me. Half white, half Mexican. When I saw your parents for the first time, I was shocked. It didn't add up." She paused from her needle work. "It's just… neither of you looks like anyone in your family."

"That's what I've always said." Pancho turned around again. "It had always been there, in the back of my mind gnawing at me. A part of me feels like an idiot for looking into it, but a bigger part of me would feel like a fool to let it go."

Debbie spun him around and dabbed some peroxide on the wound one more time. "Well, considering what Hondo said about the night your dad died, nothing would surprise me anymore."

"He talked about that night, huh?"

"A little."

"I thought maybe he wouldn't… just since it was all so far-out, I mean. It was wild, Debbie. It looked like a coyote half of the time on all fours. But when we got to it, it was just a man wearing an animal skin. And the missing car. It doesn't add up either."

"What do you mean?"

"We were flying down a dirt road. We kicked up a ton of dust behind us, but they didn't. It was weird."

"New Mexico witches ride fireballs at night," Debbie muttered. "That's what my *abuelo* said."

"Hell if I know anymore," Pancho muttered.

Debbie finished her stitches and swiveled him back around to face her. "You said you needed a favor earlier, and I know it wasn't just the stitches."

Pancho bit his lip. "I need to get into that meeting in Santa Fe to see Tumbleweed Williams. And I need some of Hondo's things to do it."

Debbie nodded, still not sure how she played into this.

"So… here's the thing. The other deputies at the station know me by now, and they also know by tomorrow morning Hondo will already be on the road to Mescalero. I walk in there imitating my brother and they'll smell a rat for sure."

Debbie was intuitive enough to see where this was going. She had been seen with Hondo at the station several times now and they all knew her there. "But if you walked in with me…" Debbie turned around to wipe her hands on a dishtowel. "Oh, Pancho, I don't know. Hondo would—"

"If Hondo knew what I knew now he'd change his mind. Besides, he can't be in two places at once and one of us has got to get to Williams before the killer."

Debbie cautiously weighed Pancho's words. She knew how Hondo was by now and knew why Pancho didn't want to wake him up for another argument he'd just end up losing. Her intuition also screamed out at her that what Pancho believed was true. Sweet though they may be, Mr. and Mrs. Dumez weren't their biological parents. "Fine. But I need some makeup first," she sighed.

"No, you don't. You look great."

"I meant for you, dummy," she said as she walked to her bedroom. "Hondo wouldn't walk into the station all beaten up from a fight. But you definitely would."

***

Thirty minutes later, Debbie and Pancho were at the station. She had covered his bruises well enough that they weren't too noticeable, especially not in the dark.

"Dorrance!" Pancho pounded on the glass for Hondo's deputy. "Dorrance!"

"Sheriff?" A lanky deputy with a mustache walked to the door, confused to see "Hondo" there this late.

"I forgot my keys. I need to grab something real quick," Pancho said.

"You hear about the ruckus at the bar? Supposedly had Soviet spies over there!" Dorrance opened the door. "Don't know if they was commies or not. They was all cleared out by the time I got there. Charlie said your brother's the one who started the fight."

"Well, believe me, Dorrance, when I get my hands on him…" Pancho made a wringing motion as he walked inside. "Little scalawags probably passed out along skid row somewhere by now."

"Still though, commies in Fort Sumner…" Dorrance shook his head.

"Tell me about it. Ever see that movie *I Married a Communist?* Giving me cold feet about this one," Pancho whispered and nodded at Debbie.

"Oh, stop it, Pa…Hondo." Debbie almost slipped, but Dorrance didn't seem to notice.

"Anyways, I just need to grab something out of my office and I'll be on my way," Pancho said as he walked down the hall. "Where is my office, anyways?" he whispered to Debbie. It had been a while since he'd actually stepped foot in the station.

"Here," Debbie hissed and tugged on his arm before they almost walked right past it.

He flipped on the light. Just like he figured, the office was the same as the last time he saw it. His father's coat and cowboy hat hung on the coatrack in the corner, and all the pictures were the same. Not that Hondo would make interior decorating his main priority, but still, he wasn't surprised to see that his brother had kept things where his father had left them. Pancho started rifling through the desk.

"What are you looking for?" Debbie asked.

"Hondo'll have his badge with him. No way I can swipe that. But my father's old badge should still be in here. Should be enough to get me into the meeting."

He found his old man's badge and I.D. in Hondo's top left drawer, which was only the second place he looked. He knew his brother would keep them somewhere as a memento and he was right.

"You know him well," Debbie observed.

"It's a twin thing."

"Is that really all you need to get into the meeting?"

"Yeah, I'll swipe one of his extra uniforms out of the closet after he leaves in the morning." Pancho pocketed the badge and the old I.D. "Okay, let's go."

"That was quick," Dorrance said as they walked back into the main office.

Pancho leaned on the counter to give him an order. "Hey, I need something else done for the Carson and Miranda investigations. There may have been two other related deaths back in '37. I want you to call the coroner's office in Prescott and ask for the autopsy report on John Miller. There's another one… Walkalong Smith. I don't know his real name, but see if you can find it and dig up his autopsy report, too."

"You got it." Dorrance scribbled down the names and then as Pancho and Debbie prepared to leave, added, "Hey, what is it you expect to find down there in Mescalero anyways?"

"Indians, Dorrance, I expect to find Indians," Pancho sighed from the doorway and then realized Hondo would never act so snarky.

"Geez, sorry I asked. You know what your problem is, Sheriff?" Dorrance said.

"What?"

"You been spending too much time with that brother of yours."

"Well, you know what they say, Dorrance. If you spend too much time with another person, you even start to look alike after a while."

X.

THE MEDICINE MAN

There was no snow in Mescalero yet. Even though Hondo was in the mountains, where one would expect to find snow as opposed to the valley where he was from, Mescalero was in the southern, slightly warmer portion of the state. The landscape was very different from the flat, red-earthed valley he hailed from as well. Here, either side of the road was flanked by rocky mountains dotted with the green of a thousand pines.

He had no contacts with anyone in Mescalero, nor did he imagine anyone from there being particularly eager to help anyone from Fort Sumner. Though it had been nearly one hundred years ago that the Apache had been sequestered at Fort Sumner with the Navajo, when it came to the frontier, old grudges died hard, and the Mescalero Apache had every reason to hold one. Fort Sumner had not been an ideal spot to detain them, and many had died. They had been sent there in the early 1860s, and by the end of that same decade, the whole thing had been declared a monumental failure. The Navajo were allowed to go back to Arizona, and the Apache were sent south to Mescalero.

Hondo's gut had told him that his best bet was to reach out to the Mescalero Tribal Police and see if anyone was willing to answer his questions. They didn't have to. It was out of his jurisdiction, after all. After a few phone calls, he was directed to an officer named Delbert Baca. When Hondo had told the man his inquiry over the phone, that being witches—he knew now not to use the 'S' word—the man's response had been puzzling.

"In the day only," the voice said.

"Excuse me?"

"I'll answer your questions. But it has to be during the day."

Hondo assumed the man had plans that evening. "That's fine. Morning was when I was heading up anyways."

"Witches eavesdrop at night," the voice on the other end of the line said, and Hondo wasn't sure if he was joking or not.

Maybe in a few minutes when he met the man in the flesh, he'd be able to tell. When he drove into the village of Mescalero it didn't match his vague childhood memory of it. One July, his parents had taken him and his brothers there. It was just like in the movies with people dancing in headdresses and everything. At the time, he thought it was always like that. Now he understood that was part of a special summer ceremony. At the moment, the town looked like any other mountain village.

Hondo scanned the tree line for the church, St. Joseph's. That was where the man had wanted to meet, since that's apparently where he'd be anyways on a Sunday afternoon. The church was easy to spot, its tan-colored bricks standing out from the dark green ponderosas all around it. He drove up the mountain road the church was situated along and parked. The service had been over for a while, and it looked like the last stragglers were leaving.

A man was sitting on a bench outside, smoking a cigarette. When he saw Hondo park, he stood and put out the butt, thoroughly grounding it into the wet earth. He was of medium height, clearly Apache with dark skin and short dark hair. Late forties if Hondo had to guess. Surely this was his contact.

"Nice of you to finally show up, white eye," the man said as Hondo approached.

"You're Delbert Baca?" Hondo asked cautiously.

"That surprising?"

"No, I guess I just thought—"

"Yeah, I know what you thought. That I'd be jumping around a teepee and going like this," Baca said tapping his mouth, mocking the traditional Indian dances portrayed in Westerns.

"I was going to say younger," Hondo clarified, then realized that could be taken as insulting as well.

"Oh, so now you're calling me an old man?"

Before Hondo could respond, Baca said, "Relax. I'm just busting your balls. I'm a cop, same as you, remember?" He extended his hand. Hondo shook it and Baca added, "I also live in 1950 just like you, not the past. Everybody not from around here thinks we still live in teepees just like in the old days."

"I wasn't sure based on what you said over the phone." Hondo grinned, referring to the comment about only meeting in the daylight.

"I was just messing with you, even though that is what some of us believe, that you shouldn't speak of such things at night. The main reason I said that is I have a game I intend on watching tonight. No, it's not the Red Skins."

"Eagles?" Hondo guessed.

"Steelers. You?"

"Packers. But I won't be home in time to watch them. I take it you already know the particulars of the case?"

"Only what I read in the papers. Scalped. Missing a hand. My question for you is, what did the papers leave out?"

Hondo reached into his shirt pocket and drew out the strange bone projectile that had killed Uncle Kit. "This."

Baca got a disturbed look on his face. "Let's take this inside. Most of the parishioners are gone now."

***

Baca held up the bone dart in the light of the church, examining it closely.

"You ever deal with any murders similar to this in the past?" Hondo asked.

Baca bit his lip. "Not exactly. There was a somewhat similar killing in White Oaks back in '37. Old Chinese guy… Au Nu I think they called him. Found mutilated in his cabin, but they never figured out who did it, or why. Don't know if he had one of these things in his neck either."

"He happen to know Billy the Kid?"

"Didn't everybody back then?" Baca leaned over with a smirk and handed Hondo the bone dart.

"Good point," Hondo relented, tucking the dart safely back in his shirt pocket.

"Yes, there are some Apache witches who fire bone projectiles like the one you just showed me. But the man you hunted down in Puerto de Luna…" Baca paused as though he was uncertain of what to say next. "What you described sounds like a mixture of Navajo and Apache witchcraft. Very strange."

"When you say mixture…"

"If it had stopped with the scalping and the bone dart, I would say it was Apache. But the coyote-skinned man, that's more in line with Navajo witchcraft."

Hondo began to rub his temples. "Have you ever heard of something like this happening before? A blend of different witchcraft techniques used by the same witch, I mean?"

Baca's usually pleasant expression clouded to one of concern. "Ever hear of a little pueblo called Abiquiú?"

Hondo shook his head.

"I'm not surprised. Hardly anyone there anymore," Baca said.

"Why not?"

Baca drew in a long breath as though he wasn't sure how to answer. "A plague, for lack of a better word. You see, Abiquiú was a settlement of misplaced Indians called the Genízaros, not unlike what happened at the Bosque in the 1860s, only it predated it by about one hundred years."

Hondo couldn't place the tribe. "Genízaros? What were they exactly?"

"A little bit of everything. Kiowa, Cheyenne, Tewa, you name it. But mostly they were former slaves. Many of them were detribalized and had been forced into servitude by either the Spanish or enemy tribes. Lost their identity, to put it mildly, and so the Spaniards forced them all together at Abiquiú."

"What happened there exactly?"

"Every variety of witchcraft you can imagine, it wasn't distinctive to any one tribe. There were reports of shooting sorcery, the evil eye, possession… men turning into animals." He gave Hondo a knowing look before continuing. "But the worst of it was the plague."

"A literal plague?"

Baca nodded. "Started with a pain in the stomach that led to extreme dehydration, insomnia, and bleeding from the facial cavities. But that wasn't the worst of it. Before it was all over, the stomach would burst. Made what you're dealing with now look like child's play."

Hondo grimaced at the thought of it. "And this actually happened? It's not just folklore?"

"The plague happened. Of course, the academics of the world today refuse to believe that witchcraft was the cause…"

"And what do you think caused this plague?"

"Probably something just like that." Baca pointed to the bone dart in his pocket.

Hondo considered the possibility. The bone darts were apparently laced with some kind of poison, but surely they couldn't induce a literal plague. "You think we could be on the verge of something as bad as another Abiquiú?"

"I certainly hope not, but history does love to repeat itself."

"Well, in the interest of history not repeating itself, would you be willing to come to the next crime scene with me? You might pick up on things that I miss."

Baca bit his lip pensively, and when he took too long to respond, Hondo asked, "Don't tell me that you're afraid?"

Baca shook his head. "It's not that. I have no doubt that He would protect me." Baca nodded at a crucifix on the wall so that Hondo would get who He was. "But, I'm afraid in that same regard, I'll also be of less help to you. You see, I'm what some of my brethren mockingly call one of the 'Jesus People'."

Hondo knew that term. It was used for Indians who followed the church over tribal customs. "So am I," he said, still not understanding.

Baca chuckled. "Yes, but where you come from it's more accepted. What I'm trying to get at is that I know someone who can aid your investigation far better than me. Name's Seven McCaw. Fancies himself a medicine man of the old ways."

"Can I see him today?" Hondo asked hopefully.

"Probably. I don't know if he's home, but you can try your luck."

"Is there a number I can call? Let him know I'm coming?"

Baca shook his head. "Doesn't have a phone. You'll just have to hope he's there when you pull up."

"And where is there?"

Baca grinned. "Nowhere."

*****

Hondo followed the mountain road, which eventually deteriorated into little more than a vague trail in the grass, to a stone dugout. It was embedded in the side of a small hill that was really more of a slope. A tiny chimney at the top was smoking away, which confirmed that the strangely named man was home. Seven McCaw? Didn't seem like an Indian name to him. Seemed like he'd heard it somewhere before, though. In an old myth, maybe?

Hondo parked his truck and stared at the little hovel. He wished again that he could've called first. He didn't like just barging in on someone unannounced. He got out of his truck, walked to the front door, and knocked. After several knocks and over a minute without an answer, Hondo resigned himself to enter uninvited. Luckily, the door wasn't locked. But then again, what was there to fear in such a secluded area other than bears and mountain lions, and they didn't use doorknobs.

"Hello?" Hondo called out. No answer. The first thing Hondo noticed upon entering was the warmth and the smell. It wasn't a bad smell, but it wasn't a terribly good one either. He looked around the room and saw the source of both the heat and the smell, that being what he initially mistook for a cauldron. Upon getting a little closer, he could see it was just a large pot. The man was making a stew, though he couldn't place the type by its smell. Whatever it was, Ma never made it. He scanned the room. He didn't know what the abode of a medicine man should look like, but somehow it seemed to fit.

In a corner was a birdcage with what appeared to be a falcon. That must have accounted for some of the unfamiliar smell, he decided. The room was full of dreamcatchers and animal skins. Hondo immediately made a note to look for any coyote pelts but didn't see any. There was no television, he noticed, or any other type of modern amenity. Unlike Baca and the other Mescalero people, it was clear this man chose not to embrace the 20th century, Hondo assumed, because he was probably born in the previous one.

Hondo heard the animal hide that draped over a passageway at the back of the room rustle. A man stepped through it but strangely didn't seem alarmed at Hondo's presence. Atop his shoulder was perched another falcon.

"I'm very sorry to come in like this. I did knock," Hondo said.

The man didn't say anything as he examined Hondo. He was much younger than he expected. In fact, he wasn't much older than Hondo, mid-to-late thirties he would guess. The black hair had a few strands of gray beginning to show. If he went by his face alone, etched with hard lines from the sun, Hondo might have presumed he was older.

Hondo spoke again. "I'm with the De Baca County Sheriff's department. I would have called ahead, only I'm told you don't have a phone."

"It's alright. I knew you were coming," Seven answered in a deep, gravelly voice. "My birds always tell me when people are approaching. And I would guess you're here to ask about the murder?"

"How did you know?"

"Word still gets around, even to a person like me. Not every day someone gets scalped anymore. Would you like some stew?" he motioned to the pot. "It's almost done."

"No, thank you. I would hope not to take up too much of your time, especially unannounced like this."

The man directed the falcon off of his shoulder and onto a perch in the hovel. "So you've come to ask me about the murder. Ask away."

The man seated himself at a small table and Hondo sat across from him.

"Thank you. Oh, I haven't introduced myself. My name is Hondo Dumez, acting sheriff of DeBaca County."

"I'm Seven McCaw, though I assume whoever sent you here already told you my name."

"Yes, it was Delbert Baca."

Seven nodded, and Hondo couldn't tell from the non-reaction what Seven thought of Baca. Clearly this was a man who kept his cards close to the vest.

"Well, as you said, you know about the murders already. Our first clue that an Apache might have been involved came from the fact that the victim had been scalped."

"Scalping was adopted by the Apache from the Commanche," Seven said somewhat sternly. "Besides, with the pervasive influence of television and movies on sick minds, how do you know that it wasn't someone trying to copy the old ways?"

"I did consider that possibility until I saw the killer myself."

"And he was Apache?"

"We could never get anyone to identify the body. Don't know his name. Nothing." Hondo sighed. "But, from what I'm told, he appeared to be Apache. Only he was dressed in the attire of a certain type of Navajo witch… one that wears animal skins."

Seven nodded. "A skinwalker."

He didn't fear the name, interesting. "I was told that skinwalkers are Navajo only and aren't really associated with the Apache?"

"You would be correct," Seven said and then paused as though he had something else to say.

"Except?" Hondo interjected when he was silent for too long.

"The Apache and the Navajo were enemies. But you can learn a lot from your enemies. When the Navajo and the Apache were forced to live side by side at Bosque Redondo, I think some of their ways rubbed off on each other."

Hondo nodded.

"The Navajo called your place 'Hweeldi'," Seven said. "It meant the 'land of suffering'. Some even say that certain Navajos took to the skinwalker way to escape its confines."

"So, you think it's possible that this could be a man who fancies himself both a Navajo and an Apache?"

"Can't really say, but it's possible."

"Rather than being an actual skinwalker, for the sake of argument, let's just say it was a medicine man who thinks himself to be one. I've been told that some medicine men can become witches?"

Seven didn't seem to take the question as an accusation. He simply nodded and said, "This is true. Many witches start as medicine men before switching over."

"Well, let me ask you this. Can one be both?"

"No, never at the same time. A medicine man may become a witch, but a medicine man cannot be both at once."

Hondo took out a notepad. "Well, how does one tell the difference between a medicine man and a witch?"

"It's fairly simple. Medicine men practice their ceremonies in public for all to see. Witches only do so hidden away from the eyes of others.

Medicine men heal sickness, the witches cause it. Medicine men make sand paintings, witches do not. Medicine men chant, witches do not."

Hondo grew frustrated. Seven wasn't really helping him to identify a witch, only a medicine man. "Well, what do witches, or someone who thinks themselves a witch, do? Because so far you've only told me what medicine men do."

"There are several different types in terms of we Apache. The first is the love witch, who uses *godistso* to cause men and women to fall in love with one another. The second type, far more deadly, is the sorcerer. A sorcerer can be a man or a woman, but because men experience the emotion of hatred more intensely than women, more men than women are sorcerers."

Hondo snorted, remembering some of his ex-girlfriends. "Well, I don't know about that, but go on."

"There are three distinct types of sorcery for we Apache. The first is *nagintla'a*, or poison sorcery. Then there is spell sorcery, and finally shooting sorcery. As the name suggests, a foreign object is shot into the victim's body. This is a trait shared by Apache witches and the Navajo skinwalker."

"Hold on." Hondo dug into his pocket for the bone arrow. "Something like this?"

Seven took the arrow and examined it quizzically. "Where did you get this? From one of the bodies?"

"All of the bodies had one. This one came from the man called Uncle Kit Carson. Is it Apache?"

Seven shook his head. "An Apache witch would usually paint the arrowhead red and blue. I'm not entirely sure about the arrows of skinwalkers, as I've never seen one before." Seven handed the bone dart back to him.

Hondo placed it back in his shirt pocket. "I know you're not Navajo, but do you know how one would become a skinwalker?"

"To become a skinwalker, if it is a skinwalker you seek, it is through the killing of a close relative, a sibling or parent, for instance. The Apache way to become a witch is simple. In that case, an Apache will pay a witch a large sum of money to become their pupil."

"And if I were to go looking for a witch, where might they gather?"

"They congregate at night mostly, doing everything you'd expect; dancing around bonfires until dawn, feasting on corpses and other nasty things I won't get into. Caves are a good spot to look, naturally."

Hondo scribbled down the relevant parts of what he had just heard. "So, I get the scalping part, sort of. But why would the perp remove the hand?" He looked up from his notepad.

"There are a few tribes that practice this. The Cheyenne in the northwest sometimes made necklaces out of human fingers, for instance. I've heard of some Apache doing this in the past, but it's very, very rare. But," Seven continued, "since the killer you saw matched the appearance of a skinwalker, I would guess it was taken to make corpse powder with."

"Corpse powder?"

"It's a deadly poison known to the Navajo and Apache alike. That's probably what those bone darts were dipped in to make them lethal. They make their poison from the remains of corpses, dried rattlesnake skin, and wood from trees that were struck by lightning… among other things. They will usually carry the poison in a small buckskin pouch, carefully hidden somewhere on their person."

"Are there any other ritualistic components to a killing of this nature that I should know about?"

Seven looked contemplatively to the ceiling for a moment and then back to Hondo. "God's holy number is seven. But to an Apache, the number four will be of significance. For instance, a witch may walk around their intended victim four times in a circle or say their name four times."

Hondo's mind immediately shot to the four wooden stakes he stumbled across outside Uncle Kit's trailer. He bit his lip, wondering if he was grasping at straws. "I don't know if this means anything, but when I walked the first murder scene, I found four wooden stakes planted in the ground that seemed… out of place."

Hondo took note of the fact that Seven finally seemed to become disturbed. "Now that, that is what your people might call the smoking gun. Before, you seemed to be describing a skinwalker… in terms of appearance, at least. But the Navajo hold no significance for the number four as we do." Seven shook his head and added, "A witch with the traits of a Navajo and an Apache alike, that is truly troubling."

Hondo put down his notepad and leaned forward. "I've been meaning to ask, would you be willing to come to the next crime scene with me? You might pick up on things that I miss."

"Next crime scene? I thought you killed the murderer?"

"I did, but I have good evidence there was an accomplice that fled the scene. The newest murder proves that to be true."

"A master and an apprentice, perhaps? Interesting." Seven looked at Hondo contemplatively. "This alleged skinwalker you killed; how did you manage that?"

"Gunshot to the chest."

Seven shook his head. "If the man was truly a skinwalker, then that's impossible."

"Oh, how does one kill a skinwalker then?"

"Well, definitely not through a simple gunshot, no matter where you shoot them."

"And why is that?"

"Think about it. They're beings that can manipulate their own flesh. As such, they can quickly heal from a simple bullet or knife wound."

"Well, what does supposedly kill these things then? Silver bullets?" Hondo asked somewhat mockingly.

"According to folklore, if you mortally wound them and speak their name that will do it. But, in my opinion, the best way is a blade, or I suppose today it could be a bullet, laced with White Ash in some way."

White Ash. The words sent a chill down his spine. Thanksgiving morning, Pancho had thrown his knife into the White Ash tree in the field, embedding it firmly in the trunk. It was the same knife he had thrown into the witch that night. What if it hadn't been his bullet that killed the man? What if it had been Pancho's knife?

"What's wrong, Sheriff? Something I said?"

"No, nothing." Hondo shook his head and smiled. "And call me Hondo."

"Alright, Hondo," Seven leaned forward with a sly grin. "Now, where is it exactly that we're going to trap a witch?"

XI.
THE KID

*T*he streets of Santa Fe were snowy and damp. Everywhere Pancho looked, the bright white of the snow contrasted dramatically against either the wet, black pavement or the tan adobe buildings flanking the streets. With Thanksgiving behind them and the first snow having fallen, Santa Fe had been thoroughly decorated for Christmas, with lights encircling all the pine trees in Old Town and luminaries topping every roof in sight.

The Governor's Mansion was located downtown adjacent to the Capitol building, so it wasn't hard to find. It was built in 1912, the same year that New Mexico achieved statehood. It looked like a miniature version of the White House, only it had tan outer walls that didn't contrast well with the white pillars in Pancho's opinion. They already had Christmas wreaths hung on the two foremost pillars and snow dusted the barren tree branches hanging over the yard.

He turned Hondo's cruiser into the main driveway. Hondo was so by the book that he had taken his own truck to Mescalero. The way Hondo saw it, Mescalero was out of his jurisdiction. Since it was his personal business, he had taken his personal vehicle. Since he wasn't using it, Pancho had swiped the keys to his cruiser and taken it instead. Besides, who would be suspicious of a sheriff in a police vehicle?

Pancho was surprised when the attendant at the front gate stopped him instead of just waving him through. "Purpose of your visit?"

Pancho looked at him as if he should already know. "I'm here for the inquiry regarding Tumbleweed Williams."

Pancho thought that would do it. It didn't.

"Name?" The attendant looked over a clipboard.

"Sheriff Hondo Dumez." Pancho clutched the stolen badge as he said it.

The attendant shook his head. "This meeting is for pre-selected delegates and the press only. I don't see your name."

"Well, I can tell you this, as the Sheriff of De Baca County I have every right to be here," Pancho responded angrily.

"What county?" the guard said, clearly unable to place De Baca.

"Geez, son, you're on security detail for the governor of New Mexico and you don't know where De Baca County is?" Pancho berated him in a manner he felt was befitting of someone used to giving orders.

"Uh…"

"Two words for you," Pancho leaned out the window, angrily twiddling his toothpick. "Fort Sumner. It's the place where Billy the Kid got shot in case you ain't heard of it. Now, as sheriff of those parts, I need to know whether or not we need to exhume the body. Because if that ain't Billy the Kid in the old cemetery, we need to know who the hell it is. And if that ain't the Kid, then that's an unsolved homicide on my soil, and don't even get me started on what that will entail. And another thing—"

"Okay, okay, sir, go on through." The attendant waved his hands exasperatedly and Pancho sped into the parking lot, grinning from ear to ear.

"Sucker."

***

Pancho immediately felt out of place as soon as he stepped into the luxurious meeting room. It was the people and the furnishings alike that did it. It even smelt rich thanks to a strong hint of mahogany wood coming from the furnishings mixed in with a slew of expensive colognes and liquors. Pancho's family wasn't rich, nor did they rub elbows with the rich. In fact, he couldn't think of any rich people in Fort Sumner at all.

Pancho scanned the room. A huge table ran along the far wall lit by several large rectangular windows. Towards the center of the room was an array of chairs, which Pancho was told would be for the press. He would be seated at the table, as he understood it, which was more prestigious. Not too shabby for not even being on the guest list. Towards the front of the room was a slightly raised area where it was clear that the governor made announcements. Today, instead of a podium, two chairs faced each other at an angle, so that they also pointed out toward the audience.

As for the people, most everyone was wearing suits, reporters from what he could tell, but they were ritzier than Tilley. A sheriff from San Miguel County was there, which was odd since the Kid had nothing to do with San Miguel County. A son of Pat Garrett was there, too, but Pancho didn't catch his first name, seemed like it started with a 'J', or maybe it was an 'O'? Wilbur Coe, the son of Frank Coe, one Billy's fellow Regulators, was there as well. All of Billy's compadres were dead by now. Only the sons of his friends, and enemies for that matter, would be on hand. Except there was one man there who looked old enough to have ridden with the Kid, but Pancho wasn't sure.

The guest of honor, Tumbleweed Williams, had yet to reveal himself. Word on the street was that a lawyer named Burleson had dug him up from Granbury, Texas. Supposedly, Williams was here to seek a pardon for his days as an outlaw. According to history, Billy made a deal with Governor Lew Wallace back in 1879 to testify about crimes committed in the Lincoln County War. However, the pardon deal fell through. And now Williams was here to collect. That struck Pancho as odd. Why would someone as cool as the Kid care about a pardon? However, according to Tilley, this whole thing was just a ruse to root out members of the Santa Fe Ring.

Pancho was himself what you'd call an armchair expert on the Kid. His own family claimed that the Kid used to stay at their old homestead from time to time. Pancho wanted to believe that, but everybody claimed that the Kid hid out at their place or stayed the night at least once. But still, it was enough to fire his interest in the old desperado. He had read every book on Billy he could get his hands on growing up. *The Authentic Life of Billy the Kid* by Pat Garrett had thrilled him the most until he learned that many of the exploits in it were made up, such as Billy breaking a pal out of jail in San Elizario, Texas. There were numerous battles with Apache as well, and always at Billy's side was a mysterious sidekick just called Alias. Pancho used to pretend he was Alias riding with the Kid and shooting bad guys in the Lincoln County War when he was a boy. The whole thing read like a dime novel, and as it turned out, it was. Pat Garrett didn't even write it; his ghostwriter Ash Upson did. What Upson didn't know he simply made up. For many years the book was quoted as the gospel truth, but modern historians had begun debunking many of the book's claims.

Pancho spotted one of them, the state historian, Marcos Mendez, among the crowd. He recognized him from the photo on the dustjacket of a book he wrote on the Lincoln County War. He was easy to pick out because he wasn't just the state historian anymore, he was also the governor-elect. Milton Mayberry, the current governor, had served his two terms and Mendez had surprisingly steamrolled his opponent, the name of which Pancho could no longer remember. Mendez had played up his historical image and also his lineage, claiming to be descended from the very conquistadors who had first tamed the territory. His campaign slogan had ironically been "Don't Let History Repeat Itself," which was a dig at the fact that his opponent would likely just be a continuation of past political failures if he were to be elected.

Mendez had a haughty air about him. He was a fair-skinned Spaniard with dark hair, and even from a distance Pancho could hear him speaking with a distinctive accent. He was conversing with the sheriff from San Miguel County, and from the way they interacted it was clear they knew one another well. The sheriff looked like a typical cowboy, a handlebar mustache decorating his face topped with a big, grey cowboy hat. As Pancho studied them from afar, they turned and took notice of him, suddenly pausing their conversation. The sheriff tipped his hat at Pancho and Mendez nodded at him. Before he knew it, they were walking in his direction. Pancho cussed under his breath, not wanting any attention.

The governor-elect spoke first. "Hello, I am Dr. Marcos Mendez, and I don't believe we've met?" He extended his hand.

Pancho took it. "Hondo Dumez. Congratulations on the election."

"Thank you," Mendez answered.

The sheriff extended his hand next. "And I'm Sheriff Winston West of San Miguel County. You're from Fort Sumner, I see. Nice of you to join us today."

Pancho took note of how he said that last part, almost like it was an accusation. He wasn't going to play any games with him. Pancho shook his hand. "Is that a nice way of saying that I wasn't invited?"

Mendez flashed a sheepish, irritated smile. "I admit you weren't on the guest list. Although, I suppose that's my fault. To not have invited the current sheriff of Fort Sumner was a huge oversight on my part. My apologies."

"I see you invited the Sheriff of San Miguel County. I wasn't aware the Kid had any history there?" Pancho said.

"He didn't, really." West smiled as though he'd been caught in a lie, then added, "I just know the right people apparently."

"Well, we're both here now, and that's all that matters, right? You think he's really the Kid?" Pancho nodded at the empty stage.

Mendez looked at him contemplatively. "You tell us first."

"Truthfully, I hope not," Pancho said.

Mendez responded with a raised eyebrow.

"If he is, I'll have a lot of paperwork to fill out," Pancho explained.

West grinned. "From what I hear, you've got enough problems down there without having to deal with a resurrected Billy the Kid."

Mendez held up a finger. "Oh, yes, that's right. You've recently had not one, but three deaths in your county recently? Two of them were old-timers connected to the Kid, were they not?"

"They were. The third was my own father. Although that was just circumstantial."

"I'm very sorry for your loss, Sheriff Dumez," Mendez said. "Another oversight on my part to forget your father was among the victims. I'm afraid with this little circus we have going on here a lot has skipped my mind. Forgive me, but I'm rather intrigued by the killer. He was Native American, no?"

Pancho nodded, trying to emulate his brother's nature as a man of few words with a short response. "Apache, so far as we know."

Mendez nodded and then dug into his jacket pocket. "I can't deny I'm rather interested in this case. If you learn anything about it, do you think you might call me about it?"

Pancho took the card. "You a detective, too?"

Mendez put a hand on his shoulder. "All historians are detectives, my friend. And something tells me your case will make for very interesting reading one day." He smiled at him. "Now, if you'll excuse me, I have a few people I need to speak with."

"As do I," West said, tipping his hat to him. "Sheriff."

They didn't wait for any type of response from Pancho and walked away into the crowd. Only after Mendez was gone did Pancho realize that the man had skillfully avoided answering questions and had instead only asked them. He may have started out as a historian, but Mendez was also a slick politician. And though Pancho wasn't a lawman like Hondo, even Pancho's mind subconsciously began to do its own detective work. Initially, Mendez acted as though he forgot to invite the Sheriff of Fort Sumner, but upon further conversation, and his keen interest in the murders, it was clear that he was well aware of the goings on in De Baca County. Something was definitely fishy about the man.

And the sheriff. The minute he said that he "knew the right people," Pancho immediately thought of the Santa Fe Ring. Maybe he was one of them? Considering the upside-down nature of his life at the moment, anything was possible.

Before he could contemplate the matter further, one of the aids came onto the main stage and made an announcement. "Okay, folks, he's coming out soon. He just needed to lie down for a few minutes. He is nearly a hundred years old, after all." A few of the reporters laughed, but the more serious men there remained stoic. As far as they were concerned, Williams was a fraud and they were there to prove it.

Everyone took their seats, and about a minute later, accompanied by the governor, came shuffling in one of the most decrepit, dejected-looking men Pancho had ever seen. He was clearly cut from the same cloth as poor Uncle Kit. He wore dirty old jeans and a tattered dress shirt that hung from his limp frame. He had a grey mustache and a full head of hair still. Did that look like Billy the Kid? It was hard to tell. After all, there was only one photo of him to go on from when he was young.

As for Milton Mayberry, he was a tall, thick man with slicked-back hair that reminded Pancho of a million other politicians. He wore a tan suit made of thick fabric that made him look even wider than he already was. Mayberry's term was set to expire at the end of this year and had been mostly uneventful until now. Pancho wondered if Mayberry was aware of the secretive Santa Fe Ring that Tilley had spoken of, or if, perhaps, he was among their numbers.

"Gentlemen, thank you for coming on this cold December Sunday. Hopefully this will all be over with in time to go and watch the big game," Mayberry said. Everyone laughed, though Pancho felt it was disrespectful to the old man who might be Billy the Kid.

The demeaning attitude continued with the first question.

"First off, Mr. Williams, how much money do you expect to make from a pardon?" Mayberry asked, and everyone laughed again. The old man looked none too pleased.

"With all due respect, Governor, many years ago, Governor Lew Wallace of this territory promised me, Billy the Kid, a pardon for acts I committed during the Lincoln County War," Williams said in a gruff voice that struggled to be heard. "Being over 90 years old now, I just want to be able to die a free man."

"Well, before I take that into consideration, what can you tell us about your days as Billy the Kid?" the governor asked.

"Well, he… I mean, I was one of the greatest desperados that ever lived," the old man croaked out and the crowd laughed yet again.

The old-timer sitting next to Pancho shook his head and then hung it in his hands. He couldn't even bear to watch the disaster proceeding on stage.

"Well, that goes without saying, Mr. Williams. I'll rephrase the question. Can you give us an in-depth but succinct description of your life at the time you were known as Billy the Kid?"

The old man proceeded to do a decent job of rambling off a typical Billy the Kid history, which also included many of the falsehoods from *Authentic Life*. This went on for a good twenty minutes or more, only interrupted by the old man occasionally stopping to clear his throat or to take a drink of water.

"Next, we'd like to ask you some questions pertaining to some of the men who are no longer with us. Let's start with Pete Maxwell."

"Who?" the old man asked.

"Pete Maxwell," Mayberry enunciated the name loudly.

"Oh, yes, the man in whose house I was shot. I mean not shot," Williams corrected, and a few laughed. It was tough to tell at this point if Williams was joking and playing into his image, or if he really was that out of it.

The old-timer next to Pancho shook his head again. "Some Billy the Kid they got there," he said in a deep, smooth voice.

"You said it," Pancho replied with disgust, his faith in the man called Tumbleweed Williams waning by the minute.

Pancho caught a twinkle in the old man's eye as if he recognized him before he looked away. Pancho studied the man out of the corner of his eye. Who was he? He smelt of whiskey and aftershave and seemed strangely familiar somehow. He might have passed through Fort Sumner in the past if he was connected to the Kid somehow. Pancho turned his attention back to the conference. Someone had asked about the Coe brothers, and Williams called one of them Charlie. Even Pancho knew both of their names were Frank and George.

By the time things were wrapping up, it had felt like watching a forty-minute trainwreck as far as Pancho was concerned. The whole thing was a farce. Finally, the moment of truth was here. Mayberry was asking how he had escaped Fort Sumner that night. If Williams gave the same story that Tilley had told him in the bar about Garrett helping him fake his death, that might prove it. Only he didn't.

"The truth is, Garrett shot the wrong man that night," Williams said. "He shot a young Mexican man named Jose Gonzales. Garrett wanted to collect the reward money, and so he simply passed the body off as mine and I rode off for Mexico. The rest is history as they say." The old man lifted up his hands as if to say, "Case Closed."

The horrific realization that Hondo had been right cemented itself. Pancho shouldn't have come. There had been no mention of Garrett letting Williams go or of a canyon of gold. Regardless of whether Williams's story matched the one told to him by Tilley, he wasn't Billy the Kid, either. He was just a confused, senile old man and, for that matter, Tilley probably was just an inmate who had escaped the asylum.

"Thank you, Mr. Williams," Mayberry concluded the interview, then turned to the crowd and gave them a knowing look eliciting a few more titters. Williams got up slowly and began to hobble off the wrong way until his lawyer friend awkwardly came to collect him. He led the old man through a door to a parlor room where Williams could go lie down again.

"If you'll excuse me, gentlemen, I need to take a moment to consult with my advisors," the governor said and exited as well through a different door. Pancho noticed Mendez go through it with him, probably to weigh in on it as a historian.

For a few minutes the crowd talked amongst themselves. Pancho was going to say a few words to the old man next to him but was surprised to find that he was already gone. Within a few minutes, the governor reemerged to make his official statement, that being, "Ladies and gentlemen, after careful consultation with several historians, and in light of what we've all just heard, no action will be taken on Williams' petition for a full pardon for Billy the Kid because I don't believe he is Billy the Kid."

"You and me both," Pancho muttered and stood to leave. He'd never felt so humiliated in his entire life. What had he done? Debbie would tell Hondo eventually what she had helped him do and why. She had to. And Hondo would probably come close to disowning him considering it was all for nothing.

Outside, Pancho dejectedly kicked a pebble across the parking lot as he watched the lawyer help Williams into a waiting car.

"Why the long face, kid?" someone asked. The hint of whisky on the breath and the sound of the voice made it clear that it was the old man who had sat next to him. Pancho turned to face the old-timer. Now that he was standing, he could see that the old man wasn't short but was still below average height. However, his deep voice made him seem bigger than he was. Superficially he resembled Williams with the same bushy mustache and grey hair, only heartier and younger looking.

"Just drove a long way for nothing it turns out." Pancho leaned back against his brother's cruiser.

"You don't think that was Billy the Kid?" The man chucked his thumb back at the lawyer's car with an ornery expression.

Pancho snorted. "As if the real Billy the Kid would care about a pardon from the governor after all these years. Or go by a corny name like Tumbleweed Williams."

The old man grinned at him thoughtfully. "You got your father's eyes and your mother's bullshit detector, kid."

Pancho froze. The old man cocked a brow as though Pancho should know exactly what he was talking about.

"You… You're Tumbleweed Williams?" Pancho hissed in a shocked whisper.

"No, that's Tumbleweed Williams." The man pointed at the car driving off. "I'm Billy the Kid."

Pancho opened his mouth to say something, but the old man cut him off. "And you're not Hondo." The man pressed his finger into the sheriff's badge on Pancho's chest. "Unless they mixed up the names I left with you."

"How did—"

"You always had a big speck in that gold ring around your eye that Hondo didn't. Makes sense you'd be the one full of shit, too. Can see it in your eyes."

This man, Billy the Kid or not, knew him far too well to just be a friend of the family. Pancho was dying to ask him how exactly he fit into his life, but before he could, he saw a familiar face. And not a friendly one.

Pancho locked eyes with one of the G-men from the bar last night who had just walked outside. There was no doubt from the reaction that the man recognized him.

The old man read Pancho's face and looked behind him. "You know that fella?"

The G-man didn't bother yelling at Pancho to stay where he was, probably because he knew he wouldn't. The man was already rounding up some cronies to help chase him down.

"Unfortunately." Pancho clutched his keys. "You ever taken a spin in a police cruiser before, Pops?"

"No, but there's a first time for everything," he said, getting Pancho's drift.

Pancho swiftly opened the driver's side door and plopped inside. "Well, get in!"

The old-timer slid inside with surprising agility and Pancho peeled out the minute the old man's butt hit the seat, the passenger door slamming shut from the momentum.

Pancho looked behind him in the rearview mirror. Already, three black sedans were following them. Pancho gunned it for the front gate, which was currently still open.

"You sure are a popular fella," the old man said. "What'd you do to piss 'em off?"

"Barfight," Pancho responded absentmindedly as he watched the guard rail suddenly begin to lower. His pursuers were shouting at the front gate attendant to keep them from leaving.

"Hondo's gonna kill me," Pancho muttered as he gunned it and plowed right through the guard rail. In no time he was out of the driveway and on Paseo del Peralta.

Pancho swore upon seeing the traffic in Old Town on a Sunday afternoon. The streets were narrow and the sidewalks were clogged with holiday shoppers. "We're never gonna get anywhere on these streets."

"You got a police siren, don't ya?" The old man looked over the dashboard and found the switch. He flipped it on and the cars ahead of them began to pull over.

"I've only ridden in the back of one of these before, today's my first time in the front," Pancho said.

"A chip off the old block." The old-timer smiled and shook his head, not the least bit concerned with the three carloads of men out for their blood. To him, it seemed like this was any other Sunday afternoon drive. Suddenly the back windshield shattered from a bullet.

"Musta been some barfight you got into." The old man peered behind him, still not terribly worried as another gunshot rang out. "Well, two can play at that game." The old man drew a revolver from his hip and began to fire. It only took one or two shots for him to hit the front tire of the lead car, swiftly putting it out of commission, just leaving the other two, which quickly swerved around it.

"Ya know, old man, I'm having a real hard time believing you're 90 years old."

"It's what they call good clean living, son. Ought to try it for yourself sometime." He fired another shot.

"Bullshit! I can smell the whiskey on your breath from a mile away."

"Helps steady my hands so I can shoot better." The old man fired off a few more rounds, making casual conversation in between gunshots. "You a good shot?"

"Knives," Pancho muttered, then made a hard right through Old Town's narrow winding roads.

"What?"

"Knives!" Pancho shouted over the noise. "I'm a knife guy."

"That's too bad." He spun back around to reload his revolver, then suddenly stopped when what seemed to be an important thought crossed his mind. "You know what's funny? I just realized that the last time I was in Santa Fe was around Christmas just like this… Or was it New Years?"

A bullet shattered Pancho's side mirror.

"Well, anyways, it was right after me and the boys got caught at Stinking Springs in 1880. Was jailed here for three months. Food was terrible. Don't ever get jailed in Santa Fe," the old man said, pointing a finger at Pancho as though that was what was really important at the moment.

As the chase continued down the narrow confines of Old Town, suddenly, from behind the lead car, emerged a twin set of motorcycles. Each one sped around the pursuing car and onto the sidewalks until they had caught up with Pancho. One flanked either side of the cruiser and both riders immediately took to bashing out their side windows with crowbars. On the second hit, Pancho caught his assailant's crowbar in his hand.

"Pull over!" shouted the man on Bill's side. Bill casually shot him, and he toppled from his bike into the streets as pedestrians screamed in terror.

"Anyways, like I said, all this really takes me back." The old man shook his head and smiled.

"What? The Christmas decorations or the gunfire?" Pancho asked, still wrestling the crowbar with one hand and the steering wheel with the other. He finally wrested the crowbar from the man's grip and then threw it down into his wheel spokes. The man went careening off of the bike and through a storefront window as more shoppers screamed.

"Both. Speaking of which, I think I can guess who our friends are, but since they're after you, I'll let you explain." The old man chucked his thumb at the two cars behind them.

"Tilley said they were Ring men."

"Who?"

"Tilley. You know, the reporter. Says he met you in Mexico?" Pancho shouted and banked hard left, his tires sliding on the wet pavement.

"That guy's still alive? I figured he kicked the bucket ages ago."

"He probably will before long with the Ring after him."

"Well, they're our problem at the moment. Where in the hell are we headed, anyways?"

"I don't know. I figured away from them was good enough."

"Once they radio in that we're in a stolen police car we won't last long. We need something faster."

"Which would be?"

"What I came here in. I got it parked about ten miles out o' town."

"I sure hope you don't mean a horse."

"Just take a left, smart ass."

"What about them?"

"You leave them to me. I been killing Ringers since well before you were in diapers."

They were coming up on a busy intersection. The light was red for their lane, but luckily, most of the cars were staying put thanks to the siren. Bill leaned out the window as they flew under the stoplight.

"What are you doing?" Pancho shouted.

"You'll see."

Right after he said it, Bill shot down a huge holiday banner hanging under the stoplight, causing it to drop down and land right on their pursuer's front windshield. They slammed on their brakes, causing the car behind them to rear-end them. Before they knew it, it had turned into a full-on pile-up.

The old man slid back into his seat. "Still got it."

Pancho looked at him in amazement. "Good clean living, huh?"

The old man glanced at him slyly and shrugged.

After about five minutes, the old man's directions led them to what looked to be any other dilapidated old ranch on the outskirts of town. He instructed Pancho to head for the barn.

Pancho pulled to a stop. "I swear, old man, if you pull a horse and buggy out of there—"

"Wait here and hold off any more bad guys that show up." The old man thumped his revolver into Pancho's chest sideways before he could finish. "I know it's not a knife," he said disdainfully as Pancho took the gun.

The old man got out of the car and Pancho followed. In the distance, he could see a barrage of police cruisers making their way down the dirt road to the ranch. This was just great. Pancho was putting a lot of trust in the old man who claimed to be Billy the Kid.

Suddenly the barn doors flew open to reveal an old biplane. As Pancho ran around to give it a better look, the old man was already climbing into it.

"Give that thing a spin!" the old man hollered from the pilot's seat, referring to the propeller.

"When the hell did Billy the Kid learn how to fly a plane?" Pancho shouted before giving the propeller a hard spin.

"Mexican Revolution. Now get in!" the old man shouted over the sound of the spinning propeller.

The police cars were racing up the road right at them, but as usual, the old man didn't seem overly concerned. Pancho clambered into the second cockpit quick as he could.

"Shouldn't we be going the other way?" Pancho said as they began taxying in the direction of the oncoming cars.

"Nope, we got plenty o' room. Besides, it's more fun this way," he said as they picked up more and more speed. They were getting closer and closer to the procession and just when Pancho was sure they weren't going to have enough room to take off, he felt his stomach lurch and they were in the air. The old man was laughing, apparently enjoying himself. Pancho looked down to the ground to see the cars swerve to a stop, one of the officers stepping out of his vehicle and waving his arms around at them as though it would do any good.

"Hey!" Pancho shouted so loud he knew it'd make his throat hoarse. "I been meaning to ask since we met. Who the hell are you to me and my brother anyways?"

"I'm your grandfather!" he shouted over the roar of the engines.

XII.
THE MOUNTAIN

Sierra Blanca loomed ominously through Hondo's front windshield, a huge stone mass of dark blue capped by bright, white snow. Seven sat next to him in the passenger seat of his truck as a sea of green pines passed by on either side of them. It was only an hour drive, but Hondo was still surprised that as stoic as Seven appeared, conversation with the enigmatic man wasn't as difficult as he feared it would be.

"So is this the sort of thing you pictured when you entered a career in law enforcement?" Seven asked.

"Not exactly. I pictured typical Cops and Robbers stuff, not Cowboys and Indians." After a moment, he added, "No offense."

Seven waved a hand as if to say, "None taken."

After a moment, Hondo shook his head. "You know, my father, he never had to deal with anything like this. Scalping and dismembering. The most exciting case of his career had been the time that Boots McGee got himself a driver's license."

Seven offered a quizzical, unimpressed look.

"Sorry, Boots is the town drunk. I just meant to say dealing with a murder is one thing… but three murders like this…" Hondo's words trailed off as he thought of the last time he saw his father alive. "The night that we fished Old Man Miranda out of the Pecos, my father never saw it coming. One minute he was just standing there looking at a dead body, and the next he looks up to see this strange man in animal skins perched in a tree. And then whoosh," Hondo slapped his neck. "I'm sure my old man contemplated the possibility of getting shot on the job, but not by something like that. I wonder what the hell he must've been thinking when he saw that thing?"

"You act like this is something new, but it's not," Seven interjected. "It's ancient, Hondo. It was around long before you and I were born and it'll still be here long after we're gone. What is it that your book says… there's nothing new under the sun?"

"Maybe, but I still can't believe all these killings are just so that the perp can make corpse powder or whatever it was out of them. Besides, if that's what they were after, why not take the whole body then? There has to be something more to it."

"Something tells me you have a theory."

"More like had a theory. The first murder made sense to me. Uncle Kit, even though he probably wasn't related to the real Kit Carson, I could see how some rogue Indian might choose to kill him because of the bad blood that existed from Bosque Redondo. The second one, Old Man Miranda, he lived in Fort Sumner his whole life, but he wasn't part of the *old* Fort Sumner," Hondo said with an emphasis on the word old. "Miranda wouldn't have gotten there until the soldiers and the reservation were gone. And Cactus Jack here ain't connected to Fort Sumner at all."

"There's no other connections that all three share?"

"Other than all of 'em being old-timers, not really."

"Are you sure?" Seven asked intuitively, as though he knew Hondo wasn't telling him something.

Hondo relented. "Not unless Cactus Jack claimed to have known Billy the Kid. As odd as it sounds, right now that's the only commonality I know of between Miranda and Carson. Then again, every old-timer claims they knew the Kid, so maybe it's just coincidence."

Hondo turned his attention back to Sierra Blanca and nodded in its direction. "So, forgive my ignorance, but when the Apache were sent here from Bosque Redondo, was this your people's original homeland?" Hondo was curious because he knew the Navajo had been allowed to return to their homeland in Arizona but wasn't as sure about the Mescalero Apache.

"Yes," Seven answered, "it was." After a moment, he nodded towards the snowcapped peak. "Do you know the legend of the mountain?"

Hondo shook his head. "Not really."

"That is the spot of origin for our people. Our garden of Eden, if you will. Have you heard the myth of the Hero Twins?"

Hondo had heard it long ago as a boy. "I think so. It's Navajo, though, isn't it? Monster Fighter and Brings His Brother Water… something like that?"

"It's Monster Slayer and Born For Water in the Navajo. In my people's version they were called Killer of Enemies and Child of Water, and both were born of White Painted Woman on that mountain. The twins then came down and slew the monsters, making the earth habitable and safe."

"I have a twin, too," Hondo said absentmindedly.

"And from what you told me, you recently slew a monster as well." Seven flashed a rare grin his way.

"Well, I don't know about that." After a second, he added, "But then again, human beings can be the scariest monsters of them all."

Hondo could tell by the way that Seven was still looking at him that he'd missed his point. "You trying to imply that history is repeating itself again?" Hondo asked. "Like you said earlier about Abiquiú?"

Seven turned from him to stare back out at the mountain. "History is always the same story over and again. The roles and character types are always the same, just with different actors in the parts."

Hondo was curious just how deep Seven's beliefs went. "As a medicine man, to you are these stories history, like the Bible for most people, or just fairy tales?"

"All history becomes a fairy tale eventually," Seven answered without really answering. "Take the slaying of Yé'iitsoh, the giant, for instance."

"Giant?"

"Yes, a giant just like the ones from your Bible." Seven cocked a brow at him. "Does that surprise you?"

"No." Hondo shook his head.

"The Hero Twins supposedly slew him on Mount Taylor and his blood ran down the mountain creating the black, jagged landscape of the malpais south of Grants."

"You said 'supposedly' there, so you don't believe it," Hondo said as though he'd gotten him.

"I don't believe that the black lava flow is really a giant's blood," Seven replied disdainfully. "But that doesn't mean that a pair of twins didn't slay a giant many years ago."

"Well, did the Hero Twins get a happy ending to their story at least?"

"Not really." Seven glanced out the window at the trees passing them by.

"What happened to them?"

Seven turned back to Hondo. "They journeyed into the underworld to avenge the death of their father and were killed by their enemies."

"Sounds like a crappy fairy tale if you ask me," Hondo replied, failing to catch the irony in Seven's statement. He felt relieved to finally spot their destination in the distance. "There's Fort Stanton."

The white-painted buildings of the complex stood out from the dormant prairie grass of the fields, which made them easy to spot. In addition to the sprawling barracks, there was also a large cemetery full of uniform white crucifixes where many soldiers were buried.

In the days of Billy the Kid, Fort Stanton was a military post that oversaw the Mescalero Apache Reservation after they had left Bosque Redondo. Since the dawn of the 20th century, it had been a hospital. Briefly, during the war, it had served as a German POW camp. Now it was back to being a hospital again, serving the nearby settlements of Lincoln, San Patricio, and Mescalero among others.

Cactus Jack, as Hondo understood it, had been interred at Fort Stanton for a brief bout of pneumonia which he had miraculously recovered from. At least Hondo considered it miraculous that an old vagabond could recover around this time of year in the harsh cold. But then again, the people who led the germiest existences were sometimes the heartiest.

Cactus Jack was an old pot hunter who seemed to stumble from one settlement to the next, eking a living out of selling pot shards to collectors and curio shops. It was unclear to Hondo if he actually knew the Kid or not, or if he just claimed to like so many other old-timers. After all, claiming that one knew the Kid in the old days usually entitled one to a free drink at the bar. Actually, it was simply Hondo's hunch that Cactus Jack was connected to the Kid. He had been privy to the circumstances of the man's death since it had matched the details in the murders of Uncle Kit and Old Man Miranda but hadn't heard one way or the other if he had a connection to the Kid or not.

All that Hondo knew was that upon release from the hospital, Catus Jack was found on the grounds dead only a night later. No one would have thought anything of it if not for the fact that he, too, was missing a hand and had been scalped.

Hondo parked his truck in what he assumed was the main parking lot, which was actually the only parking lot in this case. Inside the main hospital, after a few minutes of asking around and establishing his credentials, Hondo and Seven were shown to a nurse who had attended to Cactus Jack.

"This was his bed, not that it matters." The nurse pointed to an empty cot near a brightly lit window. She was quite attractive, with red hair and pale, freckled skin. Her accent was thick and southern, so she wasn't from around here.

"I'm guessing that what you really want to see is where he died, though?" she added.

"Eventually, but first, I wanted to ask, did Cactus Jack say anything strange while he was under your care?"

"Delirious old men are always talking strange." She smirked. "Anything specific?"

Hondo smiled. "Anything about Billy the Kid, for instance?"

"How did you know?" she said, a shocked inflection in her voice.

"Just a hunch," Hondo lied. There was nothing wrong with her knowing that the other victims had connections to the Kid, but he had learned not to "help" witnesses along or put ideas in their heads. He liked to get his information without accidentally influencing them to veer off in certain directions or to try and tell him what they thought he wanted to hear.

She looked a bit hesitant. "Well, I'm a little embarrassed to even repeat it. Sounded like something from one of those awful dime novels."

"Please, we'd like to hear it."

After a moment's hesitation, she responded. "He claimed that he knew of some kind of connection between this Tumbleweed Williams fellow and some old, buried treasure somewhere on the state line..." she paused as though she were having trouble recalling a name. "What was it? The Adams something, I think. I'd never heard it before."

"The Lost Adams?" Seven broke his stoic silence. It was the only time that Hondo had ever seen him become excited by something.

"Yes. That was it. Claimed that Billy the Kid had known where it was or something. I just humored him like I did all my other patients. Just nodded and didn't ask too many questions. Is it actually true?"

"We don't know yet," Hondo responded honestly, then asked, "Could you go ahead and show us the spot where he was found now?"

The nurse nodded, and within a few minutes had walked them out some distance to a spot just a little ways outside the barracks. It was within a small grotto of trees along the Bonito River, rippling quietly in the background. It had been a dry year, and at the moment the river was more like a creek.

"This is it," the nurse said, pointing to a drab patch of golden-hued prairie grass.

"You're absolutely sure?" Hondo asked for clarification since one spot of prairie grass was identical to the next.

"I'm sure. I'll never forget that day."

"You were the one who found him?"

"No, one of the groundskeepers did. But a lot of us took a look at him before the coroner came. Never seen anything like it. I mean, I've seen my share of accident victims and such, it's just I'd never seen a murder like that. He was scalped, which I'm sure you knew."

Hondo nodded to her while Seven inspected the area, kneeling down in the grass.

"Do you have any idea who would want to kill an old vagabond like that?" she asked.

As he listened to the question, Hondo kept his eye on Seven. He gave Hondo a look as he picked up a small stone, signaling he'd found something important. It was interesting, he'd barely met the man and they were already developing a form of shorthand.

Hondo turned his attention back to the nurse. "Probably just a mentally ill person," Hondo lied, then asked, "Y'all have any abandoned cars pop up around here recently?" Hondo was thinking of the getaway car he'd chased to Puerto de Luna and subsequently lost.

"Not that I know of." She shook her head and Hondo made a mental note to call the local sheriff's department to see if they had any abandoned vehicle reports.

Hondo decided he might as well ask her another question while she was here. "You hear any theories yourself as to who might've killed Cactus Jack?"

She bit her lip. "Well, there is one thing, but you're not going to believe it. I know I didn't."

Hondo took note of the fact that she said 'didn't' as opposed to 'don't'. Something had changed her mind. "Try me."

"One of the older groundskeepers thinks it's a… well, he says I'm not supposed to say its name out loud."

Hondo nodded again. "It start with 'skin' and end with 'walk—'"

"Yes," she cut him off fearfully. "That was it." Then lowering her voice as if it could hear her, "He thinks it's holed up somewhere down in the cave."

"The cave?"

"You know. The big cave over yonder." She pointed northward into the distance.

"I know of what you speak." Seven stood. "My people used to hide from the soldiers there long ago."

"Can you take me to it?" Hondo asked, and Seven nodded.

Hondo turned back to the nurse. "Before we go, you notice anything else odd around here that would lead you to believe that's correct? That it's hiding out there in that cave, I mean."

"Well, I wouldn't have believed him myself except we've had a lot of dead animals turn up in the last few days. Some say it's just a mountain lion on the prowl, but since they been popping up after Jack died, I don't know what to think. One of the old-timers claims he saw a ghost light outside the cave a few nights ago, too."

A ghost light? That was a new one. Maybe someone saw a flashlight within the cave and was being overly superstitious.

"Anything else?" Hondo asked. "Sometimes the strangest things of all offer the biggest clues."

"There is one more thing, I suppose."

Hondo nodded for her to continue.

"I been hearing a kind of strange noise from the direction of the cave lately. I don't know how to describe it."

"Like a fox?" Hondo asked, no longer worried about influencing her answers. It was clear by now she was sincere.

"Exactly. How did you know? And don't tell me it's just a hunch."
Hondo smiled grimly. "Because I've heard it, too."

XIII.
THE RING

"So… If you're my grandfather, then what do I call you?" Pancho asked hesitantly as he hopped out of the plane, glad to be on solid ground again.

"You can call me Bill, you can call me Henry, you can call me William. You can call me sir or mister, or even that dirty old son of a bitch…" the old man said and tossed him a satchel before adding, "Just don't call me grandpa or granpappy or anything sappy like that."

Pancho settled on Bill.

They had landed on the outskirts of Las Vegas. Not that Las Vegas—the one in New Mexico. When Bill had shouted that they were headed there to meet Williams, Pancho had momentarily become excited thinking it was the one in Nevada before realizing it was the New Mexico version. Bill had landed his plane on a desolate highway and taxied it off into the brush a ways, parking it behind a big billboard advertising the Rattlesnake Trading Post.

Right now they were walking along the side of the interstate towards one of those little Native American-themed motels with giant wigwams for rooms. That's where Williams and the lawyer were supposed to show up, but since they were traveling by car rather than by plane, it would be a while yet before they arrived. Pancho and Bill had flown straight over the mountains due east of Santa Fe, which amounted to only about thirty minutes flying time.

"So, no offense or anything, but how the hell did you end up with me and my brother? My parents, they dead or something?"

"What gave it away?" Bill stretched out onto his stomach on a small dirt slope across the interstate from the hotel. He took out some binoculars and began scanning the road with them.

"Well, you said you were the one who left us in Fort Sumner. I assumed that meant they were dead."

"You assumed correctly."

Pancho expected this to open the door for Bill to tell him all about his real mom and pop, but instead he just kept staring through the binoculars and chewing his tobacco.

Pancho angrily plopped down on his stomach next to him. "You know, most normal people would take that as an opportunity to tell me something about my parents."

Bill sighed like it was a sore subject. "Hate to tell you this, kiddo, but I didn't actually know your father as well as you think. Wasn't really part of his life until he was already a man."

"Shit, I learned more about him from that damn reporter." Pancho stood up and kicked a pile of dirt behind him.

Bill sighed. "Listen, kid, his mother never told me about him 'til he was grown, and grown men don't exactly take kindly to their daddies if they ain't been around their whole lives. I didn't really get to know him 'til the Revolution was in full swing."

"Yeah, Tilley already told me he fought in the Revolution."

"Your mom and dad both, actually. 'Fraid that's what got them killed, too."

For a moment that registered to Pancho that they died in the Revolution until he remembered that it had ended in 1920, three years before he was born. "Wasn't the Revolution done by then?"

"Officially speaking. But even though it'd been over for a few years, that didn't mean that tensions didn't still linger. Just look at what happened to Pancho Villa."

Pancho knew what he meant. Villa had been assassinated while visiting Parral three years after the war had ended in 1923.

"Now, if you're expecting some grand story about how you need to go and avenge your parents' death you can forget it," Bill continued. "It was fallout from the war thanks to the side they picked in it, plain and simple."

Pancho chucked a rock across the brush. "And what side was that?"

Bill peered back into the binoculars, still more focused on watching for Williams. "Pancho Villa's."

"Wait, my dad really knew Pancho Villa?"

"Sure did. He was one of his best fighters. Besides, where'd you think you got that name?"

Pancho settled back onto his stomach on the dune next to Bill, his anger momentarily abated. "Whoa, so I'm actually named after *the* Pancho Villa?"

"Not too many other famous Panchos to be named after," was Bill's answer.

Pancho suddenly remembered something he'd been dying to ask Bill. "Hey, I've always wondered, am I part Mexican?"

Bill turned to him with a grin. "Well, you do know I tended to favor those senoritas and your daddy did too."

"I always knew we were too dark to be full white," Pancho said, amazed and yet not surprised to find out that he had been right all along. "Hey, so what should my real last name be? I mean, I know my dad's name was Dorado Dorantes, but if he was your son…"

"If you're asking me for my real last name, I'm honestly not sure anymore. Doesn't really matter, either. I can say that now that I've gone through about a million of 'em. Besides, I picked the Dumez family for you and your brother on purpose. I knew some of their kin way back and knew the two of you'd be in good hands."

So his old man hadn't been full of it when he told him and Hondo that his grandmother used to cook for the Kid. After a second, Pancho suddenly asked, "Why didn't you raise me and Hondo?"

"I couldn't have raised you. Was too old. Didn't have a wife neither and boys need a mother, I know from experience." Bill took out a pocket watch and checked the time. It was late afternoon.

Pancho glanced nervously at his own watch. "It's been twenty minutes since we landed. Shouldn't they be here by now?"

"Should be, but I'm not too worried about it," Bill said, then after a second, added, "yet."

"Do you think they connected us to Williams?" Pancho asked, they meaning the Santa Fe Ring.

"No. My cover going in there was as an old-timer by the name of Prairie Dog Pete." Bill ceased upon the look Pancho gave him. "You jest, but they bought it. Anyways, ol' Pete supposedly knew the Kid, which was pretty easy to convince them of considering everything I know about the Kid. I made sure to be overly vocal about my skepticism of Williams, too. And I damn sure never let myself be seen with him anywhere, so he should be fine as far as the Ring goes. Seems to me they're after you, ironically enough."

"What's the deal with you and Williams anyways?" Pancho asked.

"He's with me," Bill said and then spit out a wad of tobacco. "He's a decoy. Interesting little trick I picked up a long time ago. Besides, old men are like babies, they all look alike after a while. Not even the lawyer knows he ain't really Billy."

"Why did you need a decoy to begin with, though?"

"Had too many people recognize me not long after I was supposed to be dead. Before I knew it, word was gettin' around that I was alive and well and living in Old Mexico. Figured if I got a few old-timers to pretend to be me that weren't, the other reports might lose credibility."

"What about John Miller and Walkalong Smith, were they decoys of yours?" Pancho asked, just a hint of accusation in his voice.

Bill paused. "I never meant for them to get killed if that's what you're asking. Never imagined anything like that would happen. I just wanted to stay hidden, and they were happy for the notoriety, seemed like a fair trade to me."

"Tilley claimed you—Williams, whatever—were doing this to smoke out the Ring before you died. Is that true?"

"Well, he's not wrong. I needed to figure out if Governor Mayberry was the head of the Ring, if the Ring still existed, which now I know they do. I hadn't tangled with them in years before today. The last thing that I want is to leave a map to the canyon in the hands of a government still controlled by the Ring."

"Why all this secrecy, though? Why don't we just go to the canyon now?"

Bill sighed. "I forgot how many questions kids ask."

"I'm 27," Pancho reminded him. "I'm not a kid."

Bill sat down his binoculars. "Look, it ain't something that you, me, and a few of your pals with some shovels and a case of beer can take care of. It was a big canyon."

"About that, what is the big deal about the Lost Adams anyways?"

"Hella lot o' gold is the big deal."

"Well, I know that. But there's lots of lost gold in New Mexico. Victorio Peak, the Lost Padre Mine, Chato's Treasure," Pancho rattled off the bigger ones.

"More gold in Sno-Ta-hay—that's what the Indians called it—for one. But there's more than just gold in them thar hills," Bill answered.

"What's that mean?"

Bill adjusted his binoculars to get a better look at a car passing by on the highway. "That, kid, is a long story best told over a cold beer in a nice comfy bar. Not out here."

"Well, in case anything happens to you in between now and then, how about the short version?" Pancho asked snarkily.

"Fine. Short version to tide you over," Bill sighed and then began his tale. "Whole thing happened right after my escape from the Lincoln County Courthouse in '81. Shoulda headed straight for Old Mexico, but being a dumb kid back then, I decided I wanted to go yuck it up one more time in White Oaks. And boy did I pick the wrong night to do it."

"At one of the saloons I came across a priest and an old blind man. Didn't think anything of them until I find out the old blind man is Adams, and he's taking the priest to the lost canyon of gold he found back in '64. Not long after he tells me this, some Ring men led by Jesse Evans barge in."

Pancho remembered that name. "Wasn't Evans one of your friends?"

"Sometimes," Bill answered. "Depended on who was paying our bills at the time. That night the Ring was paying his, and nobody was paying mine. But anyways, in walks Evans and some Ringers. I thought at first they were there to get me, but turns out the Ring was after Old Man Adams so he could show them the way to the gold. I did my part to save them, fair amount of shooting as you can imagine, the saloon burned down and me and Adams escaped."

"What happened next?" Pancho asked, sounding like a little kid.

Bill sighed thoughtfully and shook his head. "Lots of things, kid."

Pancho grinned. "There was a girl, wasn't there?"

Bill smiled. "You know it. Your grandmother as a matter of fact."

"No way?" Pancho shook his head excitedly.

Bill nodded. "Name was Lo. There was five of us in the group with her... Adams, the padre, our ol' cook, funny Chinese guy called Au

Nu…" Bill paused for a moment before continuing. "There was an Apache kid along with us too. Named Wolf, kinda reminded me of myself if I was an Indian." Bill shook his head sadly. "Poor kid never even made it to the canyon with us. And, as for the rest…"

"What happened exactly… in the canyon I mean?"

Bill lowered the binoculars and nodded ahead. Pancho noticed a newer-looking, dark purple '48 Ford Coupe pulling up to the motel.

"Thank God they're here," Bill said, and Pancho wondered if it was mostly so he wouldn't have to answer any more questions.

Bill stood and brushed the dust off of his jeans. "We'll give my friend a little time to take care of the lawyer and then we'll head over."

Pancho stood. "Take care of? You mean like…" Pancho lowered his voice, "Kill?"

"No, he's not gonna kill him. Who do you think we are, Bonnie and Clyde?"

"Wait, did you know Bonnie and Clyde, too?"

"No, but I did play cards not far from here with Jesse James one night," Bill said as he walked towards the motel.

After a few minutes, they saw a light flash on and off in one of the big wigwams. "And there's our cue. You're in for a treat, kid."

"Heh, based on his performance at the governor's mansion I don't know."

"Key word performance, just wait."

Bill knocked on the wigwam's door.

"Password?" the hoarse voice that Pancho recognized from the mansion uttered.

Bill said two words back to Williams which surprised Pancho.

"Oh, it's you," was Williams' response to the coarse language as he creaked open the door.

"Who else?" Bill replied, then nodded to the lawyer passed out on the other twin bed. "What about him?"

"Don't mind him. I slipped him a sleeping pill. He'll be conked out 'til tomorrow morning for sure." The old man eyed Pancho suspiciously. "Who the hell's this?"

"This is my grandson. Kid," Bill put his hand on Pancho's shoulder with an ornery grin, "meet my old pal, Jesse Evans. One of the best pickpockets in the game."

"Jesse Evans…" Pancho uttered in shock. "You're still alive, too?"

"There's a lot of us ain't dead, kid," Evans croaked out as they walked into the cramped room.

"You get it?" Bill asked Evans as he shut the door.

"Of course. I ain't lost my touch yet." Evans reached into his shirt pocket to draw out a signet ring of some kind. It looked like it had the Zia symbol on it, but with an all-seeing eye in the middle. "Governor was wearing it on his left hand just like you figured."

"See this?" Bill held up the ring so that Pancho could examine it. "That's the Santa Fe Ring insignia."

"I used to be a Ringer myself once," Evans intoned almost proudly. "Until I switched sides."

"You never had a side," Bill told him. "You just went with whoever paid best."

"And they quit paying," Evans added.

Pancho clutched the ring for himself, studying the emblem. "But ain't that pretty stupid to advertise who they are? Isn't that the whole point of being a secret society?"

"You would think," Bill answered. "But secret societies have strange rules about showing their true allegiance. Sort of like hiding in plain sight, only most people are too dumb to notice. And if you do, you get labeled as a kook for pointing it out."

Pancho thought of Tilley. It was true. His theories about the Ring had earned him a one-way ticket to the nut house.

Bill took back the ring. "Shame. The canyon'll have to remain hidden for another fifty years at this rate."

A thought suddenly occurred to Pancho. In all the chaos, he hadn't even thought to tell Bill about the skinwalkers.

"Well, I hate to tell you, and this might sound crazy, but the Santa Fe Ring isn't the only thing after you two. Ever heard of something called a skinwalker? They're these witches that wear animal skins—"

"Skinwalker!" Jesse practically shouted.

Bill's face took on a look of concern Pancho had never seen before. "Where in the hell did you run across a skinwalker?"

"Me and my brother killed one in Puerto de Luna a week ago."

Bill and Jesse exchanged a glance.

"Couldn't have," Bill said. "They all died out years ago."

Pancho shook his head. "Apparently not. Guy was dressed in animal skins and the whole nine yards."

"Well, hell!" Jesse exclaimed as he hobbled over to his bed. "In that case, I'm hitting the road tonight!" Frantically, he began to repack the suitcase he'd previously been unpacking. "Never said anything about skinwalkers, Bill, or I wouldn't o' come!"

"This is bad, kid," Bill said to Pancho. "Skinwalkers make the Ring look like a group of choir boys."

"How did you come across skinwalkers?"

"Same as you did. They're looking for that canyon, and they know I'm the key to finding it." Bill turned his attention to Evans. "And you. If you don't hear from me or see me by day after tomorrow in Granbury, I want you to mail this. It's important." Bill thrust an envelope into his chest.

Evans took the envelope. "Anything else I can do for you? Mow your lawn while you're away? Feed the dog? Have a nice bath drawn for you when you get home?" he said sarcastically.

"What you can do for me is to try not to die in the meantime," Bill said as he marched towards the door.

"Heh," Evans guffawed and pulled a six-shooter out of his suitcase. "Any Ringers or skinwalkers come after me, and I'll fill 'em full of lead."

"I know. I meant try not to die of old age," Bill said as he and Pancho walked out the door.

Evans shouted the same two words to Bill that he had used as his password earlier.

"What in the hell do skinwalkers want with gold?" Pancho asked as they hurried across the highway.

"They don't. The Ring wants the gold. The skinwalkers want something else."

"Let me guess, you'll tell me later?"

"Bingo. Right now we've got to get to Sumner."

They were nearly to the billboard that hid his plane. "What for?"

Bill stopped and put a hand on Pancho's chest. "I got a bad feeling," Bill muttered.

"Like what?"

"Like we're being watched. I left a big .44 in the cockpit, go and grab it for me." Bill's hand drifted down to the smaller revolver on his hip.

Pancho jogged over to the billboard cautiously. No one was hiding behind it, or under the plane from what he could tell. He hoisted himself up onto the wing and pulled back the little tarp draped over the cockpit. Winston West was crouched inside waiting for him.

"Surprise," he said, pointing the .44 at him.

"Oh, shit…" was the only response Pancho could muster.

West stood. "No, this is your 'Oh, shit' moment." He whistled, and several men burst from behind the brush, guns drawn at him and Bill.

XIV.
THE UNDERWORLD

*A*s Hondo and Seven walked towards the entrance of the cave, Seven handed him the tiny object he'd found at the kill site. It was a small rock with a lightning symbol etched onto it. "Interesting. What's the significance exactly?"

"One of the ingredients of corpse powder is tree bark that's been struck by lightning. The lightning symbol is powerful medicine. Sometimes they etch it onto a small black rock like this and leave it at the kill site."

"Why?" Hondo handed the little rock back to him.

Seven pocketed the stone. "Beats me. I'm a medicine man, not a witch, remember?"

The land they were traversing was an odd hybrid of the desert and the forest. The ground was dry, hard, and rocky, yet it was also dotted with medium-sized junipers. The trees amplified the sound of the light winter breeze somewhat ominously. Hondo had expected the cave to be in the side of a hill or mountain but was surprised to see that it was located at the bottom of a large sinkhole. Unbeknownst to him, it had formed nearly 1,000 years ago, revealing the entrance to the underworld that was Fort Stanton Cave. It wasn't terribly dramatic or intimidating looking.

"You mean that's it?" Hondo said, underwhelmed.

Seven nodded. "If Sierra Blanca is our Eden, that is our underworld."

Hondo contemplated Seven's choice of words considering the fable he'd told him earlier. "And what was it you said about the Hero Twins descending into the underworld to avenge their father?"

Seven got his drift. "Well, lucky for you, you're not with your twin. You're with me."

"You actually been down in it?"

"Once or twice when I was a boy. There are secret passages that only my people know. They would use them to evade soldiers in the old days."

"How long does this thing go exactly?"

"Miles."

Hondo stopped. "As in two or three?"

"As in dozens, possibly." Seven stared down at the winding trail towards the mouth of the cave which had suddenly become more intimidating to Hondo.

"No one knows how long it is. Every few years, just when someone thinks they've reached the end, some intrepid explorer will find a new corridor," Seven continued as they tepidly made their way down the steep, loose entry.

"And then, of course, there are the people that go down in there and never come back out again." Seven stopped at the entrance. "Having second thoughts yet?"

"I had second thoughts the minute you called this place the underworld," Hondo said cynically. "But, somewhere in there is the accomplice of the man that killed my father, and I intend to get him."

"You still think it's just a man. That's cute," Seven said and walked into the abyss.

As if going into a bottomless pit wasn't bad enough, Seven had to bring up the skinwalker. Hondo tried once more to convince himself that it was just another man in an animal skin and Seven was being superstitious. As for Pancho's knife being laced with White Ash killing the man in Puerto de Luna, it was probably just one of life's odd coincidences.

Hondo turned on his flashlight, illuminating the interior walls. Initially, it wasn't unlike any other cave he'd been in aside from the noise of an incessant dripping somewhere in the depths. The passages varied in size, as did the terrain. Sometimes it was easy going; other times, he had to stoop down low to accommodate the drooping ceiling. However, the deeper they went, the more alien it became.

The first noteworthy formation he saw resembled a lofty pyramid, only formed of crystallized rock and jasper. Bright, sparkling water dripped down the sides. Along the ceiling, he spotted what the cavers called starburst gypsum, so named because they looked like exploding stars, though to Hondo they looked more like crystal tree leaves.

The musty smell was the most difficult thing to get used to, but after about twenty minutes or so it seemed to become just another part of Hondo's strange new existence. His life had changed a great deal in the past week. Before that night in Puerto de Luna, Hondo would have never pictured himself spelunking in a lonely cave with a strange medicine man on the trail of a killer who liked to dress himself in animal skins. Strange was becoming the new normal for him. And after the death of his father, Debbie was the only bright spot in this bizarre new chapter of his life. However, it also struck him that his growing affection for her oddly made him more fearful than he normally would have been. Before her, trekking into this dark cave would not have been quite so daunting.

Hondo had wanted to take a long ball of string to ensure they didn't lose their way, but Seven assured him that he could always find his way out.

"What if I lose you?" Hondo had asked.

"Don't," was Seven's simple reply.

After walking about 1,200 feet or so, the two men encountered a fork in the underground road. The larger passage pointed to the northeast, while the smaller crawlspace slanted downward to their right.

"Which one would you take if you were a skinwalker?" Hondo asked.

Seven nodded at the crawlspace. "Well, in Navajo the name skinwalker technically means *naaldlooshii*, or 'he who goes on all fours'."

Hondo cussed and got on his hands and knees, crawling headfirst into the chasm. After a while the cave floor became carpeted with thousands upon thousands of crystal needles of gypsum on either side of him. Six hundred feet later Hondo was glad to be able to stand as he exited what cavers called the Crystal Crawl. Hondo's back was relieved for him to be standing upright again. He gave it a hearty stretch as he shone his flashlight along the walls of the new corridor. The beam tinted the walls with a golden hue, making the formations look like melted gold. The image took him back to the nurse's comments on the Lost Adams and Seven's reaction.

"So, what was that Lost Adams thing y'all were talking about back at Fort Stanton?" Hondo asked, knowing good and well what it was but wanting Seven's version of it to see what spin he gave it.

"You expect me to believe you're a native New Mexican and don't know the legend of the Adams Diggings?" Seven replied as they trudged along.

Hondo smiled bashfully and decided to afford Seven the respect of the truth. "Sorry. Playing dumb is a cop thing. A way of getting more sincere information out of people. I just noticed it was the one thing that seemed to strike a chord with you back at the hospital."

"How about you tell me your version of the Lost Adams Diggings first? And then I'll tell you mine."

Hondo didn't like having his own game played back at him, but he was currently at Seven's mercy in more ways than one. Plus, the man was doing him a favor by being here.

"Well, from what I remember, it was discovered back during the Civil War in the 1860s. Man named Adams turned up half-dead at Fort Wingate and told the soldiers how he had fallen in with a group of prospectors a few months back. They were on their way to a canyon that 'cried tears of gold' as their guide put it. Was a half-breed named Gotchear, if I recall. Led them to the canyon as promised, then took off mysteriously in the night. A few days later, Chief Nana and some Apache showed up and massacred everybody but Adams. That's it in a nutshell at least."

"You're right except for the bit about the miners being the first to discover it. You see, only the white man calls it the Lost Adams Diggings. Hundreds of years before they came, the Spaniards called it the Canyon del Oro. But it was known first to my people as Sno-Ta-hay Canyon."

"Sno-Ta-hay? What does that translate to exactly?"

"'There it lies,' basically."

"What lies, the gold I assume?"

"Not necessarily," Seven replied, which struck Hondo as odd.

"Is that why the Apache murdered the prospectors? Was it sacred ground or something?"

"It's not sacred. It's dangerous. Powerful medicine as they'd say in the old days," Seven answered cryptically, and Hondo got the drift that he better not press it any further. Whatever it was, it was a sore issue. Besides that, he wasn't sure how importantly it figured into the investigation anyhow.

Their trail terminated into a huge corridor. Wherever Hondo shined his flashlight, all he could see were rock walls in every direction except for that which they just came. "What now?"

"Here," Seven crouched down and held his hand over a tiny passage where Hondo could feel a slight gale of air.

"Looks awfully small," Hondo said, fearing that Seven was planning to crawl into it.

"We can fix that," Seven said, grabbing a flat rock that he used to scoop away some of the mud. It made the hole a bit larger, but still not big enough for Hondo's liking.

Seven turned to him with a devious grin. "What you're about to see, no white eye has ever seen before," he said and then plunged headfirst into the opening.

Hondo took in a deep breath and followed him through the cramped passageway, which thankfully wasn't very long. In less than a minute's time he was free of the tunnel and out in the open again.

The new passageway was thankfully large compared to the previous ones, about twenty-five feet high and equally wide. Something in the middle of the passageway caught Hondo's eye. Before him was a literal river of snow, but it was impossible.

"What is that? I know it looks like snow but…"

"White calcite. And look at this." Seven knelt and pointed out what looked to be large, muddy animal tracks staining the calcite.

Hondo knelt down and ran his fingers over the dirty paw prints. "A mountain lion?"

"Yeah, that must be it," Seven replied sarcastically. He stood and extended a hand. "Follow the yellow brick road and find out."

Hondo stood. "I thought you didn't watch TV?"

"I don't own a TV, there's a difference," Seven replied. "But even I've seen the *Wizard of Oz*."

Hondo and Seven began to walk along the white river of calcite. It was strange because though it looked just like snow to the eye, it was hard and solid to the touch. Neither he nor Seven left indentations or footprints.

Hondo didn't know how long they'd walked along that lonely river, maybe an hour or more. Time seemed to pass differently in this strange, underground world that he currently found himself a resident of.

Seven suddenly stopped and shone his flashlight on a new corridor of the cave. "Here. This is where the witch would hide."

"How do you know?" Hondo asked.

"I just know," Seven said solemnly and walked into the corridor.

Hondo followed, his right hand instinctively lowering to the revolver on his hip to make sure it hadn't fallen off somewhere in the cave.

The corridor lasted a hundred feet or less and opened into a medium-sized chamber. The room was a fitting abode for a monster, or a man that fancied himself one. In fact, it seemed Hondo was in the mouth of a giant monster as the low-hanging ceiling was lined with a million needle-like stalactites. It wasn't low enough that Hondo had to crouch, but he could reach up and touch the stalactites if he chose to.

"Look," Seven said, shining his flashlight on a bloody sight.

In a corner was what looked like a half-eaten deer leg. There was no sign of a fire anywhere in the cave.

"Mountain lion den, just like I figured," Hondo said.

"Guess again." Seven illuminated another grizzly revelation. Before them in the light was a strange necklace strung with human fingers. A few feet away was the palm of the hand, which looked like it was being dried out and saved for later.

"Just as I thought. They're cutting off the fingers for the necklace and using the palm for corpse powder," Seven said.

Out of the corner of his eye, far down the corridor, Hondo suddenly detected bright light. His heartbeat quickened. It was another flashlight. The man was coming back.

"Hey." Hondo nudged Seven in the arm as the light grew brighter and brighter, then suddenly vanished. Hondo blinked and shook his head in disbelief. No one was there, nor was there any sound. Was that the same ghost light the nurse spoke of?

"What the hell? Where—"

Seven put a finger to his lips and looked around the cave.

A skin-crawling screech emanated throughout the cavern and a man in a massive cougar pelt landed on Seven's back, seemingly from out of nowhere. Seven went down and so did his flashlight. Hondo jumped onto the man's back and immediately regretted it. In a feat of what seemed like superhuman strength, Hondo felt himself thrown into the ceiling, the needlelike stalactites stabbing into his back. His flashlight flew from his grip and landed on the cave floor, spinning in a circle. Instinctively, Hondo grabbed onto one of the stalactites, breaking it off as he fell to the ground. Hondo clutched the jagged stalactite like a knife, preparing to right himself and then stab his attacker. Before he could, a clawed hand flipped him over from his stomach onto his back. In the brief flashes of illumination provided by the spinning flashlight, he saw only a puma-like head as sharp claws slashed into his chest.

He didn't feel the same way he had felt in Puerto de Luna. There, he had been primed for a fight, but here he had suffered an ambush. Still, Hondo fought to gather his nerves and plunged the stalactite into the man's shoulder where it joined the neck. His attacker reeled back and screamed, letting go of Hondo so that he could remove the jagged intrusion from his shoulder. As he did, Hondo took the opportunity to go for his gun. Hondo drew it out and fired into the man's abdomen, the sound deafening in the tiny little cave. He heard another loud screech and the man disappeared. Hondo crawled towards the flashlight.

"Seven," he uttered into the darkness. There was no reply. He grabbed the flashlight and shined it around the room, shocked to see his companion gone without a trace. Hondo could discern the sound of what seemed to be animal paws skittering in the darkness. Then Hondo heard it. The same woosh of air he had heard the night his father died. There was a sharp sting in his neck. His hand flew to the spot, coming back wet with a small smattering of blood. He'd been hit!

He spun around to see the man advancing on him again; the cougar skin pulled down over the his head obscuring his face. Hondo went for his gun preparing to shoot again when suddenly Seven's face entered the beam of light from the side.

"Here kitty, kitty," Seven cooed. Instead of bashing him over the head or stabbing him with a knife, Seven blew a fine white powder into his face and the man tumbled backwards like a vampire that had been splashed with holy water. Hondo followed the perp's falling body with his flashlight to the floor. The man was screaming and clawing at his eyes as though they were burning. Hondo was sure his own eyes were playing tricks on him as the form before him seemed to transition between animal and human, until finally the animal skin fell from his head, revealing a younger man than the one he'd faced at Puerto de Luna.

"How did you…" Hondo didn't finish his question as he sidled up next to Seven.

"White Ash powder," Seven said simply. "When you said we were on the trail of a skinwalker, I chose to err on the side of caution."

As much as Hondo hated to believe it, it seemed to be the White Ash that had done more harm than his bullets. Still, out of habit more than anything else, Hondo pointed his gun at the wounded man on the ground before them. Since he was younger, he might live if they got him out of the cave in time.

"If you cooperate, we'll help you out to Fort Stanton. Do you understand?" Hondo asked in a harsh tone.

It replied in a language that Hondo didn't recognize, but Seven understood.

"He's speaking Apache," Seven said.

"Can you translate?" Hondo asked Seven hopefully.

"Yes, but be quick about it. He hasn't much time before the dust kills him."

"What's the antidote for this?" Hondo hissed, pointing to his neck.

Seven translated the guttural reply. "There is no antidote."

"We'll see about that," Hondo said. He was younger and heartier than everyone else he'd seen die from this poison. Maybe he could beat it. "Why did you kill those men?"

The skinwalker spoke in its strange tongue.

"He says you ought to get out of the cave while you can still walk," Seven answered.

"I don't care. Ask him again. Why were they after those men?"

The dying man hissed his response.

"He says you know why," Seven said.

"Because they all knew Billy the Kid? Why?"

"Because he's the last man alive that still knows where Sno-Ta-hay Canyon is," Seven answered.

"What's it to them?" Hondo wanted to know why a coven of Indian witches would be so dead set on the canyon.

The man gave a longer answer than he usually did and Seven issued the translation. "They want the gold, like everyone else."

For the first time, Hondo's gut told him that Seven wasn't telling him something, even if he had responded quickly with no hint of hesitation.

"Why haven't you gone after Williams yet?"

"We have special plans for him. He's for…" Seven paused, seeming to have trouble with the word. "Ma'cho."

"Ma'cho? Who the hell is the Ma'cho?"

"He says you really should leave," Seven answered.

Hondo pressed the gun to the man's temple and asked again. "Who's Ma'cho!?"

The man looked him in the eyes, and for the first time Hondo could see that even his eyeballs looked like those of an animal.

"After I'm gone, he'll be the last skinwalker," Seven translated. The man gave Hondo one last spiteful smile, then fell limp and died. Hondo suddenly began to feel himself becoming lightheaded, blackness clouding his vision. Was this it? Was he about to die like his father? His last thought was of Debbie as Seven stepped in to steady him before he could hit the ground.

XV.
THE HAUNTED MANSION

They had been traveling for over an hour now across State Highway 56. The sun had set a while back, but the sky wasn't completely dark yet, just a gloomy grey with hints of purple in the lingering clouds. The barren landscape flying by on either side of them was decorated with nothing but the black, windswept lava hills created by Capulin Peak about 60,000 years ago. Pancho actually took it as a bad sign that he and Bill weren't blindfolded. If they blindfolded you on the way to their secret lair, that could mean that they planned on letting you go after it was all over. The fact that they weren't blindfolded implied that this would be a one-way trip.

Pancho and Bill were crammed into the backseat of a nice, large sedan, their hands bound, with West sitting between them. A nameless driver chauffeured them down the highway while Mendez sat comfortably in the front passenger seat. As Pancho and Bill had discovered, the snooty historian and governor-elect was himself part of the Santa Fe Ring.

Pancho turned to West. "You know, not that you didn't make a super cool entrance back there in the plane, but you're a big man to be crouched in that little cockpit. How long were you hiding in there for?"

West shot him a wolfish look.

"You'll probably have a crick in your neck tonight. Hope it was worth it," Pancho added.

Mendez turned to face the backseat. "We'll both be sleeping like babies tonight, Dumez. You, on the other hand..." Mendez shook his head and pursed his lips sourly.

"Where are you taking us, anyway?" Bill asked. "At this point I know it ain't to the beauty shop."

"Dorsey Mansion outside of Springer," Mendez answered. "Ever heard of it?"

"Can't say I have," Bill answered while Pancho shook his head.

"It's one of our nicer properties, though a bit rundown compared to what it was in the old days," Mendez explained. "There we'll have ourselves a nice visit, won't we… what was the bogus name you gave us? Prairie Dog Pete?"

West turned to Bill. "I have to admit, that was a good one."

"Yes, it was," Mendez continued. "But we both know who you really are, Mr. Antrim. Or is it McCarty? Bonney?"

Pancho's eyes lit up in alarm. Up until now, he wasn't so sure that he hadn't just been arrested due to his association with Jamison Tilley in Fort Sumner and Bill along with him. But, clearly, Mendez knew who Bill really was.

"Sorry to break it to you, but you got the wrong guy, mister," Bill replied.

"No, your friend Williams was the wrong guy," West said.

"Yes, we know that's who you were visiting in Las Vegas," Mendez said. "And don't worry. We'll let your impostor friend go on his merry way for now. We don't need any more bad publicity with another murder. As far as the papers are concerned, by tomorrow reports of a surviving Billy the Kid will be buried, so to speak."

Mendez smiled and Pancho could tell the man was impressed with his little pun even though he wasn't.

"And meanwhile, we might just be burying the real thing ourselves," West said, looking at Bill.

"What gave it away?" Bill asked.

"You fit the description better, for one. And your history of the Kid was far superior to Williams' version," Mendez explained and then concluded, "I'm afraid you oversold yourself a bit, old-timer."

After a moment, Mendez held up a finger and added, "There is one thing that I can't figure out, though, and that's the death of your little friends scattered across the state."

"Have to admit, it is a little suspicious that you and your buddy Williams are the only two not to pop up dead," West added.

Pancho made a mental note that they obviously weren't aware of the skinwalkers, which was good he supposed. Bill feigned ignorance, too.

"Mister, if you're suggesting I been going around scalping folks then you got a screw loose," Bill harumphed.

Mendez nodded, mulling it over in his head. "I admit, I have heard rumblings of a secretive Native American sect that pledged to keep the canyon hidden."

"Canyon?" Bill said, a hint of disgust in his tone in a vain effort to play dumb. "What canyon?"

Mendez smiled deviously and turned around. "That's cute. But we can talk about that later, Billy the Kid," Mendez added the last part rather dismissively.

"Hey, that's Mr. Kid to you," Pancho said, leaning forward.

"Sit down," West hissed.

Pancho leaned back and scanned the horizon for Dorsey Mansion. A cold dirty wind mixed of sleet and black earth made it difficult to discern, but it was most likely the structure he could see jutting from the flat plains ahead. This was confirmed when they turned onto a lengthy farm road heading in that direction. They drove through a large swinging gate and into a dark, ghostly orchard that surrounded the property. It was hard to tell if the trees had simply lost their leaves during fall or had been dead for years. Somehow the latter seemed more fitting. Before he knew it, Dorsey Mansion had gone from being a tiny speck in the distance into the looming monstrosity before him.

"Welcome to Dorsey Mansion, built by the great Stephen W. Dorsey. He was a contemporary of yours, Mr. Kid," Mendez said.

"A fellow Ringer, no doubt," Bill replied.

"Naturally," Mendez said. "Dorsey was a carpetbagger from Alabama who made it into politics and eventually the Santa Fe Ring. He completed construction on his estate in 1882, right after you died, in fact."

As they approached the mansion, they drove past a medium wooden structure that seemed to be under construction. It looked like a large podium or dais. Or gallows for a hanging…

"What's that?" Pancho asked, even though he wasn't sure he wanted to confirm his fear.

Mendez grinned. "Oh, that's nothing," he said with a wave of his hand. "Just some construction underway for a special occasion tomorrow morning. Far more interesting are the water fountains ahead."

Mendez pointed to a large, circular fountain in a state of disrepair that had run dry. Atop it was a stone statue of a bobcat eating a rattlesnake. Two other smaller fountains could also be glimpsed closer to the house.

"Dorsey had those imported from France." Mendez motioned to the two smaller fountains. "He spared no expense."

To that effect, there was also a large swimming pool, obviously not in use anymore. It was full of dirty rainwater atop which floated dead leaves and brush. As for the mansion itself, it looked out of place in New Mexico. One half of the structure looked like a roughhewn log cabin, which would be at home on the prairie, but the other half looked like a medieval castle from Europe made of sandstone. There was even a turreted tower that resembled a giant chess piece; the rook Pancho thought it was called. Pancho was shocked to see stone-cut faces and actual gothic-style gargoyles decorating the top of the tower just below the turrets. All that was missing was a flash of lightning to illuminate them, but the Indian summer and its thunderstorms were gone, and winter had taken their place.

Ever the historian, Mendez explained, "The faces you see are modeled after Dorsey and his family. The gargoyles, though, and I adore this, are modeled after his political enemies." Mendez pointed to the one at the very top. "That one's based off of James Blaine."

"I hope you don't expect us to pay for this bullshit," Bill said in reference to the forced historical tour.

"Only with your lives if you don't cooperate," West said as the car came to a stop, but even Pancho knew that was a lie. It would be foolish to let them go after all this was over. Their captors only needed them to have the illusion that they might live through it all. Pancho was willing to indulge them as he planned his escape. Or, at least, he intended to plan an escape once he got a better feel for the building's interior.

He could see that the lights were on, which meant someone had to be inside. But he also took note of the fact that there were no vehicles outside, so with any luck there wouldn't be too many people there. Only one car had followed them, and if it seated five men, presumably, that would make for eight men to do away with, including Mendez and West, plus however many were inside the mansion.

They parked near the tower, which served as the main entryway. As they were led inside, Pancho got the lay of the land. The centerpiece of the foyer was an impressive double cherrywood staircase that twined before them. There was also a large fireplace, and the wall was decorated with various animal skins from Dorsey's hunting trips, Pancho presumed. He looked to the ceiling. Brass chandeliers hung from an ornate, cast plaster medallion, and one of the chandeliers had carved cut glass, which depicted a hunting scene.

"Normally I would offer to take your coats, but seeing as your hands are bound…" Mendez said in a taunting manner.

Before either Pancho or his grandfather could offer a snarky comeback, a striking young woman came slinking down the staircase. She was Hispanic, with dark, dramatic features; a fox fur shawl draped over her shoulders. She wore a curve-hugging black dress and high heels, as though she were expecting company much ritzier than what currently stood before her. To Pancho, she looked like a movie star. Apparently she did to Bill, too, who mouthed his amazement.

"Allow me to introduce our caretaker, Sangay Sinaloa," Mendez said. "Miss Sinaloa, this is—"

"There's no need. I know who he is." She marched past Mendez and right up to Bill, who she immediately slapped across the face.

"Sweetheart, you must have me mistaken for someone else, because I know I'd remember you," Bill responded once he recovered.

"That was for my great-grandmother," she said loudly and then leaned in to whisper, "She never stopped talking about you. Even on her deathbed, she spoke of how wonderful you were." Then, even lower, she whispered, "If they didn't have other plans for you, I might even…"

Her words trailed off as her eyes drifted to Pancho as though he were an eavesdropper. Pancho stared at her in disbelief. He was the young, good-looking one, and here she was ogling his 90-year-old grandfather. "What am I, chopped liver?"

"Who is this?" she asked, finally acknowledging him with a dismissive look.

"If you hadn't interrupted me, I would have said this is the sheriff of Fort Sumner, Hondo Dumez," Mendez answered.

"Correction," West said, holding up Pancho's wallet. "He's the sheriff's twin brother, Pancho."

Pancho was startled. He hadn't even noticed West swipe it.

"Very interesting," Mendez cooed.

"And he's important why?" Miss Sinaloa asked.

"He's not," Bill said. "Just a groupie of mine along for the ride, one I imagine he regrets by now."

Miss Sinaloa crinkled Bill's collar in between her fingers. "Well, normally I would give you a tour, but something tells me they're headed straight for the cellar?" Miss Sinaloa turned to Mendez.

"I'm afraid so," Mendez replied.

"Why? What's in the cellar?" Pancho asked nervously.

"You'll see. Follow me, gentlemen, and I'll explain to you just what you're missing," Miss Sinaloa said as she started off in the other direction. Two guards prodded Pancho and Bill along behind her with their guns, while Mendez and West remained in the foyer.

"Upstairs are the master bedrooms," she said, pointing upwards as they walked through a long dining hall with a huge table. She paused briefly. "The top of the tower offers a sunroom with a stunning view of the whole estate, especially at sunrise. It's too bad you can't see it," she said with a sultry eye on Bill.

Pancho rolled his eyes in jealousy and disgust. Next, they traversed a huge library with pool tables in the middle of the room. "As you can see, Senator Dorsey was a very learned man and a pool enthusiast."

"I'm a bit of pool shark, myself," Pancho said. "If you uncuffed me, I could—"

"This way to the cellar, gentleman," Miss Sinaloa cut him off contemptuously as they headed towards a set of stony steps leading downwards. Pancho tried his best to get a sense of the layout before they were forced downstairs and thought he caught sight of a large kitchen. They prodded Pancho and Bill down the stairs until they reached an iron grill door through which was located what used to be the wine cellar. Although the mansion had a certain musty smell to it overall, the cellar stank of wet mildew and stones to the extreme. Pancho was amazed by the size of it. The cellar was as big as the house.

"At one time, the cellar served as a post office for the nearby communities. You can see a few remnants of it in the form of the counter against the far wall," Miss Sinaloa explained.

"What about the dungeon?" Pancho was referring to the shackles on the wall along with what looked like an old-fashioned torture rack.

"That's a recent addition. The good doctor can tell you more about that," Miss Sinaloa explained.

Pancho was surprised when the guards behind them began to undo their handcuffs.

"You offer these tours to the public, or are we just special?" Bill asked, rubbing his wrists.

Suddenly the guard behind Pancho nudged him towards the wall with the shackles. Bill's guard did the same.

"Oh, heavens no. Only dignitaries and special prisoners like yourself," she said, still looking at Bill even though it was Pancho's hand that she was currently chaining to the wall.

"We let the public think it's haunted, so they stay away," she added. "But then again, considering the number of prisoners that have been executed down here over the years, I suppose it should be."

"Yeah, you probably scare all the ghosts away," Pancho said as she moved onto Bill.

Bill whispered something in her ear as she did his shackle to make her giggle. Pancho groaned.

The two guards made their way back up the stairs seeing as Pancho and Bill weren't going anywhere.

"Well, as they say, the doctor will be in shortly," Miss Sinaloa said, backing away with the remainder of a blush. She was still so flustered by whatever it was Bill had said that she nearly tripped on her way back up the stairs.

"What is it with you?" Pancho asked.

"Ladies love outlaws no matter how old they get."

"Who was her great-grandmother?"

"Heck if I know, kid. Lot of senoritas over the years. I bet you got one back in Sumner yourself, don't you?"

Pancho grinned. "I wish. My brother just nabbed the prettiest one in town." He shook his head at his current predicament. "I still can't believe I'm being held prisoner by the Santa Fe Ring with Billy the Kid."

"Yeah, it's a dream come true, ain't it?"

Pancho laughed. "Actually, if you want to know something funny, when I was a little kid, I used to make believe I was Alias riding with Billy the Kid. You know, the character from *Authentic Life*?"

"What do you mean, character?"

"You mean Alias was real?"

The old man gave him a sly grin. "As real as the man next to me right now."

"I knew it!" Pancho said.

"Pat and Ash may have made up some big stretchers in that book they wrote, but they weren't all lies despite what the snooty historians might tell you. Speaking of which…"

As if on cue, Pancho heard footsteps followed by the distinctive voice of Mendez. "Gentleman, gentleman," he called out. "How are the accommodations? I know it's not as nice as the rooms upstairs but I'm afraid those are reserved for dignitaries coming in later tonight."

"Oh, what's the occasion?" Bill asked when he reached the bottom of the stairs.

Mendez walked into the large chamber flanked by two guards. "Your hanging tomorrow morning, as it turns out. You saw the gallows under construction when we drove in, but I didn't want to ruin the surprise. I wish I could take credit for it, but it's the governor's idea. He thought it would be… how did he put it… poetic for you to perish just as you were supposed to back in 1881 with a noose around your neck."

"How thoughtful," Bill said.

"Excuse me, isn't that like putting the cart before the horse?" Pancho asked.

"Come again?" Mendez shot him an irritated if not intrigued look.

"You're supposed to give us the false hope that we might live through this. You know the game. You promise to let us live if we tell you what you want to know. We tell you, then you go back on your word and kill us," Pancho explained.

Mendez smiled, amused by his intellect. "Clearly, you're both intelligent men, so I'll make no such false promises." Mendez pulled up a stool and sat before them. "But here's what I can offer. You tell me what I need to know, and you get one final peaceful night of existence before the hangman's noose swiftly sends you off into eternity tomorrow morning. You don't talk, and I'll spend the entire evening making this the single most painful, horrific night of your lives. Comprende?"

"Aren't you just a historian?" Pancho asked with grotesque fascination.

Mendez stood and walked towards the old post office counter. "Yes. And among my favorite things to study are the execution and torture methods of the old days."

He unrolled a tarp sprawled across the counter, revealing a plethora of rusty-looking old knives and saws. He picked up one of the knives and turned back to face them.

"In fact, if the governor weren't so determined to see you hanged," he said, pointing the knife at Bill, "and don't judge me, I respect the irony, I'd do something more creative. If it were summer, for instance, I might bury you up to your necks and let the ants make a meal of you out in the blazing New Mexico sun for a few days."

"You could let us freeze to death," Pancho suggested. "I hear it's supposed to snow tonight."

"Nice try, but that is far too peaceful a death for ones such as yourselves." He touched the knife to his chin contemplatively. "Another one I've always wanted to try was to wrap a man in a wet cowhide and let it dry out in the sun. You see, as it does, it slowly constricts you, much like one of those South American anacondas I'm always reading about in *National Geographic*. I wonder if it would work in the cold? Oh well, it's no matter. The gallows are being finished as we speak."

A smile crossed Mendez's lips as though a lightbulb had just gone off in his head. "I tell you what, I have been reading up on the Spanish Inquisition as of late. My roots go back to Spain, in case you haven't noticed."

"Oh, we've noticed," Pancho said, "and I think the accents a little too on the nose there, pal."

Mendez ignored his remark as he walked over to the torture rack. He patted his hand on it. "You know what this is?"

"Looks like the old wash rack my mother used to wring her wet clothes through," Bill said.

"I think you know exactly what it is." Mendez grinned deviously and nodded to his two men. They unchained Bill from the wall and led him to the rack.

"Hey, take me instead!" Pancho shouted. "He's an old man, for crying out loud."

"A very stout old man," Mendez observed. "I do believe you are the Kid, but I have to admit, you don't look a day over 75 or 80."

"Well, in case you haven't heard, I been living down with the Yaqui in Mexico. Some of them folks live to be a hunerd and twenty," Bill said as he was strapped to the machine.

"Well, I'm afraid you'll have to be content with only making it to 90, Mr. Kid. But as I said, your last night alive doesn't have to be filled with unbearable pain so long as you tell me what I want to hear."

Mendez patted his hand on the torture rack. "This isn't an original, I'm afraid. Built it myself. Was a father-son project for me and my boy."

"How touching," Bill said.

"Yes, I only wish he could be here. He loves Billy the Kid as much as any child," Mendez said as though what was about to happen would be fun for the whole family.

"Oh, well. And now to talk of things long overdue," Mendez rubbed his hands together. "Tell me what it is that I desire to know."

"Well, I was born back in 1809 in a small log cabin that I helped my father to build in LaRue County, Kentucky," Bill began with an old joke on the history of Abraham Lincoln.

Mendez nodded and one of the men turned the wheel connected to the ropes, which tightened, drawing out Bill's arms and legs with an audible sound of tension. "That's only a taste of what's to come, old man. Now tell me what it is I wish to know," Mendez said.

"Fine, fine," Bill began with a hint of discomfort in his voice. "My birthday isn't really in November like they all say it is. It's actually in September, in case you want to get me something."

"I doubt you should make it that long." Mendez nodded and the man turned the wheel a second time.

Pancho cringed for Bill as he listened to the ropes tighten. He also heard a loud crack that he knew didn't come from the ropes, but Bill only said, "Thank you, son. I've been trying to pop that for years. I might just take this contraption home with me when this is all said and done."

Mendez laughed. "I'm impressed, old man. You took the first two turns alright, but the third will finally start to do some damage, so I'll help you out." Mendez leaned in close to Bill. "Seventy years ago, you were part of a very special excursion into western New Mexico. You and several others were the last men to ever see the legendary Lost Adams before it was concealed in a violent cataclysm, an act of God, some say. And if the stories are true, you made it out with a bit of the gold. Is that correct?"

Bill nodded. "Sorry to tell you, I already blew my share of it."

Mendez smiled. "Based on how you're dressed, that's obvious. But, from what I hear, you also made a map to the canyon."

When Bill didn't answer, Mendez added, "No need to confirm it, that was a rhetorical question."

Upon another nod from Mendez, his goon gave the wheel another slight turn.

"I'm right here. You could just turn me loose and let me lead you to it," Bill said, wincing through the pain.

Mendez grinned. "Oh, you'd like that, wouldn't you? You'd lead us off on a wild goose chase until you died of old age. No, old man, I want the map."

Before Mendez could respond, footsteps sounded from the stairwell. It was West. "You're wasting your time."

"Is that so?" Mendez said, clearly not used to anyone correcting him.

West walked up to Pancho and put his revolver to his chin. "You're not hitting the right pressure points."

"Him?" Mendez asked quizzically.

"Yep." West pulled back the hammer, then looked in Bill's direction. "Isn't that right, grandpa?"

Pancho shot Bill a look.

Bill retained his composure. "'Fraid you're mistaken. I never laid eyes on that young man before today."

Mendez wasn't buying it. The seed had already been planted in his mind, which was working feverishly to confirm what West had just told him. "There is a certain resemblance, isn't there? Same height, some of the same facial features. I'll be damned."

"The jigs up, old-timer. Tell us where you hid the map or you can spend the rest of the night staring at baby boy's corpse," West said.

Bill relented. "Fine. I hid it in the last place I figured anyone would ever look."

"And where's that?" Mendez asked.

"My tombstone."

XVI.
THE WOLF

"Your tombstone!?" An angry, skeptical look spread across West's face.

Pancho was dumbfounded. So that's why Old Man Miranda had been so hellbent on hiding it!

West pressed the gun barrel harder into Pancho's chin. "Old man, if you're lying…"

"Better not kill us before you can confirm it then," Bill said glibly.

"It's true," Pancho interjected breathlessly, hoping to buy them some more time. "I knew the man who made it. His name was Salvador Miranda. He's one of the old-timers that was murdered."

"Fascinating." Mendez tapped his chin. "What better place to hide something than in plain sight?"

After a moment of contemplation, he shook his head. "The book I could write about this if the general public were allowed to know about it."

West withdrew his gun from Pancho's face. "Don't worry. I'll make a little trip to Sumner before dawn."

Mendez nodded. "After dinner. Fort Sumner's only a few hours away." He paused for a moment at the sound of car doors shutting above ground outside. "In fact, I hear our guests now."

Mendez motioned to his man, who released the tension on the rack. Bill let out a sigh of relief.

"See now, that wasn't so hard," Mendez said as a guard escorted Bill back to the shackles on the wall.

Mendez walked towards the stairs but turned to his prisoners once more before ascending. "And now, you can both spend the rest of the evening getting to know one another before you die." He cackled and walked up the stairway, followed by his two goons.

West gave them a funny look and tipped his hat to them. "If it was up to me, I'd let you both join us for dinner. Your hanging is a big deal for the Ring. Men whose grandfathers you killed are upstairs right now, eager to see it happen. Speaking of which, I suppose I need to mix and mingle. Sleep tight." With a devious grin, he disappeared up the stairs.

As soon as he was out of earshot, Pancho started in on Bill. "What were you thinking hiding the damn thing in your tombstone?"

"It was a spot I figured nobody would ever look." Bill shrugged. "Besides, me and Pat knew we were gonna fake my death for a while, so we had Salvador make the tombstone with a secret compartment in it."

"Yeah, well, you picked a hell of a spot to hide it considering your grave is one of the #1 tourist destinations in New Mexico now."

"Hey, back then I didn't know that I'd be the big deal that I am. Plus, we thought it'd be funny."

"Yeah, hilarious," Pancho said. "And why the hell is it I get the impression you're not terribly worried about our current predicament?" Pancho rattled his shackles for effect.

"Because, for being a historian, Mendez forgot all about my favorite method of escape." Bill slipped his hands free of his shackles.

"How did you…"

"I'm Billy the Kid, remember?" Bill grinned. It was true, Billy the Kid was notorious for his ability to slip out of shackles with ease thanks to his large wrists and small hands. "I can teach you, too, just—"

"Bill, maybe sometime when our lives aren't at stake?" Pancho rattled his shackles again.

"I still need the key, genius," Bill responded. He rubbed his hands together and then cracked his knuckles. "This'll be just like my escape from the Lincoln County Courthouse. Course, there was only two guards to contend with that time."

"Yeah, that and you were seventy years younger."

"Well, one way or the other we gotta get outta here and get the tombstone."

"Yeah, about that…" Pancho began to tell Bill about the tombstone, but they both tensed at the sound of footsteps coming back down the stone stairway.

"Quiet." Bill slipped his hands behind his back.

"What are you gonna do?"

"Fight 'em, I reckon," Bill said simply.

"You're 90, old man, you can't fight for shit without a gun!" Pancho whispered.

"Looks like I won't have to." Bill's eyes lit up at the reveal of the figure descending the stone stairway.

"What were you two talking about?" Miss Sinaloa said as she seemed to slither towards them.

Bill didn't miss a beat. "As a matter of fact, we were talking about you."

"Oh, really?"

"Yes, I was just telling my grandson that back in the old days the condemned man was usually granted a last request. I know what mine would be tonight."

Her eyes widened. "Well, you're in luck, because I couldn't stop thinking about you," she whispered and leaned in close. "I brought the key." She held it up enticingly.

"No need, darlin,' I already slipped out." Bill let his hands slide from behind his waist to make their way up Miss Sinaloa's back.

"Oh, you're an even badder boy than I thought," she said.

"Now, howabouts we set the kid free and we can all leave this place together?"

"I'm afraid that I'm perfectly happy with my position here in the Ring." She pursed her lips. "Besides, there's over twenty men here now. You'd never make it. Just accept my gift as the condemned man's last request and come with me upstairs. We can watch that sunrise I told you about."

"Sorry, kid." Bill smiled at Pancho as Miss Sinaloa took him by the hand and he followed her to the stairwell. Pancho shot him a dirty look. He'd only known his grandfather for all of a few hours and didn't know what he was planning.

Just before they were about to disappear out of view up the stairs, Miss Sinaloa shot Pancho a taunting look and turned to Bill. "Kiss me now, I don't think I can wait until we get upstairs."

She was clearly a woman who delighted in tormenting men, Pancho thought. But the joke was on her. As she closed her eyes and tilted her head back, Bill socked her across the jaw.

"Sorry, toots," he said as he laid her unconscious body out across the steps. He stood up and shook his head. "The things we give up for our children."

He took the shackle key from her limp hands and walked to Pancho with a cocky grin. "Still got it."

"Whatever, old man. Your heart probably woulda given out before you got her bra off."

"Yeah, but it woulda been a nice way to go," he said and undid Pancho's shackles.

"Now, how the hell do we get out of here?" Pancho said, rubbing his wrists.

"Just get a gun in my hands and we'll be fine."

"Easier said than done."

"You ever killed a man before?" Bill asked.

Pancho nodded. "In the war."

"Good. So you won't be one of those saps who feels guilty for killing the bad guys?"

"I'm not really that type," Pancho said as they both leered up the stairway. A lone guard stood sentry with his back to them at the top of the stairs.

"Good. Because if these people are anything like their forebearers, they're evil, plain and simple. Even toots back there." Bill chucked his thumb in the direction of the unconscious Miss Sinaloa.

"What's the plan then?"

"You take him out silently with your knife, then I get his gun."

Pancho patted his jacket pocket for his blade. West had been so overconfident that he wouldn't escape that he didn't confiscate it. Pancho drew it out and flipped open the switchblade as he crept up behind the man. Despite what Bill had said, Pancho still couldn't bring himself to literally stab a man in the back, even if he was allegedly evil. Pancho shook his head, inwardly cussing himself as he placed the knife back in his jacket pocket. Instead, Pancho snuck up behind the man and swiftly slipped his right hand under and across the guard's neck. Quickly, he anchored his right hand to his left bicep while his left hand pressed firmly into the back of the man's head.

The guard's arms flailed, but he was incapable of crying out for help due to Pancho cutting off his windpipe. It was something Pancho had been on the receiving end of many times at the hands of an angry Hondo.

Bill shot him an irritated look as he drug him down the stairwell. "What happened to not having a problem with killing the bad guys?"

"It's different if they aren't shooting at me," Pancho hissed back as the guard finally went limp due to lack of blood flow and oxygen to the brain.

Bill rifled through the man's jacket, finding his holster and removing the gun. "You know you can't do that to all of them," Bill said, releasing the gun clip to see how many rounds were inside.

"Well, hopefully the next ones will be shooting at me," Pancho responded.

"Hopefully," Bill retorted snarkily, sliding the clip back into the gun.

"Damn, I don't like these new-fangled guns," Bill said as he found a second, smaller gun the man had on a leg holster. "Be nice to have a good old-fashioned revolver. More reliable."

They both crept up the stairs and surveyed their surroundings. They had three doors to choose from. To the left was the large kitchen Pancho had glimpsed, now bustling with the activity of half a dozen or so servants prepping dinner. To the right were double doors that led into the main dining hallway, while directly ahead was a doorway leading into the library/pool hall. Pancho crept to the door directly ahead and peeked through. Two guards were playing pool. That door was out. Pancho snuck to the door on the right, opening it quietly and peering into the dining hall. He saw a maid polishing the center of the table to make it extra shiny for dinner. Pancho heard floorboards creak and looked above to see several men walking along the balcony of the second story.

"Well?" Bill asked.

Pancho shut the door. "I counted three men with guns in there. I think we'd have better odds going out through the kitchen."

"I don't know," Bill said. "My trigger finger's getting awful itchy."

"Come on. The most intimidating guy back there looks like Chef Boyardee," Pancho said, wanting to take the path of least resistance.

As soon as Pancho said it, a middle-aged woman with a small beehive of red hair finally took notice of them from the kitchen. She nudged the burly chef next to her chopping vegetables.

Pancho grinned sheepishly. "Sorry, we got lost looking for the bathroom. It around here somewhere?" He looked up at the ceiling innocently as if it would be up there somewhere.

The woman smiled awkwardly, then shouted out, "They're loose, sound the alarm!"

One of the staff pulled what seemed to be a fire alarm that started ringing.

"Clearly, they know who we are," Bill said.

"They're just kitchen staff. How bad can they be?" No sooner than the words left Pancho's mouth, a knife embedded itself into the doorpost by Pancho's head. Before the man who looked like Chef Boyardee could throw another, Pancho had plucked the same knife from the wall and thrown it back at him. With a scream, it pinned his hand to the timber support beam next to him.

Pancho and Bill made their way towards the kitchen since it was their best exit. Suddenly, one of the suited guards who had been in the first room playing pool burst through the door. Pancho was at the right spot at the right time to flip him over his shoulder and throw him to the ground. When he went to draw, Bill shot him quick as lightning. The second man rushed into the room carrying a shotgun, and Bill promptly shot him as well.

Before they could make a run for it through the kitchen, the red-haired woman had slammed the kitchen door shut. Pancho rammed his shoulder against it. "They must've barred it shut!"

"Where's that first room lead?" Bill asked.

"The library, and we both know it's a dead end."

"Well, the dining hall it is then," Bill said.

"Are you kidding? It's probably swarming with guards now!"

"We got no other choice," Bill said as he disarmed the two dead ringers, getting his hands on the shotgun and also their handguns.

In the other room, they could hear the footsteps of what sounded to be numerous guards taking positions on the balcony. "Come out, you're outnumbered!" one of them shouted.

"What next?"

"We go into the next room, guns blazing." Bill tossed Pancho a gun, which he caught, and then another. "The only problem is, even though

I may get around good for my age, I obviously can't run anymore. I'm gonna need you to pull your weight."

"Wait, I have an idea…" Pancho's eyes drifted tellingly to a wheelchair in the corner. It had probably belonged to Dorsey when he became old and decrepit.

"Aw, hell," Bill said, clearly hating the idea but realizing it was the most logical move.

"I'll do the running and you do the gunning, just don't let me get shot, old man," Pancho said.

"Let's just hope we don't go out like Butch and Sundance. I'm pretty sure both of them are dead."

An instant later, Pancho and Bill, seated in the wheelchair, burst from the double doors and into the long dining hall. Bill had a gun in each hand plus the shotgun across his lap for backup. The guards had all lined up along the second story to ambush them. Bill wasted no time in firing at the balcony, picking men off one by one. Some tumbled and fell to the first floor below, while others dropped where they were.

Time seemed to flow differently for Pancho, sort of like the night in Puerto de Luna. He was hyper-aware of everything going on. Dinner plates and glasses were exploding along with the wood of the ornate dining table. The noise was horrible. Maybe he just imagined it, but every few seconds he felt like he could feel the bullets whizzing past him.

There were too many men for Bill alone to hit. Pancho had an idea to free up his hands. He gave Bill a hard shove, letting him and the wheelchair sail along on their merry way. In the midst of his mad dash, Pancho jumped sideways onto the slick surface of the table, landing on his back and letting his momentum propel him—the glass shards that poked into his skin be damned. He focused on aiming his guns at the men Bill missed. It wasn't the same as aiming with a knife, but he tried to pretend as though the bullets were the blade. Maybe he was better with a gun than he anticipated, or maybe it was just his survival instincts, but he hit several of the ringers dead on as he slid across the slick tabletop.

A bullet finally nicked his right arm near the shoulder as he reached the end of the table and went sliding off onto his back, dropping his gun in the process. Swiftly he glanced at his arm and could see the side of his jacket was ripped clean through on the very edge. It was only a graze, thank God, albeit a bad one. He looked at Bill, who was likewise coming to the end of his ride, rolling to a stop. A man dashed to the doorway leading into the foyer in front of Bill at the same time that a man dropped from the balcony in front of Pancho.

Pancho forced himself to stand and fight; only the man before him was already drawing his gun. Bill shot the man in front of him with the shotgun, and the blast propelled him backwards into the man holding the gun on Pancho. As the man tumbled over, Pancho seized the moment, stepping to the side to trip him, and then brought his right hand down hard across the back of his head. The man's gun flew up in the air as he did. Pancho promptly caught it and then shot the man with it.

Bill gave him a look as he rose from the old wheelchair. "Nice to see you finally carrying your weight, princess."

"Hey, he was shooting at me." Pancho nodded to the dead body, then ahead to the foyer. "Only one door away from freedom now."

"Then let's make like a shepherd and get the flock out of here," Bill said and hobbled to the doorway.

He opened it. Before them, Mendez, West, and several fat men in suits were gathered around the fireplace. Mendez sat in a big, red leather chair, West standing by his side. Pancho pointed his gun at no one in particular and shouted, "Alright, you fat old—"

Pancho halted his insult at the sound of a gun safety clicking and a cold barrel pressing into the back of his skull.

"You were saying?" West cocked a brow.

Two men had been standing on either side of the doorway they had burst through and were now relieving Pancho and Bill of their weapons.

Mendez began to clap and stood, determined to show he wasn't shaken by the commotion. "Gentleman, these are our esteemed guests I was just telling you about. Having one last little shootout outside, were we?"

"I am impressed. The old man's still got it," West said, then pointed his fingers to the two men that had disarmed them, who quickly bound Pancho and Bill's hands in the front with some rope.

"That's Billy the Kid," a fat old man smoking a cigar harrumphed. "Looks more like Billy the Old Codger now."

The rest of the men laughed except West. "A very dangerous old codger. And the new kid ain't bad either," he said with admiration. "In fact, gentleman," he motioned to his two henchmen, "bar the door shut." West leveled his gun at Bill and Pancho.

Mendez shot him a look. "You really think that's necessary? From where I stand, it's over. Though, if you had pulled it off," he said to Bill, "it would have been an even greater feat than your escape from the Lincoln County Courthouse back in '81."

"I don't know, Mendez. I still think there's a chance they could pull it off on their own yet, but my ego just won't allow for it." West suddenly turned the gun from Pancho and Bill to Mendez and shot him through the heart. Blood flecked across West's face as Mendez tumbled back against the red chair. Mendez looked down at the red splotch spreading across his white suit in horror and confusion as he sunk to the floor.

"What?" was all he managed to mumble before he slumped over dead.

"West, what are you doing?" one of the fat men cried in terror.

"Getting rid of the rats." West shot him next.

"Shoot him!" one of the nameless Ring-leaders shouted to the guards flanking Bill and Pancho. Both fired into West's torso, but he only flinched. When one of them rushed West, he didn't bother to shoot him. Instead, he grabbed him by the shoulders, forced him to his knees, and then twisted his head completely backwards in an incredible feat of strength. The man's limp body dropped to the floor. In terror, the remaining Ring men plowed past Bill and Pancho to get to the door that West had instructed his men to bar shut. West seemed to fly past Bill and Pancho to the door, dispatching every last man with his bare hands.

West turned and flashed a satisfied smile. "Well, now that our unwanted guests are out of the way, let's get down to business."

"Y'all are working together?" Pancho asked in confusion. It was the only conclusion he could draw under the circumstances.

"Not that I know of," Bill replied in shock.

"Don't recognize me, huh?" West said to Bill as he wiped a bit of Mendez's blood from his mouth. "I can't blame him. It's been a long time," he said, turning his gaze to Pancho. "Me and grandpa here go way back. A lot of good times… the search for the Lost Adams… the Revolution."

It didn't make any sense. West looked to only be in his forties. How could he have known Bill all the way back then?

"No… can't be," Bill muttered, his eyes wild.

Pancho looked at Bill. "Who is he?"

"I'll show you." West began to unbutton his shirt. "Magic is a strange thing. You can change into an animal. You can wear another man's face. You can even turn into a ball of light and fly." West slid out of his shirt, and Pancho noticed that the bullet holes where he'd been shot were already beginning to seal up.

West reached for his eyes and began to remove something from each. They were contact lenses. "But the catch is, you can't change your eyes. As they say, eyes are the window to the soul."

He looked up to reveal two distinct animal-like eyes on a human face. "That's the one thing God won't allow us to hide."

"You son of a bitch, I should have known," Bill said.

"Known what?" As soon as the words left Pancho's mouth, he figured it out. West was a skinwalker.

"You… you're a skinwalker and part of the Santa Fe Ring?" Pancho asked, confused.

"I just killed most of the Ring, son," West said as though he were a complete fool. "No, I'm not a part of the Ring." He pointed to his face. "West was before I killed him a few weeks back."

"Wait. You can change into other people, too?" Pancho said.

The man with West's face laughed. "You have a lot to learn, son."

"Why don't you show us your real face?" Bill said bitterly.

"I rather like this one for now," he said as he approached them. West held up his hand, animal-like claws slowly beginning to protrude from his fingertips. "But now that you mention it, I could do with something a little younger."

The man jammed his clawed hand into Pancho's left arm with a jolt. With his hands bound, there was nothing he could do and it felt as though the life was being sucked out of him.

"There, that should be enough." Pancho flinched as West abruptly withdrew his claws.

"What happens now? I turn into a werewolf?" Pancho asked in horror.

"No," West looked at him with sheer disgust. "I turn into you." In midsentence the man had transformed into Pancho. "With just a few drops of your blood, I get your body, your voice, a hint of your mannerisms, and even a few choice memories." The man wearing his face paused and tasted the blood on the end of his clawed fingertip. He smacked his lips like a gourmet chef trying to determine the secret ingredient in a special sauce. "In your case, I see a very pretty little waitress down Fort Sumner way. She helped you impersonate your brother. Interesting."

"Don't you dare—"

"Don't worry, I'm just giving you a little example of what I can see. Quite telling that I barely took a sample of your blood and that's the first thing that I got from you. Speaking of which, what have you been keeping from me, old man?" The man with Pancho's face jammed his claws into Bill's abdomen and he doubled over. Pancho lunged at the skinwalker, but he caught him by the neck and lifted him off the floor.

Pancho watched in horror, unable to breathe as the skinwalker stared into Bill's eyes, scenes playing out in his mind that only he could see.

"You have been holding out on us, old-timer. I see now it isn't as simple as cracking that tombstone open and getting down to business. But now I know exactly what I need to do, and where." He unjammed his claws from Bill's stomach and dropped Pancho.

Pancho immediately leaned into Bill's side to keep him steady, fighting off his own lightheadedness for the sake of the old man. The skinwalker left them to peruse the animal skins hanging on the wall.

"Now, which one do I like?" He tapped his clawed finger to his chin. "Hmmm... I haven't turned into a bear in ages, however..." The man took a wolf skin and draped it over his bare shoulders. "You can never go wrong with the classics."

Pancho watched in awe and horror as the animal skin seemed to mold itself to him and come to life. It was like the Big Bad Wolf from Little Red Riding Hood had animated itself before his very eyes. He hadn't been seeing things in Puerto de Luna after all. They really could change into animals, or half-animals. Below the wolfskin muzzle, Pancho could still see his own face on the skinwalker.

"What do you plan to do with us?" Pancho asked.

"Well, nothing with grandpa here. He's just a dead man walking now. But you… I don't want you dead just yet." Suddenly, he used his claws to slash through the ropes binding their wrists. Pancho swung at him immediately, but the skinwalker spun away from him with animal-like grace.

"Be seeing you," he said with a smile that made him look like a Cheshire cat.

His eyes seemed to glow and the man began to float off the ground, the loose animal pelt billowing along his back like a superhero cape before a bright light enveloped the room. Before Pancho could react, the ball of light burst through one of the upper windows. The gust it created drew the fire out of the hearth and onto the walls, igniting the whole room as if by magic.

"Can you walk?" he asked Bill fearfully.

"I'll need help," he rasped, clearly in pain. Pancho looked frantically around the fiery room. The doorway, in addition to being blocked, was also completely enflamed. The window the skinwalker had flown out of was too high. Pancho grabbed the red leather chair and hurled it through the window at ground level. He helped Bill hobble to it. Pancho stepped through first and then steadied the injured Bill as he followed. When Bill stumbled, Pancho picked him up and carried him out to the prairie.

"Dammit, don't you be dying on me." Pancho was shocked to feel his eyes glisten.

"Don't worry. Ain't got time to die yet." Bill watched the flames consuming the mansion with satisfaction as Pancho sat him down. "Well, that took care of the Ring at least."

Bill coughed up a bit of blood.

"We need to get you to a hospital," Pancho said.

"Even if we had time for that, we're both wanted men. Besides, you can't let him get that tombstone," Bill coughed out meekly.

"Well, don't worry. There's something you don't know, and clearly he don't either, because if he did, he would've been gloating about it."

"What?"
"I already have the real tombstone."

XVII.
THE RIVER

Pancho explained the circumstances of the previous night to Bill as they sped south towards Sumner in one of the Ring's stolen sedans. How Hugo Miranda had stolen the real tombstone from the cemetery and swapped it for the decoy; how he had given it to Pancho at the bar for safekeeping; and finally, how Pancho had buried it under their White Ash tree until he figured out what to do with it.

"You still with me, Bill?" Pancho asked, fearing the worst. The old man was slumped over in his seat. Was a day all that he got to have with him? One day to grow to care about him, to love him, and then to lose him?

Bill stirred. "Good boy for doing what you did. And good on ol' Salvador, too. One of the few I trusted."

Pancho's mind returned to the events of Dorsey Mansion an hour ago. "That man back there, the skinwalker, who is he exactly?"

Bill stared out the window, the lights of a passing car briefly illuminating his pensive expression. "He was a friend a long time ago before he became an enemy. I thought he was dead, but apparently not…" Bill barely managed to get the words out before he began to slump over again.

"Bill!" Pancho shook him again. "Bill!"

"Let me rest, kid. Let me sleep 'til we get to Sumner. I won't give up the ghost yet, I swear."

Dammit. There was so much he wanted to know. So much that only he could tell him. This was practically the first breath they'd had to take together alone since they met. Pancho let the old man be, praying that he'd still be with him when they made it home. He was speeding like the devil in between Las Vegas and Santa Rosa, a virtual stretch of nothing that was usually devoid of cops. He was still wearing his brother's uniform if they did get pulled over, though. Nor was he worried about the Ring since most of their numbers probably perished in the fire. By 11 o'clock, he sped past Lake Sumner. He nudged Bill.

"We there?" he asked groggily.

"Yeah, check it out, Bill. You're famous."

Pancho watched the old man's eyes liven like a little child's at the sight of a highway sign advertising the grave of Billy the Kid. "Well, I'll be damned. I'd heard about it, of course, but I ain't been back here since I died to see it for myself."

As Fort Sumner came into view, Pancho got the strange feeling that this would be the last time he ever saw the place. Maybe it was because Bill was dying. Maybe he was sensing Bill's own emotions. Or it could've been Pancho's subconscious, subliminally doing the math on the past day's events. He had been caught impersonating an officer, engaged in a high-speed, high-profile pursuit through the streets of Santa Fe, and had put himself on the enemies list of both a secretive ring of politicians and a deadly skinwalker. His life as he knew it was over and there was no going back now.

"Take me there," Bill said.

"What about West… I mean the skinwalker?"

"He's already come and gone, I imagine. He can fly, remember?"

"He said something when he was seeing into your memories. That there's more to the tombstone than just cracking it open?"

"It has to be done at a certain time at a certain place to find the gold. I wrote a letter explaining the whole thing. Evans has it… why I told him to mail it if he don't see either one of us soon…"

Another question crossed Pancho's mind. "I don't understand something, though. If skinwalkers can steal your memories through your blood, then shouldn't he be able to find the canyon from your memories alone?"

Bill shook his head. "They can only draw your recent memories. Just like with you, he didn't get your whole life story, just the memories that were most important to you from the last few days or hours. That's why he can't find the canyon from my memories alone. Besides, even I'd have a hard time retracing my steps without the map at this point."

"Will he go after Williams, I mean Evans?"

"I don't think so. That letter I gave to Evans explaining everything… I wrote it only a day or two ago, that's how he knows what it said.

Now he only needs the tombstone." Bill suddenly chuckled. "I guess it's a good thing you're a horn dog."

"What's that supposed to mean?"

"It means it's a good thing it was still that girl on your mind and not the tombstone you hid."

They pulled up to the old cemetery, which looked more like an abandoned cattle corral than a graveyard. It was just a plot of messy, desert earth surrounded by some barbed wire and crooked wooden fence posts.

Pancho parked and shut off the engine. "What is inside the tombstone?" he asked since he got the impression that it was more than a simple map.

"We call it the Ojo del Oro, the Eye of the Gold. You put it in the right spot at the right time, and it points the way to where we buried a portion of the gold and a map to the canyon."

"Only since you switched the tombstones, he ain't gonna have the right one," Bill continued and reached into his jacket. "Which leads me to the real tombstone. There's a special place in Granbury I want you to take it. Here's the address." Bill shoved a crumpled piece of paper in Pancho's hand.

"Why Granbury, Texas, of all places, though?" Pancho asked.

Bill smirked. "Granbury is a special place. You'll see why once you get there. Now help me get out of the damn car already."

Pancho did as he said, and Bill took in his surroundings as Pancho helped him into the cemetery. "They cut the trees down," he said sadly. "Used to be big cottonwoods here."

"Farmers didn't like them obscuring the sunlight from their crops," Pancho said.

"Fort's gone, too. Course, I heard the river washed it away. Still mighty strange to see it this way."

Pancho felt sorry for the old man, although, he was also feeling sorry for himself. Instinctively, he knew that once he left here, he couldn't come back. He breathed in deeply, wishing for the familiar scent of alfalfa mingled with the cool flowing water of the irrigation ditches. But winter had come. The fields were dormant and the canals were either dry or frozen.

"So where is it? Take me to my grave."

Pancho helped him to the spot, which was surrounded by little more than a bunch of dead, knee-high prairie grass. A chain-link fence unceremoniously encircled the Kid's grave in a vain attempt to keep souvenir hunters and vandals from the tombstone, which Pancho could see was now gone. Not only that, the skinwalker had slashed right through the fence. It had fallen to one side, the spot the tombstone once occupied now vacant. He was relieved that it was, though. That meant the skinwalker had come and gone. "Your marker's gone, obviously, but this was the spot."

Bill snorted, then clutched his chest. "That so, huh? Looks like a big pile of nothing right now." After a moment's reflection, he said, "Take me to the Pecos. I wanna see it one more time."

The river was close to the cemetery and not a terribly long walk for a dying man, but Pancho knew it would probably take the last of the breaths that he had. When they arrived at the river's edge, Bill leaned on Pancho's shoulder and looked on the Pecos with satisfaction. "Now this… this is just like I remember it. Looks like I'm right on time too."

Pancho gave him a puzzled look.

Bill showed Pancho his pocket watch. "Eleven thirty. That's the time of night I was allegedly shot, if you recall." He shut the watch. "And now it's the time that I'm gonna die."

Pancho started to say something, but Bill cut him off. "Here, give this to your brother for me." Bill handed him the watch. "You'll always have your memories of me, but he ain't got nothing."

Pancho nodded and took it, wishing Hondo could be here. "I will," Pancho said, trying not to let his voice crack from emotion.

"Don't feel bad, son. Dying ain't the worst thing that can happen to a fella. Besides, I been 'dead' for seventy years now and just now got around to actually doing it." Bill laughed through the pain.

He clutched his chest and stumbled a bit. Pancho steadied him as they both knelt down, still overlooking the river, listening to its soothing babbles and ripples. Both had spent so much of their youth listening to it, it was almost like a lullaby for them. They both watched it flow by the light of the moon, each saying their own goodbye to it.

"Oh well, I had one hell of a life at least," Bill rasped. "Know what my big mistake was back in the day, though?"

Pancho shook his head, unable to speak.

"I was too showy. If you're going to be an outlaw, be sly about it, don't make a big show of it. When I was younger, I always needed my enemies to know how good I was, how smart… wanted them to lay awake at night wondering when I'd get them. Now I know it's better to just let 'em think you're stupid so they won't ever see you coming."

Bill laughed again weakly, a little blood flecking his shirt.

Pancho finally spoke. "Know something funny, old man? When I first saw you, I kept thinking I'd met you before. I just didn't know how long ago it was." Pancho sniffled. "Thanks for picking a good home for me and my brother."

Bill grinned and nodded weakly. "Kid, do something for me?"

He nodded. "Anything, Bill."

He cocked his head to the side. "When I kick the bucket, just for giggles, bury me in that damn cemetery where I belong, so that way the tourists don't get cheated out of their money," Bill croaked out and this time Pancho couldn't help but laugh along with him.

Bill stiffened, clearly having another bout of pain.

"You okay?" Pancho asked, knowing he wasn't but also not knowing what else he could say.

"Getting close now. But it wasn't the damn Ring that got me at least," he said with some satisfaction and a wry smile. "That B.S. Evans and me made up, about the Kid wanting a pardon. I don't care about that. But I did want to leave a lasting legacy to the state other than being a dusty old tourist attraction. I want the people of New Mexico to benefit from that gold. Just promise me you'll keep it safe… the tombstone?"

"I promise," Pancho said, his eyes tearing up again.

"The letter I gave Evans will explain the rest to you… just don't crack it open until they're gone for good… the Ring and that monster, I mean."

Pancho nodded through the tears he could no longer hide. "I won't."

Bill had another spasm of pain. "God help me," he rasped. "I wish I had more time… time to help you do what needs to be done."

"To do what, Bill?"

"To kill that thing. Wouldn't of ever stuck my head out of the sand again if I knew it was still out there. Hoped it was dead by now… hoped I only had the Ring to contend with, but I was wrong."

Pancho nodded, his heartbeat picking up. He could tell this was the final stretch.

"I lied to you, kid, about your parents, I mean. It wasn't the war. It was that thing that did it... it was looking for me... did it to get at me."

"Why didn't you tell me?"

Bill shook his head. "Didn't want you chasing after it and getting yourself killed. Only now it don't matter since it found you first."

He gripped Pancho's shirt collar. "Don't let it get to that canyon... can't let him get the bones."

"Bones? I don't understand." What was he talking about?

"Don't let Mescal get to the canyon..." Bill's hand went limp and his eyes closed as he slipped into unconsciousness again.

"Mescal? Who's Mescal, the skinwalker?" Pancho didn't understand. "Bill! Bill!" He shook him.

Bill opened his eyes and smiled weakly. "Happy trails, Alias." Bill winked at him and then his eyes closed for the last time.

XVIII.
THE FUGITIVE

It was half past eight, and Debbie was still waiting for the strange man at the far end of the counter to leave. He had been here since they opened. He was shifty-eyed, paranoid looking, and wore a seersucker suit, his hat parked on the countertop. He seemed like he had something to say but was afraid to do so.

She was tense anyway. Hondo said that he'd call her Sunday night, only she never heard from him. What if something had happened to him? He was on the trail of a killer, after all. It was probably nothing and she'd see him swagger in any second. Only when he did she still had to fess up to helping Pancho impersonate him. Would he understand?

"Your boyfriend's still here, is he?" Patsey chided her playfully, cutting into her thoughts.

"Don't remind me. He's always looking at me."

"Price you pay for being pretty. But it accounts for bigger tips at least."

Debbie shot her a bashful look.

"Hey, work it while you're still young, honey," Patsey said and disappeared into the kitchen.

Debbie cautiously let her eye drift down the counter. The old man caught her gaze immediately as though he were waiting for it. He held up his coffee cup for another refill. "If you don't mind, ma'am?"

"Of course not," was Debbie's answer, although inwardly she was marveling at just how much coffee this man had drank. He'd have a heart attack if he drank anymore.

"Thank you," he said as she refilled his mug. "I been meaning to ask, you're Hondo's girl, aren't you?"

"Yes. How do you know him?" Debbie said, a hint of alarm in her voice.

"Reporter. Jamison Tilley's the name."

Debbie set the coffee pot down and lowered her voice. "You're the man that Pancho mentioned."

"I see I need no introduction."

"Listen, you shouldn't be here. They're looking for you," she whispered.

"That may be, but I'm still not in as much trouble as Pancho." The man took a swig of his coffee.

"What are you talking about?"

He sat his cup down. "You haven't heard?"

Debbie shook her head.

"He's in big trouble for impersonating his brother. Not just that, I heard he ran from the law. Big car chase. Lots of property damage." He shook his head and took another sip. "Probably spend the rest of his life behind bars when they find him."

Debbie's heart sank. What had she done? "How do you know all this?" She saw nothing of what he had just spoken in the papers this morning.

"I'm a reporter. I still have my sources, even if I am on the lam. I'm afraid I was wrong about Tumbleweed Williams, though. Turned out he was a fraud."

A few new customers walked into the diner. It was getting busy. "Listen, mister, you better go."

He looked at her quizzically, holding his mug between both hands. "You going to call the authorities on me?"

Debbie didn't know how to respond.

"Seems to me you ought to be the one laying low." He sat down his mug. "If I understand it right, you're an accomplice."

"How did you—"

"That's not important." He slipped a few bills on the counter. "As I said, you might want to get out of town yourself before it's too late because there will be an investigation, and when there is, just think of the position that will put Hondo in."

The man gathered his coat and hat and walked towards the door. Debbie had gotten her wish. The man was gone, only now she felt even more troubled than before.

***

Hondo was in the midst of a fever dream. The monster was chasing Debbie through the streets of Fort Sumner and he was trying desperately to catch up to it and kill it. Sometimes he was with Debbie and the monster was behind them; other times he was behind the monster chasing it. It looked like a half-wolf half-man, similar to the thing he had killed in Puerto de Luna, only bigger. Just as he was about to catch it, he suddenly found himself facing the monster in a cave. It opened its huge jaws to bite into him when his eyes shot open. He immediately regretted it and threw up an arm to shield his sensitive eyes.

After a moment, his eyes began to adjust as he made out the white walls and wooden floors of Fort Stanton, which were reflecting the bright sunlight outside from the large windows. He and Seven had entered the cave in the afternoon, so it had been many, many hours since he'd last seen daylight.

His eyes drifted to a man in a chair near his bedside. At first he thought it was Seven, but eventually he realized it was Baca.

"Sorry I'm not very pretty to look at," were Baca's first words. "You kept calling out for someone named Debbie. I'm guessing she must be your wife?"

"Girlfriend," Hondo answered.

It seemed as though there was something important that Hondo wasn't remembering that he needed to ask Baca. His hand shot to his neck, which had only a small bandage on it where the bone had pierced his skin. "Why aren't I dead?"

"Most people that get stuck with the bone poison pass within a few hours. Seven managed to pull it out of you right away and then drag you out of the cave."

Hondo sat up and found he didn't feel as bad as he feared he would. "Where is he, anyway?"

Baca leaned forward dramatically. "He's been fasting in a tent in the wilderness for hours, praying for the Great Spirit to grant you life."

Hondo rubbed the back of his neck. "Really?"

"No, dummy." Baca leaned back in his chair. "He just went to get something from the vending machine. He likes Ding Dongs, I think." Baca began perusing the morning paper.

Hondo sighed and leaned back into his pillow. "How long was I out for?" He ran his hand along the stubble on his jaw.

"Seven drug you out around midnight or later, I think. It's 8:30 now."

"Good. I need to head to Santa Fe."

"You're a little late for the circus if that's what you're after." Baca tossed the paper into his lap.

Hondo picked it up. He feared that he might find news of Tumbleweed William's death. Instead, the main headline read "WOULD BE KID FLUNKS EXAM" with the secondary one reading "Billy the Kid Impostor Returns to Texas in Shame."

"Scratch that," Hondo corrected, "I need to be in Granbury, Texas." After a second it dawned on him that he'd never told Baca of the connection between the killers and the would-be Kid. "Wait, how did you even know that—"

"Seven filled me in on what the skinwalker in the cave said. About how they're after Williams for his knowledge of the Lost Adams canyon."

Hondo's suspicions suddenly became aroused. "You and Seven know each other better than you let on, don't you?"

"I didn't think either one of us let on one way or the other. But, yes, we both know of the canyon as all Apache do. And, despite our very different beliefs in the spiritual side of things, we both agree that the canyon needs to remain hidden."

Though Baca seemed to like to joke about Native American stereotypes and myths, Hondo could tell he was dead serious. "So you know where it is?"

"No," Baca said.

"And we intend to keep it that way," Seven added as he walked into the room and plopped down next to Baca in an empty chair. He clutched a bag of sunflower seeds from the vending machine rather than junk food as Baca implied.

"You," Hondo said, looking at Seven. "You kept something from me in the cave. About that canyon."

Seven flicked a seed in his mouth, unintimidated. "So what if I did?"

"I asked the skinwalker what they wanted with it, and you told me it was gold. But it's not, is it?"

Seven spit out the shell he'd just cracked. "Had I given you an accurate translation of what he said, it would have been too much for you at that time. After all, you're still getting used to the fact that monsters are real."

"Besides, you're not Apache. You wouldn't understand," Baca chimed in.

"Well, since the monster almost killed me, can I be part of your super-secret Indian club now?" Hondo asked, mildly irritated. He needed his morning coffee.

Baca and Seven exchanged a glance. Seven shrugged and popped another seed in his mouth.

Baca leaned forward. "For starters, no Indian gives a rip if the white man gets his greedy mitts on more gold. That's not why Adams' party was massacred by the Apache. They were digging on cursed ground."

"Think of it as a burial ground. But not for the Apache," Seven added.

"So what? They find an old burial ground for whoever. Big whoop." Hondo sat up out of bed, ready to get out of the itchy gown they'd put him in. "Can you hand me my pants so I don't moon the nurses?" he asked irritably, motioning to his clothes in the empty chair on Baca's right.

Baca handed them over. "Remember the little history lesson I gave you on Abiquiú? On the plague?"

"Yeah?" Hondo nodded, then looked both ways to make sure the cute red-headed nurse wasn't around and slid into his trousers.

"Well, let me put it this way. The bone dart that killed your father and the others, it's dipped in corpse powder—human corpse powder. But the thing buried in that canyon… if a skinwalker were to make corpse powder out of its bones… there would be no stopping them. It would be even worse than Abiquiú."

"That's what this is about? Old bones and Indian magic?" Hondo

"No white man knows the true legend of the canyon," Seven began. "Do you remember the story I told you on the way to Fort Stanton, about the Hero Twins slaying Yé'iitsoh?"

"Yeah…" Hondo answered reluctantly, worried where this was going.

"According to our legends, when the Hero Twins slew Yé'iitsoh, his brothers buried him at Sno-Ta-hay."

Hondo remembered that name from he and Seven's conversation in the cave. "So when you said the name means 'there it lies,' you really meant…"

"Yé'iitsoh, that's right."

"And according to the legend, from then on the canyon walls cried tears of gold for the fallen giant," Baca added.

"Yé'iitsoh?" Hondo muttered incredulously. He threw his gown off and grabbed his shirt. "I thought you believed in God, not mythology?"

"Myths are just one people's interpretation of history, like the great flood story common to all cultures. In this case, I think God sent the Hero Twins to destroy the monsters. Why else would so many tribes have the same myth about them?"

Hondo looked to Seven as he buttoned his shirt. "And now you know what the skinwalkers seek, the bones of a god."

Hondo stared at the two men in disbelief, what respect he'd had for them slowly beginning to dissipate. This was too much. Hero Twins? Monsters? Sure, in the darkness, the so-called skinwalkers had looked like monsters, but they died just like men. Looked like men, too, when the animal skins fell off.

Hondo wanted to get as far away from the two as he could. Their words had made him uneasy. "Look, thank you for your help, but I need to get going."

Baca turned to Seven. "Told you he couldn't handle it."

Hondo grabbed his things, then realized how rude he was acting even if the two men were a little bit off. He turned and said, "I'll call you if I find anything else about the investigation, okay?"

The two gave him a disappointed stare as though he were breaking up the band just as it was getting started. Hondo nodded awkwardly and turned to walk away.

Monster or not, Tumbleweed Williams would be the killer's next target if the pattern held. And if the skinwalker in the cave was right, there was only one of them left to deal with. He'd better call the police department in Granbury and warn them right away about the killer, though he'd leave out the skinwalker part so they didn't think he was nuts. Actually, he'd better call his own department first and make sure the town didn't burn down in his absence. Or Debbie. He wanted to call her right away even if he should be calling the station. His mind took part in a brief bout of tug of war before he decided to call Debbie at Patsey's. Hondo found a payphone near the front entrance and eagerly slipped in a quarter. For some reason, his conversation with Seven and Baca had troubled him deeply, disturbed something in the pit of his soul. He needed to hear her voice.

She answered on the fourth ring.

"Debbie, it's me."

"Oh, thank God. I got worried when you didn't call last night."

What happened to him last night didn't qualify as a typical phone conversation. "Sorry about that... I just stayed at this crummy motel that didn't have a phone." He bit his lip. He didn't like lying to her, but that was the easiest thing to do for the moment. "I'll explain better in person. I missed you."

"I've missed you, too." Hearing her say the words uncoiled the tension knotting itself through his body. For the first time since he woke up, he felt himself relax.

Suddenly, she lowered her voice and said, "Hondo, there's something I need to tell you. That weird guy was just here."

"Who?"

"Reporter called Tilley something."

His relaxed muscles tensed again. "Is he still there?"

"He left about five minutes ago."

"Okay, I need to call the station right away. They might still can track him down."

"Hondo, there's something else I need to tell you."

"Can it wait?" He hated to cut her off, but every second counted when it came to tracking down a perp.

There was a brief pause that troubled him, but then she said, "Yeah, it can."

"I'll call you right back, okay?"

"Okay."

Hondo hung up the phone and then put in another quarter. Within a few rings the secretary answered and put him through to his deputy. "Dorrance—"

"Hey, Hondo, I mean, Sheriff," Dorrance began, not even letting him get a word in edgewise. "I'm pretty shocked we got an answer this quick, but the coroner in Prescott already called me back."

"Coroner in Prescott?"

"Yeah. You asked for anomalies in the autopsy of John Miller."

What was he talking about? "Never mind that. I need you to do a sweep around Sumner Avenue within a few blocks of Patsey's."

"Yessir. What for?"

"Jamison Tilley was spotted there less than ten minutes ago."

Dorrance laughed. "Couldn't have been."

"Why the hell not?" Hondo asked, irritated.

"You haven't heard?"

"Obviously not. What?"

"We found him yesterday."

"Where?"

"Buried out south of 84 not far off the road. Coyote or somethin' dug 'im up. Looks like he'd been buried for a week or more."

"Can't be." Hondo's blood ran cold. Not just because Debbie had seen him, but Pancho had seen him only a few nights ago as well. A thought suddenly hit him connecting Tilley to the strange happenings. Could it be? Were skinwalkers more than just men who wore animal pelts and pretended to be monsters? He looked around frantically, hoping he'd catch sight of Seven or Baca before they left.

"Well, you can take a look at 'im yourself. But you'll have a hard time arguing with me after you see him," Dorrance droned on as Hondo continued to scan the hospital. Thank God. Seven was just now heading for the front exit.

"Hold on a second." Hondo cupped his hand over the receiver as Seven caught his eye. "Hey, those skinwalkers, can they change into people, too?"

Seven cocked a brow. "I thought you didn't believe?"

"Can they or can't they?" he asked angrily.

Seven nodded. "Yes, they can. What's happened?"

Hondo held up his finger and then uncapped the phone. "You're positive that you I.D.'d the face correctly?"

"Matches the one on the poster perfectly, just deader," was Dorrance's response. "You coming back to town?"

Hondo thought of Granbury. Williams could wait. Besides, it sounded like the last skinwalker was in Sumner. "I am now," he answered and hung up the phone.

"What's wrong?" Seven asked again as Hondo frantically dialed the diner back.

"I think the last skinwalker is in Fort Sumner and he's wearing the face of a dead man."

Patsey answered this time.

"Patsey, could you get Debbie, please?"

"Who is this?"

"Hondo."

"Sorry honey, she just got busy with a table of four. I can have her call you back."

Hondo looked at his watch. "No, that's okay. Tell her I'll be home here in a couple hours. And one other thing, you see Jamison Tilley come back in, call the office."

"Is he dangerous?"

"Very. And, if they try to tell you he's dead, tell 'em they're wrong."

***

"I take it from your hurry to leave that you're a believer now?" Seven asked as Hondo walked up to his truck.

Hondo stopped to lean against the front fender. "I'm coming around. How was it you said that you kill these things again?"

"For a normal skinwalker, like the one in the cave, White Ash by itself is usually enough. But I have a feeling the last skinwalker he referred to is different."

"How's that?"

"It's all in the translation… the way he said it. I don't think he meant last necessarily as in the last one, the more I think on it, I think he meant the most important one, the highest ranking. Like wolves, they'll have an alpha or a pack leader. They are special. According to legend, to kill one of them, you also have to utter their true name at the point of death. Upon being reminded of their humanity, the supernatural evil that strengthens them becomes useless."

Hondo snapped his fingers, remembering the name uttered in the cave. "Ma'cho. That was the name the skinwalker in the cave referred to him as, right?"

An embarrassed look crossed Seven's face. "I'm afraid my Apache was a little rusty back there. I didn't remember then, but ma'cho is just an obscure Apache term for wolf. Usually we say ba'uchaahi or ba'cho, very rarely ma'cho. So rather than his name, I think he simply meant this skinwalker takes the form of a wolf rather than a coyote or mountain lion like you've encountered so far."

Hondo shook his head. "Great. Reminds me of one of those damn monster movies with silver bullets."

Seven smiled grimly. "Speaking of which, I made this early this morning." Seven drew out a necklace from under his coat. A single bullet hung on it. It was the same .45 caliber that Hondo used in his colt revolver.

"Is that one of—"

"I took the liberty while you were sleeping." Seven handed it to him.

Hondo weighed it in his hand. "It blessed by a medicine man?"

Seven ignored his joke. "In the old days, we would have killed a skinwalker with an arrow made of White Ash wood. But, these are no longer the old times." Seven took the bullet back and held it between his fingers. "The case is still filled with gunpowder like any other, but towards the tip, I filled it with what little White Ash powder I had left."

Hondo took the bullet back, then added, "I'm sorry I didn't believe you before. Actually, in spite of everything I've seen, I'm still not sure what to think…"

"But?" Seven raised a brow.

"But…" Hondo grinned and pocketed the bullet, "until then, I'll err on the side of caution. Care to come with me?" Hondo asked hopefully.

"I think you can manage on your own. Besides, you can't be in two places at once, and it sounds like someone needs to keep an eye on this Williams person."

"Really?"

"I will travel to Granbury and keep him safe. It is my people's responsibility to keep that canyon hidden. If he knows where it is, then it is our duty to protect him."

Baca pulled up next to them in his squad car and rolled down the window. "Come on, Medicine Man. I'll give you a ride back to the res."

Hondo reached out to shake his hand one last time. "Thank you for everything."

Seven shook his hand and nodded. "Don't mention it."

A thought suddenly struck Hondo as he crawled into his truck. The bullet was only half of the solution according to Seven, who was sliding into Baca's patrol car.

Hondo rolled down his window. "Hey, how the hell am I supposed to figure out this thing's real name?"

Seven and Baca both exchanged a look. Baca looked back to Hondo and shrugged. "Pray."

***

Hondo must have broken the sound barrier on his way back to Sumner. Too many strange things were going on and his gut told him that everything was about to come to a head. He made what was supposed to be a two-and-a-half-hour drive in an hour and forty-five minutes.

Once he made it to Sumner, he barged into the police station first. "You still got the body in here?"

"Well, good to see you too, Sheriff." Dorrance took his feet off his desk and stood. "Yep, got 'im in the fridge."

They headed to the back towards what Dorrance called the "fridge" where they occasionally—no, make that very rarely—stored a dead body before sending them off to the coroners or the funeral home.

"Hey, you were so riled up about Tilley I didn't get to finish telling you about the Prescott coroner," Dorrance said.

"John Miller? I never asked for any records on anyone by that name."

"Hate to tell you, Sheriff, but you were right here in the office with Debbie when you did. Late Saturday night, remember?"

Hondo's blood boiled as his detective brain and brotherly intuition connected the dots. Pancho had been so dead set on going to see Tumbleweed Williams that he'd impersonated him, and he'd apparently roped Debbie into helping him.

"Oh, right." Hondo played along so that he didn't implicate them both. "Guess I just forgot in all the commotion."

Dorrance continued, "You need to catch up on your shut-eye is what I think. Had a cousin like you. Got too stressed out, not enough sleep, and next thing you know, he's dead with an… an… what ya call it… an annarism?"

"You mean to say aneurism. Now, what were the results?"

"Miller's was same as Uncle Kit and Old Man Miranda's. Well, not exactly the same, his hand wasn't cut off, but they did find one of those bone thingies in his neck. Haven't gotten the other one yet."

"Remind me of his name."

"Smith, Walkalong Smith or something like that."

Interesting. Angry though he may be at his brother's impromptu investigation, he had actually managed to turn something up. Apparently this had been going on for years now.

They reached the small morgue and Dorrance pulled open the body drawer revealing the dead form of Tilley. The desert had done its due diligence on his features, but it was him alright. In addition to the desert-induced deterioration, his torso was badly slashed by claws of some kind.

"Looks like the coyotes chewed on him a bit after they dug him up," Dorrance said, though Hondo now suspected that the slashes and bites had been inflicted while he was still alive.

Hondo tipped the body's head slightly to the side, stiff though it was, to get a better look at the neck.

"Ain't we supposed to use gloves?" Dorrance asked, but Hondo ignored him.

There it was. A small wound at the base of the neck where a bone projectile had likely been fired.

"See that?" Hondo pointed it out. "Another bone dart, you can bet on it."

"Well, I'll be darned. That mean it was the same feller who killed the sheriff and the others?"

"Most likely." Hondo covered the body and slid it back into its temporary home. He returned to the hallway. "Hey, you seen my brother around today?" he asked tepidly.

Dorrance shook his head. "Last I heard of him was Saturday night when he got in that big fight at Sunnyside. Ain't seen him 'round here all day yesterday or nothin'."

Hondo nodded. "Thanks, Dorrance. Think you can handle things 'til I get back this afternoon?"

"I reckon," he said as Hondo stood in the doorway. The secretary had just walked up to hand Dorrance a sheet of paper, which he took to examining.

"Alright, see you in a bit." Hondo stepped outside before he could be bothered by whatever it was she was handing him. He had bigger fish to fry.

"Sheriff!" Dorrance hollered for him. "Hold up, you're gonna want to hear this."

"What?"

"We just got an APB on your brother."

XIX.
THE WRITING IN THE SKY

When Hondo pulled up to the house he felt like he hadn't seen it in ages even though it'd only been a day. And what would he tell Ma? As if she weren't having a hard enough time already, Pancho was a wanted man now. Evading the law was one thing, but doing it while impersonating an officer opened a whole new can of worms.

Patricia would be at school and Jerry was back at his ranch, so Ma would be home alone for the first time in days. The familiar whine of the screen door, which he and his father alternately always claimed they'd fix, heralded his entrance. Hondo found Ma a disheveled mess at the kitchen table, her head down and a cigarette smoldering away in the ashtray. Ma had taken up smoking since their father had died. Said it helped calm her nerves.

"Ma," Hondo began tepidly, "I'm home."

She lifted her head from the table. She'd been crying. Did she already know? She stood and wrapped her arms around him. "He's gone, Hondo, and I don't think he's coming back."

"I know, Ma, I know. I'm sorry."

"Always said the two of you could drive a woman to drink and here I am smoking instead." Ma sat back down and started her second cigarette.

"Was he here?" Hondo asked instinctively.

She nodded.

"How long ago?"

She shook her head. "You ain't gonna find him. Not that I'd want you to anyways." She smiled weakly. "Left early this morning, before sunup."

"That idiot." Hondo slumped back and sighed. "He's ruined his life. And for what? To chase down a Billy the Kid impostor?"

"It's not his fault. There's something I shoulda told you a long, long time ago."

Hondo leaned forward. "What are you talking about?"

Ma took his hand with teary eyes. "I love ya, hon, something awful, but you ain't mine. I mean you're mine, but I didn't give birth to you."

Hondo sat back, dazed. Anger and confusion welled up inside of him, his immediate thoughts going to Pancho as though this unwanted revelation was his fault. "Pancho knew," he muttered. "Pancho always knew. How the hell did he know and I didn't?"

"Because you're more trusting than he is." She patted his hand and smiled. "We found the both of yas on our front doorstep one day with this." Ma slid a weathered note to him that was as old as he was.

Hondo picked it up and read it aloud. "To Mr. and Mrs. Dumez, I knew your kin once down along the Hondo River and know you're good people. I can't take care of my grandsons, and their folks are both passed. They wouldn't have a good life with me on the lam, and so I'm leaving them with you. If you can't take care of them, please find someone who can. Sincerely, W.B."

Hondo sat the note down in stunned disbelief. W.B.?

"Left a little note on each of you with your names, too. Your father thought we should change 'em. Said whoever 'twas that left you might come back one day to take you away. But I fought 'em on it. Figured keepin' you named what you was intended was the right thing. Plus, I liked the names."

Why did this new information trouble him so much? He slumped back in his chair as Ma continued.

"That's why me and Harold moved to Hatch for a while. Nobody knew us there, and if we popped up with twin boys, nobody would know you wasn't ours. Then, one day we'd move back here to Sumner, and we did. Told folks we had you while we was away in Hatch."

Hondo's reeling mind returned to the man who had left them. He had a very strange hunch as to who it was. "You know who W.B. is?" Hondo held up the note again.

"I had my suspicions, but I didn't know for sure until Pancho went chasing after that old man claiming he was Billy the Kid the other day," Ma answered.

"No," Hondo muttered as he shook his head, still unwilling to believe anything as far out as that. First skinwalkers and now this. It was as though a veil was lifting, revealing that his ordinary world was anything but. "Can't be."

"You know how I caught your brother last night?"

Hondo shook his head.

"Heard somebody rustling around outside. He was digging a hole under my White Ash. He hid something there." She paused. "The Kid's tombstone."

Hondo hung his head in his hands. "He's taking it to Tumbleweed Williams in Granbury. But why?" And if Pancho was going there, the skinwalker would follow.

"Hondo, don't arrest him." Ma grabbed his arm.

"It's not that, Ma." He didn't want to worry her any worse, but he'd prefer she know the truth rather than thinking he was out to get his own brother. "I think he's in danger."

Her eyes darkened with more concern than haunted them already. "How so?"

"Because everyone that's ended up dead has a tie with Billy the Kid, and if Williams is the Kid…"

Ma nodded. "What can I get you before you go?"

"Nothing, Ma, I'll be fine." He stood and the doorbell rang. "What now?"

Hondo walked towards the front door and saw Debbie standing behind the screen, holding a couple of plates with tinfoil over them. He had already forgotten he'd told Patsey to tell her he'd be home this afternoon. A part of him was happy to see her, another was angry, and yet another was filled with dread. The stress of the last 24 hours, coupled with the revelations just thrust upon him had made his exhausted brain turn borderline savage.

Things were going so well. Why did his brother have to get her roped into this? Why did she choose to help him? They had gone behind his back. He felt foolish. Was he just a joke to both of them? Big, dumb, oblivious Hondo who couldn't figure out the truth like Pancho did.

"Hondo." Her eyes lit up until she saw the anger in his and her happiness faded to worry. "Patsey told me you were home. I brought this for you and your ma." She held up the plates she'd brought from the diner.

Hondo stayed where he was in the doorway. "Ain't you done enough already?"

Debbie didn't try to play dumb. "Oh, Hondo, I was gonna tell you." She lowered the plates dejectedly.

"Yeah, after the fact," he said and was shocked that his voice almost cracked.

"I'm sorry, but I thought I was doing the right thing, honest."

"Well, thanks to you, he'll go to prison," Hondo said as though it were all her fault, even though he knew it wasn't. "As if my mother wasn't going through enough already."

What was he doing? He didn't want to lose her, but he didn't want to let the issue drop either. He should have let up, only he didn't.

"You know, Debbie, the kiss I could understand. We're twins and you were drunk. But helping him with something that stupid, behind my back…"

"I'm sorry. I didn't mean to mess things up. I thought I was helping." Her eyes pleaded with him to understand. Reminded him of a beautiful, wounded doe.

This should have been his moment to smooth things over, but his confused, addled brain wouldn't allow it. "Well, thanks a lot," he said callously.

They stood there awkwardly until she said. "I'll be going now, Hondo."

It killed him the way that she said his name.

He rubbed his temples. "Look, I'm sorry. I've just had a really hard day and I have to get on the road to look for Pancho. I'll call you when I'm back, okay?"

She backed away and down the porch. "That's okay. I understand, Hondo. It was a mistake for me to come."

She walked hurriedly to her car. Hondo didn't know what he wanted. He was still mad, but he didn't know if it was really at her or not. He was too mixed up to figure it out.

He stepped off the porch. "Debbie, wait."

The phone started ringing incessantly in the background, further fraying his nerves.

Debbie wouldn't even look at him as she made her way to her car and opened the door. "No, you're right. I really should be going."

"Hondo!" Ma came running to the screen door, stretching the phone cord to its limit.

Hondo saw tears in his mother's eyes. Whatever it was, it wasn't good. He turned back helplessly to Debbie, who was starting her engine.

"It's your deputy," Ma said, her hand letting the receiver drift helplessly from her ear down to her waist. "They got him."

***

Debbie crammed her second suitcase of the afternoon shut. She hadn't cried this much since her mother had passed, which wasn't long ago in the scheme of things. That was another thing she had in common with Hondo since his dad died. In an odd way, helping him with his grief seemed to help her with her own. Everything was going so well. Why did Pancho have to come knocking on her door that night? Had she been unfaithful to Hondo in some way by helping his brother? Yes, she had liked Pancho, too, but as time went on, she realized it was mainly because he reminded her of Hondo. Being identical in appearance, how could he not?

Her anxiety-fueled brain continued to dig its dark hole of worry and guilt much deeper than it needed to be. Her thoughts turned from Pancho to the fact that Hondo's life took a turn for the worse when she came into it. She left Cimmaron because her mother had just died. No sooner than Hondo got with her and his father was killed. Did she bring this upon him somehow? Was she cursed or something?

It was no matter, anyway. She was leaving. She'd pack up her things just like she'd done when she left Cimmaron. Even if Hondo got over what had happened, like the reporter said, the investigation would be hard on Hondo, who would no doubt try to protect her. Yes, he'd clearly been angry at her, but deep down she still knew he'd put his job on the line to shield her and his brother if it came down to it. His life would be simpler without her complicating it.

There was a knock at her door. The knot in her stomach tightened. Could it be one of the authorities here to ask about Pancho already? Or was it Hondo? He had tried to stop her from leaving as she drove off. As much as she dreaded seeing him, and in spite of convincing herself that his life would be better without her, she found herself hoping that it was him. She peaked through the curtains and could see

Hondo's broad shoulders. He had his back to her and he was dressed differently than he was earlier. Could it be Pancho?

Tepidly, she opened the door, still hoping somehow it was Hondo rather than his brother. "Hondo?"

He turned around. He was wearing sunglasses even though it was overcast outside. He was holding a big stone. No, he was holding Billy the Kid's tombstone.

"Pancho?" It had to be him. "What are you doing here?"

He didn't wait to be invited in and stepped through the doorway. It made her uncomfortable.

"You ever bought a really expensive antique only to find out it's a fake?" he said.

She didn't know what he was talking about and she didn't care. "Pancho, you shouldn't be here," she said, her voice wavering with emotion.

Suddenly and purposefully, he dropped the tombstone, breaking it in half and denting her linoleum floor in the process. She jumped back in alarm.

"See what I mean?" He motioned at the broken tombstone. "It's a fake. I could smell it."

She didn't know how she knew it, or how it could even be possible, but this wasn't Pancho. Or Hondo. The energy the strange man was radiating didn't feel right and every spiritual instinct she had told her she needed to get away from him.

"You're not Pancho. Or Hondo," she said, backing against the wall.

"I'm impressed, little girl." The face was still the same, but the voice had suddenly deepened.

"Who are you?"

He took off his sunglasses to reveal a pair of bright, golden wolf-like eyes. "I'm the big bad wolf."

***

Pancho sat dejectedly in his cell. He'd failed Bill's last request to get the tombstone safely to Granbury. And he'd been caught by Hondo's dimwitted deputy, Dorrance, no less. He buried Bill in the cemetery last night like he'd asked in an unmarked grave, exhausted and beaten up though he was. After that, he'd gone home and climbed through the window of the guest house to dress his wound where the bullet grazed him. He didn't know if he was more relieved or disappointed to find that Hondo hadn't returned. He had so much to tell him if the ol' brick-head would believe him. He'd wanted to see Ma but didn't know what to tell her. However, he'd ended up seeing her anyway and was glad for it.

Pancho had buried the real tombstone in a shallow spot between two of the bigger roots of the old White Ash. As he was digging it up, Ma had staggered out in the darkness holding a lantern and caught him hoisting the dang thing out of the earth.

"What are you doing to my tree now?" Her jaw dropped when she saw what he was holding.

"Ma, it's not what it looks like," he said, gripping the tombstone tight.

She shook her head. "Always knew this day would come."

At first, he thought it meant the day that he finally went too far, but she had surprised him when she said, "I knew it since the day Harold and I found you."

Pancho was stunned; she had finally admitted it.

"How long have you known?" she asked.

He set the tombstone down and offered her a guilty smirk. "Since I was 13. Well, I didn't know, but I suspected it deep down. Didn't know for sure 'til yesterday."

She started to tear up. He rushed to her side, grabbing her arms gently. "Ma, this doesn't change nothing. You'll always be my Ma."

"You're leaving, aren't you?" she said tearfully.

"'Fraid I have to, Ma. I got in trouble something awful. I met him, though. The man who left us here. Do you know who he was?" he said with a bittersweet grin.

Her answer mirrored his. "I suspected but didn't know 'til just now." She smiled meekly. "There was a note he left with you. Had his initials on it was all, but something told me it was him." After a moment, she asked, "Where are you headed?"

"Texas for now. I'll come back if I can." Even though that's what he wanted to believe, something told him this was the last time he'd ever see her.

She sensed it, too, he could tell. She nodded meekly and stared into his eyes for a moment. Finally, she said, "Don't forget where you came from, Son."

He shook his head, his eyes tearing up for the second time that night. "Never."

He embraced her for a long time under that old tree before he'd gotten up the gumption to leave, hoping to God that his gut was wrong, that one day he could come back. He'd gotten onto the road heading for Granbury around four in the morning... until he passed out along the side of the road and slept like the living dead. Not only had he lost a bit of blood, not to mention not eating, it had been too long since he'd slept. And so, his body had betrayed him and let him slip into unconsciousness a little ways between Fort Sumner and Melrose on Route 60. That's where Dorrance found him passed out in his car. And that's how he had ended up back in Fort Sumner in the jail.

Pancho could tell that Hondo had walked in from the sound of his boots, though they sounded a little wobbly for some reason.

"You alright, Sheriff?" he heard Dorrance ask cautiously.

"Yes, dammit, I'm fine," Hondo snapped.

"Found him with this," he heard Dorrance say, and Pancho knew he was referring to the tombstone. "Is it some kind of prank?"

"Not exactly," Hondo answered.

"Listen, Sheriff, this here's a family matter. I ain't reporting it that I found him, and what you do with him is your decision. I didn't see nothing except for whatever you say I did."

"Thank you, Dorrance. Can you give us some time alone?"

"Sure thing, Sheriff," Dorrance said, a hint of cautiousness still evident in his voice. Pancho heard the front door open and shut as Dorrance left.

Pancho prepared for an argument as he heard the heavy clop of his boots coming towards his cell in the back. When Hondo came into view, Pancho could see that his eyes were bloodshot and he seemed uneasy.

"Hondo, you okay?" he asked cautiously.

His brother didn't say a word and began unlocking his cell.

Pancho stood defensively. "Hondo, before you say anything, there's a lot you don't know."

Hondo swung the cell door open. "I know that you couldn't manage to stay away from Debbie." His eyes were bleary with anger that had faded into exhaustion. As his hand reached into his coat pocket, Pancho wasn't sure what he was going to draw out.

"Now look," Pancho began. "Nothing happened between us. She just helped me get some things out of here when I knew you wouldn't."

"I know," Hondo said, revealing what he had in his coat pocket. It was a bottle of whiskey that Pancho remembered belonged to their old man. It was also half empty now. Pancho couldn't believe it. The other night Hondo had been too strait-laced to even attempt driving home after drinking, and now he had driven to work half-soused. "Come on, let's go to my office."

Pancho followed him. Hondo sat behind their father's old desk, or rather his desk now, and Pancho seated himself across from him. "The old man's whiskey, huh?"

"It seemed appropriate under the circumstances." Hondo pulled a glass from the desk drawer for Pancho and filled it. Hondo kept the bottle.

"Hondo, you're gonna think I'm crazy but…" Pancho looked up from his hands with dread to meet his brother's gaze. "I met our grandfather."

"Let me guess. He was Billy the Kid?" There was still a tinge of anger in his voice, which Pancho mistook for skepticism.

"I know how it sounds."

"I believe you."

"But if you'll just… Wait, what?" Pancho said with a delayed reaction to Hondo's unexpected response.

"Ma showed me the note. I believe you. First skinwalkers, then Billy the Kid turns out to be our long-lost grandfather. Why not?" Hondo took another swig.

"Well, you don't have to sound so disappointed by it. I mean, it's pretty cool when you think about it."

Hondo slammed the bottle down. "Cool? You think it's cool that our father died because of all this? That you're going to go to jail because of all this?"

"I didn't mean it like that, Hondo."

"Dammit, Pancho, why couldn't you be happy? Why'd you have to go poking around for the truth?"

Pancho knew what he was really saying. Hondo didn't want to know the truth. Hondo had been happy and content, and Pancho had brought his happy little world tumbling down.

"Hondo…"

Hondo stood. "Do you have any idea what you did to Ma? To Debbie? To yourself?" he shouted, his voice wavering with emotion.

Pancho finally had enough and stood, grabbing his brother by the shirt collar like he always did to him when he was mad. "You selfish bastard! It's not my fault you didn't want to face the truth!"

Hondo tried to shove him away, but Pancho held firm. "Not my fault you wanted to bury your head in the sand your whole life."

Hondo launched himself across the desk, bringing he and Pancho both to the floor. Pancho took advantage of his brother's drunkenness and managed to roll on top of him and slug him one.

Drunk though he was, Pancho had still poked the bear. Hondo screamed and got him in a crocodile roll, careening them over into an old display cabinet of their father's, which crashed to the ground. Shattered glass and assorted antiques spilled to the floor as Hondo got the upper hand again, straddling his brother.

He didn't hit him and only shook him by his jacket. "She was perfect and you ruined it!" Hondo shouted.

That's what this was really about. Debbie. "I didn't do anything with her. I just needed help and knew you wouldn't!" Pancho shouted.

"No, you want her, I can tell. You wish you were the one who saw her first!" Hondo yelled and took another swing at him, but Pancho dodged it and shoved his brother off of him and onto the floor. Hondo was too drunk to overpower him like he usually did. Instead, they both just lay on the floor, catching their breath.

"Fine, I wish I saw her first, but I didn't and I'm okay with that," Pancho rasped out. "And you know what, I'm happy that if she isn't with me, she can be with you because you're better than me."

Hondo worked to catch his breath as he stared up at the ceiling. "No, I'm not."

"I'm a screw-up. I can't hold a job. I'm always in trouble. I'm never happy sticking in one place. I wish I was content like you, but I'm just not, alright," Pancho said, then, after a moment, added, "Besides, Hondo, she's not a prize that you won. She can choose for herself, and she chose you."

After a moment, Hondo laughed. "There's a killer out there that can wear other people's faces, and here we are still fighting over a girl."

Pancho had to laugh himself. Then he reflected on what Hondo had just said. Before he left, Hondo was still on the skeptical side whereas witches and skinwalkers were concerned. "Wait, when did you learn skinwalkers can turn into other people?"

"Today. Tilley is one of them. I mean, not Tilley. He's dead, been dead for weeks."

"Son of a bitch," Pancho muttered. It was probably the same skinwalker that had impersonated West. "So, when I was talking to Tilley, he was really—"

"Yep."

"Well, watch out, because he can also change into me now. All they need is your blood, they don't have to kill you."

Hondo finally turned to look at him. "Wait, if he can turn into you, then Ma or Debbie could be in danger."

Pancho shook his head. "I don't think he'll come after them. He got the tombstone, or thinks he has the tombstone."

"What does the tombstone have to do with this?"

"There's a treasure map thingy in it."

"What?"

"You heard me."

Hondo's face lit up. "To the Lost Adams?"

Pancho flipped onto his side to face his brother. "How'd you know about the Lost Adams?"

Hondo swore. "It's gonna take forever for both of us to catch up, only you need to get out of here."

"No, I need to get to Granbury to hide that tombstone."

"You need to get it to Williams, don't you? So he's our—"

"No, not actually. He was just a decoy." Pancho stood and offered his hand. "Look, it's a really long story. How about I tell it to you on the way to Granbury and we finish this thing together?"

Hondo eyed him for a moment, thinking it over, and then took his hand.

As Pancho pulled Hondo to his feet, a great gust suddenly shook the windows as if a big airplane had just flown by. They looked outside to see a gale of wind carrying a torrent of dead leaves and tumbleweeds through the street. Suddenly a huge stone shattered the front window. No, it wasn't a stone. It was the bottom half of the tombstone replica.

"What the hell?" Hondo said, looking from the busted tombstone on the station floor to the other one Dorrance had placed behind the front desk.

"That one's a fake. And I have a hunch the skinwalker just found out," Pancho explained.

"There's a note." Hondo knelt to untether it from the string attaching it to the stone. He unfolded the note and looked up at him with a panicked expression. "The real tombstone for the girl – after dark."

"Debbie," Pancho muttered, knowing it would be her since the skinwalker had seen her in his memories.

"But where?" Hondo muttered in a panic.

Before either could utter another word, the scream of a woman on the sidewalk drew their attention.

"Look!" a boy cried.

"It's a UFO!" an old man shouted.

Pancho and Hondo rushed outside. Dorrance was among the onlookers, staring slack-jawed into the sky. "Sheriff, what the hell is that?"

"I don't know, but it sure ain't the wicked witch," Hondo said, amazed at what he was seeing.

In the grey afternoon sky, a fireball was streaking through the air trailing smoke. It was writing something. They looked like numbers. One looked like a three, followed by a five, then a one, a zero, and an eight.

"What the hell?" Pancho muttered.

"They're coordinates," Hondo said. "Thirty five north by one hundred and eight west."

A motorist staring at the literal writing in the sky crashed into a fire hydrant and water began cascading into the air.

"We need to figure out where that leads, and fast." Hondo tugged on Pancho's sleeve. "Come on."

They both ran for Hondo's truck.

"Sheriff, where are you going?" Dorrance shouted.

"Sorry, Dorrance, gotta go see a man about a horse!" Pancho hollered from the truck as they sped off.

XX.
THE LAND OF FIRE AND ICE

The red rocks flanking either side of Route 66 blazed an angry orange as the sun sank into the horizon. Soon, the orange glow of the firmament faded into a pink haze which gave way to a light blue, and then, finally, darkness. The brothers weren't far from their destination and would arrive within a few minutes. As soon as they had left the sheriff's office, Hondo had gotten a map and figured out where the coordinates led. The spot was Fort Wingate, where Adams had fled from the canyon after the massacre. It was also perhaps not coincidentally the starting point of the Navajo's Long Walk to Fort Sumner in 1863. So far, the brothers had spent the entirety of the drive playing catchup on their respective adventures.

"So, in Puerto de Luna, it was my knife that killed him instead of the bullet?" Pancho mused in shock.

"Apparently so. The blade must have gotten sap on it when it embedded itself in Ma's tree."

"So all we need to do is shoot it with that special bullet your Indian friend made then?"

Hondo grimaced. "Maybe. Maybe not."

"What's that mean?"

"Supposedly this one is special. Seven thinks it's the chief skinwalker."

"I can believe that." Pancho remembered his encounter with it in Dorsey Mansion. "Damn thing acted like the world was its office."

"The catch is, according to Seven, to kill the lead skinwalker you have to utter its true name at the point of mortal injury."

"Dammit!" Pancho struck the dash. "I think Bill was trying to tell me before he died. But he couldn't get the full name out. Only a surname… Mescal."

"You think he was trying to say Mescalero and got cut short?"

Pancho shook his head. "No, he was telling me its name. I'm sure of it. According to the legend, does it have to be the full name or just part of it?"

Hondo sighed. "The full name, I think."

Pancho cussed again.

"Don't feel bad. I thought I had it for a while, too… what was it? Ma-ko…May-cho…" Hondo squinted, trying to recall the exact word. "Ma'cho! That was it, only it just turned out to be some obscure Apache word for wolf."

"That's it!" Pancho hit Hondo on the shoulder.

"What is? Ma'cho?"

"No, Bill told me that on their way to the canyon they befriended an Apache kid named Wolf. That has to be the skinwalker!"

"Wait, if this kid went to the canyon with him, why would he need the map?"

"That's just it. Bill said that Wolf never made it to the canyon with them. I took it to mean he died, but he must mean they got separated or something. Then, later, when I asked him about the skinwalker, he told me that he used to be a friend. This Apache kid fits the bill perfectly. Besides, from what you've told me, most of the skinwalkers have been Apache instead of Navajo, which is unusual, right?"

"Right."

"And Mescal is definitely an Apache surname, so…"

Hondo grinned. "Holy cow… you're right. You've got the name and I've got the bullet. How's that for God looking out for us?" He kissed the bullet hanging from his necklace.

"Wolf Mescal," Pancho muttered in amazement as relief washed over him. "We can finally kill this thing and avenge Dad… both our dads, actually."

Suddenly, another pressing thought crossed Pancho's mind. "Speaking of that, should we tell Patricia and Jerry the truth?"

Hondo turned to him, the lights of a passing car illuminating his face. "I was thinking maybe that'd be our little secret with Ma." He smiled. "Keep at least some semblance of our old lives that way. You okay with that?"

Pancho smiled. "Yeah, actually I am."

They rode in silence for a moment. However, Pancho's mind would only allow him peace for so long. Soon it turned to another problem that needed to be solved. Though he had made his peace on leaving Fort Sumner for good earlier, now he was beginning to regret it, wanting more and more to hold onto his old life. "You think there's any way to straighten out all that business in Santa Fe? Most of the Ring died when the mansion burned down as far as I know."

"Didn't you say Governor Mayberry was one of them?"

"Yeah, but he's on his way out, and the skinwalker killed Mendez, the governor-elect. So maybe there's hope after all?"

"Time will tell, little brother. But one problem at a time," Hondo sighed and nodded ahead. "We're here."

Hondo hadn't headed for the modern quarters of Fort Wingate and had instead driven them to a few secluded ruins from the old days. Parts of the fort were still in use by modern soldiers, but this particular area consisted of abandoned barracks that dated back to the Civil War. It was far and away from the newer components of the fort, which was currently mostly used as a Native American school among other things. A few years ago, during the war, the place was bustling with activity and had served as a training center for the Navajo Code Talkers. Now only a few soldiers remained.

Two medium-sized buildings shone before them in Hondo's headlights. They looked lonely out there by themselves, surrounded only by dead trees towering over the dormant prairie grass.

"Déjà vu," Pancho muttered when he saw the old stone ruins. "Reminds me of Puerto de Luna."

Hondo put the truck in park. He yanked the bullet from the necklace and loaded it into his revolver. "Yeah, but this time we know what we're up against." Hondo clicked back the hammer of the revolver. "I'll take the shot when Debbie is safe and you say the magic word, deal?"

"Deal."

They exited the truck and walked towards the buildings, Hondo with the gun and Pancho with the tombstone. He had placed it in an old rucksack he had kept from his days in the army and carried it on his back, freeing up his hands to use a flashlight. Or a knife. Not that it would do any good. The sap from the White Ash tree would have worn off by now.

"Split up. Each take a building?" Pancho asked as they approached the two structures.

Hondo shook his head. "No, this time let's stay together."

They entered the first building on their left. It was devoid of any furnishings and was now just an empty shell. Frantically the beams of their flashlights cut through the darkness, illuminating nothing but collapsed ceiling beams through a dusty blue haze.

"Where the hell are they?" Hondo muttered.

"He's playing games with us," Pancho said. "Be careful."

"Debbie?" Hondo cried out hopefully, but there was no response. Other than the sounds of their own footsteps, all they could hear was a rat scurrying around in the darkness. Pancho caught sight of a bodily form in the path of his flashlight.

"Hondo." Pancho grabbed his brother's arm. In the beam of light could be seen the silhouette of a body hanging from the rafters. For a moment Hondo panicked that it was Debbie until he realized it was clearly the body of a man. The brothers dashed to it.

"Is it another old-timer?" Pancho asked, trying to connect it to the earlier murders.

"No." Hondo shook his head and shined his beam up onto the man's face. Pale though it was, it was clear this wasn't an old man. "He looks like he's our age."

Hondo traced the beam down the body revealing a military uniform. "He's one of the soldiers," Pancho observed. "But why?"

Hondo's detective brain began to piece it together based upon the locations of the kills. "I'm starting to think this is about more than just Billy the Kid and the Lost Adams."

"What are you getting at?"

"All of the murders—the recent ones at least—took place at a fort that oversaw the Native American population. Fort Sumner, Fort Stanton, and now Fort Wingate."

"The starting point of the Long Walk to Fort Sumner," Pancho realized aloud.

"This means something to him." Hondo suddenly noticed a note tucked into the dead man's breast pocket. He pulled it out and began to unfold it. It was hastily written in something red.

"What do you want to bet that's not red ink?" Pancho said.

Hondo began to read it aloud. "To the 'Hero' Twins."

Pancho shot him a confused look.

"Don't ask. It's an Indian thing." Hondo turned his eyes back to the note and continued reading, "Just as my own journey started here nearly one hundred years ago, so too will you begin your own long walk to my kingdom. You'll find me in a black, jagged land formed of giant's blood where no modern vehicle can traverse. Meet me at the foot of the crater where fire and ice mix—high noon tomorrow."

Hondo handed the note to Pancho. "Where the hell's that? He draw us a map at least?"

"I know this." Hondo snapped his fingers as his mind went back to his conversation with Seven. The giant's blood referred to the slaying of Yé'iitsoh. The land of fire and ice was the malpais. "It's the badlands near here south of Grants."

"There's miles of that lava flow. How do we know where exactly?"

"Where fire and ice meet at the foot of the crater. He's talking about the ice caves under Bandera Crater. You've heard of them, haven't you?"

"Yeah, I know where they are," Pancho sighed. "And we'll need horses to get there."

"Well, we both know a guy pretty well..."

They both turned to face each other. "Jerry."

***

TUESDAY, DECEMBER 5, 1950

"Ya know, at first when y'all asked me to meet you at the big arches, I was kinda hoping you meant McDonalds," Jerry said from atop his horse, that same dumb, ponderous expression etched across his face as always. Before the three brothers stretched the huge curvature of La Ventana Arch of El Malpais National Monument. Years of erosion via wind and water had created the huge natural arch that currently loomed over a sea of trees. Though it may have reminded Jerry of a hamburger joint, to Hondo and Pancho, the sandstone arch looked more like the enormous, crooked doorway to the home of a giant. It was striking to begin with, but was made even more so by the pink, dawn sky above it.

"Sorry to tell you Jer-bear, but this is only the starting point," Pancho said.

"And we have a long way to go," Hondo sighed from atop Geronimo, Uncle Kit's horse that had somehow become a strange new fixture in his life. The brothers had called Jerry from a payphone last night and told him to meet them with horses at Ventana Arch since it was the most distinctive landmark in the area. The brothers had driven south to get there late last night. They had parked Hondo's truck in the forest before it had gotten too rough to traverse and walked south to the arches where Jerry met them at dawn.

Jerry had headed north from Alamogordo, where his ranch, or perhaps they should say his in-laws' ranch, was located. As their luck would have it, Jerry married into money. His in-laws had gifted him and Marlene a nice ranch on the outskirts of Alamogordo where they kept several horses which included Geronimo. Since the brothers didn't have a place to keep him, Jerry had taken him home after the funeral. That wasn't the only thing they had asked Jerry to bring, though.

"You bring the right rifle?" Hondo asked, leaning in close to inspect it.

"Of course." Jerry patted the Colt. .45 lever action slung across his shoulder. "I still don't understand why it *had* to be this one. I got lots of better long-range rifles than this."

Hondo had specified a .45 rifle because it was the correct caliber to fire Seven's special bullet, just like Hondo's revolver.

Pancho and Hondo exchanged a look. "Eh… We'll explain that on the ride," Hondo said. Last night, over the phone, he had only told Jerry that this involved rescuing Debbie from one of the killers responsible for the death of their father. And though Jerry had seen the skinwalker that night himself, they hadn't yet explained to him that they were more than just men in animal skins.

"But first, let's go get the lay of the land." Hondo slid off Geronimo. He wanted to survey the challenge that lay ahead from the high ground atop the sandstone buttes, the challenge being the blackened lava fields of the Malpais, *malpais* being Spanish for the badlands.

The three brothers dismounted their horses and tethered them to some nearby pines. When they reached the top of the granite summit,

Hondo took out a pair of binoculars and scanned the dramatic landscape before him. It was a fitting abode for a monster. The landscape was almost entirely black and green, the black being the fiery, dried sea of lava, and the green belonging to the pines that had miraculously found a way to sprout amongst it. Elsewhere was the glowing gold hue of the sandstone buttes, still illuminated from the rising sun. Sporadically dotting the landscape were also patches of white from a recent snow that had yet to melt entirely.

North of the sandstone butte were numerous extinct volcanos, where mostly only fire-blackened lava decorated the scarred landscape. Oddly enough, beneath the obsidian sea were also caves of ice. Ironically, what was previously smoldering hot before it had cooled and hardened was now the very thing insulating the ice caves and keeping them frozen year-round, even in the heat of summer. The Spaniards had mostly avoided this area, choosing to go around it rather than traverse the rocky terrain. The Navajo didn't have that luxury. They were forced to march across it on the Long Walk, and now the skinwalker wanted them to endure the same hardship.

"Well, I can see why they call it the badlands," Pancho said.

"They almost tested the first atomic bomb here before they settled on Alamogordo," Jerry added. "Since it's already scorched earth."

Satisfied that what lay ahead matched what he saw on the map, Hondo put his binoculars down. "Might as well get to it. Burning daylight."

"Careful, you sounded like Dad," Pancho said with a smirk. The irony now rang a little differently now that they both knew they didn't share any of his genetics.

They made it back to the bottom of the butte and remounted their horses and set off into the badlands. Once they reached their destination, the plan was simple. Hondo and Pancho would wait for the skinwalker and trade Debbie for the tombstone, while Jerry would secretly take to the high grounds with a rifle. When the skinwalker appeared, and he had a clean shot with no risk to Debbie, Jerry would shoot him with the special bullet, and Pancho would utter the thing's true name.

Like every other good ol' boy in the territory worth his salt, Jerry had gone on so many hunting trips over the years that he could pick the wings off of a fly by now. Not that he was as good as Hondo, and not that Hondo wasn't the one dying to pull the trigger, but the skinwalker wouldn't expect a third man. He would only be expecting Hondo and Pancho. Although Jerry had some difficulty accepting the more supernatural aspects of what they'd told him, he had no moral qualms with killing the man responsible for their father's death and kidnapping Debbie. Besides, this was as far into the middle of nowhere as you could get. After it was done, they would bury the body and never speak of it again.

It would take hours to cross the inhospitable lava-scarred earth. It was made even more difficult by horrific chasms that formed twisted labyrinths in some spots, which they would be forced to go around. The hellish labyrinths weren't due to any supernatural force, though, but rather the natural elements. When the lava cooled it contracted into the crisscrossed walls that made up the maze. At the moment they were riding past another upheaval of earth.

"Skinwalkers sure do like to hang out in creepy places." Pancho stared at the dry, cracked earth.

"Kinda reminds me of a pan of Ma's brownies, ya know, when she overcooks them?" Jerry said, his mind still on food.

The twins shot him a look. "What? I ain't et since last night and y'all were in too much of a hurry to let me stop and get breakfast."

"Well, I'm sorry, Jerry, but we ain't gonna take time out for pancakes when a girl's life is on the line," Pancho said.

"You just worry about shooting that son bitch down, Jerry, then we'll take you out anywhere you like," Hondo said.

"And tell me again exactly where we're headed?" Jerry asked.

Hondo pointed northwards. "There, to Bandera Crater."

"Please don't tell me that we're supposed to meet him in the crater?" Jerry whined. "I mean animal people is one thing, but erupting volcanas is another."

"That volcano ain't active, Jerry," Hondo clarified. "Besides, the note mentioned the place where fire and ice meet. The fire refers to the volcano, and the ice means the ice caves underneath."

The further north they went, the more the landscape became blanketed in snow, and slowly but surely, the crater on the horizon loomed larger and larger. The volcanic field, which contained nearly

30 volcanos, was located along the Jemez Lineament. Bandera had last erupted in 1170 BC, spewing out 23 miles of lava. It was 800 feet deep and would most likely erupt again one day. However, if geologists were correct, it only erupted every 5,000 years, so they should be safe.

"This is the spot," Hondo said as the huge, snow-covered caldera towered over them. Trees grew up the sides and within the mouth of the crater, which they could see inside thanks to a V-shaped indentation split in the side of the volcano. It looked like a giant casting ladle for pouring lead.

"What now?" Jerry asked.

"You get to the high ground," Hondo pointed at the volcano, "while me and Pancho stand around out here like sitting ducks with the tombstone and hope this is the last of his games."

The brothers dismounted their horses and hitched them to some nearby pines. Pancho looked at his watch. "Got an hour 'til high noon. If this is the spot."

"It is," Hondo said. "Has to be. The ice caves should be right beneath us."

Hondo walked over to Jerry, who was getting ready to ascend the slope to find a good vantage point. He held up the bullet. "I know I've said it before, but I'll say it again. It has to be this bullet. Got it?"

Jerry took the bullet. "Geez, you do sound just like Dad," he said as he loaded it into the rifle.

"And you don't take the shot until you know Debbie's clear?"

"Yes, Dad," Jerry replied, aggravated.

Pancho snickered.

"Let's go with him, get the lay of the land," Hondo said to Pancho. "We got time."

"Alright, but you carry this damn thing for a while. My back can't take it anymore." Pancho undid his rucksack and handed it to his brother.

Hondo strapped it along his back and trailed his brothers up the snowy caldera. Jerry suddenly stopped and snapped his fingers. "Damn! I knew I forgot something."

"What?" Hondo asked in alarm.

Jerry turned around and lowered his voice. "Now, y'all don't tell nobody this, but you want to know what the best camo for hunting in the snow like this is?"

They both just stared at him, wondering what would come out of his mouth next. He looked side to side as though someone might overhear him.

"Marlene's wedding dress," he whispered. "Thing's huge."

Pancho and Hondo sighed in disgust.

"O' course, I felt right strange and stupid laying out in the snow in it, but those bucks never saw me. Perfect snow camo."

"Jerry, just hurry up and get your ass up the mountain." Pancho pointed uphill and trudged towards him.

"I dressed in green forest camo. I stick out like a sore thumb!" Jerry stomped his foot angrily into the snow and the ground suddenly gave way beneath his feet, taking Pancho with him. Hondo watched in shock as a sinkhole swallowed his brothers whole.

***

Pancho had been taken completely off guard. He could barely register what had happened as he tumbled downhill into a chasm, his vision obscured by the snow that fell through with them. The situation was completely out of his control. Just when Pancho thought he'd stop tumbling, he tumbled some more. Jerry had been the straw that broke the camel's back to open a sinkhole that had probably been forming for the past few days thanks to the snow.

Finally the assault on his overwhelmed senses came to an end and he stopped rolling. Pancho wasn't so sure that he hadn't momentarily been knocked unconscious as he shook his head and then surveyed his strange new surroundings. They had fallen into one of the ice caves. The air was cold and heavy, and it felt as if it was pressing right against his cheeks. It was so quiet he could hear his own heartbeat.

He turned to his right and could see his brother coming to. "You okay, Jerry?"

He nodded his head and then shook it, coming out of the same haze as Pancho.

The decline had been gradual enough not to seriously injure them, just bang them up, but was also too steep to climb out of once they reached the bottom. The light at the end of the tunnel was far, far away, obscured by volcanic dust combined with an icy haze within the cave. It reminded him of the sky during an eclipse.

"Hondo!" he shouted upwards.

His brother's silhouette loomed over the hole. "Pancho! Are you guys okay?"

"We'll live. Do you think we fell into a trap?"

"I don't know," Hondo shouted back. "I'll get some rope. Stay there!"

"Where the hell would we go?" Pancho said, irritated.

Then he heard it. It was a noise that sent a spiritual chill through his blood rather than a physical one. It was the fox-like titter he had heard that night in Puerto de Luna. Jerry's eyes lit up. He recognized it, too.

"You remember that sound, don't you?" Pancho asked.

"Should we wait for Hondo or go after it now? I got the bullet, after all."

Pancho bit his lip, not sure what to do. Suddenly a feminine scream echoed through the dark passageway.

"There's our answer!" Pancho said.

Pancho grabbed Jerry's arm and hoisted him up. "He gonna kill her?"

Pancho shook his head. "No, something tells me that was his way of telling us where to go. But we damn sure better hurry." Then he turned his head to the surface and shouted, "Hondo! They're down here! We're going ahead!"

"What!?" Hondo shouted back, but there was no time to explain. He'd figure it out that he needed to get his butt down here.

"Come on, Jerry." Pancho took out his flashlight and took off down the cavern. He quickly found that stepping swiftly was a bad idea when he slipped to the cave floor. Pancho marveled at the texture. It was cold and smooth.

"What the hell?" From the cave floor, Pancho illuminated the trail before them.

"Ice… pure ice," Jerry remarked, amazed.

Pancho took Jerry's hand and stood. "Well, so much for hurrying. Come on."

The two men walked as quickly as they could across the trail of ice. When the ice disappeared into lava rock, they traversed the ground hastily until they reached another section of frozen, flat terrain. Parts of the icy ground were so colorful that it looked like they were walking on a trail of turquoise. Though the ground was usually slick but level, the ceiling varied in height, necessitating that they occasionally duck down to dodge icy stalactites. As they navigated a particularly slippery section, they took note of petroglyphs dotting the cave wall. Some looked familiar, like the spiral symbol so common to petroglyph sites, while others featured strange-looking creatures. As he walked along, one caught Pancho's eye of two men teaming up to attack a strange, bird-like man with a blowgun. Another seemed to show a wolf on two legs, a skinwalker, obviously.

"Sure, guys, I'll leave my wife and child at home to come along with you to rescue your mutual girlfriend from a potentially active volcano haunted by werewolves. Why not?" Jerry muttered behind him.

"She's not our mutual girlfriend," Pancho retorted.

"Coulda fooled me on Thanksgiving."

"And I've said it before. They're not werewolves, they're called skinwalkers."

"Well, if it can turn into a wolf, don't that make it a werewolf then?"

"They can turn into any animal they want, not just wolves. Bears, deer, anything. But this one… this one is definitely a wolf."

They had reached a fork in the tunnel, each path leading into its own dark passageway. "Which way now?" Jerry asked.

As if in answer to their question, a cry for help suddenly broke the icy cold again.

"Hondo!" It was Debbie's voice, only it seemed to come from both tunnels somehow.

Jerry shot him a confused look. "How—"

Pancho shook his head. "These things can mimic people, not just animals. Their voices… everything."

"Which tunnel is she down then?" Jerry asked.

Pancho stepped tepidly into the tunnel on his right and called out, "Debbie, is that you?"

Again came the wailing cry of "Hondo!" from both tunnels. Then suddenly, the tunnel wall shook. Pancho jumped backwards deeper into the tunnel as the entryway collapsed into a heap of debris.

"Jerry? Jerry?" he called out frantically in between coughs while also waving the dust out of his eyes.

"Pancho, I'm fine! But, what about you?"

Pancho could barely hear his brother's muffled call through the rocks. "I'm okay," he shouted back. "I guess the cave decided for us." Or the skinwalker, he thought.

"I'll dig you out!" he heard Jerry shout.

His flashlight shown the result of the collapse. There would be no digging their way out, not without wasting precious time. "It's no use!"

Suddenly, he heard the familiar titter come from down the lava corridor. He wouldn't have to worry about Jerry facing the skinwalker alone. The monster was at the end of this tunnel, not Jerry's.

"You go on, look for Debbie!" he shouted.

"I ain't leaving you!" he shouted through the rocks.

"I'll be fine. You find Debbie and wait for Hondo! Now go!"

Pancho turned to face the tunnel before him, ignoring his brother's cries. Oddly, he wasn't frightened of what he was about to face. Whereas the skinwalker they saw at Puerto de Luna behaved like an animal out to kill them, this being could be reasoned with. It liked to talk. And Pancho could keep it talking until Hondo arrived with the tombstone… and hopefully Jerry with the bullet. Or, if not, if the opportunity to kill it didn't arise, hopefully the creature would keep its word and let Debbie and his brothers go after it got the tombstone. Pancho reflected back to the encounter he'd had with it at Dorsey Mansion. It had freed him of the rope binding his hands even though it had no further use for him. It had said it didn't want him to die just yet. Why? Soon he might have his answer.

Pancho traversed the tunnel for several minutes until it opened into a massive cavern. Pancho gasped in awe. Despite all the strange sights he'd beheld in the past week, this one was still the most terrifying. Before him stretched a vast lake of ice which had a strange, green tint that set it apart from the more turquoise-colored trails he'd walked previously. Across the vast lake of green ice, Pancho could see a huge black wall of lava rock. Nestled high above in its confines was a structure that at once looked like a castle but also vaguely reminded him of the Puyé cliff dwellings, only cruder. Carved into the steep lava rock was a series of rungs meant for climbing. He couldn't be sure, but he thought he heard a flute coming from the ruins.

"God help me." Pancho took in a deep breath and prepared for the arduous climb. More than ever he was glad he had handed the tombstone off to Hondo so that it was his burden now. After several minutes of climbing, he finally hoisted himself onto a flat surface again. Catching his breath, he surveyed his surroundings. Only two things stood out to him. One was what looked to be a large, shallow bowl of some kind. He suddenly realized what it was: a giant cauldron. He shuddered to think of what it may have been used for in the past. The other was a natural stairway formed out of the molten lava. It led to the only entrance that he could discern. With a sigh, he decided to face what was within and climbed the short staircase.

As he stepped inside the entryway, it was pitch black, the sound of the flute song serving as his only guide. Soon he reached a torchlit room, barren aside from an altar stone in the middle. At the head of the room on a crude obsidian throne sat the skinwalker playing the flute. With its head down, it looked as though a wolf was playing the instrument. However, the pelt didn't look alive like it had at Dorsey Mansion and seemed to be dormant at the moment. Sensing his presence, the head lifted revealing a familiar face beneath it. There sat the man he had once called Jamison Tilley.

"Hello, Pancho," the skinwalker said with Tilley's familiar voice. "Was feeling sentimental. Thought I'd wear something familiar."

Pancho studied the face he once knew as that of Jamison Tilley's intently. It had the same features other than the eyes, which blazed with the golden, animal glow without the contact lenses to hide them. It was amazing how dramatically one's countenance could change a person's face. Gone was the paranoid, scared old man he had met in the bar, replaced with a wolfish, overly confident visage.

"That was you the whole time, wasn't it? I never even met the real Tilley, did I?"

"Afraid so." It set the flute aside. "I hated being Tilley, by the way. Man was pathetic, but then again, aren't you all?"

Pancho ignored its swipe at the human race. "How the hell did you know who I was? Who I really was, I mean?"

The skinwalker settled back into its throne. "I've been chasing down leads on the Kid for years, as I'm sure you now know. Lucky me, after I had Uncle Kit killed, I decided to question your brother about the murder—as Tilley, of course. See if the law was onto us yet. And to my great surprise, I could smell the same blood running through your brother's veins as the Kid. Speaking of the Kid's blood, I take it he didn't make it?"

"No," Pancho answered bitterly.

"Too bad," the creature said, its voice tinged with disinterest as it inspected its nails. "Where's the tombstone? I don't see it."

"It's coming." So is something else, you bastard, Pancho thought inwardly.

"It had better be for the girl's sake."

"Where is she?"

"Don't worry, she's alive and well in the crypt. I put her on ice, as they say."

Pancho's blood boiled. "Old man, you better not have harmed a hair on her head or—"

"Or you'll what?" the skinwalker interrupted him. "Take another ineffective swing at me like you did at Dorsey Mansion?" He laughed. "Don't worry, she's fine. It may shock you to hear that nothing would make me happier to see you and her make it through this. All I need is that tombstone and everything will be... how do you hicks say it, hunky dory?"

"Hunky-dory, huh? Well, riddle me this, old-timer. Once you get your paws on that tombstone, how the hell are you gonna dig that canyon out? Gonna turn into a giant dog or something?"

It shook its head disapprovingly. "You really think someone as conniving as me doesn't have a plan? You're nearly as devious as I am, I bet you can figure it out. I can turn into anyone I want after I get a bit of their blood on my hands, so to speak."

Pancho's mind suddenly flashed back to that night at the mansion, specifically the memory of Mendez's blood splattering across West's face when he shot him. "The new governor. You're gonna take on his form."

"Bingo," the skinwalker answered, shifting into Mendez, his thick Spanish accent taking over. "Should be fun running the entire state, not to mention what's left of the Santa Fe Ring."

"And as governor, you can use the state's resources to dig out the canyon..."

"I have to admit, you figured that out rather quickly. I somehow doubt your brother would have." Mendez's face eyed him slyly.

"What are you getting at?"

"I'm saying you remind me of myself." With that, he had shifted back to Pancho. "And, you take after our mutual friend the Kid much more than your brother, I'm afraid."

"Mutual friend? That's a funny choice of words for someone you murdered in cold blood." Pancho wasn't just buying time, he was seizing the opportunity to get to know his enemy, to confirm that this was indeed the Apache man named Wolf Mescal that Bill spoke of. Because if it wasn't...

"Well, as the old adage goes, there's two sides to every story. Billy and I went way, way back. We're the same age, actually. Met him back in '81 and saw quite a bit of myself in him. We were both orphans who had to fend for ourselves; we both spent considerable time in Fort Sumner, albeit for very different reasons."

Pancho watched as the skinwalker changed into his true form, a young Native American man, confirming what he needed to be true, that he was indeed the Apache called Wolf. His features were handsome, with long dark hair. His eyes seemed to become even more intelligent on their rightful face. "Nice thing about being a skinwalker, you can appear as young or as old as you please. But this is the real me, or the real me as I appeared back when I first met the Kid."

"How'd you two meet, anyways?" Pancho asked to learn more about his foe.

"We were both on the trail of the canyon, but for very different reasons. There was a priest who was escorting Old Man Adams back to the site of his infamous diggings. At the time I was posing as the priest's little altar-boy helper. Eventually the Kid joined our party along with a few others to the canyon. Things were going well until they found out what I really was and one of them put a bullet through my skull. They thought it killed me, but all it really did was slow me down and make me forget... In time, as my memories returned, I thought perhaps I could find the way to the canyon myself. Only a great cataclysm occurred, or so I hear, that so vastly altered the landscape it had become unrecognizable." He shook his head. "So, as you can imagine, I've been searching for that canyon for a long, long time."

"And why exactly is that? Gold?" Hondo and Bill both had said the skinwalker was after some mystical bones allegedly buried there. Pancho was just taking a page from his brother's playbook, playing dumb to get his opponent to open up.

"Gold?" the skinwalker answered mockingly. "I have no use for gold. For me, this is about revenge."

"Revenge? You already killed the Kid, who else is there to murder? Me and my brother?"

"Oh, there are many, many people left to kill, but you and your brother aren't necessarily among them." He smiled. "Let me explain. Once upon a time in Fort Sumner lived a very special boy. No, not you, Pancho. I'm talking about me. Although I was born in Arizona, I became what I am now along the Long Walk."

"You should have seen it." He shook his head. "The land I came from was proud and beautiful, but off they herded us like cattle to the flat, boring earth of your country. The journey was a nightmare. Ceaseless walking all day, and every night when we made camp, the children would wail and the old people would groan. Then every morning there'd be that damn bugle to wake us up and get us to marching again.

"Sometimes the elderly would drop dead along the trail and be no more. That was nothing, though. They'd lived their lives."

Pancho watched as the skinwalker's eyes seemed to fade into the past, reliving every moment he spoke of. "I remember once as we crossed a river the waters swept into a buckboard transporting a load of infants. They were washed down the rapids, never to be seen again. And then there was my own mother. We were only a day away from the Bosque when she collapsed in a heap and the soldiers left her for dead in the snow. I wouldn't leave her, so I stayed behind, preparing to die myself. And then I saw my salvation. Do you know what it was?"

"Let me guess, a skinwalker."

"Correct, but not just any skinwalker. He was the very first of his kind, already ancient by then. Though he wasn't able to save my mother, he marked me as his own and then walked me to the Bosque where he left me."

"Don't tell me, and then you had a grand time there running around on all fours as a little wolf cub until they sent you back to Arizona?"

"Hardly. You see, even before he changed me, I was already something of an outcast among my people. My mother may have been Navajo, but my father had been an Apache. Even though I was a child of both tribes, the Apache and the Navajo hated each other. No one wanted me, so I had to fend for myself those four long years.

"Conditions on the Bosque were atrocious. The bitter water of your river made us sick. The poison weeds killed my people's sheep. The Apache had already cut down the best of the trees for shelter. By that first winter, nearly all of the livestock were dead, as were the old and frail that had miraculously made it through the Long Walk.

"At the time we simply thought it was the ineptitude of the soldiers. Little did we know that they were subservient to the idiot bureaucrats in Washington who didn't know what to do with us. But eventually the first skinwalker returned for me. When I asked him in anger why he had left me in such a terrible place, he told me he wanted me to experience the hardships of the Bosque. To let my anger simmer and build itself into a monster so that one day, I could take revenge on those that subjugated us."

"And just what exactly does this revenge entail?"

"I'll wait for your brother. I'd like for him to hear it. Speaking of which, were you taught how one becomes a skinwalker?"

"I missed that part of the class. You'll have to enlighten me."

"You must first be marked in some way by the skinwalker." He held up his hand as claws extended from the tips of his fingers.

Pancho looked down at the claw marks on his arm. "But, you said—"

"I said you wouldn't turn into an animal. And you won't unless you proceed onto the next step."

"And what's that?"

"The killing of a close blood relative."

XXI.
THE LAST SKINWALKER

Pancho was chilled at the implication of the skinwalker's last statement, wondering just where this was going as he continued his tale.

"It all dates back to the tale of the very first shapeshifter. The story is a bit like Cain and Abel," he continued. "To attain the power, the original skinwalker killed his brother with a cursed dagger carved of bone. Upon taking his sibling's life, he was granted the gift of shapeshifting… and immortality."

"Immortality? Tell that to the two dead skinwalkers me and my brother killed already," Pancho chided him.

"Well, with every gift comes a curse. You see, the first skinwalker killed his brother in the shadow of the White Ash tree. As penance, it was decreed that the skinwalker should die from the White Ash. But it takes more than that to kill a true skinwalker such as myself created by the original." He smiled snidely. "Do you know what that is?"

Pancho's machismo urged him to answer with the skinwalker's given name then and there, but he bit his tongue. Some of Bill's last words to him had been to not let one's ego get in the way when dealing with one's enemies. Instead, Pancho merely nodded and answered, "Your true name. Any chance you want to tell me what it is?"

He offered a toothy smile. "I think not. Besides, if I told you, I'd have to kill you."

There it was again. That reluctance to kill him. "I don't get you. I mean, you've killed my adoptive father, my grandfather, my real parents. Why not me?"

"Because I see something special in you, Pancho." He leaned forward. "You know, even though I didn't dig my claws into you for long, I still got quite a sense of who you are, what you want. You suffer from the wanderlust. I can go wherever I please, whenever I please. So could you."

"Why would I ever want to be like you?"

"It's the only way you can ever be free." The skinwalker extended his hands towards him and they began to shift subtly into Pancho's own. "That soldier I slaughtered at Fort Wingate, I did that with these hands. Your hands." He withdrew them and leaned back. "Your fingerprints are all over him."

"You son of a bitch."

"Made sure a few of the students at the school saw me, or you, I mean, hanging around, too. When the police find that body and investigate, you'll be the prime suspect. I mean, you were already in trouble for that business in Santa Fe. For that, you'd go to prison for a while, but not this. For this, you'll get the chair." He shook his head. "You're going to be on the run for the rest of your life. Would certainly come in handy to be able to change your appearance, wouldn't it?"

Pancho shook his head defiantly. "I won't sell my soul, even if it costs me my freedom."

"I know something that might tempt you even more than your freedom."

"What's that?"

"The girl. I know how bad you want her."

His voice had a strange effect on him, like the little devil on his shoulder whispering in his ear but ten times worse. The skinwalker spoke the truth. Pancho didn't hate his brother for loving Debbie, but he couldn't deny he wished he could have made the connection with her first.

The skinwalker leaned forward enticingly. "As I said before, to be as I am now, one only need to take the life of a loved one. Kill your brother, possess the girl for yourself, and live free for centuries."

"Sorry, no dice, pal. You're the last skinwalker, and you're gonna stay that way," Pancho said, his voice beginning to waver with anger.

He settled back into his throne. "Oh, I'm not the last skinwalker anymore. I made a new recruit at the mansion. You've met her before."

Miss Sinaloa came walking into the room, a fox skin draped over her shoulders, only this time it teemed with life and seemed to crawl across her. Her striking eyes were made even more so as they literally glowed with evil. And whereas before she had appeared immaculate, her hair was wildly amiss and her dress was charred from the fire at the mansion. She truly looked like a wild woman now as she leaned against the skinwalker's throne.

He gave Pancho another sly grin. "She's a real fox as your slang would say."

***

Hondo carefully made his way down the steep decline using a rope that he'd anchored to a tree. If this was their only way out, they'd need it to climb back up. It flayed his nerves to be going this slow while Debbie's life was on the line, especially with how things had ended. It would kill him if that was her last memory of him, thinking he'd blamed her for everything that had happened—especially now that Debbie's own life was in jeopardy thanks to him and his brother. He couldn't risk slipping and damaging the tombstone and ruining the deal with the skinwalker, either. From what he understood from Pancho, what was inside wasn't a typical map, but something Bill had called the Ojo del Oro, or Eye of the Gold. It sounded delicate.

The irony suddenly hit him that he was back in another cave and he wished that Seven was here. Seven had said that the Hero Twins met their end in the underworld on the trail of the monster that killed their father. In terms of the skinwalker that had murdered their adoptive father, Hondo and Pancho had killed it that night in Puerto de Luna, and he and Seven had killed the accomplice in Fort Stanton Cave. However, if what Pancho had told him earlier was true, the skinwalker they were after now had killed their real father. The coincidences troubled him. Was this history repeating itself as Seven suggested, or was it simply a case of life imitating art?

Upon that thought, Hondo's foot finally made contact with solid, level ground. He whipped out his flashlight and wasted no time in exploring the corridor. His right leg suddenly began to slip out from under him, stretching painfully as he tried to keep from falling over. He pointed the flashlight at the cave floor and was shocked to see turquoise-colored ice. He righted himself, cinched the rucksack a little tighter to his back, and began to traverse it swiftly but carefully.

Just as parts of the ground were pure ice, he noticed that moisture wept from the ceiling as well. In an interesting contrast, the stalactites coming from the roof were jagged and dangerous looking, while the icy stalagmites jutting from the ground were clear and rounded at the ends. It didn't take him long to come to what looked like a cave-in. He could tell it was recent from the way his flashlight illuminated more dust in the air than usual in addition to the piles of rock.

"Pancho? Jerry?" he cried out, afraid one of them might be trapped behind it.

No answer. He'd have to hope they had both gone into the open tunnel before him. At first, the passage was nothing special. Well, it was still an ice cave. That was special, but it wasn't any different from what he'd seen before. Eventually the tunnel widened into more of a corridor. The walls were lined with human-sized cavities in which laid forms that were only half human. Each cavity contained the skeleton of a man, and perhaps a few women, with animal pelts and skeletal remains atop their heads. He couldn't believe what he was seeing. He'd heard of Indian Burial Mounds before, like that big one… Spiro Mound he thought it was called, but nothing quite like this. This was a literal skinwalker crypt.

Just as he caught himself slowing down to take in the macabre sight before him, a scream suddenly pierced the silence. It was Debbie.

***

Debbie's mind had been in a frenzied, dream-like state for hours, suffering the same parade of nightmarish imagery over and over again. A wolf wearing Pancho's skin. An evil looking woman wearing a fox fur leering down at her. Black jagged lava rock and crystal blue ice. And a sensation like flying. Then, she finally opened her eyes to find a strange man standing over her.

She immediately slapped him and screamed out of instinct. He screamed back. It was Hondo and Pancho's younger brother, Jerry. For some reason, awakening to the sight of Jerry almost seemed stranger than the shapeshifting man she'd met earlier.

"Jerry!?" She was sitting up now, clutching her chest, feeling her heart racing.

"Well, what'd you do that for? I'm only here to rescue you," he said, clutching his cheek.

Debbie touched her face. Her cheeks were icy cold. "I'm sorry. Where am I?" She looked around the icy tomb in amazement.

"You ever hear of that ice cave beneath the volcana outside of Grants? Well, believe it or not, that's where you are." He offered her a hand to help her off of the platform she currently sat atop.

She took his hand and slid off, her joints slightly achy. She took in her surroundings. She had been sleeping atop a black stone altar, it looked like. A jagged curtain of ice hung before it as if to hide her. Elsewhere in the room she could see casket-sized holes dotting the walls. It was a crypt. She rubbed her hands across her bare arms. She was wearing short sleeves when the skinwalker had taken her.

"Oh, here," Jerry removed his hunting jacket so that she could wear it.

She wrapped it around her shoulders. "Thank you."

Jerry shook his head. "I knew I should've worn Marlene's wedding dress," he said, and Debbie thought perhaps she was hearing things.

"Debbie!?" a voice broke the silence, and either Hondo or Pancho came skidding into the room across the icy floor. Only in her haze and abject terror, rather than recognizing Hondo for who he was, Debbie's fear-addled brain screamed that it might be the skinwalker come back.

"It's him! The skinwalker!"

"It is!?" Jerry began to fumble with his rifle.

"It's me, you idiot," Hondo said to his brother.

Debbie was still terrified, remembering the brutish man that had kidnapped her.

Hondo grabbed her by the shoulders. "Debbie, it's me! It's me!"

She looked up tepidly to see the familiar gold-rimmed green eyes she'd become accustomed to rather than the animal eyes that had terrified her yesterday.

She pressed her face into his shoulder as his arms wrapped around her, her heartbeat finally beginning to slow. "Oh, Hondo, what happened? I saw a man that looked just like you and Pancho only it wasn't."

"I know, honey. I know," he said, running his hands through her hair comfortingly. After a second, he tipped up her chin. His eyes were full of regret. "Debbie, I am so, so sorry. I'm sorry for what happened. I'm sorry for how I reacted at the house. I know you were just trying to help, I was just..."

"You were going through a lot."

"It's still no excuse."

He leaned in to kiss her and Jerry cleared his throat. "Guys, one, it's a little awkward with me here watching, and two, aren't there like werewolves and shit running around down here?"

"Good point." Hondo looked at his brother. "Where's Pancho?"

"I don't know, there was a cave-in," Jerry answered.

Hondo placed his hands on Debbie's shoulders and hunched down to look her in the eye. "Look, I'll explain everything later, but I have to go back for Pancho." She nodded and he turned to his brother. "Jerry, you get her out of here. There's a rope at the opening of that sinkhole. And give me that bullet."

Jerry removed a bullet from his rifle and handed it to Hondo.

"Don't you need more than one?" Debbie asked, mildly confused.

"This one's special. Another long story." Hondo loaded it into his revolver and then holstered it.

"How are you going to find him?" she asked, meaning Pancho.

Hondo shrugged. "I don't know. Dig him out if I have to."

"There's no need for that," a sultry female voice interjected from a dark passageway illuminated by two glowing, animal-like eyes. A slender but shapely woman emerged wearing a form-fitting black dress that looked as though it had been burned in a fire. It was the same woman she'd seen in her nightmares. Though initially she thought it was just a part of her dream, she could now see that the woman really did have a live fox draped over her shoulders. It looked as though it had been charred, too.

"I can show you the way, Hondo. I can show all of you the way," she said from the dark channel.

Hondo aimed the gun at her. "No, just me. Take me to my brother, let them go, and I don't shoot you where you stand," he threatened.

She looked at the gun dismissively. "Bullets cannot harm my kind. And all of you are coming. After all, our host is waiting."

***

After much walking, the woman had led the trio through a series of passageways that eventually turned from ice and rock into the interior of some kind of structure. It reminded Debbie of a pueblo in a way, only carved out of black lava rock.

"What is this place, the Taj Mahal of the skinpeople?" Jerry asked as they shuffled through a torchlit corridor.

"You will not speak in the presence of the master unless spoken to, understood?" the frightening woman responded without turning around. Even though they followed her from behind, the living fox fur around her neck had turned to watch them. Debbie shivered.

Jerry reached out to touch it and it snapped at him. Jerry's hand shot back. Hondo shook his head at his brother, a signal to play it cool, then tapped the revolver still holstered to his hip. The woman hadn't considered it a threat, and so hadn't removed it. But Debbie seemed to gather there was something special about the bullet in the chamber. She also gathered that Hondo didn't want to waste it considering that he didn't shoot her.

They entered a larger room. Pancho was standing in the middle near what appeared to be a stone altar. He at once looked relieved and distressed to see them. He had probably been hoping that they had gotten away but was also glad to be in the company of his family again. Then Debbie saw the skinwalker perched arrogantly atop an obsidian throne. Though she had never laid eyes on this particular man in her life, somehow she knew it was her abductor. He looked them all over appraisingly but didn't offer any type of greeting as they went to stand by Pancho.

"Good work, my dear," the skinwalker said to their escort. While the fox-draped woman spoke into the skinwalker's ear, Hondo did the same to Pancho.

"What are we gonna do about toots over there? I only have one bullet," Hondo whispered.

"Don't worry, I know her real name," Pancho answered, which puzzled Debbie. What did the name have to do with anything?

Debbie flinched when the woman turned around to face them. Her attention was solely focused on Hondo. "You there, the good looking one."

"We're identical," Pancho hissed at her.

"Set the tombstone on the altar there so we can see it," the woman commanded.

Hondo undid the rucksack and placed it on the altar. He unveiled the tombstone. "You got what you wanted. The tombstone for the girl. Seems to me it's time for us to leave."

The skinwalker finally spoke. "Leave? You've only just arrived."

"Well, you're not exactly being a very good host." Pancho grinned deviously and stepped nearer the throne. "You haven't even introduced yourself yet."

Debbie watched as Hondo let his hand slip to the revolver, ready to draw. Now was the time. Debbie said a silent prayer.

"That's not true," the skinwalker answered, outstretching his hand towards them. "I think we've all met under different guises." He cast a glance at Debbie.

Pancho turned to Jerry and Debbie. "You'll have to forgive him, he's a little touchy about using his real name. But allow me to introduce you to the one and only Wolf Mescal." Pancho turned snidely to the skinwalker expecting to see a shocked reaction.

Instead, the skinwalker offered him a pitiable, mocking look. "Oh, you poor boy." He wagged a finger as a devious grin spread across his face. "I see what's going on here. You thought you would utter my true name, big brother would fill me full of lead, and then I'd die. That might work on a normal skinwalker, like my associate here, but as I told you earlier, I am a true skinwalker. To kill one such as myself, you need White Ash and my real name, and I'm afraid poor grandpa Bill only knew the half of it as they say."

Pancho and Hondo shared a horrified look.

The skinwalker shook his head as he continued. "A skinwalker only shares their true name with other skinwalkers. Though my surname was indeed Mescal, and Wolf is... how do you say...tangent to my real name, Wolf is more of a nickname as your people would say. It's a shame I can't say it. It really rolls off the tongue."

Hondo slowly removed his hand from the revolver as the skinwalker eyed him. "It's torturous, isn't it, to be so close only to fail?" it taunted him.

Though Hondo looked mortified and defeated, Debbie noticed that Pancho appeared more contemplative, as though his mind was hard at work.

Suddenly the skinwalker shifted his form into that of a deep-voiced old man with a mustache. "Don't worry, though. You can take some solace in the fact that your grandfather can get what he always wanted." He outstretched his hand towards the tombstone on the altar. "The gold in the canyon will go to the peoples of New Mexico as he always wished. Not that it will matter by then."

The skinwalker shifted into the form of a Hispanic man with a heavy accent. "You see, I, or Governor Mendez, I should say, will be regarded as a hero for unearthing the gold for the entire state. But meanwhile, I'll get what I really want." The skinwalker shifted back into his true form.

"The bones of Yé'iitsoh," Hondo said. "You want the bones to make corpse powder out of to cause a plague, just like the witches at Abiquiú."

The skinwalker gave him a surprised look. "Did you actually figure that out on your own?"

"I had help," Hondo answered. "But where you plan to unleash it, that I figured out all on my own."

The skinwalker cocked a brow. "Enlighten me."

"It's the forts, Stanton, Sumner, and Wingate, isn't it?"

"Clever boy. I have to admit I may have misjudged you, Hondo. That's right. Making corpse powder is a complicated process, and the bones of a normal human being simply wouldn't do."

"But with the giant in that canyon…" Hondo began.

"I can make enough to kill thousands," the skinwalker said.

"Excuse me?" Jerry raised his hand. "I know I may not look like the smartest guy in the room, but couldn't you just have gotten some dynasaur bones or something?"

The skinwalker dug his claws into his obsidian throne as though he wanted to rip Jerry's face off. "You white eyes wouldn't understand. To you, Yé'iitsoh is only a myth, but to my people, he was a fearsome god, slain unjustly, some might say, by the Hero Twins of old. The powder of his bones will serve as his revenge as well as my own. And the first place I'll unleash the deadly poison is within the waters of the Bosque near good ol' Fort Sumner. I'll let it out into the Pecos and the irrigation canals. Your water will be poisoned, your crops will die, and then so will you. In other words, there will be pestilence and famine upon the land just like in the days of Egypt."

"Well, that's justice, alright," Pancho began angrily, "killing a whole town's worth of people that had nothing to do with your plight. All those families arrived there long after the fort was done and gone. Same with the doctors and nurses at Fort Stanton. And the Indian school at Fort Wingate now."

"True, but when those settlements and the people there all die, it will make a statement to the world," the skinwalker responded.

Hondo shook his head angrily. "You were never going to let any of us go, were you?"

The skinwalker cocked his head contemplatively at Hondo before responding. "You think that because I told you of my plan that means I can't let any of you live? Not true." He indicated to Jerry and Debbie. "Besides, who would believe a simple waitress or a hillbilly that the new governor is a skinwalker that plans to poison the state?" He shook his head arrogantly. "It'll just be another conspiracy theory from the mouth of hicks."

"What about us?" Hondo asked since the skinwalker didn't indicate to either he or his brother.

"One of you will join me, and the other… will die."

"What are you getting at?" Hondo asked while Pancho remained uncharacteristically quiet.

"One of you must take the other's life so that the others may live." The skinwalker outstretched his hand, indicating her and Jerry again.

"No!" Jerry shouted and moved forwards. He stopped when the woman held up a finger and the fox on her shoulders hissed at him.

"Don't do it!" Debbie said, grabbing Hondo's arm.

"I'm offering you a good deal, my sweet," the skinwalker addressed her. "If I were truly cruel, I would make you mine. But I'm allowing the winner to claim you. And, even if you don't get the one you want, he'll look just like him at least," he cackled cruelly.

"Fine, take my life then," Hondo said desperately. "I'll give it willingly."

"You don't understand, Hondo." Pancho finally broke his silence as he slid off his heavy jacket. "We've both been marked by a skinwalker." He rolled up his sleeve to reveal a clawed imprint that looked like it would scar one day. Debbie had seen the same markings on Hondo's back. "You take my life, or I take yours, we become one of them."

Pancho suddenly turned to the skinwalkers. "Only thing is, if that's the way it has to be, that's fine with me." He turned back to Debbie, his voice wavering with emotion. "You're right. I want her, always have, and if one of us has to die anyway, I might as well get what I want."

Debbie gasped. Was he serious?

"Pancho, what are you doing?" Hondo replied, shocked.

"Nothing that you haven't done to me since we were kids. Sold me out, thrown me under the bus because you think you're morally superior to me." Pancho thumped his chest as he stepped toward his brother aggressively. "Pancho the drifter who can't keep a job while you think you're some high and mighty hometown hero."

"Oh, I like the drama," the skinwalker cooed in Mendez's thick Spanish accent.

Hondo's eyes had turned into pools of betrayal and pain. "Sold you out? When have I ever—"

"Don't play innocent, Hondo." Pancho circled the altar stone. "Like that day in the pool hall when you threw me to the wolves to let me get my ass kicked by the McPhersons!"

Hondo's distraught look suddenly seemed to turn to one of contemplation. It was making sense to Debbie now. Pancho was playing a game of words with his brother, a game that only Hondo understood. She had watched the two of them enough to realize that sometimes they spoke in code. On the surface, to an eavesdropper, their conversation might sound like something else entirely than what it was. They would say one thing while really meaning another. And the pool hall, Debbie vaguely remembered that story from the night in the bar. The brothers had played some sort of a trick on the McPherson boys. What kind of a trick did they have up their sleeves now?

Hondo let his hand slip back down to his revolver. "Okay, if that's how you feel, then I say we have us a good old-fashioned duel to honor our late grandfather, another worthless criminal just like you."

The skinwalker clapped his hands. "I love it! Just like in the Old West."

"Fine." Pancho stooped over to remove something from the inside of his jacket. It was an old, gold pocket watch. He looked at Debbie. "In fact, sweets here can count us down. See which one of us wins you." Pancho winked at her and tossed it. Nervously, she caught it. "What time is it?" he asked.

Her hands trembled as she opened the watch. "11:59."

"One minute to high noon, perfect," Pancho said.

"Aren't you getting ahead of yourself? You need a gun for a duel," Hondo said, his voice tinged with anger that Debbie now suspected was a put-on.

Pancho whipped out a shiny blade. "I don't need one. I have a knife."

The two brothers began to circle around the altar. Debbie and Jerry backed away while the skinwalkers watched intently from the throne.

"What's the time, toots?" Pancho asked.

"Forty-five seconds to noon," she replied, both thankful but still nervous to be in on their little game.

"Count us down at ten seconds," Pancho said.

"You really think you can beat me with a knife?" Hondo asked.

"I did that night in Puerto de Luna. I threw my knife into the skinwalker that killed Dad before you could fire a single shot. Just another thing you failed at."

"Are you sure you really want to do this?" Hondo asked him. But Debbie could tell he was really asking Pancho if he was certain of the plan, whatever it was.

"What was that nickname our father had for me?" Pancho said, and Debbie could tell that another question had been asked in code. But what?

Pancho continued his angry monologue. "Impulsive Pancho, acting on the fly, never looking before he leaps. I hated that name."

Jerry's face contorted into a sneer of confusion. He wasn't in on the game. To himself, he muttered, "Wait, Daddy never called—"

"Seventeen seconds," Debbie said loudly to edge out Jerry's comment.

"Hear that? Only 17 more seconds and I don't have to put up with your macho bullshit a second longer, Pancho," Hondo hissed angrily.

Debbie caught onto the subtle way that Hondo had emphasized the word macho. Was that the answer to Pancho's hidden question in some way?

Pancho grinned deviously. "Well, too bad, because I don't think I can wait a second longer to end this."

Hondo nodded. "Well, I guess there's only one thing left to say then, isn't there?"

"Goodbye, big brother." Pancho made a sudden move as if to go for his knife while Hondo whipped the gun from its holster lightning fast and pulled the trigger. Debbie flinched.

***

Just like the night in Puerto de Luna when he had felt hypersensitive to everything going on, Hondo swore he could see the bullet fly from the chamber. Pancho's grab for the knife was just a fake out so he could dodge to the side, allowing the special bullet to go sailing past him and towards the skinwalker they now knew to be Ma'cho Mescal.

When Pancho asked Hondo what nickname their old man used to call him by—and considering the old man had no nicknames for Pancho—Hondo caught his brother's clue right away. Earlier, the skinwalker had said that Wolf was more of a nickname, though it was tangent to his real name. It had been Pancho's coded way of asking him to remind him of the obscure Apache word for 'wolf' that Hondo had spoken on the car ride to Fort Wingate: Ma'cho. At that moment, it suddenly made sense. Only a few minutes ago, the skinwalker had taunted them about not knowing his real name, telling them that it rolled off the tongue. And that was his fatal mistake. Wolf Mescal didn't exactly roll off the tongue, but Ma'cho Mescal certainly did. When Hondo had said he was tired of Pancho's "macho" bullshit, that was his coded way of answering his brother's question.

It was an educated guess at the thing's name, but it was a damn good one. He was about to find out whether their gamble had paid off as the White Ash-laced bullet sailed into the skinwalker. The monster flinched and the woman next to him gasped as the bullet plunged into his chest. His eyes seemed to become brighter, the angry fire in his soul burning through them. He stood and stepped forward from his throne. "You fool, I already told you a bullet cannot kill me."

This was the moment of truth, what it had all come down to. Hondo held his breath and let Pancho do the honors. "What about a White Ash bullet with your name on it... Ma'cho Mescal?" Pancho said.

Upon the utterance of his true name, Ma'cho Mescal's face took on a hateful, rat-like countenance. He shook his head. "No...No..."

"Our parents and the Kid send their regards," Hondo added with a smirk and lowered the gun.

Ma'cho peered down at the smoking hole in his breast with disbelief. As he looked back up at the men who had just signed his death warrant, the light in his eyes flickered on and off and his body seemed to convulse with a supernatural electricity. It looked like a lightning storm was coursing through his veins. Not only that; the entire cavern began to convulse and shake with him.

"That's not good," Pancho said.

"Time to go," Hondo said and grabbed Jerry and Debbie. Pancho put the tombstone back in the rucksack and slung it across his back, tight.

The skinwalker had by now fallen to his knees, his body changing rapidly and painfully from one form into the next. A lifetime of identities and murdered men flashed before Hondo's eyes until the being reverted back to his true self, only now weathered and ancient looking. The female skinwalker knelt by his side as he contorted in pain. Angrily, he outstretched a clawed hand at them as the wolfskin on his back came to life once more, seething with anger. Suddenly, a stalactite from the ceiling came tumbling down. The she-fox jumped backward as it struck Ma'cho Mescal, who shattered into a cloud of ash and dust and was no more.

"You killed the master!" the enraged woman yelled, taking on a predatory stance. "For that, you must be killed!"

Pancho pointed a finger at her. "Hey, I know your name, too."

"Yes, but you have to mortally wound me first." She continued her advance as they backed towards a passage leading out of the room.

"Good point." As quick as Hondo had drawn his gun earlier, Pancho threw his knife into her shoulder.

Angrily, she plucked it out, unphased.

"Guess that White Ash sap doesn't last for long," Pancho mused.

"Come on, let's go!" Hondo yelled and herded them through the open passage. Hondo looked behind him to see the volcanic rock collapse just in time to seal the female skinwalker inside before she could follow.

"This thing erupting?" Jerry asked as they made their mad dash down the passage.

"No!" Hondo shook his head. "This… this is supernatural! It's not the volcano."

He stumbled as he came to the termination of the ghostly structure, which opened out onto a short staircase made of hardened magma. They treaded down it as quickly as they could amidst the violent earth tremors.

"What now?" Jerry asked.

They were on a ledge that sloped down into the main cavern defined by the huge green lake of ice. There was nowhere to go. To get to the bottom, they'd have to climb down arduously and slowly, and there wasn't time for that. The whole cavern was about to come down.

Hondo shook his head and embraced Debbie. "Only God can help us now."

"How about we go for a ride?" Pancho said.

"In what?" Hondo asked.

"That." Pancho pointed to what looked like a gigantic cauldron perched on the edge of the ledge.

"Yeah, I'm pretty sure people got sacrificed in that thing, Pancho. That's a big no from me," Jerry said.

"Well, you know what they say, the Lord works in mysterious ways. Come on!" Pancho hopped inside and waved his hands.

Hondo helped Debbie hop in as Jerry asked, "How do we get this thing going?"

"Just like Dad's old Studebaker—one of us has to stay out and push!" Hondo said alongside Jerry.

"I hate this!" Jerry pushed hard along with his brother towards the edge. They both hopped in as the cauldron went sliding down the sloping obsidian wall, its terrified passengers screaming. Soon the cauldron went from sailing down the cliff-slant to skidding across the ice lake. It was heading right for a huge maw of conjoined stalagmites and stalactites that looked like the giant, salivating mouth of a monster.

"Brace yourselves!" Hondo cried and laid himself over Debbie as they went sailing through the huge maw. They broke through the icy teeth like they were nothing, the raining fragments doing them no harm.

Hondo lifted his head and looked around in amazement as their makeshift chariot slid down an icy passageway of bright blue ice.

"You were right, God did help us!" Jerry shouted gleefully.

"Yeah, but the devil ain't done with us either. Look!" Pancho pointed to the sides of the cave wall.

A terrifying, unnatural sight assaulted their eyes. The fox woman was defying gravity and scurrying upside down across the roof of the tunnel.

"Jerry, see if you can shoot that thing!" Hondo ordered his brother since he still had his rifle.

Jerry loaded a round as it came closer. "I thought you said only special bullets could kill them?"

"I know this one's name!" Pancho yelled.

"I thought that only worked on the other one?" Jerry shouted back.

"Just shoot the damn thing!" Hondo yelled.

Jerry aimed his rifle, taking shot after shot at the she-fox, but it was too fast. Suddenly, a bright light enveloped the cave, briefly blinding them. In an instant, she had transformed into a fireball to shoot from the wall and onto the cauldron. She landed on it with such force that it split it in half, sending Jerry's section off on its own wild ride while putting the rest of them into a disorientating spin.

The intensity of the spin nearly slung Debbie off, but Hondo caught her. As Hondo held tight to Debbie to keep her from spinning off, the she-beast attacked Pancho, flipping him over until he was flat on his stomach to get at the rucksack.

"Give it to me! If my master is dead, then I will at least fulfill his purpose!" She tore through the rucksack to get at the tombstone and hoisted it out. Immediately her hands began to sizzle. She held on for a moment and then dropped the tombstone, her hands still smoking. She looked to Pancho as he spun around to face her, horror and confusion etched upon her face. Hondo wondered what was happening.

"Sorry, forgot to tell you, I buried it in the backyard," Pancho said with a grin. "Right under our White Ash tree."

"No! No!" she hissed, shaking her head in disbelief.

"Lady, it's about time you took a hike!" Debbie shouted and then punched her right in the face.

The fox woman screamed and went flying off the back of the rock, tumbling behind them just as a portion of the cave roof collapsed, sealing her in the skinwalker tomb for good.

"So long, Miss Sinaloa!" Pancho shouted out down the icy passage.

"Where did that come from?" Hondo asked.

"I knew you both were probably too old fashioned to hit a woman," Debbie said with a smirk.

"Good girl!" He kissed her forehead just as their descent finally began to slow at the same time that the tremors were beginning to cease. The ground was leveling out and turning upwards again instead of downwards, finally slowing their descent.

"I guess this is where we get off," Hondo said as the thing finally skidded to a stop.

They stepped off the split cauldron and looked around for Jerry. They saw his portion of the giant pot, but not Jerry.

"Jerry! Where are you?" Pancho shouted.

"Here," Jerry managed to cough out. They worried he was mortally wounded for a second, but a moment later, they found him hunched over behind the cauldron, throwing up. "This is why I don't never go to amusement parks!"

Pancho patted him on the back and surveyed the cavern they currently occupied. "Where the hell do we go from here?"

"There." Debbie pointed ahead, catching a glimmer of light in the distance shining from an opening in the roof of the cave. The surface world beckoned, now all they had to do was climb up to it.

***

After returning to the surface, the quartet had walked from where the ice caves had released them back to the horses at the foot of the volcano. From there, they had ridden south towards a sandstone canyon not far from where Hondo had parked his truck the night before. They stopped to let the horses drink from some melting pools of snow. It was also at this spot that one of them needed to head east for Hondo's truck while the others continued south to Jerry's.

"I guess this is where we part ways," Pancho said from beside his horse.

"You sure you can't just come home with us?" Jerry asked his brother forlornly.

Pancho shook his head. "It's too risky for y'all to be seen with me. In case you hadn't noticed, I made the papers this week in a big way, Jerry."

"The only place you belong is in the funny papers." Jerry leaned in to embrace his brother.

"Hey, don't let those space monkeys at Holloman boss you around, alright?" Pancho ruffled Jerry's curly hair as he pulled away.

"I'd say don't get into any more trouble, but I know that ain't gonna happen," Jerry said, mounting his horse. "I'm gonna hit the trail and get my truck ready. Y'all don't dilly-dally too much, ya hear?" he said to Hondo and Debbie. He grabbed the horse's reins, clicked his heels, and shouted, "Hi-ho, Silver and Away!" The horse reared up and nearly threw him off before it dashed into the sandstone canyon and they all laughed.

Pancho walked up to Debbie and took her by the shoulders. "Debbie, I'm sorry, but it never woulda worked between us. Now, I know he's not as handsome as I am, but he'll have to do."

"I think I can manage." She smiled and looked at Hondo, then she and Pancho embraced.

"Oh, and one more thing." Pancho held up a finger as he pulled away. "Don't ever let him eat dairy after six."

Hondo rolled his eyes.

"I'll try to remember that," Debbie said, then looked at Hondo and added, "I'll give you two a minute.

"That's a pretty girl you got there," Pancho said as she went over to attend to Geronimo. "I'm happy for you, I really am."

Hondo smiled with a nod. "I know. When will you be coming back?" he asked hesitantly, afraid of the answer.

After a moment, Pancho finally answered. "I ain't coming back, Hondo."

"Hey, don't give up. It's gonna take some doing, but we can prove your innocence," Hondo argued. "I'll vouch for you on everything… we'll take on the Ring together."

Pancho shook his head. "There's something you don't know. That soldier we found at Fort Wingate… the skinwalker killed him with my hands. My fingerprints are on his body. Explaining the Santa Fe Ring is one thing, but you start spouting off about skinwalkers and they'll send you to the looney bin."

Hondo opened his mouth to argue, but Pancho cut him off. "You know that's the way it's gotta be."

Hondo wasn't sure what to say. "I've spent my whole life with you, Pancho. Even when you're not with me… you are. I can't explain it."

Pancho hit him on the shoulder. "Exactly. It'll be like any other time that I've ever been gone."

"Yeah, except then I always knew you'd come back."

They both eyed each other for a moment, the unfathomable reality setting in that this really might be the last time they would ever see one another, then embraced.

After a moment, Hondo pulled away. "I'll go check on Williams in Granbury as soon as I can. You better get to Mexico and take that thing with you."

"I'll keep the tombstone hidden away. I promise."

Hondo started to hand him his wallet, but he shooed it away. "I don't need the money, I'm good."

"Not the money, dummy. My I.D. in case you get pulled over in my truck."

Pancho took the wallet. "What about you? What if they think you're me?"

Hondo nodded at Debbie. "I think she'll vouch for me."

Pancho mounted his horse and took the reins while Debbie and Hondo climbed up on Geronimo.

"Hey, I almost forgot," Debbie suddenly said. She tossed Pancho his pocket watch.

He caught it, looking at it thoughtfully. "No, I'm the one who forgot. He wanted you to have it." He tossed it to Hondo.

Hondo caught it with a puzzled expression. "Who?"

Pancho grinned at his brother's obliviousness and shook his head. "You know who."

Pancho spurred his horse and took off into the forest.

"Are you okay?" Debbie asked as they watched Hondo's twin disappear into the trees.

"I'll be fine. Something tells me I'll see him again… eventually." He turned to her. "Besides, I think this is actually the first time we've ever really had a chance to be alone." He shook his head. "I'm an idiot. I should have asked you out the moment I saw you. Before my life got turned upside down by wolf-men and she-foxes."

"You did pick a heck of a time to finally make your move," she said with a grin.

"You know what? Let's start over. I'm Hondo Dumez, acting sheriff of Fort Sumner, and I would really, really like to show you around town."

"Just me?"

"Just you."

"I would love that."

Just as she leaned in to kiss him, a shout broke through the canyon walls. "Hondo!" It was Jerry. "Hondo!"

Hondo sighed. "If it isn't one brother, it's another."

A breathless Jerry came running up to them. "Sorry, the horse got spooked and bucked me off." He chucked his thumb back towards the canyon. "Think I could ride with you?"

Hondo turned to Debbie. "Think you can handle being sandwiched between two Dumez brothers on a horse?"

"It wouldn't be the first time."

Jerry shot them a confused, mildly disturbed look. Hondo and Debbie laughed as Jerry hopped onto the back of poor Uncle Kit's horse.

"So, I gots a question for you," Jerry asked as they trotted into the canyon.

"Shoot," Hondo said.

"So, Pancho told me those things can become any animal they want just by wearing the skin?"

"Yessir."

"Well, I was thinking, if I was one of those things, I wouldn't turn into a wolf or a fox. I'd turn into a skunk. Now that would scare me. Call it a… skunkwalker."

Hondo stared up at the noonday sun and sighed. It was going to be a long ride.

EPITAPH
THE HAND

A storm was coming. Hondo could see it brewing along the dull, gray horizon. Soon the snow would fall, trapping him here if he wasn't careful—here being back in the mountains of Mescalero. As such, he'd need to make his visit short. He liked Seven, but he damn sure didn't want to get snowed in with him. Besides, tonight he and Debbie were going out. Alone.

He shifted his gaze to the morning paper, which sat atop the dash of his truck. The main headline read: TUMBLEWEED WILLIAMS DEAD AT 90 YEARS OLD. Right next to it was an article on the death of the governor-elect, Dr. Marcos Mendez, though only Hondo truly understood the irony. The article claimed Mendez had died in a tragic accident when Dorsey Mansion caught fire. What he was doing there, the article tactfully neglected to mention.

Clustered among the secondary stories were two more articles that caught his eye. One was a semi-humorous account of a UFO sighting over Fort Sumner. The other told of an earth tremor in the vicinity of Bandera Volcano. No one but himself and a few others knew that all four stories were connected.

The paper wasn't the only interesting reading that Hondo had done that morning. He had also received a letter in the mail. A very special letter. Pancho had mentioned that Bill instructed his pal Jesse Evans AKA Tumbleweed Williams to mail a letter to them if he didn't hear from Bill or Pancho. With Bill dead and Pancho and Hondo tied up in the malpais, Evans had mailed the letter as told.

Apparently, it was the last thing he did before he died. The papers reported that he was found dead on the roadside while walking home from the post office. The papers also reported that it was a simple heart attack that did it. And the papers, as Hondo suspected, were wrong. He had called the Granbury sheriff's department to inquire if the murder might be related to the ones that had plagued New Mexico recently. Though the poor Billy the Kid impersonator hadn't been scalped, he had suffered the same mutilation that the others had in the removal of his left hand. The sheriff's department explained to Hondo that they had managed to keep that detail from the press and intended to keep it that way, which was just fine with him. In turn, Hondo suggested that they should check for a bone dart in the neck during the autopsy.

As for Bill's letter, it was addressed to Pancho and gave further instructions as to how and where to open the tombstone when the time came. "When it comes to the gold, trust no one," was the final line before Bill signed off. For some reason, Hondo imagined a deep rich voice when he read it.

Hondo would hide the letter somewhere safe, just as Pancho had done with the tombstone. Hondo's main point of concern now was, who had killed the man called Tumbleweed Williams? Though skinwalkers were the obvious answer, the time frame didn't line up since both were accounted for in the malpais when Williams was killed. Even if the damn things could fly, Hondo still doubted it was one of them, which presented him with a new mystery to solve. Seven's hovel was only a few more minutes away.

He pulled up just as the first flecks of snow began to fall. It looked just like it did the last time, the small chimney smoking away. Hondo exited his truck, flipped up his jacket collar to shield his neck from the bitter cold, and walked to the door. He didn't bother knocking this time and simply walked inside.

Seven was stirring another pot of stew.

"I've been expecting you," he said.

"Let me guess, one of your birds told you?" Hondo stomped the little flecks of snow off his boots.

"Hell, no. They wouldn't go out in this weather." Seven shook Hondo's hand. "I knew you'd come to ask about Williams."

Hondo took off his coat. The hovel was warm from the fire he cooked the stew over. "What happened?"

Seven motioned for Hondo to sit at the table. "Can't say. By the time I got to Granbury, he was already dead. I went to the spot where he was found but didn't find anything suspicious. Heart attack, I heard."

Hondo sat. "I'd have a heart attack, too, if I was him. Papers aren't reporting it, but the sheriff's department says he was missing a hand like the others. Wasn't scalped, though. No autopsy yet, so can't say as to whether there was a bone dart in his neck or not."

Seven nodded gravely. "What do you plan to do?"

Hondo shook his head. "I don't know. As it stands, Williams was the last of the old-timers. There are no more to kill. He was also the last loose end, apart from me, you, and my brother."

"Speaking of your brother, where is he?"

"I don't know... don't want to know so I don't have to lie when they come asking me, and I know they will. He took the tombstone with him wherever he went. So, the secret of the canyon is safe."

Seven nodded. "That's good. I do regret not being able to meet him, though."

"Maybe one day. Something tells me I'll see him again. You know, twin intuition and all that."

"What did happen exactly?" Seven asked. "When you faced the last skinwalker, that is."

Hondo recounted his story to him best that he could and shook his head when he finished. "I can't deny that some days I still wake up thinking it will turn out that all this was a dream."

Seven was shaving a potato to drop into the stew. "Ah, yes, and let me guess, in your dream I would have been the scarecrow and Baca the cowardly lion?"

Hondo grinned. "I don't know, you seem more like the friendly wizard from those old books with the hobbits in them." He paused contemplatively. "What we faced was just as wild as any fantasy."

Seven shook his head. "You white eyes crack me up. You believe so unceasingly in God and angels above, but the minute you see a devil here on earth you just can't believe it."

"Well, it's a strange thing to find out that the fairy tales of your youth were right all along and your adult beliefs were what was wrong."

"And what fairy tales specifically were those?"

"Billy the Kid didn't die, the Santa Fe Ring still exists, and monsters are real."

Seven stopped shaving the potato. "And the Hero Twins?"

Hondo bit his lip. "Nah, sorry." He shook his head. "Ever hear the old expression that sometimes a flat tire is just a flat tire? In other words, God didn't do it and neither did the devil. Coincidences do still happen."

Seven shrugged and started to plop the potato pieces into the stew. "And what of our friend Williams? I don't think we can chalk that up to coincidence."

"I agree. But it still bugs me that I can't put a finger on the killer. Both of the skinwalkers should have been dead before Williams even left his front door."

"Maybe whoever did it is completely unrelated."

"Like a copycat?"

"Possibly. Or, worse, it's just a new cycle beginning again."

"History repeating itself, all that?"

Seven nodded and continued to stir the pot.

"It'll just be the same old story again. The good guys and the bad guys." Hondo stood, preparing to leave.

"Except they never tell you that the bad guys sometimes have a good reason for doing what they're doing."

Hondo slid his coat back on, startled. "You saying you agree with the skinwalker wanting to poison the Pecos?"

Seven shook his head. "No. He wanted to right a wrong, just didn't know any other way of doing it."

"Well, let's just hope you and I can right this wrong before it gets out of hand." Hondo put his hat back on. "Anyhow, I need to be going. Snow's coming down hard."

Seven dipped a ladle into the boiling pot. "Are you sure you wouldn't like some before you step out?"

Hondo sniffed the air tepidly. "I don't know. It smells a little better than last time I was in here."

"I'm trying something new. Secret ingredient."

Hondo grinned but still shook his head. "No, thank you. I may have survived a bone dart, but something tells me your cooking might be another matter."

Seven laughed heartily at his friend's remark. Hondo tipped his hat and then stepped out the door.

Once he was gone, Seven grabbed his tongs and lifted a dismembered human hand from the stew. "You don't know what you're missing, Sheriff."

JOHN LEMAY was born and raised in Roswell, New Mexico, the town where aliens and a flying saucer allegedly crashed in 1947. LeMay is also a direct descendant of James W. Patterson Sr., one of the first postmasters of Fort Sumner. LeMay is the author of over 30 books, many of them on the history of the Southwest such as *The Man Who Invented Billy the Kid: The Authentic Life of Ash Upson*, and *Tall Tales and Half Truths of Billy the Kid* to name only a few. He is also the editor/publisher of *Strange West Magazine* and a Past President of the Historical Society for Southeast New Mexico.

www.ingramcontent.com/pod-product-compliance
Lightning Source LLC
Chambersburg PA
CBHW071353200726
48293CB00008B/2629